# LEGIONARY

by Gordon Doherty

www.gordondoherty.co.uk

Published by FeedARead.com Publishing – Arts Council funded

A CIP catalogue record for this title is available from the British Library.

*In loving memory of Patricia McDermott.*

GORDON DOHERTY

## Historical Note & Pretext circa 376 AD

### The Eastern Roman Empire

In the 4th century AD, the Roman Empire existed as two halves; the East and the West. Both halves were subject to an immense inward pressure from the people Rome once called barbarians. Now with armies equal to the once invincible Roman legions, these peoples amassed along the outer provinces of the Roman world, pressed by a massive population shift from the Far East.

In the Eastern Empire, it was primarily the Gothic kingdoms to the north and the Persian Empire to the east who threatened to overrun Roman territory. Thus, the empire had to think defensively for the first time in centuries, forced to abandon territorial expansion and instead define permanent borders, to bolster forts, watchtowers and palisades and defend for their lives.

In support of this new border system, Emperor Diocletian and latterly Emperor Constantine (the Great) reformed the army into two broad categories. The *comitatenses* were the descendants of the old legions, the mobile crack troops, shifting to meet threats where they penetrated these new borders. The *limitanei* were their poor relations, the men paid, armoured and armed relatively minimally. They were tasked with manning the patchwork of hastily constructed or old, crumbling forts, watchtowers and walls that marked out the *limes*, the limits of the Roman world, waiting and watching the mists of the lost lands beyond, knowing the next mass invasion was not a matter of if, but when…

## High Command Structure of the Eastern Imperial Army

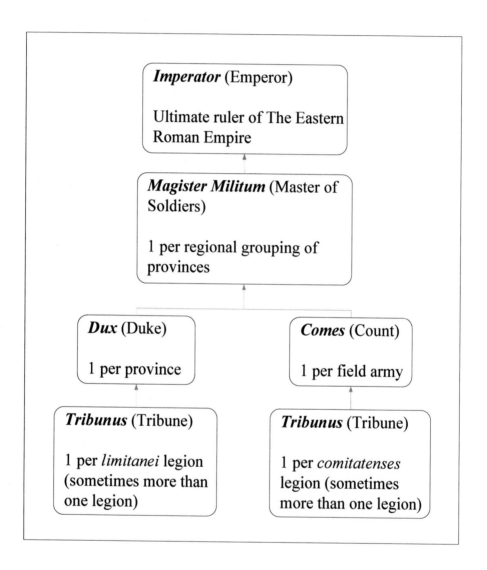

## The Legions

Evidence of unit numbers in the later Empire are equivocal as the flux in military organisation at the time meant *vexillationes* (small detachments from the traditional legions), morphed into new style *comitatenses* or *limitanei* legions in their own right. However, research suggests as follows;

An average legion of *comitatenses* consisted of between one thousand and two thousand men. A legion was commanded by a *tribunus,* and a *comes* would command a collection of *comitatenses* legions as a field army.

A legion of *limitanei* could vary hugely dependant on the extent of the *limes* they were stretched to cover, but evidence suggests they, too, averaged between one thousand and two thousand men. A *tribunus* commanded a legion, and a *dux* would command the various *limitanei* legions in a geographical region.

The rank of *primus pilus* (chief centurion) of the first century of the first cohort of a legion was held in the highest regard as the most dangerous front line position available.

## The XI Claudia

Julius Caesar originally recruited the XI Claudia (The Eleventh Claudian Legion) as far back as the mid-first century BC for the impending invasion of Gaul. It is likely that this original legion fought in the famous Siege of Alesia and the Battle of Dyrrhachium at Pharsalus before disbanding some twenty years later. The legion was reformed under Augustus and they went on to be based at various locations along the Rhine and in Dalmatia (modern day Croatia). However, by the late 4th century AD, the legion had migrated to settle on the lower River *Danubius* at the city of Durostorum in modern day Bulgaria. While camped at the city, as well as defending their stretch of frontier, some *vexillationes* would be despatched to fight around the empire.

As to the structure of the legions, by the late 4th century AD, the Roman army had been in a state of flux for several years, and uniform command structures in the legions were hard to identify, but the senior posts of *tribunus*, *primus pilus*, centurion and *optio* were all thought to have been in place at this time. Underneath these senior posts, the classical legion structure was still in evidence; cohorts of four hundred and eighty men (apart from the double-strength first cohort), each divided into six centuries of eighty men.

The diagram below gives an outline of the XI Claudia circa 376 AD, assuming a full complement of legionaries and discounting units of *foederati* and auxiliaries, who would often bolster this number.

# LEGIONARY

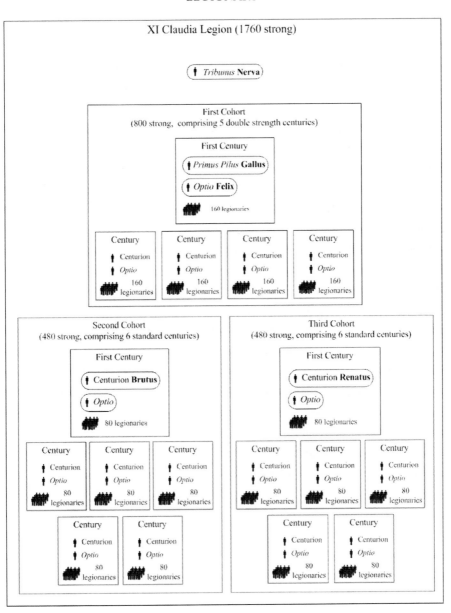

## XI Claudia Legion (1760 strong)

Tribunus **Nerva**

### First Cohort
(800 strong, comprising 5 double strength centuries)

#### First Century

Primus Pilus **Gallus**

Optio **Felix**

160 legionaries

**Century** — Centurion — Optio — 160 legionaries

**Century** — Centurion — Optio — 160 legionaries

**Century** — Centurion — Optio — 160 legionaries

**Century** — Centurion — Optio — 160 legionaries

### Second Cohort
(480 strong, comprising 6 standard centuries)

#### First Century

Centurion **Brutus**

Optio

80 legionaries

**Century** — Centurion — Optio — 80 legionaries

**Century** — Centurion — Optio — 80 legionaries

**Century** — Centurion — Optio — 80 legionaries

**Century** — Centurion — Optio — 80 legionaries

**Century** — Centurion — Optio — 80 legionaries

### Third Cohort
(480 strong, comprising 6 standard centuries)

#### First Century

Centurion **Renatus**

Optio

80 legionaries

**Century** — Centurion — Optio — 80 legionaries

**Century** — Centurion — Optio — 80 legionaries

**Century** — Centurion — Optio — 80 legionaries

**Century** — Centurion — Optio — 80 legionaries

**Century** — Centurion — Optio — 80 legionaries

## Religion

Circa 337 AD, towards the end of his reign as emperor of a briefly consolidated Roman Empire, Constantine established religious tolerance of Christianity. However, even before this, and for the best part of the next century, the first major schism in the Christian church took place in the form of the conflict between Arian and Trinitarian beliefs. Concisely, Arius, a Christian presbyter from Alexandria in Egypt, taught that God (the father), and Jesus (the son), did not exist together eternally, and that Jesus was a mortal creation of God. This was in direct contradiction to the traditional Trinitarian teachings that God, Jesus and the Holy Spirit coexisted as one divine being. The Arians were seen as a minority sect, but several high profile figures, notably Emperor Valens, supported the Arian cause during his reign as emperor of the East.

Despite this schism, the majority of emperors (with the exception of a few, notably Julian the Apostate) and their high-ranking subordinates embraced Christianity soon after Constantine's edict of tolerance. However, the citizens of the empire and the rank and file of the army transitioned more gradually. Indeed, the old gods were still being worshipped some half a century after Constantine's death, with the Persian god Mithras remaining a firm favourite of those in the legions.

## Key Landmarks in *Legionary*

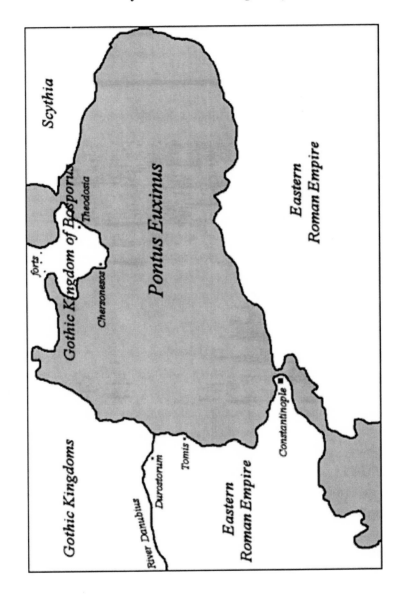

## Glossary

*Ave*; A reverential Roman salutation.

*Aquilifer*; Senior eagle standard bearer of a Roman legion.

*Beneficiarius*; Naval officer responsible for administrative duties on a ship.

*Buccina*; The ancestor of the trumpet and the trombone, this instrument was used for the announcement of night watches and various other purposes in the legionary camp.

*Caldarium*; A room with a hot plunge bath.

*Candidati*; The personal bodyguard of the Roman Emperor and descendants of the old praetorian guard.

*Chi-Rho*; The Chi-Rho is one of the earliest forms of Christogram, and was used by the early Christian Roman Empire. It is formed by superimposing the first two letters in the Greek spelling of the word Christ, chi = ch and rho = r, in such a way to produce the following monogram:

*Classis Moesica*; The fleet that controlled the waters from the Lower *Danubius* to the northwestern *Pontus Euxinus* as far as the Bosporus (modern-day Crimea) peninsula.

*Comes*; Commander of more than one *comitatenses* legions.

*Comitatenses*; The Roman field armies. A 'floating' central reserve, ready to move swiftly to tackle border breaches when they occur. See section entitled 'The Legions' for more information.

*Contubernium*; A grouping of eight legionaries within a century (ten contubernia per century). These soldiers would share a tent and would receive disciplinary action or reward as a unit.

*Danubius*; The modern River Danube.

*Dux*; Regional commander of *limitanei* legions.

*Equites*; Roman cavalry.

*Foederati*; Broad term for the variety of 'barbarian' tribes subsidised from imperial coffers to fight for the Roman Empire.

*Follis*; A large bronze coin introduced in about 294 AD with the coinage reform of Diocletian.

*Gladius*; Short sword used as primary legionary weapon up until the mid 3<sup>rd</sup> century AD.

*Hunnoi*; Huns.

*Imperator*; Meaning 'commander' or effectively 'emperor'.

*Intercisa*; Iron helmet constructed of two halves with a distinctive fin-like ridge joining them together and large cheek guards offering good protection to the face. See the helmets worn by the legionaries in the cover illustration as an example.

*Kingdom of Bosporus*; Modern day peninsula of Crimea, situated on the north coast of the *Pontus Euxinus*.

*Kithara*; Lyre-like string instrument from Greek antiquity.

*Limitanei*; Literally, meaning 'frontier soldiers'. Light infantry spearmen. See section entitled 'The Legions' for more information.

*Lorica Segmentata*; Broad, segmented iron body armour worn by the legions prior to the 3<sup>rd</sup> century AD.

*Magister Militum*; Literally, 'Master of Soldiers'. The man in this role would report directly to the emperor and command each regional *dux* and floating *comes* situated within the broad geographical grouping of provinces he presided over.

*Mithras*; Mithras was the Persian god of light and wisdom. Many Romans worshipped Mithras, particularly soldiers. Followers of Mithras believed that he was born with a sword in his hand.

*Nummus*; A low-value copper coin of late antiquity.

*Optio*; Second-in-command in a Roman century. Hand-chosen by the centurion.

*Palatini*; Literally, 'Palace soldiers' tasked with imperial escort and protection duties.

*Phalera*; A gold, silver or bronze sculpted disk worn on the breastplate during parades by Roman soldiers who had been awarded it as a kind of medal.

*Plumbata*; Lead weighted throwing dart carried by Roman legionaries, approximately half a metre in length. Each legionary would carry three of these and would launch them at their enemy prior to sword or spear engagement.

*Pontus Euxinus*; The modern Black Sea.

*Primus Pilus*; The chief centurion of a legion. So called, as his own century would line up in the first file (*pilus*) of the first cohort (*primus*).

*Propontus*; The modern Sea of Marmara.

*Qin*; The ancient Chinese peoples who waged war with the *Hunnoi*.

*Remiges*; Oarsmen in Roman navy. Contrary to popular belief, they were usually free men.

*Spatha*; A straight sword up to one metre long, favoured by the Roman infantry and cavalry.

*Strategos*; Greek word meaning military general.

*Tengri*; The *Hunnoi* god of the sky/god of the heavens.

*Testudo*; Formation where infantry place shields around all sides and overhead of their unit, thus providing protection from missiles from all directions.

*Tribunus*; Senior legionary officer. In the late 4th century AD, a *tribunus* was usually in charge of one or more legions of *limitanei* or *comitatenses*.

*Timpani*; Also known as kettledrums, these instruments consist of skin stretched over a copper bowl.

*Vexillatio*; A detachment of a Roman legion formed as a temporary task force.

*Via Egnatia*; Highway constructed in the 2nd century BC running from Dyrrachium on the Adriatic Sea, all the way through Thrace to Constantinople.

*Wodin*; The chief god of the Norse pantheon. Analogous to the Roman Jupiter or the Greek Zeus.

# Chapter 1

## Summer, 363 AD

Constantinople stewed in the midsummer sun. The Augusteum writhed with squinting faces, basted in sweat and seasoned with dust; a thick tang of roasting garlic and the fuggy stench of drying horse dung permeated the air. Raised market stalls clad in vibrant fabrics pierced the throng, sucking the hungry shoppers in like swirling currents. Hemmed in by the towering grandeur of the Hippodrome, the Imperial Palace and the Baths of Zeuxippus, the market square was a surefire hotpot for moneymaking.

Dead centre, with no respite from the midday inferno, one craggy-faced trader grinned as he scanned the eyes of his rapacious clientele; nobles, senators, businessmen and almost certainly all of them crooks. He could feel the weight of their purses – eager to be lightened. The trader's gold teeth glinted in the sunlight.

'Bring 'em out!' He bawled over the hubbub.

Two incongruous figures dressed only in loincloths were pushed up onto the rickety timber platform; a towering Nubian, scarred on every inch of his charcoal flesh and a stumpy, pale Germanian. The crowd broke into a keen rabble.

Without turning from his audience, the trader swept a hand back towards the platform. 'Slaves are the foundation of any man's business. An' today, my friends, you're boun' for a bargain.' He jabbed a finger at the Nubian. 'Will it be the mighty warrior from the distant sands of Africa – a power'ouse who will serve as a brave bodyguard or a fine labourer,' he shifted his hand towards the Germanian, 'or the 'ardy northern swordsman – this 'un'll fight for you till 'is 'eart bursts!' He revelled for a moment in the rising hum of interest. 'Or will it be the agile youth, a boy of legionary stock...' His voice trailed off as the crowd began to mutter in confusion.

Then he turned to the platform and the conspicuous space beside the Germanian and the Nubian. The crowd broke into a chorus of laughter.

'Where's the boy?' He hissed to his trade hand.

'I'm sorry, master,' the scab-coated figure yelped as he swiped into the slave-cart parked by the platform. 'He's being...difficult!'

The trader growled, thumping over to the cart. The laughter rose into a chorus of cheers as, with a snarl, he wrenched the wiry form of a boy from the cart, dangling him at arm's length by the scruff of a filthy tunic. With a shaven head, a beaky nose dominating his gaunt face, and sharp, hazel eyes tucked under thick brows, he had the look of a malnourished hawk. The boy kicked and punched in a fury, spurring the crowd into raptures.

'Only in 'is seventh year,' the trader fought to regain control, dumping the boy on the platform, while his trade hand clipped an ankle-manacle into place, 'the boy comes as the son of a seasoned legionary. Don't be fooled by 'is frame. This lad's got years ahead of 'im, and a bargain at 'alf the price!' At last, the crowd seemed to be coming round to him once more.

'C'mon – all three could be yours, let's start the biddin'!' He roared. 'Who'll be takin' 'ome the bargain today?'

Pavo gazed down at his torn and calloused feet. Tears blurred his vision and dropped to blot the filthy platform, where countless thousands of slaves had stood before, and would do so after him. The fight in him was dying, he realised, as the heckling grew ever more deafening. First, the Nubian was shoved down from the platform and off into the crowd as a deal was brokered. They hadn't spoken since they had been thrown together in the trader's cart three days ago, but last night the giant of a man had silently handed Pavo a piece of tangy root to chew, just when hunger had started to gnaw at his belly. A kind man. He didn't look to see where the Nubian was being taken. Slaves didn't look up.

Now, the Germanian was being prodded from the platform by the end of a staff – a chorus of congratulations rang out from one of the nearby cliques of toga-clad businessmen. The previous evening in the cart, the Germanian had been still like a marble carving. The fight had already gone from him, Pavo reckoned. He could see it in the deadness of the man's eyes.

Pavo shivered. He had seen that look once before: the day Father did not return from the Persian campaign. Instead, a gaunt, unsmiling legionary had ambled through the narrow tenemented street, face coated in dust and sweat pooling in his frown. The soldier had walked along, asking for a Numerius Vitellius Pavo. In excitement, Pavo had run to him. The soldier had looked at him with those same dead eyes, then handed him a purse containing the legionary funeral payout.

Mother had died giving birth to him, and he had never known her, but for the glassy glint in Father's eye when he spoke of her. Now he had nobody, nothing. Nothing, except the recurring dream. The same harrowing scene most nights, with Father stood in his armour on an empty dune, his face burnt from the sun and his eyes staring longingly, seeing Pavo, but also looking right through him. He gulped back a sob. In the eight months since Father's death, the modest room in the tenements had been repossessed, so the gutter had been his bed and vermin meat his sustenance. All the while, he had clung to the pride of Father's memory. A broad-shouldered man in his prime, he had towered twice as high as Pavo. He would return on leave from the legions, scoop him up and bear-hug him, and Pavo would nuzzle into the tousled chestnut locks – thick with the scent of wood smoke and dust from his travels. As always, Pavo coloured and bolstered this memory, sickened at the thought of it fading completely.

'Sold!' The trader yelped, punching a finger forward to pinpoint the buyer.

Pavo glanced up. Behind the shimmering golden grin of the trader, a short, corpulent figure waddled forward. His bald pate glistened in the sunlight like a shelled egg and his pallor was an unhealthy, pitted yellow, the same colour as the remnants of hair matted to the back and sides of his head. The purple-rim of his toga caught the eye – a senator.

Then a sharp pain shot through Pavo's spine. 'Move!' the trade hand barked from behind him, pulling the freed manacle to one side and shoving him down the steps. Pavo stumbled forward and down onto the dust of the ground, the skin scraping from his knees.

'Easy with my property,' the rotund man hissed.

Wincing, Pavo squinted up at his new owner.

'A fine purchase, Senator Tarquitius,' the trader purred. 'I 'ope you'll be back next time - word 'as it I'll be receivin' some Scythians for next week.'

'You would just love it if I had nothing better to do than fill your purse wouldn't you, Balbus?' The senator sneered.

'Well, if you *will* beat the ones you buy to death...'

'Keep your voice down...' Tarquitius' eyes darted all around. 'Fronto,' he barked to the rock-faced bull of a man who accompanied him, 'get this wretch into the cart!'

Pavo braced himself as Fronto stretched out a hand like a ham and wrenched him up onto his feet. Then, the senator snapped his fingers and strode forward in self-majesty through the bustle of the market. Eventually, the crowd thinned, the rabble dulled, and at the edge of the square he beheld Tarquitius' slave-cart; another grim cobbling of timbers and rust, powered by an emaciated donkey, clinging to the tiny sliver of shade under the walls of the great baths. Squinting into the penumbra of the cart, Pavo could just make out the selection of pale, drawn and defeated expressions of the others tucked inside. From one master to another. So this was to be his life. As he made to step inside, the fight was dissolving in his heart. Then Tarquitius squealed.

A withered crone stood in the senator's path. Sixty years, if not more, her face was puckered like a prune, her eyes milky, yet piercing. Her razor-like nose was within a hair's-breadth from the senator's.

'See that the boy comes to no harm from your hand,' she rasped.

'Out of my way, hag!' Tarquitius protested, sweeping her to one side, but she gripped his chubby wrist with her talon-like fingers. Tarquitius yelped. Fronto jostled, hand on his sword-hilt, awaiting the order of his master.

Pavo's tears suddenly dried and his interest keened. The crone held Tarquitius' arm fast, and stretched up on her bare and gnarled tiptoes to put her furrowed lips to the senator's ear. She whispered to him for only a few moments, and then calmly she walked over to Pavo, her eyes unblinking and fixed on his. She pressed something into his hand. With that, she wandered off into the crowd, her tousled and patchy grey locks dissolving into the melee of market goers.

The senator turned, slowly, his face milky pale, eyes wide, the fat rolls under his chin quivering. He stared at Pavo. Pavo stared back.

'Back to the villa,' he muttered quietly, his gaze drifting off into the distance.

Pavo frowned, stepping onto the slave-cart gingerly and sitting without a word next to the filthy and cowering slaves already in there. As the cart shuddered into life, he turned over the crone's words. Then he looked at his clenched fist, uncurling his fingers slowly as the cart jostled. A battered bronze legionary *phalera* – a thin bronze disc issued as a military reward, smaller than a *follis* – stared up at him. The text was chewed and battered, but he screwed up his eyes to read it in the flitting light from the slatted cart roof.

*Legio II Parthica*, it read – his father's legion. Pavo's skin rippled.

His eyes hung on the text as intrigue gripped his thudding heart. What did it mean? Confusion danced through his thoughts.

But one thing was certain.

The fight would never leave him.

# Chapter 2

## Late winter, 376 AD

The prow of the *Aquila* roared and shuddered as it carved a path out of the ocean and through the sandbank, before finally settling to a halt. The old Kingdom of Bosporus greeted her, hurling the bitter rains of the storm across her deck. Under the murky late afternoon sky, a grimacing row of legionaries clung to the sides of the ship. The howling wind filled the air as they peered across the shadowy texture of the hinterland, the long grass writhing in the gale. They gripped their shields, flexed their sword hands, all the while judging the shadows of the forested inland.

Standing at the prow was the tall and lean figure of Manius Atius Gallus, Chief Centurion, *primus pilus*, of the first cohort of the XI Claudia legion, dressed in leather boots, a ruby tunic under a mail vest, and a plumed *intercisa* helmet tucked under his arm. As he gazed upon the land, he squeezed the incessant rainwater from his peak of hair, charcoal, flecked with grey at the temples. His gaunt features, wolf-like in the gloom, betrayed nothing but a thin-lipped iron glare, yet behind the ice-blue eyes, he wondered what this dark corner of the world might think of the lone bireme on its shores. It had been fortunate to say the least that they had slipped into this bay without encountering any Gothic war ships, but from here on in, anything could happen.

'Park the oars!' He roared, remaining at the stern, eyes fixed on the land, ears trained on the goings-on behind him. First, there were the scuttling footsteps as the *beneficiarius* worked his way along the deck, and then the rhythmic clatter as the *remiges* lifted their oars clear of the water, sighing as they rested their weary arms. *Not perfect*, Gallus mused, comparing it to the drill back in the docks, *but acceptable.*

Once more, he gazed inland. The peninsula had fallen into darkness more than one hundred years ago. The invading Gothic tribes, the Greuthingi, as they were known, had declared their sovereignty over the peninsula with the delivery of the Roman ambassador's head to the emperor's palace. Since that day, the empire had seen the rise and fall of scores of emperors, her territory sliced like an apple into eastern and western halves and her mighty legions evolve almost beyond recognition. Nobody was quite sure how much this place had changed in that time, but reports indicated that the old Roman frontier fortification system still stood, lying dotted like decaying teeth across the eighty miles or so of the peninsula neck. Yes, there had been trade and diplomacy in the many years since this place had last been under direct Roman influence, but the Goths of Bosporus had fallen silent some time ago, and a hundred years could breed many ills. Gallus could only wonder what the shadows held.

He held his back straight and his face expressionless, burying the gnawing excitement and fear deep within. How would this group of men behind him handle the sortie, far from the XI Claudia fort on the banks of the *Danubius*? While the rest of the legion, some two thousand men, remained stretched out over the great river's borders protected by walls and reinforcements, here with him were the double strength first century of the first cohort – the one hundred and sixty considered most able, thrust out into the wilderness. Discounting the smattering of calloused veterans though, the numbers counted for little. Gallus turned and ran his eyes over them; barely one in ten were over twenty years of age, such was the fatality rate on the frontiers, and dressed only in filthy, sodden tunics and boots the youngsters looked every bit the farmers and labourers they were. He bit back his doubts; this was a brave new dawn for the empire, and Gallus was all too proud to lead it. In this day and age, for a *vexillatio* of *limitanei* border troops to be given a mission deep into foreign lands...well, that was quite something. Quickly, he tempered the urge to smile, keeping his lips quill-thin, maintaining the iron stare instead. Then, he placed the intercisa helmet on his head, with the shark fin of iron and the plume adding another foot to his towering frame.

'That's the stuff,' he encouraged the men as they set about tying down the rigging, thumping his hands together. But there was no cheering, no banter. He clenched his jaw at the silence.

He had been a late starter in the army, joining when he turned thirty. The post of primus pilus had fallen to him after a rapid succession of deaths of the previous incumbents. Practically every Gothic raid over the Danubius had propelled him further up the ladder; from legionary to *optio*, to centurion and now here, the role of the primus pilus. In just four years, he had risen to be the man whom all in the legion should look to for inspiration. He saw one young legionary grapple with the supply cart, his hands trembling. They were anything but inspired. *It's not you, Gallus, they're just scared*, he repeated in his head, thinking of the last words his predecessor had offered him; *you can lead them*. The old nerves that he had felt in his first officer posting as a junior optio had returned; parched mouth, self-doubt and paranoia. Regardless of this, his iron features stayed cold as ever.

His ears pricked up at a nervous cough – the rigging and deck space of the ship was in order and the men were ready, standing in formation, staring dead ahead. 'Good work! Now unload the ship,' he barked with a nod to the supply sacks and crates, 'then form up for the march.'

The men shuffled across the deck. The ropes for the gangplank were hurled over the rim of the vessel and onto the shore. The century split in two, half thumping down onto the shingle and half unloading supplies to them. The odd roar of encouragement split the air from the handful of veterans in the century, but apart from that, the silence was painful.

He looked over to his optio, Felix. The swarthy, diminutive, fork-bearded Greek was holding the silver eagle standard with a damp ruby-red bull banner rippling from the crossbar, readying to give it to the *aquilifer*, whose job it would be to carry the standard on the march. 'Felix,' he beckoned, 'give me that, I have a job for it!' He grappled the staff and strode over to the gangplank, surveying his men as they busied themselves assembling the supply cart.

'And let's get this eagle planted in the sand,' he cried, leaping over onto the shingle with a thud. 'It is time for the XI Claudia to make her mark on this land!'

The century turned to him as one – a sea of stunned faces. Gallus felt the cold fingers of doubt race up his spine as he tried to hold his posture, until, after an agony of only a few moments, a chorus of cheers erupted. The cheering died into a rabble of banter as they jostled and bumped past each other as they worked.

A thump landed behind Gallus. 'Nice touch, sir,' Felix whispered with a grin.

Gallus barely flicked up the sides of his papyrus-thin lips in return, but he knew his trusted optio valued that like a thousand bear hugs from any other. The Greek had shed blood with him along the length of the Danubius for so long that they understood each other like brothers. He turned to eye the precious few select men of the century that he could count on in the same fashion; Zosimus the hulking Thracian with a nose like a squashed pear and permanent stubble; Avitus the bald, catlike little Roman and Quadratus the towering Gaul – his thick blonde moustache a throwback to his long-lost ancestors. All had their own stories, but each of them had shared his pain in the ranks since the day he had flung himself into his military career.

Life for Gallus before the legions was like a fading dream, the days before the gods had seen fit to take her from him. *Olivia*. The morning before they had set off in the *Aquila*, he had crouched before the temple of Mithras, eyes gazing through the idol in front of him. Eternal life and honour, the deity promised to loyal soldiers. *Screw your honour, give me back Olivia!* Then he grimaced, emptying his mind of those thoughts, wiping the rainwater from his chin until his knuckles whitened.

'Oh for...' Zosimus growled, vexed at the ill-fitting cart wheels. 'Quadratus, get your back under this side so I can get the wheel on the bloody axle!'

Quadratus, reddened and fumbling at the opposite wheel, scuttled round to Zosimus' side of the cart, only to drop his side of the vehicle on the legs of another young legionary who yelped out a rather ladylike scream. A roar of nervous laughter halted work momentarily.

Gallus welcomed the distraction. 'Zosimus! Try not to decimate my century before this mission has begun.'

'Sir!' Zosimus' grimace flushed slightly as he strained to slot the wheel into place.

The rest of the century was forming up into ranks, slotting armour in place, buckling belts and harnessing weapons. Gallus paced the ground in front of his men, screwing his eyes up at the murky grey sky. He looked to his ranks; capped with their intercisa helmets, dressed in mail vests over white tunics, woollen trousers and leather boots. They carried the deadly combination of a *spatha* sword, a spear and a collection of *plumbata* darts, slipped in behind their ruby painted oval shields. His mind flitted to the paintings and frescoes of the legions of old. Gone were the *lorica segmentata*, the square shields and the *gladius*. Also gone, some would say, was the invincibility of that lost age. He took a deep breath and unravelled a parchment map as the last of the century shuffled into place.

'We have three more hours of daylight, by my reckoning. That gives us two hours marching time, which should see us to a small clearing in the forest to the north.' He paused, glancing up at his rain-sodden ranks. The men's faces said it all. Eyes darted back and forth along the tree line and fingers edged along shields restlessly. Alone on the vast beach, their number looked pitiful. Hastily, Gallus crumpled the map into his pack, biting back his frustration.

He paced before them, silent but glaring, as he thought back to the inspirational words of his predecessors. Then he boomed, 'Hold your chins high and fill your lungs with air. For we are part of the greatest military machine this world has ever known. Every forest we have entered, every sea we have crossed, every desert we have endured and every mountain we have scaled – we have been victorious. Not without setback, that is for certain, but the fact that we are here at the borders of the world today shows that we have prevailed. It is those barbarians who cower in the undergrowth who should feel fear right now, should they even be so brave to look down on us.' He saw pride flicker from the uncertainty on their faces, then puffed out his chest and seized the moment.

'Remember…we are the *pride* of the XI Claudia!'

He turned to face the forest and pumped the eagle standard into the air, as if mocking the unknown shadows ahead. This ignited a roar of approval from the ranks, and inside his chest, his heart thundered. He spun to his optio and clicked his fingers. 'Felix, organise fifty men to stay with the ship, then line up the rest – they're coming with us inland.' Then he turned to the beneficiarius. 'Take her round the peninsula, we meet on the eastern coast, as planned, three days from now.'

'Yes, sir,' Felix nodded.

'Yes, sir,' the beneficiarius agreed.

He frowned as all the mutterings of discontent, skulduggery and what-ifs during the briefing from *Tribunus* Nerva scampered across his mind. Despite the bullish bravado, which Gallus loved him for, the commanding officer of the XI Claudia could turn even the most trivial of events into a drama. However, this time there were genuine layers of agenda and politics involved. *Dux* Vergilius had meddled from above and Mithras only knew who was pulling his strings.

'And Felix,' he waited for the optio to draw closer before adding quietly. 'Be on your guard,' he locked eyes with the Greek, 'we're walking into the lion's jaws.'

# Chapter 3

While Constantinople bustled with activity on a very ordinary late winter morning, a lean, tired faced man with receding, close-cropped chestnut hair ambled up to the Palace of the Holy See. He stopped at the side gate and eyed the urban guard furtively.

'I'm here to see the bishop. He is expecting me,' he muttered, pulling his rough hemp robe a little tighter.

The guard looked apprehensive. 'Oh. And you are...?'

The robed man shuffled in discomfort. 'You don't need to know.'

The urban guard tilted his helmet back, scratching his forehead with a grin. 'Thing is, I'm afraid I do. I'm under orders not to let anyone in, unless they have an appointment. And any troublemakers...' the guard drummed his fingers on his scabbard.

'*Bosporus*,' the man hissed, eyes darting around the passing citizens.

The guard looked puzzled for a moment, and then his face dropped as he recognised the password. 'I'm sorry, sir,' he said, pushing the gate open.

Senator Peleus suppressed the urge to glare at the guard – lest he might be recognised. Instead, he kept his head down, made his way across the courtyard and over a bed of gravel directly to a rusting cellar door. The latch clicked as he heaved it open – unlocked as arranged – then he descended the steps into the gloom. He carefully paced along the candlelit corridor at the bottom, passing storeroom after storeroom, stacked with crates and bundles. Then he saw the ostentatious bulwark that was so clearly the treasure vault door. Going by its thickness, the Holy See was more than financially sound, he noted. Towards the end of the corridor, Peleus veered into the unused section of the vault network, distinguished by its darkness. He walked blind, feeling for each pillar, counting. *Two, three, turn left, one, two, three, four.* Claustrophobia clawed at his throat as all around him was silent and pitch-black. Only the chill air and cool damp of the floor tickled his senses. *Only one more pillar*, he repeated in his head, reaching out. At the same time as his fingers touched the cool pillar, a welcome halo of orange candlelight was revealed from the vault to his left. He shuffled into its paltry warmth and waited.

The location was unbecoming of men of such high station. Dank and musty, the dripping brickwork glistened all around him like the night sky. *The life of a sewer rat*, Senator Peleus shivered, pulling his robe a little tighter around his slender frame.

From above, the dull and distant clopping of palace slaves going about their business reverberated around the cellar vault. Yet, while they worked in the sunlit land of the living, their master was to conduct his business down here with a senator. *How absurd!*

Even more absurd was the fact that Peleus had never taken such a risk, indeed any risk, in his entire career. Until now. And this risk would be shared with every soul in the empire. The promise of wealth and power had seemed so much more glamorous when he had talked it over with the bishop at the festival, hubris and wine coursing through his veins. Now there was only the chill reality of what they had set in motion. *It's not too late*, a voice screamed in his head. He tried to remember the count of pillars, and then turned to step away from the candlelight.

Behind him, a shadowy figure emerged from the gloom.

Outside the main gate of the Palace of the Holy See, a gangly, hook-nosed and shaven-headed young man stood in front of the two urban guards, looking to each one expectantly.

'Yep, he's legit,' the first guard grunted to his colleague, 'the bishop said to expect a slave from Senator Tarquitius. Search 'im though.'

Pavo raised his arms with a sigh of resignation as the second guard began patting down his frayed brown tunic. Clearly, he carried only the wax tablet in his hand, but slaves will be slaves and the urban guard will be whoresons, he chuckled to himself. Then he winced as the guard ran fingers over the fresh scabs on his ribs. He gazed up at the main gate and then the ornate structure inside. This would be his first visit to the palace. Despite

GORDON DOHERTY

passing it almost every time he was sent on one of these errands, its magnificence never failed to captivate. Indeed, he considered, it rivalled even the Imperial Palace in sheer size.

'He's clear,' the guard grunted, 'smells like he's been rolling in camel turds though.'

'Funny you should say that. I *have*, just for you...' Pavo beamed.

'On your way, stinkin' runt,' the first guard shoved the gate open and the second bundled him forward.

Pavo inhaled the fresh medley of winter blooms lining the courtyard. If only he had time to dawdle, he mused. No, hand over the wax tablet, pick up the package, and head straight back by noon. Otherwise, as his ribs testified, Tarquitius' animal bodyguard, Fronto, would use him as a whipping post yet again. So no time to sneak in a little reading session at the library either, he sighed. There was a tiny sliver of give in his schedule though, he mused, feeling the coiled wire concealed under his tongue.

He hopped up the steps, waving the wax tablet at the guards on the door.

'Secretary's office is straight through,' the guard nodded to the door at the end of the hallway.

The air inside was pleasantly warm thanks to the underfloor heating, despite the cavernous ceilings. He noted the small and very ordinary oak door about half way along, touching his tongue to the concealed wire once more. Each of his footsteps sent a clattering echo around the vast space, quieting only as he entered the modestly sized office at the end. Between a tight spiral staircase and a window on the far side of the office, the secretary, a squat and puffy faced old man, sitting by a table covered with sealed papers and a stack of scrolls; his brow furrowed as he studied one.

'Message from Senator Tarquitius?' Pavo offered.

The secretary looked up, angered at the interruption. 'Hmm?' Then his face lightened. 'Oh, yes.' He ducked down under the table and rummaged before reappearing with a small canvas purse. He held his hands out for the tablet and dropped the sack into Pavo's grip, then scribbled something on a piece of parchment, tore it free and handed it to Pavo and returned to his scroll without further comment. Pavo wondered at the metallic clunking from the weighty purse. Probably enough currency to buy his freedom a thousand times over, he mused. Then his mind turned to his other business.

Turning back into the corridor, he checked all around; no guards looking his way. He slipped off his sandals and tucked them into his belt; now his steps were silent on the floor and the guards at the main entrance oblivious to his presence. He rooted the wire from his mouth with a finger, uncoiled it into a two-pronged fork-shape, and then slipped it into the lock, placing his other hand on the handle. He twisted until something caught on the prongs and then turned, but the wire bent like a limp rag. *Damn it!* Even his thoughts seemed to echo along the hall and he shot another nervous glance at the door guards, but they were still turned. He reshaped the wire and tried again. This time, with an iron clunk, the lock moved and the handle turned. The door edged open in merciful silence. He held his breath and slipped into the darkness it concealed. With a muted clunk, the door was closed again, and he was on a shadowy staircase, punctuated only by an occasional candle. The cold stone grew damp underfoot as he descended, until it became decidedly wet as he reached the bottom. A network of cellar vaults disappeared off into darkness in front of him. He made his way carefully forward. The treasure room was just beyond this shadowy honeycomb. The treasure room and the golden idol of Jupiter. A shiver of fear and anticipation danced up his spine.

Only a week previously, Pavo had been sitting on the edge of the Augusteum resting against a palm, swigging from his water skin. Having run to the senate house and then to the walls to drop off packages, he had earned himself some precious time. He had resolved to catch his breath and then head for the library, but a hand had gripped his shoulder.

'I have a job that needs taking care of, and I hear you're always keen to earn a few extra coins?' A jagged Greek voice asked.

Pavo had looked up to see a broad nose poking from a hooded cloak. 'You must have mistaken me for someone else.'

'I don't think so,' the Greek continued, unperturbed. 'My client is unhappy that something which belongs to him is in the hands of the Holy See. The door to the treasure vault has a flaw in its lock. Take this wire…'

Forty *folles* were to be his for retrieving the idol. Probably a scant fraction of the value of the piece, but a slave could never hope to sell the idol. More importantly, those forty folles were another step towards buying his freedom. Well, if his money did not go missing again, as it had last year when he had almost accrued enough.

Pavo stumbled on a loose flagstone, yanking him back to the present in the dark, cold cellar vaults. How long had he been walking? Had he taken a wrong turn? He cursed his own absent-mindedness. Then his eyes settled on a dim orange glow up ahead. Then, as he stalked forward, something flickered in the light that halted the blood in his veins; some amorphous figure, as tall as a person, *writhing* in the gloom. He crouched as he approached, feeling his way around each pillar until he heard it – a soft gurgle.

His heart thundered as the shape took form in the candlelight: two heads, one facing Pavo, eyes bulging, mouth retching, blood sputtering from its lips; the other, white haired, faced away from Pavo, hugging the first and jerking violently once, twice and again, each time another jet of blood would lurch from the first head's mouth. Pavo covered his lips and stumbled back in disgust, the purse thudding onto the ground.

At once, the shape split into two. The first part was a bleeding head with staring eyes on top of a tall, lean body, pockmarked with stab wounds. The second part was a white-haired old man in equally white, pristine robes, his hand and the dagger in it coated in a starkly contrasting crimson. The tall figure crumpled to the ground with a last rattle of breath. The old man stared at Pavo. Then he stalked forward. Pavo mouthed silent syllables, scrabbling back on the heels of his hands. The old man emitted a howl and rushed for him, dagger raised. Pavo grabbed the purse, scrambled to his feet, and hurtled into the darkness of the vaults.

The blackness offered nothing as he bounced from pillar to pillar, while the rapping footfall of the old man seemed to be always only a dagger swipe behind. Pavo tossed the purse to one side, the contents clunking down and spraying across the cellar floor. At last, the old man's footsteps slowed at the distraction. Pavo would die for the loss of the purse. Nevertheless, it was that or dying on a dagger tip here and now.

He scrambled on until a chink of light beckoned him in one particular direction, a candlelit corridor. Running onward, he barely noticed the treasure vault as he sped past it, on through an array of storerooms, then up a flight of stairs before bursting through a rusted door and out into the stark daylight of the palace grounds. He skidded and fell onto a bed of gravel, blinking.

Birds sang over the steady hum of the crowd outside, and the bored guards stood by the gates and doors, ignorant of Pavo's nightmarish encounter. As his breath stilled, disbelief swirled inside him. Had that all really happened? Surely he had to go back for the purse – otherwise, execution was a certainty. The crisp normality of the late winter morning persuaded him, and he stood to go back to the cellar door. But the door burst open at that very moment, and the snow-white haired and white robed old man stood, panting, face creased in fury, with a golden Christian Chi-Rho cross dangling around his neck. He extended a bony finger at Pavo.

'Stop the thief!' The man roared.

At once, the guards were jolted to life, haring in on Pavo, spathas sliding from their scabbards. For barely the blink of an eye, Pavo considered reasoning with them, then turned on his heel and sprinted for the main gate. From that direction, two guards came at him and they jostled as he tried to barge past. Then one of them chopped their spatha down, slitting a fine red line on Pavo's shoulder. He leapt back and spun; swords came at him from every direction – apart from the palace door. He thundered across the courtyard and in through the cavernous corridor. He burst into the secretary's office, hurdled the table, leaving a screaming secretary and a blizzard of scrolls and papers tumbling through the air in his wake, before launching himself up the staircase.

It was narrow and spiralling, and his limbs leadened as quickly as his breath grew fiery. However, the clatter of urban guards right behind him spurred him on until he stuttered to a halt as the staircase ended on a rooftop balcony. A red-tiled roof sloped up behind him and a three-story drop onto flagstones yawned in front of him.

'You're dead, thief!' One guard cried as he rounded the last spiral of stairs.

Encouraged by that and similar comments, Pavo hurdled over the balcony edge and slapped prone onto the roof, only to feel the tiles slip under him. He clawed at the tiles above as his legs began to slide from the edge, kicking into thin air. A swarm of guards buzzed on the courtyard below, sensing a reward for catching the intruder.

The crack of a breaking tile pulled his eyes back towards the balcony. One guard had ventured carefully across the tiles and stood over him, grinning like a shark, and holding out a hand. 'You've got two choices, thief. You take my hand and I'll give you a quick death. Or, you can let go,' he flicked his eyebrows up and nodded down to the courtyard.

Pavo gritted his teeth and let go.

He thrust an arm out at the wall in a dead man's desperation. Swathes of ice-smooth marble mocked him as it glided past. He screwed his eyes shut and waited on the shattering impact of the flagstones. Then, with a crunch of bone and gristle, his arm was nearly jolted from its socket, and his world became still again.

Prying one eye open, he looked down. The guards gawked up at him, dangling from a snarling carved lion head, barely a story up. *Bless Emperor Valens and his embellishment program.* At the palace gates, a crowd had gathered to take in the excitement. Seemingly, it was better to watch a slave being beaten to death than to spend the day earning an honest crust. Then they began to cheer as the guards silently grinned and drew their bows.

The twang of bowstrings harmonised with a stony crunch as the carving shuddered loose from the wall under his weight. One arrow ripped his earlobe; the rest whacking against the marble, while Pavo pivoted round and straight through the sectioned glass of a window directly below. Shards pierced his skin as he slid across the floor inside, but fright had him on his feet and racing, he was on an inner balcony, one floor up, and the corridor below was clear. Sensing an unlikely escape, he hopped over the balcony and fell onto the floor below with a grunt, then bounded for the main door of the palace. *Unguarded! They're all looking for me back there!*

As he burst through the doorway, sunshine bathed him – never had it felt so warm. Then, by his side, a glint of metal flashed. Urban guard armour. A dull crunch tore through his head.

'...that'll teach 'im,' a voice chuckled.

Hitting the ground like a sack of rubble, his mind swam in ever-blackening circles. Then he heard footsteps approaching.

'He's barely a grown man?' a frail voice spoke. 'And he's built like a gazelle, you fools – what does the Holy See pay you for?'

Pavo pried open an eye just enough to see the blurry figure of the old man with the snow-white hair.

'It won't happen again, Bishop Evagrius,' a shamed guard replied. 'It's the slave from that senator.'

'Senator Tarquitius,' the bishop spat.

'Shall we slit his throat?' The guard offered enthusiastically, grinning at Pavo as if he was a cut of raw meat.

The bishop hesitated, looked around at the gathering crowd of administrators, guards and slaves, and then sighed. He leaned in closer to the guard and spoke in a hushed voice. 'Unfortunately the situation is delicate. This slave must die, but he's not my property. Take him to Tarquitius' villa. See that the senator opens his throat by sunset.'

A gold Chi-Rho cross was swinging from a chain around the bishop's neck. Pavo's vision turned tunnel-like, fixed on the Christian symbol. His mind sank deeper into a muddy haze. Pavo lifted his head groggily and opened his mouth to speak, when a sword hilt smashed into his face.

All was black.

The mild breeze of the afternoon swirled around the villa from the open shutters. Pavo's legs wobbled as another screaming wave of pain washed from the lump above his left eye, crowned with dried blood caked into his bristled scalp. Yet he stood firm, for today, he was to face his fate.

His master's pristine villa contrasted absurdly with the slave quarters in the cellar. The filthy packed dirt floor, pooled with stagnant water, was his to call home – his and three other slaves, packed into the tiny space. Brackish water, hard cheese and fouling meat scraps were brought to them once a day. Toil in the wildly ostentatious gardens and around the villa was the diet at all other times. A bleak life, but one that he could almost tolerate, were it not for the beatings. His only grace was that, so far, Tarquitius and his senatorial cronies had not turned their sexual attentions on him, but almost every other male slave had been left bleeding and haunted after being dragged away for a night. Every morning he had run his chapped fingertips over his only possession; the legionary phalera – tracing it lightly for fear of rubbing away the precious engraving. He wore it around his neck on a leather thong. Despite everything, and in his father's memory, the fight had never left him.

That he was living his final moments was not so much of a surprise. What puzzled him more was that he had survived so many of the illicit 'jobs'. It had begun five years ago, when he was just fifteen, after a chance meeting with a shadowy character outside the Hippodrome. He had started taking on sorties for the Blues and the Greens – the pseudo-political gang rabbles who held sway on the streets of the capital. Once before, while on a job for the Greens, the Blues had caught him, then proceeded to beat him into unconsciousness, leaving him for dead in the gutter. He remembered that sensation; the numbness, the feeling of darkness creeping slowly through his flesh. He had lain there all night, and only when the morning sun touched his skin was he able to move, to crawl back to Tarquitius' villa. He shuddered at the memory and prayed that if he was to die today, that it would be a quick death.

Purposeful footsteps hammered towards the door behind him. Pavo jolted as the doors shot apart, crashing against the walls. The footsteps rapped up behind him and then stopped dead. Silence curled its fingers around his neck, but he resisted the urge to turn around.

'Pavo! You treacherous little runt! I keep you, feed you…have you any idea what you've done? Have you?'

The broad, toga-clad figure of Tarquitius strode into view to seethe in front of him. Thirteen years had done little to improve the senator's sickly appearance. More than matched for height these days, he struggled to avoid Tarquitius' bloodshot, bulging eyes.

'A senator's name is not to be sullied!' Tarquitius barked in a tone so high pitched that his voice crackled off towards the end of the sentence. 'A slave will not shame his master! A thief is disgrace enough – but to insult my name by stealing from the bishop?'

Pavo tried to suppress the small itch in his throat, but it grew into words that tumbled from his lips. 'I stole nothing. A man was murdered…'

'Silence!' Tarquitius' cry reverberated around the room and his hand whipped up – the stumpy knuckles hovered in a fist, inches from Pavo's face. The two stared at each other.

'What are you waiting for?' Pavo spoke, his voice trembling. Every other slave had suffered terrible wounds from the same hand. Some had been battered into total paralysis and some to death. Fronto the slave master had broken nearly every bone in Pavo's body over the years, but Tarquitius had never hit him. Not once. He thought of that day in the slave market and the crone. *See that the boy comes to no harm from your hand.*

Tarquitius' eyes narrowed and he lowered his hand. 'You play a dangerous game, boy. The bishop *expects* your throat to be cut. No, he *demands* your blood!' He hissed, his breath reeking of garlic. 'I cannot let this go unpunished. The bishop wants you gone from this world, and that is what must happen.'

Pavo's skin crawled.

'Fronto!' He snarled, the name bouncing around the villa, searching the corridors for the slave master.

So there would be one last bout of pain. Just like the beatings. The physical agony was nothing to him now – just a routine, really. Yet the darkness of death crept on his skin as it hared in on him.

'My name will be sullied if the senate house finds out about this,' Tarquitius grumbled.

Pavo blinked, eyeing the senator, something was different about his tone.

'But…you are to be…freed,' Tarquitius spat the words like a sinew of troublesome meat. 'Freed and exiled.'

Pavo's stomach fell away. Freedom? That distant memory.

'Don't get too excited, boy,' Tarquitius' mouth curled up into a grin. 'Exiled to the edge of the empire. Invasion territory. Your days will be spent with the limitanei.'

'The border legions?'

A posting to the border legions was thought little more than a delayed death sentence, with the limits of the empire awash with rampant barbarian hordes. However, his heart tasted only sweet liberation, spiced with fear of the unknown. He lifted his hand to touch the bronze disc through his tunic.

'When you fall at the end of a sword, then my hands are clean,' Tarquitius warbled, his chin quivering in stubborn belief.

The crone, Pavo realised. His life was being spared – no, probably just prolonged for a short period. All because of the crone. His head echoed with a thousand questions, but one roared the loudest.

'What did she say to you?' He probed. 'That day – what did she say to you?'

Tarquitius' face whitened and his eyes bulged. His tongue jabbed out to moisten his trembling lips. But before anything could come out, Fronto bowled into the room behind him, a stench of sweat announcing his arrival.

'Master?'

Tarquitius continued to stare wide-eyed at Pavo, but addressed his slave master. 'Get this boy out of my villa and down to the docks. Wear hoods and be sure you go unrecognised. Purchase a berth for him to travel on the next ferry to Tomis. The border garrison at Durostorum will be glad of another piece of barbarian spear-fodder.' He turned to Pavo. 'I have sent a messenger to tell them to expect you, so turn up, or there'll be a slave-hunt on top of you within days, and they will show you no mercy, boy.'

He turned away, but then spun back, drawing eye to eye with Pavo, grinning terribly. 'You will be dead within the year, boy, I can assure you. But should you show your face in this city again...' he began, wide-eyed.

Then his face dropped.

'...and you will die horribly.'

# Chapter 4

The first century crunched rhythmically over the bracken forest path. They had woken that morning under sodden tents. At least the rain had eased from the driving sleet showers of the previous day to a tame vertical drizzle. Now, late afternoon, the light was beginning to fade as they moved under a canopy of leaves, and a musty whiff of damp vegetation hung in the air. At the head of the column, Gallus systematically scoured the way ahead; the men had marched without rest since dawn and now time was the enemy. Without a safe campsite, they would have to employ a double watch tonight.

'Can't see a bloody thing, sir,' Felix rasped, batting another branch from his face.

Gallus kept his eyes forward, trudging on. 'The map definitely puts the first fort here, maybe just a bit farther ahead...I don't know, the forest has swallowed up every other bloody landmark we were supposed to have passed,' he pinged a finger off the parchment map, 'this map must date from the Trojan War!'

'Standard fare for a recon mission, eh?' Felix sighed, craning over to examine the sodden parchment. 'Open plains and valleys to the south and we're instructed to go crashing through the forests!'

Gallus traced a finger over their route again in hope of a revelation. Three Roman forts lay across the neck of the diamond-shaped peninsula, but the etching also indicated watchtowers, trading posts, roads and settlements. He had chosen not to veer from this one 'highway' in search of these – not so wise in hindsight. He cursed to himself silently.

'We're headed almost due east and this path is, or used to be, Roman. Unless some bugger has dug the thing up for fun, we'll reach the fort before nightfall,' Gallus asserted despite his own doubts. Yet he could sense his optio's unease. 'We're not here to engage the Goths, Felix, simply to ascertain their positions along this frontier.'

37

'Yes, sir,' Felix replied, 'just wish we could see *something* – not much of a reconnaissance if all there is to report is bloody trees,' he spluttered and then moaned as yet another branch whipped into his face, leaving a sprig of leaves in his forked beard.

Gallus' eyes were trained on the map and the large red dot on the southwest edge of the diamond; the fortified citadel of Chersonesos, the old Roman capital. Now it was rumoured to be the Goths' main trading centre. Tribunus Nerva had explained that the mission sponsors had favoured this complex countryside reconnaissance over the alternative; sending a single spy into the city disguised as a merchant to measure the Gothic strength. Gallus sighed; Emperor Valens and the shadowy figures that surrounded him saw the first century as little more than pawns, happy to face the implications of orders thrown down from above like scraps of meat. He bit back the urge to moan.

'If leaves and branches are all we have to face here, Felix, I'll be a contented man.'

He had to stay positive. Gallus knew there was still work to do with his new century to form them into a cohesive unit of men – men who could trust each other in battle. Nerva had set this only as a secondary objective for Gallus during the mission brief. However, to Gallus it was key to their survival in this foreign land and to the future of the limitanei, the border legions, as a whole. A hotchpotch of recruits, veterans and comitatenses dropouts, the XI Claudia were withering. As small an operation as this was, a successful reconnaissance could sow the seeds that might see the XI Claudia return for a full conquest of this old province. It could inspire the thousands of men in the other border legions, spread along the frontiers in draughty forts with nothing to aspire to but staying off the end of a Gothic spear.

He turned to his optio as an icy trickle of rainwater spidered down inside his tunic. 'It's cold, wet and painful, aye, but Nerva wants us to be the leading light for the Danubian legions, wants us to breathe a bit of belief back into the frontiers.'

Felix lifted his eyebrows. 'Aye, and wants to pay us triple, I hope?'

Gallus offered him a cocked eyebrow. 'What, so you can fill the coffers and drain the barrels at *The Boar?*'

Felix chuckled, then dropped back and took the silver eagle standard from the aquilifer again, hoisting it so that the ruby bull banner caught the gentle breeze. 'Up the pace, lads. Baked pheasant and garum dates for grub tonight!' Mocking catcalls were hurled from the veterans, and the recruits to the rear buckled into a chorus of laughter.

Gallus felt a rare sparkle of warmth course through his veins at the brief glimpse of camaraderie. Since his wife's death, the legion had meant everything to him. He could only numb the loneliness in his heart by becoming part of the military machine. The hazy days of his upbringing in Rome, when life had colour, were slipping away. To be old and grey, settled on the porch of a small villa by Capua in the Italian countryside, sipping wine with their children and grandchildren at play – that was the dream he and Olivia had shared. Now, it was the sweet memories of his precious few years with her that were fading like a dream.

Suddenly, something whipped across his face. Stunned for an instant, Gallus raised his hand to his cheek – dark-red stained his fingers. All around him, the forest writhed as he eyed the arrow quivering furiously in the tree to his side.

'Ambush!' He roared. As the word left his mouth, the air filled with a swarm of hissing missiles, punching into the pack of legionaries. A handful fell with a grunt, arrows shivering in their exposed necks and limbs.

'Shields!' Gallus cried. The rest of the men collapsed into a shielded column, three lines of men, presenting shield bosses to their attackers; those in the middle using their shields as a roof. Those too slow to slip into position were punched to the ground under the hail.

Gallus crouched, teeth gritted, as volley after volley of missiles hammered down upon them like iron hail. He glanced along his side and then back to the other side. To his right, a young legionary gripped his shield by the rim, and it wavered on every arrow strike, his knuckles slipping. Gallus reached over to grapple the shield handle in example, but recoiled in disgust when an arrow zipped in through the gap above the offending shield and crunched through the holder's eye. Another man down. Then another, and another. The mini *testudo* contracted further and further as Roman bodies toppled with every bombardment. Gallus growled at the impotence of their situation. These men had entrusted their lives to him, but they were being picked off like mosquitoes. First century or not, they were not combat ready, unable to maintain a solid testudo, even. Every avenue of attack he could think of would mean dropping their shield wall for a moment at least. That meant certain annihilation. Yet to stay put meant they had only moments left in any case.

'Sir! They're moving,' Felix croaked, now crouched back to back with his centurion. Gallus risked a glance out of the shield wall as the rain of arrows slowed, and spotted the darting movement behind the tree line. Was this the build up to a charge?

A crack of thunder rippled across the sky and with it came a torrent of rain and a fork of lightning. No advance came. Again, Gallus stole a glance above his shield. The tree line was empty.

'Felix, what's happening over on your side?'

The optio gasped. 'They're retreating, sir; they're running northward!'

Gallus cocked an eyebrow. 'Running away? What the...'

His words tailed off and he touched a hand to the earth. He felt a tremor, growing in intensity. His eyes widened as he saw the foliage ripple up ahead. Something was coming for them, and it was coming for them quickly.

'Cavalry charge – right on top of us. Form a line three deep...' then he hissed, so only Felix could hear, '...or we're dead!'

Ignoring the cramp in their tired limbs, his men sprang from the crouched testudo shell, and pulled round to face south, spears dug into the mud like a threadbare porcupine. The freezing rain clawed at their faces as they beheld the dark mass hurtling towards them.

Gallus' eyes narrowed as he tried to take in the charge; a hundred or more stocky riders with long dark wispy jet-black locks billowing behind rounded caps and clad in skins; what looked like composite bows and javelins looped on their backs, with long cutting swords and daggers hanging from their belts. As they thundered closer, Gallus' features wrinkled at their faces; flattened, broad, and yellow. Their cheeks appeared to be symmetrically ripped with a triple line of angry scar tissue and their eyes were almond-like and unblinking. The riders on the wing of the charge had lengths of rope looped into lassos on their belts.

'Hold steady!' Gallus roared over the rumble of hooves.

As Gallus filled his lungs at the last, his mind flitted with visions of Olivia on their wedding night; Olivia carrying their child. Then, the shadowy form of mother and child on the pyre. *I'm coming to be with you.* He leaned forward, feeling his men bracing along with him, when suddenly, like a storm dropping, the onrushing cavalry broke into two halves. They washed past the stunned legionary group, and on at the same breakneck pace to the north.

Gallus expelled the breath in his lungs, his mind reeled. 'What the...' he glanced at Felix. 'They're after the archers!'

His line slumped in utter relief. Some men belly-laughed in shock, others vomited in the mud. Felix looked down the track as the rain became sheet-like.

'Who...what are we dealing with here, sir?'

Gallus gazed down the track with Felix in bewilderment as a crash of lightning illuminated their faces.

'The lion's jaws, Felix. The lion's jaws!'

# Chapter 5

Darkness settled on Constantinople as the revelry from inside the Imperial Palace rolled out over the rooftops. Senator Tarquitius drew the crisp night air into his lungs, resting his elbows on the balcony to marvel at the burgeoning city as he sipped watered wine from a fine silver chalice.

Things were certainly looking up for him since his expulsion of that damned slave Pavo; the crone's words haunted his nightmares still, but at least now he knew he could not harm the boy and her curse could not take effect. As for the rest of her rasping diatribe…well, that could wait.

Now, here he was in his element. All the ingredients were present; Roman aristocracy, slackened morals and high spirits. This potent recipe had provided him with the ideal political stepping-stone here in Constantine's *Nova Roma*. Even the steeliest opponent would drop his guard after a skinful of wine and the close attention of an exotic slave girl. Eventually, promises would be made and secrets revealed to his crystal-clear mind. Political careers soared and crashed on such sensitive information. Tarquitius had taught the senate a valuable lesson with his dealings; he was a player in this age of imperial upheaval.

The blossoming of the Christian faith had gripped the minds of the people and provided another channel entirely for the brave and ambitious to seize power. To adopt the worshipping of a Judean that their ancestors had brutally murdered seemed to fit snugly with the expedient madness of the empire of recent times. Only a few generations previously, citizens had cheered as the lions ripped out the throats of Christians bound to posts in the arena. Now, Rome had pompously nominated herself at the head of the faith, and in direct contact with the Christian God. Now, a new breed of madness held sway with Emperor Valens; Arianism, the stream of Christianity the emperor favoured, had been forced upon the faithful from the plebs all the way up the ecclesiastical tree. Unhappy clergy tend to be more receptive to the ideas of a senator, he mused. Now, he smirked, the fruit was ripe for picking.

A shriek of laughter pierced the air together with a crash of breaking glass. Tarquitius' ears twitched as he heard approaching footsteps. Gently, he slid back into the shadows and watched the doorway.

A white cloaked and hooded figure emerged, awaiting some form of greeting.

'Senator, are you here?'

Tarquitius smirked, and then silently slid into the pale light afforded by the torch above the doorway. The cloaked figure remained unaware of his presence until he spoke in a cool tone.

'Tired of the orgy already?'

The cloaked figure spun round, startled.

'Senator, you nearly scared the life from me.'

Tarquitius grinned, revelling in the chill of the engagement. This partnership was a frosty one; frosty but necessary in order to obtain the greatness he was born for.

'Good evening, Your Eminence. I apologise for startling you, but you can never be too careful in a tender situation such as this.'

The cloaked figure lowered his hood to reveal craggy features, framed by a thick crop of snow-white hair. Tarquitius wondered at his own ingenuity in forging a partnership with this character; Bishop Evagrius, Patriarch of Constantinople, a mortal apparently in direct contact with God.

The bishop smiled. 'Indeed, noble senator, I trust the only people who know of this meeting are standing here?'

'Of course, Your Eminence,' Tarquitius replied, echoing the bishop's tone. The concealed presence of his bodyguard Fronto in the darkness by the door meant indeed that all those who knew of this encounter were indeed on this balcony.

'Then let us discuss the progress of our common objective. What of the Bosporus reconnaissance?'

Straight to it, thought Tarquitius. The fragile facade of this holy man hid a steely core, and he had certainly used this to bash his way through the hierarchy of the Holy See. *Kindred spirits*, Tarquitius mused. Evagrius raised an eyebrow at the extended silence, but Tarquitius allowed another moment to pass before he replied. He, not the bishop, would dictate this conversation.

'Our allies report that the reconnaissance force has been located and is currently being tracked. The Goths have a scattering of war bands patrolling the old frontier, but our allies are easily strong enough to protect the reconnaissance from such small numbers.'

Evagrius frowned. 'And what of the main Gothic armies? It is imperative that the expedition does not witness their conflict with our allies. We need to present Bosporus as an open door, a harvest ripe for the reaping.'

Tarquitius clenched his teeth at the scrutiny. This was supposed to be an equal partnership. He drew a deep breath in through his nostrils, adjusting his back upright, thrusting out his rubbery chins, and then set his eyes upon the innocent gaze of the bishop.

'Our allies have been instructed to divert the reconnaissance expedition from the path of the Gothic armies at all costs,' he replied, angering himself with the tightness in his voice, 'as we agreed, Your Eminence. And the Gothic armies themselves will be tackled in due course.'

'Keep a cool head, Senator. The path to the imperial throne will be clear if we pull this off. The emperor is hungry for foreign success and will be all too keen to rush his thin forces to claim Bosporus. But the people...the people are ripe for revolution. Then the floodgates will be open...' The bishop's eyes sparkled rapaciously. 'So much rests on this that perhaps we should not hang our hopes on our allies alone,' he held out a bulging hemp purse and a scroll of parchment. 'Take this, you will need it to smooth your next visit to the senate house.'

'Your Eminence?' Tarquitius asked as he took the two articles gingerly.

'The scroll will explain all, Senator,' he nodded, before his eyes fell cold again. 'But keep in mind that this venture is costing the treasury of the Holy See of Constantinople vast sums. If anything goes wrong, then this reconnaissance party, our pawns, will have to be crushed like ants. And I will be forced to look for a scapegoat.' A gentle smile bearing absolutely no warmth crept across the bishop's face. He continued. 'Greedy senators make the best scapegoats.'

A fury boiled inside Tarquitius' chest, and his eyes darted to the dark shadow that moved by the doorway. He quickly raised his hand, and Fronto slid his sword back into its scabbard with a grunt.

Evagrius raised an eyebrow. 'So you brought your thug along to protect you? This doesn't bode well for preserving a trusting relationship, does it, Senator Tarquitius?'

Again, the tone bit sharply at Tarquitius' pride. Right now, He could order this conniving old man's throat to be slit from ear to ear, if he wished. However, he knew the path to greatness meant toleration of characters like this until they had served their purpose. Then, when he gave the order, it would be all the sweeter.

'All is going to plan, Your Eminence. That is all you should be concerned with. It would be wise to remember that your goals are in my hands as much as mine are in yours.' He glared at the bishop's tranquil features. 'Fronto!' He barked. The Herculean figure emerged from the shadows again, grimacing at the bishop as Tarquitius marched along the balcony to the doorway. The bishop returned a gentle smile, before Fronto turned and followed his master.

All alone on the balcony under the night sky, Bishop Evagrius placed his hands together to pray. The trio of archers positioned on adjacent balconies read the signal and lowered their bows. Senator Tarquitius was to live on, for now...

# Chapter 6

Gallus sat cross-legged by the campfire, the next to useless parchment map of the Bosporus peninsula dangling from his fingertips as he gazed at the dancing flames. Several paths forked out through the woods before converging on the westernmost fort on the peninsula neck. He lifted a spit from the fire and tore a chunk of mutton off with his teeth. Each path was a roll of the dice, and the first roll had been crushing. Their numbers now dictated that they had to play it safe.

Only sixty-two men were left of the original detachment of one hundred and ten that had set off from the *Aquila*. They had prepared a miniature square of palisades and ditches in this clearing, and were operating a rota of double watch, as he had feared. But there was no way he would allow them to be caught like sitting targets again, Gallus swore to himself, his teeth grinding through the tough meat.

Glancing over to the huddle of off-duty legionaries, Gallus loosened his frown as he tuned into the unmistakably gruff tones of Zosimus; the ox-like Thracian regaled the group with a tale of two Cretan women, their strange sexual habits – and his indulgence with both of them after knocking out their husbands. Bursts of throaty laughter pierced the crackle of the fire at every twist of the sordid anecdote. The giant soldier and his comrades displayed the steely ruthlessness he loved them for - the bitter experience of the day undetectable so soon after the ambush.

These men had lost friends and trusted colleagues today, and their own lives had hung in the balance, yet they were still together as a unit. Gallus sighed at the sparkle dancing in the eyes of his men; years of bloody loss could toughen even the softest of hides.

Gallus caught Felix's eye as his optio wandered over. 'I can't take any more of the filth they're coming out with. Honestly, enough to make you heave up your grub, that is.'

Gallus tried to wipe the vexation from his face, nodding towards the log on the opposite side of the fire.

'And I reckon you could do with talking over what happened today,' Felix ventured.

Gallus relaxed his frown and nodded. The optio was more attuned to the mood of the others in the century, and he could read Gallus like a book, despite the iron glare. *Damn him*, Gallus smiled inside. He began before the Greek sat down. 'An in-and-out recon mission this was supposed to be. Half my men are lying back there in the woods, without a single one of those whoresons even taking a scratch.'

The optio thumped down with a sigh, his weary eyes fixing on Gallus across the fire. 'Sir, we'll send back a party tomorrow to bury our comrades. What happened today frustrated all of us, but not one of the men would have done anything differently. Defence was our only option, and it was down to you that so many of us survived.'

Gallus shook his head with a wry chuckle. 'It's just galling – I'd give my last *nummus* to hear that those horsemen had cut down every one of those whoresons further up the path.' He straightened up, picking up the splintered, blood tinged arrow shaft from his pack, scrutinising the iron tip in the firelight. 'We need to address the bigger issue here, Felix – just who are we dealing with? Those archers were Gothic going by the arrowheads. But those horsemen,' he sighed. 'Who were they? And why did they give us, a legionary column in the middle of nowhere, a body swerve? We would have been easy pickings for them.'

Felix nodded, his gaze falling into the flames. 'I think the Gothic archers were tracking us from the moment we entered the forest, waiting until we were in the thick to shower us with their arrows. The horsemen I can't be so sure about, stocky buggers, from the east I reckon...' The optio's voice trailed off.

'Yes,' Gallus nodded, 'not what we signed up for.'

'Not just that, sir. I think I've seen their like before, when I was posted out to the frontiers in North Armenia. That place was riddled with little market towns and trading posts, and there were all sorts of barbarians coming in from the steppe to barter hides, meat, slaves, spices and gems. Mithras knows where they picked it all up from. Probably best not to know.'

Gallus nodded, his lips curling in bemusement. 'Just what the empire needs – another race to grind on her borders.' He ran his hands through the retreating peak of his hair. 'I smelt a rat as soon as Nerva delivered the brief. He was nervous – knew something was wrong. His hands were tied by Dux Vergilius and whoever else had the emperor's ear over this one. This stuff is over our heads – and outside our remit, Felix, and I don't think we can deal with it now. We're going to complete this mission, and then get out of here. But first we have other business to take care of. Nerva said no detours, but…'

'The Goths?' Felix raised an eyebrow.

Gallus nodded. 'Time for revenge.'

# Chapter 7

'Oi, you couple of fairies! This is as far as I'm goin',' the cart driver grumbled as the rickety heap of wood and wheels slowed at the crossroads.

Pavo squinted at the dawn sunshine as he woke. His second morning of freedom. He shivered at the early chill and made it half way through a yawn before he noticed the snoring blonde-mopped young man resting on his shoulder. Shrugging him away, Pavo stood to stretch his spindly legs and ran his palms over his freshly cropped dark bristles. The bed of hay and grain sacks hadn't been the most comfortable, but he had slept like a baby since leaving the port of Tomis – especially after the stomach churning boat journey to get there from Constantinople. He touched a hand to the black bruise on his ribs as he slid towards the cart edge; Fronto had indulged in one last session of pummelling him. But it was the last one, and that at least warmed his heart.

'Much appreciated,' Pavo croaked to the driver, leaping to the ground. The driver glared at him and held out a hand. Still unused to holding money that he alone owned, Pavo rummaged in his purse and dug out two follis of the ten Tarquitius had bitterly handed over to him before he left the villa. He tossed the coins to the driver. Oddly, the driver nodded back to him, as he would to any citizen or freedman.

The cart set off without delay. His travelling companion, still dismounting, stumbled onto the road in his filthy tunic, with a ragged satchel over his shoulder.

'Oh for…what was his problem?' The blonde lad cursed.

Pavo shrugged, smiling, rummaging in his satchel to pull out two boiled eggs that he had bought at the docks in Tomis. He peeled the shell from one and munched into the white, eyeing the lad; probably a similar age to himself, with a tumble of blonde curls hanging on his forehead, framing emerald eyes and rosy, chubby cheeks like a cherub bust. But it was the inherently cheeky grin that caught the eye.

'Ah well, I hope he gets as far away as possible before he realises the coin I gave him last night was fake,' the youth snorted. 'Sura, Decimus Lunius Sura, unofficial King of Adrianople – here to hinder the legions,' he grinned, stretching out his hand. 'Didn't mean to pass out on you like that, but you were sound asleep when I hitched a ride. So what name do you go by?'

'Numerius Vitellius Pavo – here because…er…because the streets of Constantinople couldn't handle my greatness,' he replied, cursing his poor show of wit as he clasped Sura's hand. He didn't really have a proud history to share.

'Okay,' Sura nodded uncertainly, wrinkling his forehead and plucking the other egg from Pavo's hand. Before Pavo could protest, Sura had cracked off the top of the shell and sunk his teeth into the white. 'Well, I hope you're up to the walk?' He mumbled through a full mouth, jabbing a thumb over his shoulder to the plain stretching out ahead.

Pavo turned away, unable to suppress a chuckle at this lad's swagger, then he hopped up onto the verge at the roadside to take in their surroundings. The River Danubius snaked across the land from the west until its rapids poured into the shimmering waters of the *Pontus Euxinus*. The silhouetted bulk of the town of Durostorum hugged the banks of the river; the squat stone bulwark of the XI Claudia fort lay dead centre of the plain between the crossroads and the town, a rocky island in the sea of cornfields about twelve stadia ahead of them. He traced his eyes over the train of merchant carts along the road to the fort; a constant flow in both directions – headed in with wine and food and back out laden with legionary wages.

*When you fall at the end of a sword, then my hands are clean.* He shivered at Tarquitius' words.

They walked, they bantered then they ate some more when Sura pulled a chunk of bread from his satchel – dry but welcome, and washed down with a skin of chill water. Then as the shadow of the fort loomed closer, both fell quiet. The fort, weatherworn and half-clad in spidering green moss, dominated the landscape for him. He cast an envious glance at Sura by his side; the Thracian's face didn't betray any hint of the fear Pavo felt gnawing at his insides again. The legions were sold as a glorious career path, but the truth of military life was brutally summarised by the sight of young men mutilating themselves on the city streets to avoid conscription. It was hard to believe the texts he had read telling of a time when the army was the most sought after vocation in the empire. Sure he was free, but survival was a transient concept in the legions.

'Watch out!' Sura yelled, shoving him to the roadside. A trade cart hurtled between them, its rider standing tall – taller than any Roman, with his blonde topknot billowing in his own slipstream. A spray of grit and dust whipped up and over their faces.

'Bloody Goths!' Sura spat. 'Seems they can't make up their mind whether to trade with us or make war. Those big buggers are exactly the types we'll be up against after we've signed up. They're everywhere, I hear.' Sura turned to Pavo with a manic sparkle in his eyes. 'You scared?'

'No!' Pavo started.

Sura grew a wry smile and nodded slowly. 'I'll make you a deal,' he said, looking Pavo up and down, then nodding towards the legionary fort. 'Let's face it, neither of us is built like a legionary…you're more like a baby deer with those legs,' he prodded a finger at Pavo's slender knock-knees, scuffed and bruised. 'So if we're going to get through life in the legions, we can't let the veterans mess with us. You watch my back, and I'll watch yours, eh? Deal?'

Pavo noticed an unfamiliar feeling in the pit of his stomach – this was the first time someone had spoken to him as a friend for over a year. Back at the slave quarters under Tarquitius' villa, Kyros the Cretan, maybe ten years Pavo's senior, had played dice with him at night and shared food. Together they had suppressed the bitterness of slavery and kept each other's spirits up for many seasons. Then Tarquitius had bludgeoned him for stealing stale bread from the pantry until blood haemorrhaged from his eyes and ears.

He bit back the cold memory, accepting Sura's outstretched hand. 'They aren't too complimentary about the legions from where I come from. They say the soldiers are either local farmer boys, too young even to shave, or scum scraped from the city gutters; beggars, brigands and cutthroats - the scummier, the better.'

'Didn't put you off though, eh?' Sura chirped, slapping Pavo on the back.

'Look, I didn't choose this…'

'Aye, aye. And as I said; I'm King of Adrianople,' Sura mocked.

'Adrianople? I heard that lot couldn't hold a torch to the street gangs of the capital,' Pavo sighed dismissively, hitching up his pack. 'The Blues and the Greens; vicious buggers – and I had to deal with them on a daily basis.'

'Course you did,' Sura picked up a piece of slate and hurled it. He was already in flight by the time it skated off the back of Pavo's head.

'You dirty camel's arse!' Pavo roared, bounding for his attacker.

Pavo launched himself forward as Sura stumbled down the rough banking at the side of the road. They crunched together, head over heels down into the parched roadside ditch. Pavo swung for Sura's gut, only brushing knuckles against tunic, and falling face-first in the dust. Sura roared with laughter. Enraged, Pavo shot out an arm, grasping Sura's ankle, wrenching him from his feet and onto his back. Triumphantly, he scooped up a handful of dust, cramming it into Sura's mouth.

'Breakfast on me, and there's a nice portion of donkey turd in there for you,' he yelped. Suddenly, the neighing of a horse and a gruff voice boomed over the pair of them.

'Names and ranks?'

Both of them sprang up to face the voice. Squinting through the sunlight, Pavo made out the bull-like form of a mounted officer in full dress centurion armour; a bronzed cuirass over a dark-red tunic and a horsehair crest billowing across his helmet.

'Names and ranks? Don't make me ask again!' The centurion barked through his tombstone teeth. Pavo noted his heavy brow seemed set in a permanent frown.

Sura spluttered the clods of dirt from his mouth, to which the centurion cocked an eyebrow.

'We're on our way to enlist in the XI Claudia legion, sir!' Pavo jumped in. 'I'm Numerius Vitellius Pavo.'

'Decimus Lunius Sura,' Sura croaked.

'Couple of skinny runts coming to enlist, eh? Dunno what the army is coming to,' he muttered. 'Centurion Brutus, chief centurion of the second cohort,' the officer grunted, rubbing his stubbled anvil of a chin, 'and I can only beg Mithras that you don't end up in my ranks. Out of the ditch and follow me in.' He nodded to the gatehouse of the fort, the ruby-red bull banners flapping in the breeze from the flanking watchtowers, where a set of six grim-faced legionaries glared down on them. 'Or would you rather stay out here to roll about in the donkey shit by the roadside?'

Pavo and Sura swapped a nervous glance and then scrambled up the banking. Sura followed Pavo's lead, standing straight as a flagpole, chin up and chest out.

'Ready, sir!' Pavo chirped, but his grin dropped as the centurion's steely glare remained.

'We'll see about that,' he said, calmly turning his mount towards the legionary fort at a gentle trot.

# Chapter 8

Night cloaked the forest and only the hooting of an owl pierced the silence around the crumbling fort. The crisp air tingled on Gallus' skin as he lay prone in the bracken. Risking another glance over the foliage, he scrutinised the inside of the fort through the jagged crevice that had rent the south wall.

A fire in the centre of the flagstone courtyard danced, silhouetting the Gothic warband gathering around its heat – every one of them towering like giants, their topknotted blonde locks adding to their other-worldly appearance. But they wore no armour or weapons, he noticed keenly. He flicked his gaze up to the dark shapes strolling the battlements; these men were clad in red leather cuirasses and longswords and bows hung on their backs. Fifteen of them in total, a large watch for such a small fort. Did they know something was coming for them?

He had sent a small party back to the site of the ambush at dawn, to give their comrades a proper burial. *Mithras bless you, Felix.* Yet he suspected the spectre of the Goths would rise again when they reached this first fort. Then, a gentle scuffle behind him signalled the return of Avitus from his scouting mission.

'I've circled the fort, sir,' he panted, wiping the sweat from his bald pate and slipping his helmet back on. 'There is no larger force in the vicinity, and I count ninety inside the fort, all fighting men. They are definitely the ambush party we came across yesterday.'

Gallus clenched his fist against the hilt of his sword.

'Prisoners?'

Avitus nodded firmly, his lips pursed. 'Just the one, sir. Young lad called Proteus. A farmer boy, only signed up with us weeks ago.'

Gallus ground his teeth. A farmer boy; words that could describe most of the legion these days. The men he had sent back for the burials had returned, reporting that only forty-seven bodies lay in the forest – yet forty-

54

eight were missing. He and Felix had debated earlier that day on whether to engage the Goths. Now the decision was made.

'The quicker we move the less pain our man in there will suffer. Take up your position, Avitus.'

As Avitus slid down next to the other legionaries on the ground, Gallus took one final scan of the area. He waited, eyes trained on the Gothic watchmen on the walls. The silence grew agonizing until at last, the pair on the front wall turned in towards the gatehouse. Gallus cupped his hands over his mouth and whistled a trilling note twice.

Splitting into two groups, the legionaries scuttled for the two corner towers of the front wall of the fort, stilling themselves against the chill of the stonework. Gallus, leading the right-hand group, screwed up his eyes at the towers; the timber tower houses on top of the stone walls had long since decayed and this would be their way in – giving them a semi-fortified high ground to hold at the same time. But one slip, one yelp, any mistake and they'd have nearly twice their number to deal with in a straight fight. Gallus looked to the far end of the wall and prayed that Felix and his men were ready in the blackness.

Felix counted behind tightly closed eyes. *Four, five, six...*

'Go!' He hissed to a startled Zosimus. The big Thracian then swung a length of looped hemp rope up to a timber stump on the outside edge of the tower, where it caught silently. He yanked it twice and then grunted. 'It's all yours, sir,' he whispered.

Felix flashed a wry smile; being the shortest legionary in the century meant he was always the first name on the sheet where stealth was required, as with poor Avitus on the other side of the fort. 'Smallest buggers in the century versus the tallest warriors in the world,' he cursed bitterly. He filled his lungs as he looped and knotted the rope around his torso, kicked off his boots and passed his helmet to Zosimus before hoisting himself to walk up the wall, wincing at the scuffling and scraping of his bare feet on the masonry. His arms stiffened as he started pacing upwards, his eyes fixed on the lip of the tower. Flakes of dry and rotten wood sprinkled in his eyes as his weight on the rope ground at the stump up above. Gently placing one foot after the other Felix settled into a rhythm, and his heart steadied a little. Then there was a terrible groan of bending wood. He froze, praying for the beam to settle. Then there was a sharp crack.

His world whooshed upside down, a blinding white light filled his vision as his head cracked off of the stonework and his sword slipped from its sheath, clattering against the wall. Gruff yells broke out from the battlements above. As Felix's head stopped spinning, he quickly realised he was dangling like a fish on a line, but then he was jolted upwards. Panicked, he grappled at the rope, kicking out to get a foothold on the wall again.

Lurching all too rapidly towards the top of the wall, he stiffened in horror; a snarling blonde-locked and bearded Gothic guardsman glared down at him with icy-blue eyes and a snarl. The blood pounded in his ears and he started kicking out from the wall to increase his weight. Still he rose until he could smell the ale from the Goth's breath. He closed his eyes as he felt himself being scraped over the parapet and onto the battlements, clenching his fists in grim expectation.

'Whoa!' Hissed Gallus. 'Easy, friend – you're safe!'

Felix opened his eyes to his centurion and Avitus, huddled on the battlement behind their shields under a bombardment of missiles from the insides of the fort. The Goth remained hanging over the wall, now with a spatha lodged in his back and his blonde hair dripping red. Felix ripped the weapon from the corpse.

'Get down,' Avitus growled, yanking the optio under cover just as a volley of arrows sclaffed off their shields. Pinned down, they glanced in hope at the edge of both towers – no reinforcements yet. But now the wall-guard had raced to the scene of the incident. Seven of them.

'Push up or we're dead!' Gallus barked pointing to the narrow section of battlement still with covering parapet on both the inside and outside.

Avitus locked shields with his centurion and they raced forward, butting into the midriffs of the Goths, who stumbled backwards. Felix crouched between them; the narrow battlement meant their flank would be safe, but the weight of Gothic numbers would quickly tell, pushing them back out into the hail of arrows.

'Be ready, Felix,' Gallus panted.

Felix braced as two huge axe-bearers charged at them. Two crashing blows rained on the mini shield wall, sending the Romans staggering backwards. Then, as the giants swung their weapons again, Avitus and Gallus lifted their shields apart for Felix to lurch out, a spatha in each hand, thrusting them into the ribcages of their attackers. The Goths staggered backwards, gurgling and then toppling onto the courtyard of the fort. A thud sounded from the other end of the battlements and the remaining five Goths on the wall spun to the source; Roman reinforcements. The wall guards wavered, every moment seeing more Romans pour onto the walls behind the shielded trio. One barked an order and they turned and fled down the ladders to their mustering kinsmen in the courtyard below.

Felix grinned at his centurion – the wall was theirs! But Gallus nodded briskly to the rope.

'Ready?' The centurion hissed.

Felix risked a glance at the end, dangling in the courtyard below; surrounded by the swell of Goths. 'Oh right, forgot about this bit. Great,' he spat, taking up the rope.

Gallus cupped his hands to his mouth and let out another double whistle. A rumbling grew from the rocks where they had hidden moments before.

A wrap of *plumbatae* came crashing over the wall on either side and the legionaries distributed the lead weighted darts among their number. Each legionary took his plumbata at the ready.

'Let 'em have it!' Gallus roared.

Felix watched the volley of darts rain down, sinking into the Gothic front line and driving back their swell from the end of the rope. He mouthed a silent prayer to Mithras and leapt from the battlement, his palms searing as he descended the rope. The Goths watched in an impotent fury, their eyes sparkling with rage behind their shield wall as the optio slipped down onto the courtyard. Felix felt his limbs turn to jelly as he slapped onto the flagstones just as the rattle of plumbatae stopped like a spent hailstorm. He glanced up to see Gallus, wide eyed, holding his plumbata-free arms out in apology.

The Gothic commander stood tall and pointed his sword tip down at Felix, face torn in rage. 'Charge!'

Felix, wide-eyed, scrambled for the main gate, scraping in the darkness for the bolt.

'Gut him like a pig!' The Gothic commander screamed as his men poured forward.

Felix winced as he tore open his hand pulling at the wrong end of the bolt. He felt the earth rumble as the roaring Goths raced at his unprotected back, hearing even the intake of breath as they drew back their swords to strike. Then the bolt chunked free.

He rolled out into the night and the Gothic warriors tumbled out behind him. Utterly disoriented, he scrambled up to his feet.

'Duck!' Growled a familiar voice, cut off by the twang of a scorpion bolt.

Collapsing instinctively, Felix felt his hair parting under the slipstream of the iron bolt as it whipped over his head and sunk into the Gothic pack just emerging from the fort gates. Felix blinked up at Quadratus, his blonde moustache raised as he grinned from behind the makeshift scorpion.

'Thanks for the warning!' Felix croaked, stumbling forward.

'Like to keep you on your toes, sir,' Quadratus grunted as he set off another bolt.

Gallus clenched his fists as the scorpion pinned the Goths back into the fort and against the back wall. 'We've got 'em – take the flanks!' He cried, waving his men towards the ladders.

'Avitus, keep four men and hold the walls – watch for reinforcements. Zosimus, you're with me.'

His men were off before the order was even finished, pouring down the ladders to flank the mass of Goths, now in disarray. Pinned between the twin rapiers of spatha and scorpion, the Gothic battle cry waned. A flurry of stabbing, gurgling and iron smashing followed. Gallus butted up and forward with his shield, crunching into the face of the Gothic commander. Seizing the moment, he pulled his shield to one side and thrust his spatha at the throat of the man. The blade stopped just as it nicked the Goth's skin. All around them, a clatter of swords hitting flagstones rang out.

'Mercy,' the Gothic commander growled, bitterness lacing his words.

Gallus glanced around; his men jostled, their spathas hovering, ready to finish the job. The remaining Goths, barely in double figures, stared groundward, awaiting their fate.

'Collect their weapons,' Gallus conceded, gasping. A bitter sigh rose from the legionaries. 'Collect their weapons and bind their hands,' he barked, 'and find where they are holding our man prisoner.'

'That was a hard thing to do, sir,' Felix offered quietly beside him, 'but the right thing.'

'I'm not even sure of that, Felix. Remember yesterday?'

'The men have had revenge, sir. They'll always grumble when the red mist is down.'

Gallus eyed his optio. 'Indeed. It's not blood I want now, Felix. I want answers.'

# Chapter 9

Pavo spat the metallic bloody gloop into the sand of the training field and ran his tongue over the shard of remaining tooth. His fingers brushed his left side and he winced at the flaring agony from his ribs.

'Get up, stinkin' whoreson!' Brutus roared. The centurion booted a cloud of dust into Pavo's face. 'Seems we have a kitten here, wants to go away to lick his wounds?' He paced steadily, addressing the square of legionary recruits fixated on the brutality. Even now after a week of pain, they were still in shock at this sadist; short, but built like a tree trunk, his cropped scalp glistened with sweat and his broad face was a ball of indulgent fury. He really seemed to revel in their misery. Indeed, glowing red under the sun, he resembled some kind of demon.

It had been a whirlwind seven days since they had first walked through the fort gates. Pavo had glanced up at the flapping ruby bull banners billowing from the gate towers and felt momentarily majestic – then bumped straight into a legionary hauling two heavy buckets of steaming faeces. He and Sura had queued up with a rabble of similarly wide-eyed and fresh faced unknowns clad in filthy tunics and little else, all waiting to put their mark on the slip of parchment that would sign away their lives for the next twenty-five years. *Twenty-five years indeed*, a common joke amongst the veterans given life expectancy was two to three years. Two dark-red itchy hemp tunics, one comparatively luxurious purple edged white tunic – for parades and official sorties only, a pair of used leather boots and a frayed leather belt they received in return. The dangerous bits, the spear, the spatha sword and the plumbatae darts, weren't dished out until later, apparently until the idiots had been weeded from the ranks. The first few days had been gentle – drill practice and bunk assignments followed by functional but welcome grub in the mess hall. Then training had started, and Pavo's world had tumbled into a living Hades.

He ran a finger over his bleeding gums and squinted at Brutus, whose face curled into a grin; no way out this time, he thought; the four walls of the fort seemed so close, so high. No disappearing back into the grim anonymity of slavery. He noticed Sura peering over with an apologetic resignation.

Brutus casually raised his foot to Pavo's face and pushed him backward onto the ground. 'Get this runt out of here,' he called to two of the recruits. They scurried over and pulled at Pavo's arms. Pain rifled through his bones. The fight in his heart gnawed at him.

'I'm not finished!' he croaked, wriggling free.

'Hello?' Brutus chirped, cocking his head to one side. His eyes ran over the terrified recruits, every one of them dropping their gaze. Then his eyes fell on Sura, who was desperately shaking his head at his friend. Brutus whipped back round to Pavo.

'See, your Thracian bum boy here thinks you should bugger off, too. Get out of here before I come over there and knock the rest of your teeth in!'

Pavo's tongue felt like a leaf of parchment as he stumbled to his feet; the training field spun around him in the growing midday heat. His legs wobbled and almost buckled and his vision tunnelled, but he gritted his teeth. Dazed yet determined, he let out a roar, and threw himself forward. He saw Brutus' pupils narrow and, like a cobra, the centurion slid clear and was gone. From nowhere a crunching blow to the back of his head brought him slamming into the dust, where he hacked up a mixture of blood, saliva and bile. A mixture of groaning and laughter erupted around the recruits.

'And this, you *maggots*, is how you pacify a barbarian.'

Pavo squinted up, panting; Brutus strutted Caesar-like in front of his recruits. Frustration boiled in his blood at the arrogance of the man. But then he saw the thinnest sliver of opportunity; his eyes settled on Brutus' scabbard. He pushed to his feet and stalked towards him. *Still time to even the scores!*

'And if the barbarian refuses to lie down and accept the rule of the empire,' Brutus regaled, eyes closed and one arm extended, clearly envisioning himself in the role of Cicero, reaching down to draw his wooden training sword, 'then we serve them a portion of sweet, sharp sword.' It was a priceless instant; Brutus' face dropped in horror, as his hand patted an empty scabbard.

Pavo hatched a toothy grin. 'Looking for this?' He sighed, twirling the hefty wooden sword from hand to hand. Silence blanketed the training field and only the distant clanking from the canteen could be heard. Brutus' blank expression held momentarily and then began to redden. Sensing the scarlet fury he knew would come next, Pavo laughed, and threw the sword over to the centurion handle first. Like a splash of cool water, the crowd broke into a rabble of cheering and laughter. Slowly Brutus, too, melted into a smile. An evil smile, but a smile all the same.

'Okay dirtbags, training's over for today. Off to the canteen for dinner – I hear it's horse-turd pie today!' He roared at his own joke, before tucking his sword in and marching off, in a vain attempt to recapture his dignity of moments before.

Pavo began the trudge back to the barracks. A few congratulatory pats landed on his back from sniggering recruits. His head ached, his mouth tasted foul and his body felt like a pile of shattered pewter, but he had dug some pride from the training session.

'You've got a bloody death wish!' Sura spluttered, sidling up next to him, 'Brutus'll have you out on the sand every day now – he'll be after a bit of revenge for that little stunt!'

He looked up at the pure blue of the sky, and chuckled. 'Haven't done myself any favours have I?'

He turned to Sura, but a blinding white light filled his head as a hammer blow landed on his jaw. He was in the sand again before he realised what had happened; a bull-like recruit stood, fists clenched, in front of him. It was the broad shouldered Spurius; his short crop shimmered with sweat, his eyes were hooded under his v-shaped brow, and he grinned through yellowed teeth, stretched out under a broad and battered nose. He beckoned Pavo to his feet. Behind, Sura wriggled in the grasp of the elephantine and oak-limbed recruit named Festus.

Spurius examined his blood spattered knuckles. 'Numerius Vitellius Pavo. The slave scumbag.'

Pavo winced, shooting a glance at Sura. Sura's face flashed with shock but then quickly morphed into fury again as he kicked out uselessly at Festus' grip.

'I've got contacts that'd pay a fortune for more of this,' Spurius growled.

Pavo touched a finger to his lips – fattened and stinging. He had made a lot of enemies during his misadventures in the city; some of his missions had been for the thrill alone, but then there were those darker briefs he had been given in the shadowy alleys – big money had been lost and gained through him. 'You're from the street gangs?'

'Constantinople born and bred. You're wanted, and I'm going to collect the bounty.'

'We're here to fight in the legions, same as you, we're all equal here,' Sura barked, his legs kicking out in vain as Festus roared with laughter.

'I don't give a flying turd what you're here for. Remember the Blues? Well they want to make an example of the smart-arse who nicked their standard for the Greens.'

Pavo's mind reeled back through the troublemaking in the capital. It was last winter and he had been sitting at a filthy, rickety table outside *The Eagle* – a filth hole of an inn near the Hippodrome – picking at some fetid mess they had served as food. A gravel voice had startled him – it always happened this way. 'I hear you're the man for a bit of a sortie. Fancy earning a purse of bronze?' The thug had asked. Pavo recognised him from the racing – always at the head of riots, leading the Greens into the fray. He had eyed the bulging purse of folles the man held. The job entailed sneaking into the Blues' headquarters, in an attic above a butcher's shop on the north edge of the Augusteum, where he drugged their two apelike guards and made off with the antique bronze eagle standard they prided above all else.

'He remembers,' Festus spat back. 'Now sort him out, Spurius.'

Pavo blinked back to reality and cowered at the sight of Spurius pulling his fist back to strike. But, in a breath, the man's expression changed to a gaping smile accompanied by a mock-friendly slap on the jaw. Pavo looked over his shoulder and saw the reason; Centurion Brutus sidled past on his mount, eyeing the confrontation.

'Keep it moving,' the centurion grumbled.

Spurius and Festus strolled for the barracks. Spurius casting a malignant glance back over his shoulder.

'Still think you're ready for this, lad?' Brutus grunted.

# Chapter 10

In a final echo of winter, a heavy snow had settled over the land of Bosporus. The thirty eight men of the XI Claudia and the handful of Gothic prisoners plugged on through the pillowy drifts, zigzagging around swamp and marshland on one side and hills on the other to inch further east across the peninsula neck. The rescued prisoner Proteus lay limp on a stretcher, his legs crippled and his skin pale through loss of blood – the boy had only muttered in a fever since they rescued him from the fort.

They rounded the base of a hill and a pure white plain yawned out before them. Gallus marched up front alongside Felix; the pair gritted their teeth to prevent chattering in the icy headwind that met them from the plain, the full wrath of the cold raking through armour and clothing.

'What d'you think Proteus meant by it...*run?*' Felix mused.

'Something has gotten into these Goths – that's for sure. These men fought like cornered wolves,' Gallus nodded back to the train of prisoners, then shook his head and lowered his voice. 'The lad's not likely to make it, you know,' he whispered.

Felix nodded in resignation. 'If we can get to pitch camp somewhere sheltered tonight, he may come round given heat, food and water. At least, long enough to tell us more.'

The wind whipped the falling snow into a stinging blizzard, and Gallus pulled his woollen cloak tighter. 'It's top priority for all of us, Felix. We're dying out in this freezing Hades.'

The second fort was supposed to be somewhere in this region, but the white plain rolled out unbroken.

'More bloody snow...' The optio halted in his tracks, slapping an arm across Gallus' chest.

The crisp and unblemished snow ended abruptly; a dark smear of activity stained the plain to the north. The second fort took on an immediate insignificance in comparison with the thousands of people swarming around it. Smoke scudded across the sky from the east.

'Halt!' Gallus barked, raising a hand. He waved the column in to tuck into the hillside. 'We've got company, lots of company,' he spoke steadily. 'Avitus, Zosimus, get the prisoners tucked in to the side. Keep watch in either direction. Felix, you're with me,' he ordered, beckoning his optio. The pair jogged up to a lip of snowdrift, dropping to their stomachs just before the ridge. Gallus' mouth dried as he took in the scene of devastation on the plain ahead.

A ragged Gothic exodus swarmed around the broken remains of the fort, led by an army numbering thousands of horsemen and infantry, followed by a train of women, children and oxen tripling the overall number. To the east, the land was a charred checkerboard of burnt farmland stretching off into the horizon. Even the driving snow could not disguise the broken huts and telltale humps of mass graves pitting and scarring the land in between.

'These people...they're being *driven* from their land,' Felix gasped. As the wind howled around them, a faint sobbing could be heard along with the drumming of hooves. 'What is it – plague, pestilence maybe?'

'There's more to it than that, Felix; those graves are warrior graves,' Gallus pointed to the humps, pricked with swords, hundreds of them. 'They've been beaten in battle...and beaten badly. Now they've adopted a scorched earth policy on their own farms – desperate measures.'

'Intelligence didn't mention warring Goths tribes here?' Felix quizzed.

'No, it is, or *was* a unified kingdom according to...' a weary look wrinkled his features, '...our *intelligence*. I think they were faced with something they knew they couldn't defeat. We need to talk to our Gothic prisoners.'

'They haven't spoken a word, sir. They'll die first – stubborn bastards, worse than the lot over the Danubius.'

'They *will* talk...' Gallus was cut off by the gasp of one of the crouched legionaries behind him. Turning, he caught the briefest glimpse of a figure high on the hillside, turning his blood colder than the chill air. Like a cobra, the figure ducked back and disappeared.

'Felix, was that...'

The optio's face was grave. 'Yes, sir, the riders from the forest...'

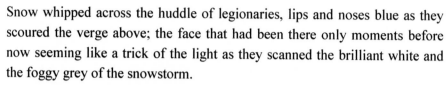

Snow whipped across the huddle of legionaries, lips and noses blue as they scoured the verge above; the face that had been there only moments before now seeming like a trick of the light as they scanned the brilliant white and the foggy grey of the snowstorm.

Zosimus scaled the shear face up to the verge – despite his enormous weight and the bitter ice that clung to the rock face he moved like a spider. Gallus and Avitus tumbled up the winding path to intercept the stranger from the other side. The snow took on a fury like never before, and they struggled to see even paces ahead.

In a brief moment of respite as the wind changed, the tip of the hill was clear, and Gallus blinked as he saw the form of Zosimus hanging by his fingertips from the verge – as the dark figure on the hilltop hared in.

'Zosimus,' Gallus roared. His words swallowed by the storm winds as the figure swiped a blade at the defenceless legionary. A dull roar echoed over the howling blizzard as it kicked into full gear again, and Gallus closed his eyes as he saw the big Thracian fall limply to the rocks below. Another brother fallen.

'Sir, we've got him cornered,' Avitus cried out.

Gallus shook the confusion from his head. He nodded, drew his sword, and pointed his fingers in a V. He stalked out to the left of the dark figure, and Avitus took the right.

'Drop your weapons, you're surrounded!' The figure spun round in a half-crouch, coiled like a spring, sword in hand. Gallus stalked forward, his spatha raised and trained on the man. The stranger's stony expression was gradually unveiled in the murky light. Curtained by long black hair, he bore the distinctive features of the riders from the forest: skin both dark and buttery, face flat and almost square, with almond eyes, a small, squat, distinctly un-Roman nose and a thread-like moustache hanging around his lips, upon which the driving snow began to settle. But it was the angry triple welt of scars on each cheek that stilled the breath in Gallus' lungs.

A cluster of legionaries, led by Felix, shuffled up around them.

'Felix? The prisoners?' Gallus howled over the blizzard.

'Sir, we saw Zosimus fall!' Felix gestured to the foot of the hill, his face grim. 'There are fifteen guarding the prisoners, but we thought you might need some extra muscle?'

'There's only one of them, Felix, but I don't see his horse – there must be more of them around. Stay alert.' Gallus then turned to the stranger. 'Drop your weapon, or you'll be dead before your next breath,' he barked.

The man's glance darted at the men encircling him, his eyes growing and his toothy grimace widening. He backed off pace by pace until his heel kicked snow from the verge onto the rocks below. With a grunt the stranger buckled, dropped to his knees and cursed in a jagged foreign tongue.

Gallus stepped over to him, lifting his sword to his throat. 'Who are you?'

The stranger looked up to his captor, rage welling in his eyes.

'I have failed, honour is lost!' He rasped in a broken Greek.

'Who are you, and who are your people?' Gallus pressed, forcing his sword point to mark a white crease against the man's skin.

'I am the first of the storm; my kin will destroy your people like a plague. *Tengri* the sky god watches from above, and he wills your end. You will be swept away like kindling,' he spat.

'Who is your leader and where are your people?' Gallus pressed on. 'I warn you, I want answers, not threats!'

At this, the stranger's eyes sparkled, and his weak rasping grew into a bellowing laugh as the blizzard picked up fiercely. Gallus held steady as a chill ran through him. Suddenly, the laughter stopped and the stranger bore a bold grimace.

'Your people will destroy themselves. *Already* they plot their own destruction yet they don't even see it…and…they want us to help!'

Gallus' brow furrowed. 'Enough of this game playing, you will talk! If you don't want…' Gallus recoiled as, fast as a striking cobra, the stranger whipped a dagger from his boot and thrust it into his own jugular. A torrent of dark blood spouted from the wound, and the life drained from his body in seconds. The legionaries stood in silence as his body toppled forward into the scarlet snow. Then a chorus of screams rang out from below. The legionaries scrambled to the edge of the hilltop. Gallus punched a fist into his palm; the Gothic prisoners lay in a splatter of blood along with the fifteen legionaries left to guard them and the crippled soldier, Proteus. Arrows still quivered in their chests and necks. A clutch of the mysterious horsemen sped away, swords stained red.

'Felix, take ten down there and check for survivors.' His optio's face was grim. Clearly, all below were dead. 'And proceed with caution.'

Gallus looked around as his men muttered in fear. Before it could swell into panic, he swallowed his rage. 'We're in the middle of something big here. It was and still is our prerogative to get back to friendly territory to report this.' He looked to the north; the Gothic horde was moving off, thankfully oblivious to the goings-on above them. He then looked to the east.

'We bury our men first, and then we move on to the eastern coast without delay. A small detachment can scout the last fort on the way. The boys we left behind on the shore will be bringing the *Aquila* round to the eastern neck of the peninsula tomorrow night to the agreed rendezvous point. Then we can go home!' The legionaries shivered, nodding in approval.

Just then Felix padded up to the hilltop. 'Sir, Zosimus, he's alive! He just let himself fall to dodge the blade. He's cracked some ribs and his shoulder, but he'll mend!' The legionaries let out a roar of approval.

'Let's get the fat bastard onto a stretcher then; I'll take the first shift on carrying him. To the coast and the *Aquila*! Who's with me?' The legionaries broke the driving blizzard with a chorus of support.

Gallus held his steady gaze until the last of his men had turned away and only then let his face fall. The coast and the *Aquila* were so very far from here.

# Chapter 11

Father stood before him, but not the father he remembered from the earlier times he had been here; he looked different. This time he was standing in the eye of a sandstorm, stock still and wearing only tattered robes, his hair was unkempt and white and he held out one hand while the desert raged around him. Pavo had felt himself being drawn closer and closer still, feeling the sand grains whip against his skin and the wind roar in his ears. The noise grew deafening until he came close enough to make out Father's features. Then he recoiled; there was something wrong with his eyes, they were shaded, dark. Then Father looked up, directly at him, his dark and hollow sockets staring. Pavo woke, sat bolt upright in his cot and gasped for breath while the legion slept around him in the silent barracks.

He shivered at the still vivid image – the dream had haunted his sleep for years. Father had always been calling him, but each time, he seemed darker, angrier. He frowned, running his fingers across his bristled scalp then feeling for the bronze phalera on the end of the leather thong around his neck.

Taking a deep breath, he glanced around the barracks to ground himself. They had been at the fort for just a fortnight, but the bitterness of life under a slave master in Constantinople seemed an age ago, long replaced by the toil under a different master in the form of Centurion Brutus. Cruel as Brutus was, it was his job. But it was the altogether more sinister threat from Spurius and his club-fisted friend Festus who seemed more direct replacements for Fronto, he mused, rubbing the dark-blue bruises the pair had left on his ribs the previous day. The other recruits would have been ambivalent about their agenda, he was sure, had it not been for Spurius' muscle, but they too had sided with the angry young Greek when push came to shove. All except Sura, Pavo mused as the Thracian snored, sleeping soundly as usual despite the pummellings he had taken from Festus. *For what*, Pavo wondered, thinking back to their oath outside the fort on that first day they met, *for a half-cocked pact made in jest when he barely knew me?*

Sunlight crept under the doorway. Pavo forced deep, slow breaths into his lungs as the orangey tendrils slithered towards his bunk. A modicum of calm was descending on him when a powerful, ripping fart echoed around the barracks, followed by the pained coughing of the poor sod who had taken the brunt of its aroma. No amount of deep breathing would make today any easier; a quick march was on the agenda; twenty miles of treacherous terrain – bog, forest and hills – carrying the full burden of legionary armour, rations and camping gear. All that on a stomach of hardtack biscuits and cheese – the meagre and all too familiar portions rationed to the recruits not out of necessity but apparently 'all part of the training'.

He again glanced at Sura; the two would have to spur each other on through today's punishment and – he glowered over at the snoring Spurius – watch each other's backs. His eyes hung on the thug momentarily, until the crunch of the morning watch on the flagstones outside startled him.

The *buccinas* howled out the morning wakeup call and at once, the barracks stirred with a chorus of grumbling and cursing. Pavo tensed his jaw as the silence ebbed away and the reality of the day ahead took a grip on him. He slid from his bunk, greeted by a confused moan from Sura.

'What're you doing out of your pit?'

'Couldn't wait to break my back and fling myself through mud,' Pavo shot back with a sardonic grin, tightening his bootstraps then slipping into the less filthy of the two coarse standard issue tunics. Casting nervous glances around the barracks, he gathered up the weighty equipment they had been assigned yesterday – certainly not the pristine armour his father had enjoyed. The rusting mail vest alone strained his wiry limbs and dug into his shoulders, and he had yet to add on the burden of the battered and punctured intercisa helmet, the solid mass of an oval shield – the paint-flecked surface scratched and scarred beyond recognition, and his wooden training sword. He winced at the thought of adding the rest of the standard campaign kit to that lot: a snub pickaxe and a rusting sickle, a coil of rope, an earth-shifting basket – all bulk that would chafe at his skin throughout the march. Even the rations were bulky and heavy, with Brutus insisting on a standard twenty-day ration pack to 'give 'em a feel for the pain of a real march.' The leather backpack was stuffed with hardtack biscuits, bread, salted mutton, water and sour wine.

As he kitted up, and let his shoulders broaden to take the load and firmed his expression; no trace of weakness could be betrayed. The trainers would verbally destroy anyone who lagged behind, but there was more to be worried about than a bollocking in front of the other recruits. His eyes darted over to Spurius, who slipped on his rusting scale armour as if it was a silk cloak as he joked with Festus.

'Can't believe we're still carrying the wooden swords,' Sura muttered. 'Weighs like a bloody rock; just shows they can't trust us not to cut ourselves, eh?'

'Or each other,' Pavo murmured, turning to sit on Sura's bunk with a nod of the head to Spurius.

'Eh? Oh forget about him,' Sura hissed. 'Listen, I've got a plan. If we make for the front of the column at the start of the march, we'll have one of the officers eyeing us all the way. The column will stretch out as the march goes on and legs get tired, so it'll be hard work to stay up there, but it'll keep numbskull over there from trying any funny business. In any case...'

Pavo's brow furrowed as Sura's words trailed off.

'What're you and your boyfriend moaning about, Pavo?' A horribly familiar voice grunted from behind him. He half expected a punch in the back of the head. When it didn't come, he knew he had to turn around and face Spurius. And take a beating. He felt his fear subside into boiling anger – he saw Fronto, he saw Tarquitius. Before he could check himself, he pivoted to face Spurius.

'What're you so bitter about? So some of your cronies from the city have offered you a couple of coins to kick my head in – is that all you're worth? I'm not bringing my issues into the army with me, so why should you? How's about you just get lost and bother someone else who cares? Like the pigs in the village!'

The barracks fell silent and still, all eyes on the pair. Then a nervous snigger escaped from one of the watching recruits. Pavo felt their stares burn his skin, but none more than that of the grimacing Spurius, whose anger twisted into a terrible yellow-toothed grin.

'In a hurry to get your face kicked in?' He sneered. He snapped his fingers and as before, Festus grappled Sura in a shoulder-lock.

'Just me and you, one on one,' Spurius hissed. Then, growling like a rabid dog, he sprang forward, grasping at Pavo's throat with his hands, throwing them both to the floor.

Pavo's lungs emptied as they hit the flagstones and a rabble of excitement broke out from the onlookers. Gasping through the raining blows to his face, he flapped his arms somewhat uselessly at Spurius' sides. A dull crack filled his head just as he tasted blood trickling into his mouth from his nose and Spurius hefted his arms back, bent to hammer down for the next blow. If he blacked out…it didn't bear thinking about.

With a grunt, Pavo clenched his stomach, finding just enough leverage to ram his knee up and into Spurius' groin with a dull thud. The barracks chorused a collective gasp of shared pain, and with a whimper, his attacker fell away. Dazed, Pavo scrambled back and up onto his feet. Then, a gust of fresh morning air swept the room as all eyes turned to the barrack door.

'What the…?' The silhouette of Brutus filled the doorway, glowering at the goings-on. 'You heard the call! You're going to pay for this today – there's a quaint little swamp upriver that you'd just *love*.' His footsteps grew steadily louder, until they stopped inches behind Pavo.

'Is there a problem here?' Brutus spoke gently.

Pavo turned slowly to face the centurion.

Brutus trembled, his face red and his eyes bulging. Then his features fell stony. 'Care to explain why you're covered in blood and filth when you should be out on that piggin' square?' He roared. 'Anyone else want to explain that?'

'He fell as he was gathering his equipment, sir,' an anonymous voice called out. Brutus pulled a sardonic grin at the answer, and then looked Pavo up and down.

'It's true, sir, I fell.'

Brutus shook his head slowly, and then looked up again.

'And you kicked seven shades out of yourself and these three morons while you were at it? Can't even bloody lie properly!' He nodded in disgust at the startled trio of Sura, Festus and Spurius. 'Enough of this rubbish. Get yourselves out in that square immediately.' He eyed Pavo again, shook his head then turned and strode from the barracks.

As he left, Spurius shouldered past Pavo with a grunt. Sura exchanged a glare with Festus and then the bull-shouldered recruit wandered off.

'You okay?' Sura asked.

'I have to be, haven't I – don't see me getting the day in bed, do you?' Pavo replied as he clipped his pickaxe and sickle to his belt. Then he touched his fingers to the numbness of his battered face.

'Well get your gear together.' Sura handed him his pack, before sliding on his own. 'It's not over yet.'

Pavo splashed down from a gnarled tree stump into a putrid soup of bog water. At once, he was up to his neck in the sulphurous swell and his armour and kit morphed into stone, pulling him greedily down. He spluttered mud from his lips, blinking the filth from his eyes as he saw Centurion Brutus and his troops shoot off into the distance – and then the following recruits splashed down to miss the hazard and were gone, too.

'There goes the plan,' he croaked, flapping at the stump. The pace of the march had been just about bearable, but the terrain was the true test. He and Sura had managed to stay near the front for the first few miles until Sura had dropped back, tiring. Now the plan was well and truly scuppered.

With a groan, he pushed forward, launched his shield from the bog onto the track, then stretched his fingers to claw at the stump, grappling the gnarled roots to pull himself out and onto his knees with a grotesque squelching. Panting, he started slopping the mud from his vest, savouring the moment of respite from the pace of the march until a set of footsteps thundered up behind him. His skin crawled, *Spurius, Festus!* Then the footsteps ended with a graceless splash.

'Bollocks!' a mud-coated figure gurgled from the bog. *Sura.*

His friend had inexplicably landed face-first in the bog, and was now thrashing gracelessly. Pavo looped an arm around the stump and craned back into the thick mess, wrapping a forearm under his friend's shoulder and round his neck. This time, his muscles really felt the strain as purchase was harder to come by. He wrenched backwards, ignoring Sura's exaggerated choking fit. Grunting, heels scraping for leverage on the bank of the bog, they finally came loose just as Pavo's vision began to spot over.

'Urgh!' Sura spluttered, caked in the dark sludge, and bleeding from his knees.

'I know it's not too pleasant,' Pavo shot a nervous glance down the track – empty, for now, 'but humour me - let's start running again?'

Sura, staggered to his feet, shooting daggers.

'Spurius?' Pavo hissed in exasperation.

'Oh, aye, right. Sorry. Don't think he's passed us yet, has he?'

'Don't know – I was too busy floating face down in that shit when the others passed. Come on, we can talk while we run.'

They set off at a jog again. 'A good, hard kicking, Pavo, that's what the whoreson needs. Then he'll think twice about bothering you, or me for that matter, in future. If we could just get him or Festus on their own...' Sura gasped as they picked up the pace.

Pavo grunted in semi-agreement, his eyes fixed on the muddied armour of the recruits just ahead, but not so far ahead that they couldn't be caught. *Safety in numbers*, he thought. He glanced back over his shoulder. Nothing. A clear run to the end and safety by the looks of it. A giddy confidence laced his blood – then his heart leapt as he faced forward again, star jumping over an oak stump he had nearly run into. A fit of giggles worked loose from his chest and he turned to tell Sura, when a dark shape swung from out of nowhere and smashed into his nose, filling his head with white light and a deafening crack.

Blackness swamped his mind. Through the bleariness, he saw a tree branch quivering gradually to a standstill above him, outlined by the blue-grey sky. Flat on his back, he craned his neck up; several paces away he made out the figure of Festus – raining blows on the grounded Sura. Dread grappled his heart. He made to scramble to his knees when another figure darted out in front of him to boot him in the chest. Spurius.

Pavo grunted, thudding back onto the dirt.

'Time to take a serious beating, maggot!' Spurius snarled, whipping his wooden sword out and smashing it against the still juddering branch, spraying shards of bark.

Pavo scuttled backwards on the heels of his hands. Spurius stalked forward – cool, unspent and suspiciously free of mud; they had no doubt taken a shortcut. Not for wasting any time, Spurius lunged, swiping his sword down at Pavo's midriff. Rolling clear of the brunt of the strike, Pavo yelped as Spurius' sword burned his flank. The pain sparked realisation in him – he had to act. This time Spurius roared as he thumped forward like a rhino. At last, Pavo found composure; he sprang to his feet, jinking to safety just as Spurius' sword splattered into his mud imprint.

'You're going to be drinking your food when I'm finished with you!' He spat.

Then, from behind him, Festus piped up. 'And that's just for starters – there's money on your head.'

Pavo forced himself to focus, despite the wailing that accompanied the peripheral image of Sura being beaten to a pulp.

'My head? You're here to assassinate me?' Pavo felt his gut ripple. The forest had never seemed so dark or lonely.

Spurius nodded slowly, a finality written all over his broad features. 'Remember what happened to Pulcher of The Greens?'

Pavo's throat tightened as he remembered the day at the races. Pulcher, the man who had hired him to steal the bronze standard, had been conspicuous by his absence. Then the very standard itself had been raised from the Blues crowd, complete with the grey, scabbed, staring head of Pulcher himself.

'You would work for the scum who do that to people? Don't have a mind of your own?' Pavo hissed, grateful of the anger that overwhelmed his fear once again. Drawing his own wooden sword, he steadied himself. 'What if I was to promise you a couple of coins to torture and kill someone – would I suddenly be your master? Is that all you're worth? Is that what your mother hoped for when she bore you – a brainless murderer?'

Spurius' face wrinkled in scarlet fury and his brow knitted into a tight v-shape. 'Nobody's my bloody master!' he barked. 'I just do what I've got to do...' then his pupils dilated. 'And don't you ever talk about my mother!'

Pavo's brow furrowed – the man was driven, but coins were not his motivation. No, something was tearing at him from inside.

He stalked to the right, and then back to the left, as Spurius jinked and jostled – moving like a cat despite his bull-like build. Having only his recent legionary training to rely on here, Pavo focused on the eyes, then the sword hand, then the feet of his opponent. There had to be a technique to this, he prayed. Knowing his opponent only had a short window before the rest of the recruits and officers would catch up, Pavo played the defensive game, skipping back for every step Spurius took towards him, watching his opponent's face glow redder at every turn.

Spurius broke the pattern, ducking to Pavo's left. Pavo skipped backwards, raising his sword and tipping the hilt towards Spurius' outstretched head – the strike was on! But his attacker read the move perfectly – it was just a feint before he whipped over to Pavo's right, swinging the edge of his sword straight into Pavo's ribs. A disembodied scream of agony rent the air over the thick cracking of a bone. He glanced at his unused shield, lying caked in mud as his legs wobbled, and gave way to the wave of nausea and blackness washing over him. He heard himself splash into the grime, but didn't feel a thing. In the numbness of semi-consciousness, blows rained down on his already pulped face.

Dim images of Spurius' frothing face came and went, twinned with hard as stone hammer-blows into his body. Then the blunt darkness was ripped away at the noise of cold hard iron being slid from a scabbard. Pavo's eyes opened as slits; Festus was handing Spurius an iron sword. Spurius grappled the hilt with both hands, eyeing its length.

'Don't bugger about – finish him!' Festus growled. 'I'll get the bloody lash if they find out I brought that thing out.'

'Aye, and what d'you think I'll get for this?' Spurius grumbled back, juggling the sword in his grip.

Pavo noticed something ripple across the thug's face as he spun the blade over in his hands. Was it, surely not...*reluctance?*

'In the name of...' Festus snarled, snatched at the blade and whipped it over his head, then bared his tombstone teeth. 'Lights out time,' he grunted matter-of-factly.

Pavo's body lay anchored to the ground like lead, every bone screaming out to move but crippled in agony. He winced in a desperate attempt to roll over, but sank back into the path of the onrushing sword swing. Grimacing, he waited on the blackness, the pain that was to come.

But nothing. Then the canter of hooves.

'Brutus!' Festus hissed.

Pavo cracked open an eye to see Festus empty handed. A dull clank a few paces into the foliage signalled the location of the sword. He stumbled to his feet, his face caked in mud and blood and feeling like fire.

'This seems to be your specialty, looking like a whore's breakfast!' Brutus boomed, scowling at Pavo's pathetic form. 'I've already bloody finished the march and had time to come back here – and I'm twice your age. Who's going to tell me what this carry-on's all about?' Immediately, Festus stood to attention and addressed the centurion.

'The idiot tripped, fell, and bloodied his nose again, sir.'

Brutus' gaze steeled. 'Did he kick the shit out of himself while he was at it...*again?*'

Pavo glanced over the scene; Sura, with a face like a cauliflower, Festus, still snarling, and Spurius – Spurius looked haunted. Whatever was going on in the man's head it wasn't pretty. He looked Brutus in the eye.

'I fell, sir. My colleagues were helping me up.'

Brutus snorted, looked them all over, as his mount bucked and whinnied.

'I'll be expecting all of you back at the fort in one piece,' he shot them all an iron glare, and then glanced over Pavo once more, shaking his head. 'Latrines for a week, all of you,' he snapped, before spurring his horse back into a gallop along the track.

Spurius' eyes burned into Pavo.

'Your time will come.'

Pavo pulled short, desperate breaths as the terror faded. He fought to contain the sobs that pulled at his throat. Sura trudged over to him.

'Look at the state of you, can't tell what's skin and what's cut. They were going to kill you!'

Pavo cut him off, rage simmering in his eyes, chest heaving. 'I don't get it, Sura, I really don't. There's something seriously wrong in that animal's head.' His body shaking, he eyed Spurius and Festus as they lumbered on ahead.

'But I know one thing for sure…It's him or me!'

# Chapter 12

The senate house echoed with the daily rabble as Tarquitius took to his feet. He had studied the faces of this collection of grey-haired men; happy to be part of the hustle and bustle, to rise to comfortable mediocrity, but never more. A purple-fringed toga and a seat on the marble steps was enough for them. Tarquitius' hair, or what he had left around the sides, was still flecked with the gold of youth, and here he was, about to surpass these old men.

A hundred minor debates simmered as he decided it was time for them to take notice. Taking the golden effigy of an eagle from his cloak, he carefully screwed it on to his staff. A smirk rose from one corner of his mouth as he stood.

'Senate of Constantinople,' he said quietly, making no impression on the rabble as he stepped onto the circular floor space.

'Senate of Constantinople,' he barked this time. Again, nothing. His face betrayed a snarl as he hurled the staff onto the senate floor.

'Senate of Constantinople!' He bellowed. The clatter of the staff and effigy echoed throughout the room along with his lament. The squabbling voices died. Tarquitius strode down the steps and onto the floor, stooping to pick up the staff; all eyes were fixed on his movements. He felt ten feet tall.

He burned his stare into each of the senators, circling the floor. Then, when they began to cough and shuffle in discomfort, he raised the staff horizontally with one hand at each end, before bringing it down over his knee with a crack. A collective gasp filled the room. Their faces said it all, he thought; *lambs, not men of action.*

'Senate of Constantinople,' he spoke in his original gentle tone. 'The empire needs you now more than ever,' he lied. 'Her very existence hangs in the balance, far from here yet at the same time perilously close.' Murmurs of concern rippled around the hall. 'The great river Danubius to the north holds back a swell of barbarians and the Goths grow ever more restless along her banks. Their ferocity cannot be underestimated, but what of the countless tribes behind them, numbering millions upon millions, driving from the east.' He stopped and let his echo reverberate and die. Not a sound in reply could be heard. 'It is only a matter of time before our defences are breached. Your homes will be fired, your daughters raped.'

At once, a rabble broke out. 'Sit down, Senator Tarquitius. We have faith in our border legions,' one of the senators yelped over the rest. 'It is civil unrest in the urban centres that we must address today. The Christian fundamentalists have burned the Arian Church in Philippi!'

Tarquitius continued as if the man had never spoken. 'Ah yes, the border legions, the famous limitanei,' he mocked, 'scoundrels of the empire brushed to its borders to serve alongside cowering farmer-boys.' He quickly dismissed the flitting mental image of Pavo and the briefest memory of the rasping crone in the market. 'Trained in weeks and clad in rusting armour from ages past.' He gazed at the brave senator, who foundered, his lip trembling as he sought a riposte. Tarquitius continued, now with a grave tone. 'They match our aggressors neither in number, nor in ability.'

Another senator cut in. 'What are you here to say, Senator Tarquitius?'

Tarquitius turned to his latest challenger. 'Isn't it obvious, my brothers?' He looked up to the back of the senate room to the figure of Bishop Evagrius, silhouetted in the shadows of the archway entrance above the steps. He continued. 'Rome builds, and thus she must protect herself. For we must stand up and roar back at our enemies.' Evagrius emerged from the shadows, his eyes narrowed and piercing as Tarquitius' speech intensified.

'I ask you, my fellow senators, to commission a new legion. A legion born and bred to attack and destroy, not to sit on our borders peering nervously from behind expensive fort walls. A legion with licence to cross our frontiers and cripple these barbarian wretches; a legion of comitatenses, to allow our empire to throw off the shackles and breathe deeply once more.'

The stunned senators looked to one another and sure enough, the rabble broke out once again. Tarquitius let it all wash over him. Aulus, one of the most senior and respected senators, stood up and shouted the loudest.

'What you propose is simply not possible. The coffers are dry as it is, and we are already taxing the citizens too highly – reports of rioting in the Greek provinces come almost daily. We are all aware of the danger that threatens the empire from its borders, but in these difficult times we can only address this threat by further fortifying our borders.' A handful of his peers rumbled in agreement.

Tarquitius nodded seemingly in appreciation.

'I will not argue with you, Senator Aulus, for what you say is fact. We all have our opinions on whether this is the best course of action. So let us decide this in the true spirit of the senate. Let us put it to the vote.'

Aulus' brow furrowed and his hands dropped to his sides as the room bubbled with a chorus of agreement. The senators shuffled to their feet to begin the vote. Tarquitius, however, was already hatching the next stage of the plan. His eyes met with those of Bishop Evagrius, whose gold had already determined the outcome of the vote. Both men afforded a sly smile.

# Chapter 13

Gallus and his trickle of remaining legionaries, just forty-one souls, jogged across the plain approaching the eastern point of the diamond-shaped Bosporus peninsula, with the midday sun and verdant grasslands bringing welcome warmth to their hearts – the frozen wastes beaten back as the coming spring gradually reclaimed the peninsula. Zosimus lay happily on his stretcher, while four legionaries heaved him along at the rear of the column. It had been a torturous march.

Avitus, having tethered a grazing mare – doubtless an orphan of war going by its decorated reins – came galloping up from the coast. 'She's here!' He cried, punching the air in delight. This brought a roar of joy from the legionaries.

The mast of the bireme became visible through the heat haze bathing the horizon, and slowly the ruby-red bull effigy that adorned the sails burst into view – at the sight of this the legionaries gave another whoop of joy.

'I've never been so glad to be facing a long sea journey, Felix,' Gallus sighed.

'I'm with you on that one, sir. Can't believe I'm actually pining for old Durostorum too – I'll be straight into the town, no distractions, right into *The Boar and Hollybush* for my fill of that swill they call ale…and then there's the women!' Felix chuckled, stroking his beard with a distant look in his eyes.

Gallus admired his optio's enthusiasm, then braced himself – the Greek wouldn't like this. 'The delights of Durostorum will have to wait for a few more days, Felix. We are dropping off the men at Durostorum. Then me, you and Tribunus Nerva are tasked with reporting our findings…to the very top,' Gallus replied.

'Constantinople?'

'The snake pit itself. Dux Vergilius will be there and,' Gallus flicked his eyebrows up, 'Emperor Valens too. Tribunus Nerva will speak to the emperor on behalf of the XI Claudia, so we just need to stay quiet and look soldierly.'

'A meeting with the emperor, indeed…' Felix puffed his cheeks out, subconsciously eyeing the filthy tunic he wore under his rusting mail vest, '…and *then* a visit to the alehouses,' he cackled.

The column of legionaries reached the sandy shore as the sun shone directly overhead. The group of fifty who had stayed behind to man the *Aquila* came splashing through the surf to greet their comrades. Their cheers dulled as they realised that more half of the inland party had been lost. The cold reality of life in the army. It took a gruff roar from Zosimus to right the mood.

'Gimme some of that soured wine, mouth's like a fart in the desert!'

They descended into a bantering rabble, soaking tired feet in the cool waters. After a short while, Gallus made the call to start loading up the ship and fill barrels from a meltwater stream for the journey back to Constantinople.

Later, the sun dipped into the western horizon as the *Aquila* readied to depart. Gallus stood at the stern, eyes scouring the landscape as the boat pushed off. He churned it all over once again; the Goths, the riders and the phantom war that seemed to be all around them yet never there. Still there were no answers. Then the words of the mysterious warrior on the hilltop echoed through his mind.

*I am the first of the storm; my kin will destroy your people like a plague.*

A flash from the beach turned his head. His eyes widened; on the shore, from where the *Aquila* had set sail, a small party of the dark riders trotted through the foaming shallows. He gritted his teeth and hammered a clenched fist onto the lip of the boat.

Felix came to his side, screwing his eyes up to scan the water's edge. 'What's wrong, sir?'

'I think we've been herded like cattle Felix,' he hissed, pointing to the distant figures. 'They've been right behind us every step of the way.'

# Chapter 14

Pavo grimaced, blinking the sweat from his eyes under the afternoon sun. He gulped at the hot air, surveying the damage to the training dummy in the centre of the yard. The sorry heap of rags and sand bags hung in tatters. His hacking, stabbing and butting at it with his training sword had started shortly after lunch, when he sneaked from the back of the column sentenced to latrine detail. Spurius and Festus had kept a low profile for the last few days while Centurion Brutus had his eye on the situation. This presented Pavo a perfect opportunity for a little extra training – not the drill and formation stuff but robust, one-on-one fighting.

And it was damned hard work. His sweat-soaked tunic clung to him like mail armour and his legs trembled; he gazed up at the dipping sun and slumped to the dust. *Enough for today.* He began the trudge back to the barracks, when he heard the unmistakable gruff laughter of Spurius from the latrines.

Pavo turned to eye the dummy, envisioning the hulking figure of his nemesis. He tried to burn the menacing scowls of his tormentor onto the image. Whatever his problem was, there had to be an end to this.

Snorting, he launched himself at the dummy, crashing the side of the sword into the imaginary Spurius' midriff. He ducked under the would-be counter swing and then attempted to spring round to his opponents' flank, but his legs betrayed him, tangling and casting him rather ungraciously in the dust. He sat up and wrung his hands across his stubbled scalp.

'Idiot!' He cursed, spitting dust.

'Well done. Made a good job of defeating yourself there,' a voice called out from the side of the yard. Pavo looked up, startled. Leaning on the short wooden fence was Centurion Brutus.

'I've done my share of the latrine detail,' Pavo stammered. 'I was just trying to put in some extra practice.'

Brutus snorted, strolling around the fence and onto the yard. 'I don't remember giving you a set number of latrines each to slop out?'

Pavo reddened, his tongue welded to the roof of his mouth.

'At ease, lad.' Brutus spoke gently. 'Numerius Vitellius Pavo, from the streets of Constantinople I believe. A freedman, too?' Brutus cocked an eyebrow.

Pavo still felt surprise when someone or something reminded him of his freedom, and the hot shame and invisible shackles of slavery still cuffed his mind. 'Freed only so I could come here and be killed,' Pavo sighed. 'My father was a legionary, though,' he added, puffing his chest out.

'My father was a slave,' Brutus stated, his face stern. 'Worked himself to death, he did – bought freedom for my mother and I with his death payout.'

Pavo gulped, scared to speak.

Brutus pulled a one-sided grin. 'You want to learn how to look after yourself properly, right?'

'Right. I mean, yes, sir,' Pavo replied, his mind spinning – the sadist wore just a hint of warmth on his craggy face.

'I've served for over twenty years in the XI Claudia, each and every one of the battles I've fought in, I've survived, and the poor sods that have faced me have died. D'you know why?' Brutus asked. Pavo shook his head. Brutus took his training sword from his scabbard.

'Because I know how to use this, and, more importantly, I know *when* to use it.' Brutus looked Pavo up and down, and then pointed over to the training dummy with his sword. He picked up Pavo's shield and approached the beleaguered effigy. 'You've got brains, lad, more than most of this lot,' he swiped his sword over the barrack buildings. Then his face wrinkled a little, 'going by that stunt you pulled when you nicked my sword…well…it's either brains or stupidity.'

Pavo felt his face flush.

'But chucking yourself desperately at an opponent says a lot. It says you're brave, maybe, but it tells your opponent you've run out of ideas. The barbarians of Germania and the tribes across the river – they all used to fight like that, and they've all been beaten…well it's a different story now they've learnt!' Brutus chuckled, stalking around the dummy, shimmying behind his shield. 'Swinging your sword about like you've sunk a bath of ale shows an easy pick of kill points for me to exploit. I just need to bide my time,' he grunted, 'and while you're all arms and legs, I can just strike decisively...once!' Brutus suddenly appeared from behind the shield, jabbing up and into the dummy's midriff. Sand spilled from the burst bag.

Brutus turned, grinning at Pavo. He always wore that trademark evil grin at the training sessions. 'Also notice that you're exhausted, and now imagine I'm the next ugly whoreson in an enemy army of thousands, all queuing up to gut *you*. You simply don't have the energy left to resist me. On your guard!'

Pavo's limbs roared in protest, but Brutus was poised and ready – no backing out. He sighed, got into a combat stance, and waited.

The two men began to circle each other. Brutus' eyes bulged, fixed on him, anvil jaw set like a carving. Pavo locked onto a slight dip of Brutus' right shoulder – he was going to hit his left. Instinctively, Pavo dived, swinging his training sword into what he expected to be Brutus' unprotected left flank. Instead, Brutus pulled from the faint, easily parrying the wooden blade; Pavo found himself flapping in midair, with both his arms wide out to his side, his neck and chest completely exposed. Fast as lightning, Brutus brought his sword down onto the centre of his chest with little more than a gentle tap.

'Kill,' he calmly called as Pavo slapped onto the dust. 'Not a drop of sweat on my brow either, you'll notice?' Pavo again sat up in the dust. 'As well as by-the-book legionary tactics, you've got to be a bit dirty, too, eh?' Brutus grinned. 'Spurius and his monkeys will have you for breakfast every single time you fight if you present yourself like that.'

Pavo shuffled up to lean on his elbows at the mention of Spurius. So the sadist centurion did know what was going on.

'I get it. Any chance of some more tuition?' He croaked.

'I've got other runts to batter into shape,' Brutus said, 'but I'll teach you what I know. I can't give you twenty years of legionary warfare experience though. That you'll have to gain for yourself.'

Pavo pushed himself to his feet up again.

'Where do we begin?'

'You should begin by calling it a day. You've learned a good first lesson – don't be a hero – play safe and if you can, be a dirty bugger.' Brutus scratched his head for a moment, his eyes darting around the sand. 'You know what I mean…er…a boot in the stones is worth two on the feet…'

'Yes, sir,' Pavo nodded. His skin prickled with pride and at the same time he had to suppress a laugh at the centurion's clumsy metaphor.

'And get back to cleaning the bogs – I want a pristine setup for my evening turd!'

'Yes, sir,' Pavo sighed, his shoulders sagging.

Brutus nodded briskly before marching off. Pavo hesitated for a moment before calling after him.

'Thank you, sir.'

Brutus did not turn or respond.

Pavo strolled from the training yard in the dying light, the slightest hint of support from his centurion and it felt like there was an army behind him. As he approached the latrines, he heard Festus choking – probably cleaning out a particularly fetid latrine. He smiled. Perhaps the whole world wasn't against him after all.

# Chapter 15

Gallus stared at the ornate cutlery. He felt all eyes on him in the cavernous palace hall as he eyed the array of utterly foreign implements flanking the mysterious shellfish in front of him; it seemed like the zenith of the Roman Empire waited with bated breath on his choice.

The Emperor Valens sat at the head of the table, dressed in a purple silk robe, his hair snow white and combed forward in the traditional style, dangling over austere, high arched brows and cobalt eyes. His seat was flanked rather ominously by two standing figures in white tunics, armed with spears and scabbards; the *candidati*, cream of the *palatini* and sworn to defend the emperor to the last. To the right, the aged Bishop Evagrius of Constantinople was seated beside the blubbery Senator Tarquitius. Facing the imperial and ecclesiastical lineup were, along with Gallus, the other representatives of the XI Claudia; Optio Felix, with his beard combed to two perfect points and Nerva, the jowel-faced, shaven headed tribunus, head of the legion. Unlike Gallus, Nerva had turned down the chance to wear full military decoration and instead he wore simple red robes and his usual intense expression on his face – one that always made Gallus a little nervous, given the tribunus' firebrand reputation. One last figure made up the table; the balding, rotund and ageing dux of Moesia, Vergilius – already glassy eyed and ruddy cheeked from quaffing wine, the crimson blotches contrasting sharply with his sparse and unkempt white locks.

Gallus eyed the dux; upon stepping off the gangplank of the *Aquila* and onto the city docks, a messenger from Senator Tarquitius had brought the good news; the senate was willing to back the proposal to send an invasion force back to the Bosporus. Since the senator first had Vergilius' ear over a year ago, the dux had been obsessed by the prospect of the XI Claudia going on the offensive. Cheap rhetoric, other officers had called it, but Vergilius' eyes had sparkled as Tarquitius spoke of the military legends of ages past.

The wine loving, palace dwelling dux was in charge of the limitanei legions all along the eastern Danubius, officially. And despite the dux's ineptitude he also held a dual post as *Magister Militum per Illyricum*, incredibly making him master of the nearest sibling dux – the dux of Dacia Ripensis. All this made the incompetent sot Vergilius the one man linking the armies of the north with Emperor Valens himself. And all because he embraced the Arian strand of the Christian faith, Gallus mused – at least that was how Nerva had put it, but the thick gold cross hanging around the dux's neck lent weight to the theory. Yes, Christianity was enshrouding the empire from the top down it seemed, while the rank and file stayed true to Mithras. But as the dux had spiralled upwards incoherently and unchecked, it was the men below him like Nerva, the tribuni who led the individual legions, who truly held the borders together.

Gallus glanced across to Evagrius, who was using the small, curved knife to crack the shell in front of him. Breathing an inner sigh of relief, he followed suit. The emperor didn't seem too interested in his food, prodding at the shell without conviction. Then he looked up to address his guests.

'So let's not wait for the sun to set before we hear of it; what happened over there? I've heard rumours of warring Gothic factions and ruined forts. Those people just won't settle, no matter how much we throw at them,' he mused, eyeing a faded scar on his forearm.

Gallus perked up at once, sensing all eyes falling on the three of them, but he held his silence and looked to Tribunus Nerva. He had fought alongside Nerva many times since he had been a young man, mainly along the Danubius frontier, fending off Germanians, Goths, Suebians and Alamanni. Ten years junior to his commander, Gallus looked to him as a role model; unfailingly, Nerva had shown himself to be willing to throw himself into the heart of the battle and risk his life on the front line. After so long, Gallus could even overlook the older man's failings, his stubbornness and blinkered approach to tactics.

As Nerva began to recount the reconnaissance report, Gallus looked across to the emperor. Valens too held an awesome record of military success behind him in his rise to the throne – a welcome buck in the trend of feckless emperors that had seen the empire crumble in the years before his ascension.

Although the empire lay fractured between the East and the West, with men like Valens at the helm there was always hope.

Nerva's tone changed and he slowed as he broached the point of the dark riders on the peninsula.

'There is an issue with an unidentified people that Centurion Gallus encountered. Only small parties were ever sighted, but they were heavy cavalrymen, and there is the possibility that it is they, and not rival Goths, who are driving out the local populace.'

Gallus felt words push at his lips. But, knowing it was against all protocol to speak over his tribunus, especially in front of the dux and more so the emperor, he bit his tongue. He was jolted, though, as Senator Tarquitius spoke out sharply, cutting off Nerva mid-sentence.

'This region has been in the wilderness and in the hands of barbarians for many years now. We have to expect a variety of unknown peoples in the region. What would be a concern would be if they were in a great number. Fortunately, the reconnaissance reports only small bands of these people,' he paused just long enough to stir the inevitable question from other side of the table, but again continued just as the breath filled Gallus' lungs, 'but in the event of a larger force, the recently commissioned comitatenses legion will be patrolling into Scythia and beyond. The I Dacia will be a fine addition to the imperial army, and they could easily come to the aid of the XI Claudia if need be – eh, Vergilius?' He nudged the dux, who simply looked up from his empty cup, eyes red in inebriation.

Gallus' mind spun as he took in the politician's words. A new field legion in the current climate? He glanced at Nerva, also wearing a wrinkled brow.

'Comitatenses?' Nerva gasped. 'Forgive my bluntness, but they don't come cheap. Thousands of men needing rigorous training in field combat, and then armed and armoured in the best equipment we have.'

'All hail the I Dacia!' Vergilius boomed, wine spilling from his raised cup.

The emperor shot a glare of contempt at the dux and then sighed. 'Indeed, this will seem a rather violent steer away from recent policy. But,' he added, looking up with a glimmer in his eyes, 'we have new resources.'

Gallus eyed the emperor; Valens wore a steady expression that betrayed little of his thinking. That itself told Gallus a thousand things about the man.

'Tell them, Vergilius,' Tarquitius nudged the dux again.

Vergilius snapped his fingers and a slave darted over to fill his cup with unwatered wine. Then he spoke, his words were rounded and over pronounced with the effects of alcohol. 'The Thervingi Goths to the north of the Danubius are split. Their two *would-be* kings, Fritigern and Athanaric,' he pulled a wide-eyed and sardonic expression, 'are tearing at each other. It's a bloody power struggle – but all the better for us.' The dux grinned, bringing a chorus of sycophantic laughter from the senator. 'But it gets better; after years of battering our weary limitanei, Fritigern has seen the light,' the dux raised a finger high as if addressing the forum, 'and has agreed to become an ally of the empire. With his allegiance, we have access to thousands of highly skilled Gothic fighters, who can form the basis of this new legion, and many more.'

'More *foederati?* With all due respect, my emperor – Gothic mercenaries cannot replace Romans,' Nerva spoke firmly, addressing the emperor and hiding his anxiety well.

'Seeded with the better Romans from our legions, they will become effective Roman troops,' Vergilius interrupted. 'The XI Claudia must have a few prime candidates for Roman role models?'

Gallus had to bite his lip once more while Nerva waited in vain for support from the rest of the table before replying. 'We have some fine soldiers, indeed. But we can't afford to lose any manpower. Our number is below eight hundred already – we can barely call ourselves a legion anymore. And what of the cost – the cold, hard gold required to pay for this new legion,' he paused momentarily, 'and our expedition?'

Vergilius spun his chalice and he gazed at the wine lapping the rim. 'Ah yes, the reconquest Bosporus.' The dux leant forward keenly. 'Well, our holy bishop has solved one of those problems for us – the Holy See will fund both initiatives...entirely. A gift from God, if you will!'

Gallus' eyes darted across the face of the bishop; his features lay settled in a peaceful smile under a pure white crop of hair, his expression in direct contrast to that of Nerva, whose features were pinched, lips wriggling in search of a reply.

Valens cut through the tension, his voice steady and unaffected by the wine. 'Let us proceed with the reconquest of Bosporus. The empire needs to move outward and forward. With their specially commissioned fleet, I trust that the new I Dacia legion will be within sailing distance of the peninsula to support the XI Claudia, should they be needed?'

'Indeed, they will!' Vergilius cut in.

Tarquitius coughed, leaning across the face of the dux. 'Permit me, Emperor. There was the...*other* element to the Gothic truce, too?' Then he turned to Vergilius again.

'Ah, yes,' the dux slurred, 'While Fritigern has chosen the path of a wise man; Athanaric remains relatively cold to us. But he knows the value of diplomacy - he has offered to supply an able strategist from his own court to lead this new legion.' He nodded vigorously at the widening eyes of Nerva, 'Wulfric may not be Roman, but he is highly capable from what I hear, and what's more,' he grinned wildly again, 'this move guarantees us a truce with Athanaric's Goths. A vital prerequisite to any expedition to the Bosporus given the temporary fragility that would leave our borders in.' The dux's words had become staccato and bullish as he finished, his face reddening and his eyes watering.

A gentle smile rippled across Bishop Evagrius' face, and Senator Tarquitius raised his chalice.

'To Tribunus Wulfric and his new legion, the I Dacia,' he toasted, 'and to the Bosporus mission!'

Emperor Valens remained expressionless.

Gallus glanced to Nerva; concern swirled on their faces.

# Chapter 16

The town of Durostorum glowed like a beacon on the banks of the Danubius as the blackness of night set in. Legionary watchmen stood alone in the darkness atop the watchtowers stationed at every third of a mile along the riverbank – alone, but all too alert to the barbarian danger that lurked on the northern banks. There hadn't been a raid in days now, and that meant trouble could not be far away. All the while, behind them, the town's nightlife rumbled on in a heady cocktail of noise and colour.

At the centre of the town, *The Boar and the Hollybush* inn, sporting the traditional vine leaves and ale stirring pole emblem at its open doorway, was bursting at the seams. Built of hefty stone blocks and roofed in the local thatched style, the inn looked like it had stood on that spot in the town centre for a thousand years. A pair of *kithara* players plucked an upbeat ditty and a pair of *timpani* rattled out a jangling rhythm. Legionaries and townsfolk packed the hay scattered ground outside, ale being ferried out to them across a sea of hands to a chorus of cheers while a tang of roasting goat, stew and stale vomit permeated the air.

Inside, Pavo sat at a long table, gripping a goblet of half-watered wine. He was surrounded by a mob of rather seasoned legionaries from the XI Claudia; scarred, burnt, grizzled and proud of it. Having returned from their mission to the far-flung land of Bosporus that morning, they were keen to hit the town. To say they were rowdy would be somewhat of an understatement; every so often, the table rocked and jumped, tipping goblets and vases to the chorus of raucous laughter as the legionaries would regale their colleagues and the assortment of local women with tales of their sexual misadventures.

Pavo's head swam as he drained the last of his cup. With each sup of wine, his nerves had dulled – almost to the point where he felt up to joining in with the banter. One more mouthful first, he reasoned giddily, tipping his cup back and letting his mind fill with the obscenities he could use to litter his sentence. As he tilted it back down, the curvaceous figure of the young redheaded barmaid again filled his view and at once, his mind emptied. *Beautiful.*

'Roll your tongue in, Pavo,' Avitus cackled. 'Think you'd never seen a pair before!'

Pavo turned to the short, bald veteran who had introduced himself a short while ago. 'As if! Worked my way around the best lookers back in Constantinople, I did!'

'Course you did, lad. Course you did,' He slapped a hand on Pavo's shoulder.

As a slave, he would often wonder at the beautiful but sour-faced senatorial stock who would visit Tarquitius' villa with their fathers, yet they would merely eye him in distaste like a scraping from the sole of their sandals. One 'outside' chore had been a bit special though; two years ago, at *The Eagle*, near the Hippodrome, he had just returned from a surveillance mission for the Greens. Having stalked a top man of the Blues as he drunkenly staggered back to his home, Pavo watched as he pulled the key from the tiny crevice by the shutters; that information had been like gold dust to the Greens. And the buxom lady, at least twice his age but with curves in all the right places, who was plonked onto his lap as a reward, seemed all too happy to congratulate him. For some time that evening, he had felt alive like never before, as they hungrily thrust against each other again and again. Afterwards though, it had been awkward – what was there to talk to her about? How could a slave hope to entertain a free woman? She had quickly bored of him and just as fast as his spirits had soared, they plummeted again as he trudged back to Tarquitius' villa and the slave quarters.

This girl, though, she was different.

Emboldened by the wine, he sneaked a wink at her. To his absolute delight, she responded with a smile, amber locks tumbling across her milky white face. Then he noticed Sura standing behind her, making a thrusting gesture with a look of pained ecstasy on his face.

Enraged, Pavo wobbled to his feet, slapping a palm on the table to steady himself, when he felt a hand grip his forearm. The bull-like legionary to his left glared at him. His battered nose wrinkled in distaste as he looked Pavo up and down.

'You with us?' He grunted as he lifted his goblet to his lips with his club-like fingers, the smallest of which was missing a half above the knuckle.

Pavo allowed the initial wave of fear wash over him and then gulped the dregs of his wine to fuel a reply. 'Yes, I'm with the Claudia,' he said with a forced casualness.

The legionary raised an eyebrow, wrinkling his forehead. 'Which century?'

'Er…' he started, sensing all eyes on him. No point in lying. 'I'm one of the new lads…still deciding which century to put me in.'

The legionary stared at Pavo, his face stony, and the rabble around them fell silent. Suddenly the legionary's face creased as he bellowed in laughter. 'You're a recruit! You're not with the Claudia yet, lad!' He roared.

Pavo's skin burned and he shot a glance to the barmaid – she hadn't heard, he noted with relief. Then he glared back at the gnarled tank sitting next to him, feeling his veins run rich with wine now. 'I'm as good a fighter as any of you here, and we'll be recruited into the centuries in the next few weeks!'

The legionary pointed the stump of his little finger at Pavo. 'This is the sign of a legionary; someone who has seen some action, and left a bit of himself on the battlefield to prove it. You're a raw recruit, no good to anyone yet. Eh, Avitus?' He retorted with a half-smile, winking to the smaller legionary across the table.

'Leave it out, Zosimus. I bet he could kick your arse!'

Pavo knew he was being toyed with. He decided to play the game.

'Is being an ugly whoreson also necessary to be a legionary?' He grinned, eager to keep the banter flowing. The huge legionary's face fell stony – and then grew scarlet. It was possible he had gone a little too far.

'Right, you little bugger, outside now!' He slurred at Pavo, shooting to his feet. The gathered troops all let out a roar of drunken approval that broke down into a gaggle of laughter.

'Come on! Everyone outside to see Zosimus getting his arse whipped by a recruit!'

With a collective whoop, Pavo found himself being lifted from his feet and swept outside by the exodus of legionaries.

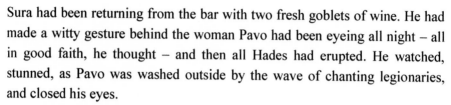

Sura had been returning from the bar with two fresh goblets of wine. He had made a witty gesture behind the woman Pavo had been eyeing all night – all in good faith, he thought – and then all Hades had erupted. He watched, stunned, as Pavo was washed outside by the wave of chanting legionaries, and closed his eyes.

'Oh bugger!' He murmured.

'Is that your friend?' A soft voice asked. It was the fiery vixen.

'Aye – always getting himself into bother,' Sura sighed, brushing his hair back from his eyes subconsciously.

'There are an awful lot of men angry with him,' she mused.

'Aye, he needs my experienced hand to guide him through life,' Sura chuckled, arching his brow and puffing out his chest. 'So what's your name?'

She looked cross. 'It's Felicia. And yours?'

'Decimus Lunius Sura, unofficial king of...' he began uncertainly.

'Well, *Sura,*' she cut in, 'aren't you going to help your friend?' She was definitely cross.

'Well, I...' he began.

'There's a horse out the back,' she cut him short again, pointing to the open shutter behind the bar. 'Bring it back before dawn.' With that, she planted her lips on his. After a lingering moment, she leant back. 'Off you go now.'

Sura's eyes grew as she cut through the crowd to the bar. After a moment, he shook his head clear and he stumbled back from the crowd to make for the black of night via the shutter. As he climbed out, he looked back, still bemused.

Felicia wore a mischievous grin.

Pavo swayed on his feet, nearly as drunk as his foe, who could barely hold his head up. The cool of the night air swirled around them, numbing Pavo further.

'I'm going to show you...' Zosimus murmured into his chest, waving a finger wildly in the air.

Pavo surveyed the situation as well as his cloudy head would allow him; surrounded by a circle of massive legionaries, grinning in drunken anticipation – a sea of teeth and sparkling eyes. This wasn't the time to display the techniques that Brutus had been teaching him, they would have to wait. If he were to back down, he would look like a fool in front of this circle of what he hoped would be his future colleagues. Only a swift, telling blow would do. The jaw, neck, and stomach presented themselves as likely places that would down the inebriated figure of the legionary. Then the failsafe popped into Pavo's head from the afternoon with Brutus. He took one step forward, and then swung his right foot with all his strength and coordination straight into Zosimus' groin.

A cushioned thud sounded and the crowd of legionaries let out a chorus of 'oooh's' and then fell silent. Zosimus simply let out a whimper before crumpling to the ground.

Pavo stood back. How many times had that little manoeuvre saved him, he marvelled.

'There, I showed him; I am worthy of the Claudia!' He roared confidently, jabbing a thumb into his chest. The circle of legionaries turned to him, grinning like sharks. Pavo gulped.

'All moves are fair play at *The Boar*, surely?' He pleaded.

'Yep,' one of the circle grunted, 'and we're about to show you a few more.'

'Get him!' One of them roared, and at once, they sprang towards him. Pavo ducked under the myriad shovel hands that shot out to grab him. A smash of legionary heads from above triggered a chorus of enraged roars.

Then a voice called out. 'Pavo! Grab my hand!'

Pavo glanced through the forest of legs, his head swimming; Sura pelted towards him on horseback, hanging from the saddle, holding out an arm.

He rolled between the legs, throwing himself directly in front of the horse's hooves. 'Whoa!' he cried, skidding back from being trampled and grasping the lifeline of Sura's arm. His shoulder groaned in protest as he was whipped from the ground and crunched onto the tough leather saddle.

'*Mithras!* Talk about a taste of my own medicine,' Pavo grumbled as a sickening pain spread from his groin.

Sura spurred the mount into a bolt and the legionary rabble slipped into the darkness behind them with a chorus of curses. 'Next time I think you should only take on a century, rather than an entire legion of veterans, single-handedly,' Sura slurred as they made for the legion fort.

Pavo let out a chuckle, feeling suddenly invincible.

'Oh, and you've got Felicia to thank for this one!'

Pavo felt a wave of jealousy burn his neck. 'The barmaid?'

'Aye, we were chatting for ages. Nice girl…good kisser.'

'Just shut up and ride!'

# Chapter 17

Gallus stood in front of an ornate, polished bronze mirror. He fastened his cuirass into place and then took to polishing the dulled sections of the breast moulding. It was very different from his day-to-day battered and rusting mail vest, but anything that wasn't pristine in the Imperial Palace would mark him out as a wretch from the border legions. He saw the metal shine up at last and gave a sigh of semi-contentment, his eyes setting on his reflection – his gaunt features looked even colder than he had remembered and the flecks of grey by his temples seemed to have multiplied into definite streaks. How long since that face had bore a warm smile. *Olivia.* He rubbed his eyes. He pushed the memory back.

He turned his thoughts to the previous evening. The feasting had ended before sundown after a seventh course of stewed dates and yoghurt, but the chatter had rolled on late into the evening as they had sampled more and more of the delicious range of vintage wines from the imperial cellar. He wasn't a big alcohol drinker, but had been wary of causing offence refusing the slave-girls who constantly buzzed around the table and he had soon come to appreciate the potency of the stuff.

Valens, the man behind the purple cloak, had proven to be a surprisingly warm character once the business of war and politics had been addressed. The bishop, of course, maintained a holy sobriety. First impressions of this man suggested that he might be a harmless character, but his eyes had a glint of impeccable sharpness in them that Gallus could not quite gauge as being cunning or simply alertness. The presence of Tarquitius at the table had caused the majority of the alcohol abuse. His constant calls to sample more of the fine wine had always been answered, though Gallus had noted with a keen interest that the man himself took to diluting his portions with up to five parts water while the dux by his side took his wine neat. Tarquitius persisted in moving the subject of conversation back to the military situation along the

Danubius, and it was clear that agendas were being pressed more forcibly as the night wore on. Whether it concerned the XI Claudia's fortunes crossed his mind a few times, but in the end, the wine carried his thoughts away.

Satisfied that he was impeccably polished, Gallus pulled at the chamber door and stepped into the towering hallway. This place was designed to make a man feel smaller than a mouse, and it worked. As usual though, he straightened his back and held his head high, marching confidently past the occasional sneering candidati. Then he came to an open *caldarium*, where the playthings of the emperor and his retinue lay strewn; cups, clothes and shoes scattered everywhere. Then, as he passed the pool, a group of giggling girls sank into the water to hide their naked breasts from him. Gallus afforded only a batted eyelid before moving on – years of celibacy had taught him precise self-control. To kiss Olivia's sweet neck one more time he would forgo all other pleasures of the flesh. He stepped over the mixture of goblets and robes punctuating the floor, while a single unfortunate slave darted around in a vain attempt trying to reinstate perfection before Valens could lay eyes on the mess.

Gallus moved on past a particularly stern looking candidati, through to the garden terrace. Valens leaned on the balcony overlooking the city, his purple robe billowing gently in the spring breeze as he surveyed his capital through the heat haze. Beside him, a pair of slaves waited patiently with a vase of what looked like iced water and fruit pieces. There was no sign of Nerva, Tarquitius or the bishop.

'Come and see this, Centurion,' Valens called.

Gallus took a deep breath, shook the fog of his hangover from his mind and walked from the cool interior of the palace and out into the baking morning sun to join the emperor at the edge of the balcony. The air was sharp with the salty tang of the waters of the *Propontus* and the docks below fizzed with activity. All excitement centred on a fleet of some fifty newly constructed triremes lined up against the harbour wall, boarding planks linking them to the dockside. Slaves scurried back and forth across them laden with cargo like a train of ants. Near the first ship – a grand looking thing, painted with an emerald boar emblem – stood a stocky, red-haired figure, in full gleaming decorative armour. *Wulfric*, Gallus assumed.

'You're a man with the heart of a soldier...a true Roman,' Valens enthused, cupping an arm around Gallus' shoulder. 'This is Rome as it used to be, and can be again. The transport fleet for the new I Dacia legion.' Valens chirped, brushing his palm across the scene below.

'The new legion? It's been mustered already?' Gallus asked.

'Well, just the command structure...and the supporting navy, of course. The fleet is being prepared to move up to the Danubius delta, and will select recruits for the new legion along the way.' He shook Gallus' shoulder firmly. 'Only a core will be sourced from your legion, so don't worry. And I'll see that your fort is supplied with plenty of new recruits.'

Gallus suppressed the meld of protests that swam into his mind; stripping the borders to create one floating legion? How many places could this one legion protect at once? He bit his lip and searched for a different tack. Then he noticed something under the veneer of Valens' enthusiasm. The emperor had shrewdness in his eyes, almost as if he wanted to coax a reaction.

'And what of these Goths who are to be supplied by Fritigern?' Gallus played along.

Valens' lips curled a little at the edges, and his eyes keened, locked on Gallus' face. 'Then the fleet will move up the Danubius to pick up Fritigern's men. Once they are kitted out, we are ready to deploy the legion. Quick responses to any border attacks, Centurion,' he purred, 'that's the key to keeping the rest of the northern tribes back – send the fear right through them with swift, decisive action!'

Gallus nodded, but he could sense now that Valens was definitely testing him, and the rhetoric was deliberately cheap.

'And Wulfric?' Gallus nodded to the armoured figure at the dockside. One of Athanaric's best men, standing like a peacock in the heart of the empire.

'That's our man,' Valens nodded, his face dropping. 'By all means I'd rather have your tribunus in there to lead them; any Roman would get my vote, but politics wield the heaviest sword. Damn it if that's not always the case.' The emperor's tone was laced with a trace of venom. 'An emperor can no longer rule as one.'

Gallus felt his mouth run dry. Fritigern's men filling the Roman ranks made him uneasy, but this one man of Athanaric's filled his heart with trepidation. 'Do you trust the Goths?'

Valens turned to him; his face had fallen stony. 'Do you?'

Gallus searched Valens' cobalt eyes; did the emperor share his doubts? 'I tend to mistrust until trust is earned, my emperor.'

Valens' face curled into a sardonic smile. 'A wise philosophy, Centurion. And one I fear I should follow.'

Gallus shifted uncomfortably.

Valens turned back to the docks, but his eyes stared a thousand yards. 'Well, Centurion Gallus, I have a lot of thinking to do. But the question is valid; do we trust them?'

Gallus shuffled in discomfort as the question hung unanswered.

Finally, Valens spoke. 'We have to, Centurion, we have to.'

# Chapter 18

Brutus leapt backwards under the swipe of the wooden sword and then dropped to his left side to steady his fall. Like a locust, Pavo hopped forward and rested his sword in Brutus' ribs.

'Surrender?' Pavo chirped. Now this was being alive!

A gust of afternoon air coated them both in a red dust and Brutus glared up at him, his face boiling in a scarlet fury. Pavo gulped at the bloodshot eyes of the centurion, before the craggy face broke down into a heaving cackle.

'You nippy little bugger! I knew I could teach you a trick or two. Here, give me a hand up,' he grunted, offering his tree trunk forearm. Pavo reached out – and felt Brutus' sword in his chest before he even knew he had made a mistake.

Brutus pulled him in so the two were face to face. 'The men you will fight will be dirty buggers; they'll try every trick in the book to open you up and spill your guts.' Brutus pulled him closer. 'So heed my words, don't ever be nice to anyone with a sword in their hand. Not even me.' With that, Brutus released his grip.

Pavo closed his eyes and shook his head. 'You're right. I'd be skewered by the likes of Spurius by now.'

'That arrogant little turd? You know enough to pummel the shit out of him now. He's a decent lad who's got problems, but he needs to be taught a lesson, I reckon. The trick for you is to get him on his own, without that grunt of his trailing him around – that Festus one is pure animal, stone cold – slice your throat for a follis.'

Pavo shot a glance down at his own body – still gangly despite the training. Brutus shook his head.

'Forget all the muscle bollocks; he's had the same training as you. The only edge he ever had on you was sheer bloody arrogance and the ability to fight dirty. And that's what I'm telling you that you have to do. Kick him in the balls and make him thank you for it before he even thinks about attacking you.'

Pavo laughed. 'Actually, I've had a bit of practice at that recently.'

'I heard about you lowering Zosimus' chances of having children. Top soldier he is, and I'd doubt my chances against him on the battlefield, but the man's a lumbering fool whenever he visits *The Boar*. He got what was coming to him.'

'So he isn't out to find me and break my neck then?' Pavo asked.

'He doesn't even remember who kicked him in the nuts! All of his friends do, but they won't tell him,' Brutus waved his hand dismissively. 'They find it hilarious!'

'I might venture back to the inn sometime soon then,' Pavo mused.

'Why are you so keen to go back to that hovel anyway? It's got to be the wine or…a woman?' Brutus jibed.

Pavo's eyes widened as he tried to think of a way out of the subject, when out of nowhere a shout rang round the yard.

'He's after the one with the big tits!'

Brutus and Pavo looked up. Sura, swinging his sword, swaggered towards them, chuffed with his timely entrance.

'The barmaid? Ah, a fine choice, well known to the Claudia,' Brutus mused.

'And to me,' Sura added casually.

Pavo felt a burning in his chest. He made to stand up and retort, when the centurion slung his training sword round to point at him.

'Two against one it is!' Brutus roared and then winked at Sura, who reached into his scabbard with a grin.

Pavo rolled his eyes and then flicked to battle mode. He kept his eye on Sura who threw his sword from hand to hand, while tracking Brutus with darting glances as the centurion darted around behind him.

'See that patch of horse shit over there, Sura?' Pavo quipped. 'You'll be wearing it!'

Sura let out an exaggerated hoot of laughter. 'Nah, because you'll be eating it.'

'Listen to the gladiators, eh?' Brutus chuckled. 'Couple of sheep-shaggers!'

Pavo grinned as he realised they were both off guard. He let his legs buckle under him, and pivoted on the spot, bringing his wooden sword hacking into the hamstrings of Brutus. Pavo's sword spun from his hand, tumbling across the yard behind Sura, while the centurion unleashed a howl of pain and toppled to the sand, hugging his legs.

'Twice in a day? You're on latrines for life, lad!' he cursed through gritted teeth.

'Ha!' Pavo chirped. Then he turned to Sura; his friend stood, stunned.

Pavo glanced at his empty hands and then at Sura – his friend was in no mood for mercy. He gulped back his doubts and stalked forward.

'All right,' Sura chuckled, tossing his sword from hand to hand. 'Come on then, I'll try and not leave you with too many bruises – might need you fit to come and collect me after I spend the night humping Felicia.'

Pavo skipped and slowed towards his friend, until they were almost within touching distance. Sura ducked to the right, going for the kill on Pavo's left. Pavo ducked outside of the would-be blow. As the wooden blade scraped across his skin, he cupped his hands together and brought them crashing down on top of Sura's outstretched arm. The sword toppled from his hand, and Sura stumbled to the ground with a howl and then a flurry of swearing.

'Another kill.' He calmly stated, inspecting his fingernails.

'What in Hades have you been teaching him, Brutus?' Sura moaned.

'*Brutus?*' The decked centurion roared. 'It's *sir*, you little runt!'

'Sorry, sir,' Sura added sheepishly. 'Fancy teaching me some of that,' he coughed, standing up. 'I much preferred it when he fought like a pregnant donkey.'

# Chapter 19

The docks of Durostorum swelled with bodies as the impressive I Dacia fleet dropped anchor. Having sailed up the western coast of the Pontus Euxinus, they had drifted inland via the Danubius delta that morning. The market traders flocked from their usual spots deeper in the city at the promise of heavy legionary purses.

A hot and very bothered Centurion Brutus barged his way through the mob towards the magnificent flagship's berth – the crew swarming like ants to dock the vessel. The heckling of market traders rattled in his eardrums as he navigated the throng in the claustrophobia of the intense midday heat.

At last, he burst into precious space and a cool breeze bathed his glistening skin. Brutus marvelled at the trireme; freshly hewn and treated timber; fresh linen sails emblazoned with an emerald boar; gleaming ballistae perched on the decks like coiled snakes and a small wooden archer platform hung about one-third way up the main mast. Most striking was the prow, with a massive, sharpened-iron ramming prong, sparkling in the sunlight. Brutus had only heard of this new mobile army of comitatenses via Nerva's memorandum that had arrived just this morning from Constantinople. He hadn't thought too much about it, but this fleet looked very capable – someone had poured plenty of gold into the initiative. Surely not the emperor though, he reckoned. Valens had only weeks ago denied the XI Claudia a troop transfer request for fifty experienced fighters to replenish their scant number.

Suddenly, the flagship's gangplank smashed onto the dock. The bustle died, all heads turning to the noise. Brutus craned his neck to see what was happening; six towering legionaries filed from the vessel and barged back the majority of the crowd before fanning out at the lip of the dock. They wore beards and blue ink *stigmas* on their skin – not of Roman stock for sure, but not an uncommon thing in the army these days, he mused. The soldiers looked around expectantly.

'Oh bugger, this is my cue!' He hissed under his breath. He spun round, feverishly trying to locate the dock watchtower. Screening the sun from his eyes, he finally found it, and at once started gesticulating to the two buccina-wielding troopers, who were obviously more interested in the events on the dockside.

'Pay attention you lazy...' Brutus growled. He glanced around him, spotted a beaten staff resting against the side of a market stall and hefted it like a javelin.

'Imperial business – sorry,' he muttered at the gawping stallholder. He loosed the staff through the air and watched it sail up and straight into the chest of one of the dozing watchmen. With a high-pitched yelp, the watchman and his partner were at once alert and scouring the crowd with venomous eyes, until they found the boiling glare of Brutus. Their faces turned pale and they fumbled their instruments to their mouths.

The buccinas blared as a group of three figures emerged from the deck of the ship. Two more tree-like legionaries flanked the equally imposing officer in the centre. Tribunus Wulfric, Brutus guessed. The stocky tribunus cut a distinguished figure in his hybrid Roman-Gothic armour. The fiery red beard and inky eyes gave him the look of a hungry predator. Not one to relish meeting on the battlefield, Brutus surmised.

'Officer coming through,' he grunted, bursting past the last line of onlookers. The party descended halfway down the gangplank as the centurion, red faced and breathless, arrived to greet them.

'*Ave!* Acting Chief Centurion Brutus of the XI Claudia legion at your service. In the absence of Tribunus Nerva, I'm responsible for greeting and welcoming you to the City of Durostorum.'

Wulfric smiled. '*Ave,*' he replied with an unmistakably Gothic twang. 'Tribunus Wulfric. Here to skim the cream of the XI Claudia!' At this, Wulfric's men burst into raucous laughter. Wulfric grinned, making no effort to quieten them.

Brutus, stunned at the lack of protocol, maintained his stony expression. 'So I understand, sir. If you'd allow me to escort you to the legion fort, we can introduce you to the other senior officers and then discuss the recruitment.'

'My men and I will come to the fort later today. First we have some unwinding to do,' he replied, nodding uphill towards *The Boar and Hollybush*, conspicuous by the cheering of early punters inside. This time both the men and the onlooking crowd erupted in laughter.

Brutus prayed for the ground to open up beneath him; his first taste of command at this level and this Wulfric was treating him like a fool. Inside he boiled with rage, but he held it back just long enough to get one more sentence out; 'As you wish, sir. In that case, I'll invite the senior officers of the legion to join you.'

The grin faded from the Goth's face, and he nodded. 'Very well.'

# Chapter 20

A doorstop of bread thumped onto Pavo's plate. He traced a slow glance up to the cook who had provided him with the baked monolith.

'You've excelled yourself again, I see.'

The cook grimaced and slapped his fist on the counter. 'Move along,' he hissed.

Pavo dropped his gaze and moved on with a snigger. The next cook behind the counter waited patiently with a pitifully thin strip of cheese in his hands.

'Give him some special sauce to go on it, Cyrus,' the first cook cackled. The second cook started brutally horking up the contents of his throat.

Pavo sighed, nodded and moved on, cheese-free. Laden with a not-so-hearty dinner, he moved along the meal-line to the wine barrels, where a queue was beginning to form. It had been a killer of a day, with another all-terrain forced march, then a gruelling session of combat training and camp construction. His limbs were still wiry but the muscles were now like gnarled rope, and despite all the pain and fatigue, he had never felt so fit. More than this, in his mind he felt so different; a real will not just to survive, but also to live. Being a freedman was good. Hard but good.

He rested his back and head on the stock of empty wine barrels, closing his eyes, waiting for the queue to crawl along. Then a voice came to his attention above the rabble, almost as if it was inside his head.

'We're being recruited soon, so you might not get another chance,' the voice said. 'If you're going to take him down tonight – and you know what'll happen if you don't – you'll need my help,' the voice continued. 'And we need to take down that cocky bastard, Sura, too.'

Pavo's heart leapt and his eyes blinked open. He looked along the queue – nothing. The voice seemed to be coming from inside the wine barrels? Turning, he traced the echo of the voices; then he saw it – through the gap in the barrel-stack he just made out two shadowy forms huddled in the darkness of the corner. Spurius and Festus.

'Tchoh!' Spurius spat, his eyes darting around the canteen at the swarm of recruits. 'Will you keep a lid on it? We'll talk about this later.'

Pavo felt his veins ice over as he broke from the queue. Where was Sura? His eyes shot around the mess hall. All around him, recruits were intermingled with legionaries, heckling, babbling and hooting with laughter – not a care in the world it seemed. His heartbeat tripled until at last he spotted his friend chewing happily on a piece of solid bread. Pavo tried to stroll casually to the table. He slid into the bench facing Sura.

'I thought you were getting a kicking from the cooks...' Sura trailed off and his brow wrinkled. 'What's wrong?'

'We've got to get out of the fort tonight – or we're dead.'

# Chapter 21

*Whoresons!* Brutus screamed inside.

Wulfric and his men were loud. Loud, arrogant and rude. And that was quite something coming from him, he thought. Certainly, the ale had helped loosen their tongues, but this was a deliberate hand in the face of the XI Claudia.

The other Goths Wulfric had brought with him to be his centurions were a real bunch of hard men. Two had been in the western imperial guard; another had fought in Pontus as a gladiator, recruited at Wulfric's request after he had impressed in a tournament at Trier.

'Slit your throat for a follis,' Wulfric had enthused of him, slapping the grinning man on the shoulder.

To Brutus' left and right, Avitus and Zosimus were seated, both still groggy from their night on the town following the return from the Bosporus mission, but the best men available while Nerva and Gallus enjoyed their trip to the capital. Brutus sympathised as Zosimus swirled his cup of water in distaste, but they had to stay lucid while these strangers drank the place dry and sobriety was probably the best way to keep a lid on Zosimus' hair-trigger temper while Wulfric and his men hurled thinly veiled insults at them.

Wulfric swung his bloodshot eyes round to Brutus and stabbed a finger into his shoulder. 'So how many of your men d'you think will be fit enough for my legion?' He slurred.

Brutus refused the bait and turned on his finest tongue. 'When the senior officers are back in the morning, we can discuss this detail,' he replied as a local crashed over the table next to him, shrieking with laughter and fountaining ale over his friends, 'in a proper environment.'

'In the meantime we've got the grunts looking after us then, eh?' Wulfric swept his finger across Brutus, Zosimus and Avitus. His men roared.

Brutus again felt his heart thud. It would be interesting to see if the Goth showed the same level of disrespect to Gallus. *Gallus*, he mused, cold son of a bitch. But then, nobody messed with him. Perhaps a mention of the primus pilus' name might quell the atmosphere a little. Why stop there, he wondered, dropping Nerva's name would surely do the trick.

'No, it's just that *you're* in no fit state to talk about it now. Tribunus Nerva will be able to demonstrate the talent of our legionaries, tomorrow. As I said.'

Wulfric pulled an expression of mock attentiveness – eyes wide. 'Nerva? The man is a loose blade. I would be surprised if he could show me any talent, since your limitanei have been sitting in this cesspit for the last … how many years? It's comitatenses we are looking for, soldier, not militia.'

Brutus' blood boiled, and he cursed himself as he felt his skin glow red as usual. The warm friendly bustle and alcoholic rabble of the inn carried on around the thick pool of tension, but inside the centurion, a torrent of rage swelled. Before he could check himself, he was on his feet, his clenched fist hammered into the table. The inn fell silent and all eyes swung onto them.

'Right, you stinking whoreson,' Brutus growled. 'I don't know how a runt like you has made it to the rank of tribunus of the Roman army, but it's safe to say that on any other rank you'd be on the wrong end of the lash for that kind of talk,' he clicked his fingers, the snapping sound reverberated in the silence, 'like that!'

'Sir,' Avitus hissed, eyeing the gape-mouthed locals, stilled by the outburst. Brutus kept his stony stare on Wulfric, who glared in return. Wulfric's men grinned, their hands by their sides, but their fingers writhed near their scabbards. Then, a cool draught of evening air gusted over the scene, in concert with the creaking of the wooden inn door.

'Am I interrupting?' A familiar voice boomed. Brutus dropped his stare when he saw Wulfric's face switch into a smile. He turned to face the stern gaze of Tribunus Nerva, flanked by Centurion Gallus. 'Care to fill me in on the details?' Nerva continued.

Wulfric smiled again at Nerva. 'Your chief centurion was just telling me how ferocious the Claudia can be. Care to join us? Then we can introduce ourselves properly.'

Nerva cast a disdainful look across the table. 'Tomorrow, in the fort headquarters. Dawn. It would be wise to save our discussions for when we have clear heads,' he barked. With that, Nerva nodded to Gallus, turned heel and left, as quickly as he had arrived.

Brutus caught the raised eyebrows of Gallus as he made to follow the tribunus. *It's down to me to sort this out*, he sighed. He looked over to the bar, nodding to the landlord. Then, rolling his eyes up slowly to settle on Wulfric again, he forced a smile onto his face.

'Well, Tribunus Wulfric, we'll be leaving you and your men to ready yourself for tomorrow. Your quarters at the fort are prepared for you, whenever you decide to call it a night.'

Wulfric looked as if he had found a bar of gold. Until the bell for closing time pealed violently – three hours before actual closing time. Wulfric's face dropped and the punters broke out into a rabble of jeers.

'Oh dear, seems like it's time to call it a night,' Brutus spoke through a taught expression.

As if their legs were leaden, Wulfric and his sour-faced party shuffled up from their seats and swaggered to the door.

'Tomorrow,' Wulfric called back over his shoulder.

'What is all this about, sir?' Avitus asked as the door swung shut on the emptying inn.

Brutus remembered the garbled memo he had received from the messenger; Goths, new legions, lavish spending. 'Politics, Avitus,' he sighed. 'Bollocks we don't need to know but bollocks we have to suffer.'

A cool midnight breeze rippled through the fort. All was silent, save for the odd cough and shuffle from the legionaries on guard duty.

Pavo pressed himself against the cold stonework at the foot of the guard tower on the southeastern corner, his teeth clamped together to stop the chattering. Pitch and shadow danced around him on the deserted training yard, with only the pinhole canopy of starlight and the torches on the guard towers above piercing the dimness. He risked a glance around the edge of the tower to the guardhouse; no sign of Sura and the hatch-door he had gone to investigate remained locked. He strained his eyes, scouring the dull shapes to find his friend, when a snap of twigs from across the training yard jolted him back round, heart racing, fists clenched. Nothing. Only a swirling of the dark shadows behind the barrack buildings where the rest of the legion lay in their bunks. He gazed at the emptiness, determined to see what his imagination taunted him with.

The hastily hatched plan was fragile at best; based on gossip from one of the older legionaries, the disused hunting pit in the forest appeared to be their best bet – now they just had to lure Spurius out there. What would happen next was another matter, and he couldn't see Spurius politely agreeing to sit down and broker a truce.

Pavo had risen from his bunk, lifted his latrine sponge and strolled from the barracks as naturally as he could manage with the eyes of Spurius and Festus following his every step. That pair were not for sleeping tonight. The icy night chill danced around the neck of his tunic, and he pulled it up a little, shivering – then a hand came crashing down onto his shoulder.

'We're all set, the guards have moved off to the corner towers. Move!' Sura hissed.

'In the name of...I nearly soiled my tunic!'

'You should have; it'd mean you could run faster.' Sura hissed.

Gulping his heart back in, Pavo scurried after his friend. The watch on the walls above had hit a quiet spot; one guard at each corner, staring out over Durostorum and the eastern cornfields respectively. Apart from that, all clear. Now it was time for action. His filthy bunk seemed like a warm paradise in comparison to this dark chill.

Sura put his fingers to his lips as he gently slid the latch on the hatch-door and lifted it free of its lock. The door swung open in merciful silence to reveal the shadowy moonlit world outside. An audience of darkened trees waited, their leaves writhing gently in the breeze, beckoning them across the plain.

'Go, now!' Sura hissed.

Pavo balked at the sudden urgency. Glancing over his shoulder, he saw it, a pair of human shadows haring towards them. His blood froze and a pang of terror prickled his skin. Spurius!

Pavo fell through the doorway, bundled by Sura. As the hatch-door slapped shut, Sura only just remembered to raise a hand backwards to cushion it closed. As soon as it stilled, a clenched fist from inside punched it open again.

'Come on!' Pavo hissed, grabbing at Sura's forearm and stamping at the fingers of the rogue hand. The two set off across the open ground, speedy but silent, towards the trees. Behind them, they heard a dull thud of footsteps. They simultaneously burst into an upright sprint, abandoning stealth.

'Oh, bugger!' Sura croaked. 'Don't look round!'

Pavo fought the fear and focused straight ahead, burying the urge to roar to the wall guards. In the forest, he had a chance of escape. He bit his bottom lip hard and tasted the metallic wash of blood as he willed his limbs onward. The branches reached out to him, only a hundred paces to go, when a frustrated growl from behind accompanied a sharp whirring and then a spinning training sword scythed past his ear.

'In the name of...' he yelped. They were only paces behind. He crashed into the thick mass of branches closely followed by Sura. The drop in speed felt like hitting a stone wall as the foliage rallied against them, rebounding to push them backwards then shackling them as they drove into its mass for what seemed an eternity. Scratched all over, they stumbled out onto a clearing and a faint track.

'You're dead, Pavo!' Festus croaked as he fought through the foliage, only an arm's length behind, his breath clouding over Pavo's shoulder.

'Which way?' Sura cried, darting his eyes down the path in both directions.

Panting, Pavo shot a glance at the stars; he circled his hands, ignoring the barrage of insults from behind. In the forest to the west of the fort, the old legionary had said to his friends. He saw the dim glow of Durostorum light the sky further down the path.

'West – this way. Come on!' He barked, shoving Sura forward just as Spurius ripped free of the branches and launched himself onto the path with bear-like arms outstretched.

'I can't see a bloody thing, how do we know where it is?' Sura spluttered, squinting at the pitch-black ground.

'Just run and keep your eyes on the ground ahead!' Pavo stretched his stride until it hurt. His eyes traced the dimness of the path – he could barely see his own feet, let alone the...

'Pavo! Jump!' Sura cried.

The ground disappeared beneath him as his world spun and then with a dull crunch he landed, shoulder-first in a pile of animal bones. *Not good*, he reasoned, wincing at the sharp, stabbing pain racing through his back. He had landed right in the hunting pit. *Great plan*, he cursed himself. Within a single breath, two massive hulking shapes crashed down on top of him. This was bad, very bad.

'Pavo! Get up, get out of there!' Sura called from up above. Pavo's vision came together and he made out his friend's silhouette in the starlight above. His heart and mind were already crawling out of the pit, but his legs stayed pinned firmly under Festus. The groggy giant grunted and shook his head. Pavo kicked out, squirming towards the pit wall.

'Give me your hand,' Sura cried from above, hanging over the pit edge, gripping a stray tree root with his other hand. Pavo thrust out his arm to the shadowy saviour. Their hands slapped together, and they shared a grin. Then the root ripped free. Sura howled as he toppled into the bundle of bodies.

Pavo saw just a blinding light as a limb crashed against his skull. A flurry of swearing, spitting and scuffling ensued before they broke apart, each scrambling to a corner of the rectangular pit, Pavo's eyes tuned into the darkness and he made out Sura slumped in the opposite corner, dazed. Spurius and Festus ignored Sura and turned for him. He gripped the pit wall in panic, the dirt crumbled in his hands.

'You're for it now, Pavo,' Spurius growled as they closed in on him.

'Nice place this,' Festus spat, 'could see a recruit having a nasty accident here.'

No way out. Staying alive was all he could hope to do. He grasped at what felt like an animal thighbone from the pit floor, hefting it up and over his shoulder, ready to strike.

'That's no match for *this!*' Festus crowed, sliding a spatha slowly from his scabbard, the blade catching the starlight just long enough to illuminate his stump-toothed sneer. 'Time to finish the job from the other day.'

A shuddering thwack rang out, followed by whining and then an ungainly thump, but there was no pain. Pavo started; Sura stood where Festus had been, swaying, eyes spinning from the fall, holding a heavy strip of tree-root in his hands; Festus was a dark lump on the ground, unconscious and snoring like a boar. Spurius' eyes widened and he stepped back.

'Not so keen on two against one, eh?' Pavo spat. Then he looked to Sura with a grin, only to see his friend's eyes roll in their sockets before he, too toppled into the dirt.

Spurius grinned back. 'That was handy, eh?'

His heart racing, Pavo paced to the side as Spurius drove them to circle each other.

Spurius shimmied and Pavo's knees almost buckled; the darkness, the raw terror here was so far removed from his sessions with Brutus.

'Not so clever in a real fight, are you?' Spurius hissed, reading his mind.

'You try getting closer to me and you'll find out.'

Spurius snorted derisively, and then pulled a feint and another shimmy, before suddenly he sprung, barging Pavo to the ground, then began raining blows.

*Damn it!* He cursed as his back thudded into the pit floor. *All that training...for this!* Pavo blocked out the dull thudding – only pain so far, nothing lethal. This fight could still be won. He felt his arms being brushed away as he tried to shield himself, and kicked out, pushing Spurius back. But like a hunting lion, the bulky soldier sprung straight back on top of him, fists raised.

'Why don't you just finish it?' Pavo croaked.

Spurius grappled at his tunic collar, wrenching him from the dirt and right up to his face.

'Why don't you just...just *disappear?*' He spat. With a tortured howl he cast Pavo back and slid to the ground against the opposite pit wall.

Pavo sat up, his ears ringing and his face numb, and stared at his enemy; Spurius ran his fingers across his cropped scalp, kicking his heels into the mud.

'What in Hades is going on with you?'

'Just bugger off, for your own sake,' Spurius grumbled, his face buried in his chest.

Pavo's mind spun. He eyed the tree root at the far wall – an easy escape. Then he glanced to Sura – still out cold, and then to Spurius and Festus. He couldn't leave Sura here, but couldn't get him out alone.

'Spurius, I don't care what your problem is anymore. I just want to make sure Sura here is okay.'

Spurius chuckled dryly.

'Help me get him out of this pit and I'll help you with Festus.'

Spurius frowned with a look of disbelief. 'D'you think I care if that cretin lives or dies?'

Pavo followed Spurius' glare – burning into the snoring Festus.

'I don't get it, okay? Will you just help me with Sura?' With that, he scrambled up the dirt wall. Slapping onto the earth above, he afforded a few sharp breaths before prising himself to his feet. He turned to look back down into the hole and drew a breath to try to coax Spurius once more. But something rammed into his back and instantly he was face down in the ground again. A set of hands wrenched his arms back.

'What in the name of Mithras is happening here?' A voice raged. Pavo twisted his neck round to see a mounted centurion glaring down at them in utter disdain, his wolf-like features illuminated in the moonlight.

'I've got him, sir!' The legionary on his back roared.

# Chapter 22

The sun peeked over the horizon, coaxed by Zosimus' buccina cry. He pulled the instrument from his lips and filled his emptied lungs – *that'll wake 'em*, he chuckled to himself. He rested on his shield, glad the urge to sleep had finally left him. The guard from last night had been thrown into jail for letting a group of recruits slip out of the fort during the night. Zosimus chuckled again as he reminisced on his own distant days as a troublesome recruit, and then jumped to attention at the echo of a rhythmic march coming from the east gate. Centurion Gallus strode beside Tribunus Nerva towards the officer's quarters, both men wearing a hardened stare.

'I can't believe we're actually late – pray to Mithras Wulfric is still comatose somewhere.' Nerva cocked an eyebrow to his primus pilus as he placed a hand on the door. 'Ready for this?'

'How do we play it, sir?' Gallus spoke quietly.

'Keep our cool. We need to understand where he's coming from,' Nerva whispered, then added with a tilt of the eyebrows, 'even if what he really needs is a good chinning.'

Gallus grinned as the door strained on its hinges, and then his face fell, stunned; sitting around the scarred oak table in the centre of the meeting hall, Wulfric and his men looked fresh and well into their discussions. A parchment map was pinned open with a goblet and a dagger, and a variety of carved wooden figures lay dotted across the etched landscape.

'Good morning,' Wulfric offered, not bothering to turn and face them.

Gallus glanced to his tribunus; Nerva bit back a frustrated sigh before mounting a cool smile.

'Good morning, Tribunus Wulfric. I'm glad you could join us,' he replied swiftly, cutting across the room and breaking into the huddle, discarding all etiquette. Gallus followed suit, watching the Goth's eyes as Nerva bulldozed into the matter.

'So you're considering your options for recruitment, yes?' Nerva snapped.

Wulfric's eyes narrowed and he moved his lips to speak.

'Okay,' Nerva cut in, 'you'll be hard pressed to get a full complement of officers from Moesia alone,' he sighed, lifting the two figurines positioned over the large dot of ink marking Durostorum. 'If you want a strong legion, and I presume you do,' Nerva waited just long enough for Wulfric's face to flush in fury, 'then you've got a three to four month sortie up and down the river. There are plenty of battle-ready officers along the frontier. The key is not to strip any one section too heavily. Not with the threat of invasion hanging at every ford and bridge these days. Where you recruit, you must also provision.'

Gallus swallowed the grin trying to envelop his features. Nerva could cut the brash figure in the middle of a pack of lions.

'Your opinion is noted, Tribunus,' Wulfric seethed. 'But we have a specific brief, and time is of the essence if we are to achieve it. Battle-readiness inside two weeks.'

'Preposterous,' Nerva swiped an arm through the air. 'Not worth the recruitment fees.'

'I have my orders,' Wulfric spoke slowly. 'Directly from your emperor.'

Nerva fell silent, stumped. '*Our* emperor, surely?'

'Of course,' Wulfric nodded, a grin crossing his face as his colour lightened to normal. 'Shall we get down to business?' Wulfric suggested, waving his open palm over an empty stool.

Nerva sat, and then eyed the seven figures surrounding him. Then he looked to Gallus with the slightest of nods.

'Shall we leave our officers to their business?' Gallus offered, eyeing Wulfric's guards.

Wulfric looked him up and down with vague interest. The air grew thick again before Wulfric flicked his index finger.

'Very well, one to one it is.'

Gallus caught the glint of relief in Nerva's eyes and then turned back to Wulfric's men. 'If you care to follow me, I'll take you on a tour of the fort and our morning training session.' With a series of grunts, the five guardsmen scraped their stools back, stood and filtered towards the doorway.

'While you're out there,' Wulfric cut in, 'mark the names of the best soldiers you see. We'll be taking them.'

# Chapter 23

Pavo's vivid dreams were ripped from him, and stark reality came flooding back with a dull clanging of iron. He lurched bolt upright, pawing the sleep from his eyes.

'What in Hades?' he croaked as the iron clattering grew louder and faster. At the same time, his body provided him with a rippling report of the previous evening's injuries.

'Awake yet, dung-breath?'

Pavo's heart sank as he recognised the dank stench of the fort prison. Even worse, Spurius lay in the adjacent cell, glaring, rattling his knuckles along the bars. He slunk back onto the cold and crumbling cell wall, squinting through swollen eyes at the parchment-thin slots near the ceiling. The sliver of light they allowed in sent a fiery pain through his head and he shuffled on the damp and hard hay-mattress to escape the glare.

'You shouldn't have made things so complicated last night,' Spurius sighed.

'Aye, sorry for that,' Pavo spun around, his nausea rising into rage, 'should've just let you kill me, eh?'

'Well you're alive, so stop moaning.'

Pavo shook his head in disbelief and then prised himself from the disgusting bed, then shuffled over to the iron barred cell gate. He pressed his face against the bars – providing a cool relief to the cuts and bruises to his face. Outside he could see only a corridor stretching off to the left.

'You keen to get out? If I were you, I'd be praying they don't come for us for as long as possible.' Spurius sucked air through his teeth. 'Forty lashes if we're lucky.'

'Why are you even talking? Animals don't talk,' Pavo threw back over his shoulder. Then his blood cooled – the rest of the cells were empty. 'Where's Sura?' He croaked.

'Relax, he's in the hospital. Just pray he's not in the bunk next to Festus,' Spurius mused in semi-interest.

Pavo slumped down on the bunk again. From the shadows, he afforded a look at his enemy; Spurius' naturally craggy features were embellished with a rash of scratches and bruises, his mouth was twisted in an agitated wrinkle, but his eyes were most interesting – under the permanently creased brow they gazed in melancholy at some bronze figurine he wore on a chain around his neck. Pavo looked at the legionary phalera hanging round his own neck and wondered what story Spurius' trinket held.

'So what's this all about, Spurius?' He ventured.

'Eh?' Spurius grunted, his face pinching into the more familiar aggressive gurn.

'One minute you're spitting venom at me, threatening to kill me – the minute you get the chance you decide to let me go? That's twice now.'

The air grew thick as Spurius simply stared back at him in silence, before he finally replied. 'It's a long story...you wouldn't be interested.'

'Try me,' he said.

Spurius let out a long, tired sigh and his expression became saturnine. Just as he took a deep breath to speak, the outer jail doors creaked open – both of them shot up to the cell doors.

A deep babble of voices echoed along the corridor. Pavo strained to see the source of the commotion. Five figures in black armour stood around a centurion – it was the one from last night, his stony, sunken, wolfen features unmistakable. Pavo's neck burned in embarrassment – what could he possibly say to excuse the whole sorry scenario?

As the party strolled past the empty cells, their voices became clearer and Pavo recognised the jagged tongue – Gothic. They slowly worked their way down to Spurius' cell.

Pavo eyed the men; all of them towering near the jail ceiling, they wore the beards and flowing fair hair of the northern tribesmen. Their armour was Roman, but embellished with painted symbols and dripping with trinkets. The largest of them eyed Spurius and Pavo, before shaking his head.

'Deserters? Cowards in other words. Not for us,' he spoke in broken Greek, 'you got any murderers?' He grinned as his colleagues roared at this.

Pavo felt his skin burn – deserters? His tongue strained against the urge to blurt out the story – now was not the time.

The centurion stepped forward. Pavo nervously eyed his long and pointed features, his firm jaw and the piercing ice-blue eyes spoke of determination and going by the bounty of phalerae hanging from his breastplate, he was pretty important. The centurion grimaced. 'Well I don't know what your criteria are, but the jailhouse and the hospital are hardly going to provide fit and worthy officer material. You are free to request a drill inspection of any men of the Claudia, but I suggest we move on to the barracks now. The active legionaries will be preparing for training – that's where you will source the men for your legion.'

The five Goths nodded grudgingly, and then turned to walk back down the corridor. The centurion followed them with a sigh.

'What's happening?' Pavo ventured, pressing his face against the bars of the door.

The centurion pivoted, his glare burning into Pavo.

'If a soldier addressed his primus pilus in such a manner, I'd have him lashed. From a deserter though, I'm not surprised.' Then the centurion's face wrinkled in a sneer as he eyed Pavo's gangly form. 'Or are you some kind of starved beggar we picked up in the countryside?'

Pavo's eyes widened. He backed up from the bars, his throat dried up and he shook his head.

'I'm sorry, I...I'm a new recruit, sir. Numerius Vitellius Pavo.'

'Recruits will be the death of this army,' he grumbled. 'I know all about you. Missed my evening meal because of the ruckus you caused last night. So do yourself a favour; it's Centurion Gallus – don't forget it, because I'll have my eye on you. Troublemakers don't last long in my ranks. Lucky for you I've got bigger problems to deal with right now.'

As the centurion turned to stalk down the corridor, Pavo slumped back onto the bunk with a groan. Centurion Gallus; he'd heard the name countless times in the mess hall, the inn and in the training yard. A man with a heart of stone, they said. Ruthless, they said. A man they would follow without question, despite the odds, they said.

A man who despised him.

'Not the brightest introduction you could've made, Pavo,' Spurius mused.

# Chapter 24

Centurions Gallus and Brutus flanked Tribunus Nerva at the side of the training court as the trio stonily observed the Gothic examination of the legion. Flies swarmed in the mid-morning heat. Brutus spat one from his lips.

'Don't think I can take much more of this, sir.'

'They want to break us like a wild horse,' Nerva agreed, his eyes narrowing. 'They're prodding in all the right places, for sure.' He sighed as he watched Wulfric barge one of the centurions from his place, facing his century, to bark his own commands at the men.

'How did the dust settle then, sir? Are we going to be left with any legionaries at all?' Gallus asked.

'Wulfric has taken his orders to mean that everyone else in the empire bar the emperor himself is a second-class citizen. Effectively…we cannot deny him anything he requests. The brief was to have Roman officers and Gothic ranks, but Wulfric has taken the orders and shaped them to his whim.'

'Does the emperor know how damning this is for his borders?' Gallus shook his head. 'They might only be after a handful of our men, but we are already barely a token force.'

Nerva sighed. 'I think our friend, Senator Tarquitius, has had a little too much bend of Dux Vergilius' ear. This notion that the Goths will obediently follow a truce when our defences are threadbare is fundamentally flawed. It's the cheap rhetoric that the politician uses to colour his arguments that's carried this.'

'What has a senator got to gain?' Brutus shrugged. 'It'll be Wulfric, Vergilius and the emperor who get the glory of any victories in the field. It'd make me sick like a dog to see a whoreson like Wulfric leading a triumph though,' he grumbled a little too loud.

'I'm not sure about this,' Gallus spoke warily, his tone hushed. Nerva and Brutus turned to him keenly. 'Sir, I think Tarquitius is being played, just

126

as he in his own way is playing the dux and the emperor. Where Wulfric sits in all of that, I'm not sure. But someone must be pulling all the strings in this mess.'

All three fell silent, looking over to the figure of Wulfric; now resting on the barrier, the Goth observed his guards putting the legionaries through their paces – now they were on their third round of fifty press-ups. The jagged barking of the Goths grated, but the Romans were maintaining their cool despite the blistering heat. Wulfric's eyes were narrowed and focused. Gallus noticed the sharpness in his expression; for sure, this man was searching for the breaking point of the legion, but he was no brainless lout.

'What will this mean for the reconquest of Bosporus if we lose number here?' Gallus asked as he scanned the training field. Scarcely one thousand men, including the latest rabble of recruits. The remaining eight hundred or so of the three cohorts of the legion were still spread thinly along the Danubian watchtowers and fortlets and could not be summoned from those posts.

Nerva turned to look Gallus in the eye. 'I asked the emperor the very same question. He only said that provision would be made to ensure the mission went ahead. And I think we all know where that path leads to...' he sighed.

Gallus' heart sank; foederati, the scourge of the army in recent times. Just as with the new comitatenses legion, the XI Claudia would be topped up with powerful warriors from the forests of Germania and mercenary Goths from the northern plains. They augmented the numbers quickly, but what you got was a throw of the dice; tales of mutiny, anarchy and ill-discipline far outweighed the few success stories.

'On the bright side, we've always got Brutus' new litter to add to our operative number,' Nerva added.

'Not if the two runts who are in the jail are anything to go by,' Gallus replied. 'If they can't control themselves in here they won't be much use on the battlefield. That one, by the name of Pavo, didn't even address me by rank this morning.'

Brutus frowned but Nerva cut in before he could speak. 'I think there might be more to that story than meets the eye. Brutus reckons the lad has potential.'

127

'No offence, Brutus, but I'll believe it when I see it,' Gallus offered.

'The lad has had a hard time since he got here,' Brutus reasoned, then shrugged, 'but I suppose that's the point, eh?'

# Chapter 25

The back streets of Constantinople, just off the Atalos Gate, were dim at best at this hour, only a few ill-tended lanterns swung above doorways. The night chill drifted in like an icy breath and every corner and shadow swam with the unknown. A hooded figure shuffled across the pool of light in front of a sleepy brothel then slipped into the blackness of the alleyway by its side. All was silent for a moment until the clanking of armour announced the arrival of soldiers. Two urban guardsmen flanked Senator Tarquitius.

'Wait,' he raised his hand as he eyed the brothel. He stood stock still, shivering, his eyes darting uneasily. A piece of rubble clattered out in front of them from the blackness. Tarquitius started, while his two guards clasped the hilt of their swords. Tarquitius moved a hand over each of their scabbards.

'At ease,' he whispered to Fronto, eyeing the shadows by the alley.

Bishop Evagrius was enveloped in the darkness, dreamlike and ethereal. Tarquitius moved towards him, his heart pounding.

'This surely isn't a safe haunt for members of the Roman Senate?' Evagrius spoke gently. 'I'm sorry; I didn't mean to startle you.'

Tarquitius frowned until a grey light shaped the bishop's features. 'Let's make this quick. Where are the funds?'

Evagrius smiled, and only when Tarquitius frowned, he replied. 'A church vessel laden with gold has been despatched. It will arrive on time, and it will serve its purpose.'

Tarquitius gritted his teeth.

'And I should interrogate you on your progress?' Evagrius suggested. 'Oh, sorry, I forgot. You have no further part to play.'

Tarquitius' eyes bulged and he seethed at the bishop's coolness.

'I've played my part, I've risked my name.' He took a step forward. 'Let us not forget; I could end this whole affair whenever I so desire.' He paused as the bishop flicked his eyes up sharply and nodded. Confused, Tarquitius twisted to glance over his shoulder, but he saw only his two guards alone and alert, as expected. He turned back to the bishop. 'All it would take would be a nasty mugging on the back streets of the emperor's great city, for a church leader to be found dead tomorrow morning.'

He watched the bishop's eyes with glee, anticipating the fear and the inevitable climb-down. Instead, his blood ran to ice; from behind him came a gurgling and then a crumpling thud, shortly followed by another. Turning slowly, his eyes fell to the two figures on the ground, one lay with an arrow piercing his chest, and another with two in his throat. Both were stone cold dead. Tarquitius felt his head spin as he turned back to face the patriarch of Christianity.

Bishop Evagrius wore a dreadfully inappropriate smile.

'Let us not forget the power of the Church, dear senator,' he whispered gently, before slipping backwards into the shadows. 'And understand that a gentle political death can be far less painful than the real thing. Your services are no longer needed, Senator. Step back.'

Tarquitius' eyes widened. Acutely aware of his surroundings, a shiver of terror raced over his skin as he imagined what he couldn't see in the darkness. Time stood still, and his heart thundered. The bishop had vanished as quickly as he had appeared. The senator's primal fears hit boiling point and his legs convulsed into a stagger that broke into a run.

# Chapter 26

'Pull yourself together, runt!' One of the legionaries grunted.

Pavo felt his legs buckle again, but forced himself straight as the two soldiers dragged him ruthlessly across the training court. He shook his head clear, blinking at the starkness of the afternoon light after hours in the dimness of the jail. The shouting and general bustle of training swirled in the air to his left, and mocking cheers hurled Pavo's way from the recruits were cut short by a roar from Brutus.

Pavo felt his skin burn in shame, and then he saw their destination – the officers' quarters. The doorframe tore a gash in his left shoulder as he was bundled into the room without ceremony. Before him, around a large rounded oak table, stood Centurion Gallus along with an even more ornately decorated officer who was shaven headed and jowl faced, but the wild glint in his eyes was what marked him out – as if he wanted to lurch across the table and grasp Pavo by the throat. Tribunus Nerva, he feared, a firebrand who would issue the lash himself, going by the stories he had heard. Their faces were fixed and stony. His knees smashed against the flagstones of the floor as the guards dropped him suddenly to salute the officers.

'On your feet!' Gallus roared. 'You're marked out as a troublemaker, a bad apple, soldier.'

Pavo felt his tongue loosen – desperate to spill the whole sorry saga, when the door clicked behind him and Brutus walked in to join the panel of officers scrutinizing his sorry stance. The first utterings of a reply tumbled from his mouth only to be sharply repressed by a heavy elbow in his back.

'Shut your mouth, the primus pilus is speaking!' The giant soldier behind him growled. Pavo caught Brutus' glare; stern-faced, his eyes widened just enough to underline the warning.

'We need only obedient legionaries in the Claudia, who will serve her and her officers without question. While in the fort you are under orders to follow protocol.' Gallus sighed and shook his head. 'And being caught beating another recruit to a pulp outside of the fort after the curfew...'

Pavo looked Gallus in the eye and shame burned on his skin. This was not the path his father would have wanted him to take. He could only hope Brutus might have passed a sympathetic word on his behalf.

'...and to be caught out by the primus pilus,' Gallus shook his head, 'demonstrates not only unruly behaviour, but sheer *stupidity!*'

Pavo's mouth dried like parchment. Lashes would be a relief in comparison with this humiliation. Months of red raw flesh on his back could only hurt him physically. It would be just another layer on top of the network of scars on his torso from his time under Tarquitius' roof.

'The typical punishment for this misdemeanour is not pretty. One hundred lashes,' Gallus paused, 'and the first three will lick the flesh from your back.'

Pavo gulped. So it was to be.

Gallus glared at him. 'But that fate has conspired to save you is a blessing you should not forget. Centurion Brutus assures me that you have previously shown yourself to be more than the sorry runt that these events might suggest. Together with that, our legion is being stripped of key men by our Gothic friends out there,' Gallus paused, clenching his fists with a glance to Nerva, 'just while reports are coming in of rogue Gothic warbands crossing the river all over the province – Thervingi who are not happy with their leader's truce with Rome, apparently. And it's not just Fritigern's lot; Athanaric's men are only too happy to join in, it seems.'

Pavo shuffled from foot to foot in discomfort as the officers shared dark looks, their frustration palpable.

'We're on full alert for Gothic raids and need every man fit for duty. Back to the barracks, soldier.'

'Yes, sir. Thank you, s...' Pavo began.

'But don't think you're in the clear,' Gallus cut in, 'You're on the precipice. Should there be a next time, I will have no say in it,' the centurion leaned forward, eyes searing, 'the lash won't even come into it. You *will* be executed.'

'Yes, sir,' Pavo shivered.

# Chapter 27

Sura surveyed the dice on the mess table, grinned like a shark and then raised his eyes to Pavo.

'As much as I hate doing this to you, that'll be another ten follis.'

Pavo stared straight-faced at his friend, biting back his stinging pride as he pushed his last coins over. He softened as he again set eyes upon the swollen, discoloured lumps still peppering his friends' features. He had only been released from the hospital that morning – so maybe a little tolerance of his usual boasting was in order, Pavo mused.

'King of Adrianople – master of dice,' Sura enthused, wide-eyed as he swept an arm across the table to collect his winnings. The watching recruits released an exaggerated gasp. 'Though a tougher opponent would be a nice challenge.' At this, the onlookers burst into a rabble of laughter.

'All right, one of you bright sparks try to beat him!' Pavo swept his empty cup from the table, shooting to his feet. 'He's cheating like a beggar, there's no way anyone can win at dice consistently.' He scanned the recruits' faces, searching for support – but turned away in disgust at their inane grins.

'Well sod the lot of you then,' he snapped, stomping over to the empty mess table.

'Wait, Pavo,' Sura called, following him. 'I was saving this for later, but I've got some good news for you,' he beamed, tucking his purse into his belt.

Pavo cocked an eyebrow, waiting on some witty put-down 'Oh?'

'So cynical, you want to let your guard down a little,' he replied, swiping a half-finished platter of bread, goat's cheese and olives from the opposite table before sitting down. 'One of the lads was telling me. They were taking an order from Centurion Gallus, and they overheard a discussion between him and Brutus while he was waiting. Your name cropped up.'

Pavo's stomach churned. 'Not sure I like the sound of that? Gallus looks at me like a piece of dirt – I can't seem to do anything right around him.'

Sura laughed. 'Don't worry. Apparently Brutus was praising you to Gallus, says you're better than the average grunt.'

Pavo hung on to every word. 'And a troublemaker, apparently. Thank Mithras I've made a good impression on Brutus, at least. What else?'

'That's all, but come on; better than a kick in the stones, eh? Anyway, I'm sure you were just an afterthought at the end of a long list of *my* points of greatness.'

Pavo looked up. 'Think that'll have any bearing on how Spurius sees us?'

Sura remained expressionless.

'No, I thought not. Something isn't right, still. It's like sometimes, just for half a moment, he actually has a conscience.'

'Must have missed that,' Sura snorted, shovelling a handful of bread and goat's cheese into his mouth and jabbing a thumb at one of his bruises. 'The state of my face suggests otherwise.'

'In that pit, he was like a bear until it was just the two of us left standing. Then when we were in the jail he was, I don't know how to put it; it was as if he was there and not there at the same time? He cursed me to Hades at first but when he'd got that off his chest, he didn't seem interested in breaking my neck...for once.' Pavo shook his head. 'This place is driving me nuts.'

Sura leaned back on his chair, bringing his hands round to the back of his head. 'Well, you won't notice then if I cheat you shamelessly at dice,' he quizzed, cocking an eyebrow mischievously. 'Will you?'

Pavo twisted his face into a mock scowl. 'You dirty...'

With a bang, the mess hall door burst open; Centurion Gallus filled the doorframe and the fire danced as a cool gust whipped around the hall.

'I need ten recruits,' he barked. Pavo took a quick head count – exactly ten recruits present. Gallus continued; 'And it looks like I've found them. Form ranks in the yard, full battle equipment.'

'Sir,' Pavo ventured, 'what's the situation?'

Gallus, halfway out the door, spun back, his eyes narrowed. 'No time for questions, soldier – you're needed. That's all you need to know.'

With that, the door swung shut, the gust washing the sleep from the warm air of the room. Pavo looked around the sea of wide-eyed recruits. His mouth dried as he pondered his next move; so many faces, some friendly, others not so friendly. He shot up to his feet.

'You heard the centurion, what are you waiting for?' He croaked. All eyes fell upon him and at once he felt awash with redness. The silence hung around him like stinging nettles for just a moment that felt like days.

'I'm with Pavo. Let's move!' Sura yelled, startling the recruits in to life. Pavo sighed, a warm wash of pride flooding his veins as each of the recruits nodded to him on their way out the door towards the barracks. With a slap on the back from Sura, he followed them out.

They scuttled across the deserted training yard and into the barracks, which were soon filled with a muddle of crashing and clattering armour as the ten recruits slung their gear on. Pavo fumbled at his helmet strap, his fingers feeling like bloated loaves of bread. A bead of sweat raced down his face as he saw the others ready and moving for the door.

'Bugger it,' he muttered, tucking the straps into the cheek guards. If Gallus noticed, he'd be in trouble, but if he was the last one to stagger out he'd look silly anyway. He rushed to join his colleagues, just as the recruit at the head of the group balked.

'Stop, Gallus is outside. Form a line and march out.'

Pavo felt a wry grin ripple over his lips; a few months in these drafty barracks and they were all vying for the officer's attention.

Outside in the yard, Centurion Gallus' face betrayed nothing but determination. 'We have a situation to the west,' Gallus barked. 'A band of Gothic raiders has been reported south of the river. They have pillaged and burnt a country villa belonging to the dux. I'm calling on recruits to deal with this because I don't have enough legionaries left to call on. Centurion Brutus has ridden ahead with twenty men. We will be bringing up the rear, together with another ten men you would do well to learn from.'

'How many Goths, sir?' Pavo piped up, shuffling to stand as straight as possible.

Gallus glared at him, then eyed the other recruits carefully, raking his stubbled chin with his fingers, shaking his head. 'Doesn't matter. What matters is that we get enough of us out there to deal with this. There's no time to lose.'

As he spoke, the steady crunching march of ten hardened legionaries echoed through the air. Pavo looked up to examine them, struck by their hulking frames. Was that what happened to you after a few tours of duty, he mused? The lead legionary of the ten looked familiar. Zosimus, the man who Pavo had crippled efficiently at *The Boar and Hollybush* two weeks previously. Zosimus' eyes hovered on Pavo, a hint of puzzlement etched on his broad face, before he turned his eyes forward with a slight shake of the head.

Centurion Gallus turned once more to face the recruits. 'We will be moving in to reinforce Centurion Brutus and his men, who I'm sure will have the situation under control by now. I'll be leading these ten fine legionaries and my optio, Officer Felix, will be leading you. I expect you to do your legion proud.' Gallus then turned to Felix and gave him a nod. 'Form a column, marching at triple time.'

The countryside lay silent but for a whistling spring breeze. The sweet aroma of woodsmoke rolled across the meadows and cornfields from the smouldering remains of the nearby villa. Brutus gritted his teeth, his fists clenched as he scanned the emptiness around them. The legionary by his side shivered, yet the air was warm.

'Bloody Vergilius!' The centurion growled. 'The whoreson never even visits the provinces he supposedly commands. Yet us lot are punted out because some bloody Goths have torched his bloody summer villa. Bloody sheep-shagger should be out here to deal with it himself!'

The corn rattled again, as if teasing the puzzled twenty. He turned, unnerved as the horses shuffled.

'He can sense something,' the rider whispered to his centurion while eyeing the swaying fields.

Brutus stroked his own mount, 'Easy, boy.'

The wind died at that instant, and Brutus' mount's ears pricked up. He whipped his head up to see dark shapes rise from the crops along their flank. Leather cuirasses, conical helms, bows and longswords all around him.

His hand fell to his scabbard, but the roar to call his men to arms never came, as the sharp, cold punch of a Gothic arrow into the centre of his chest toppled him from his horse. Brutus felt his body crumple to the ground, and a sensation of at first warmth and then a trickling cold snaked through his limbs. As he lay prone, his fellow riders rallied in vain as the Goths picked them off like ripe fruit. One by one their bodies toppled around Brutus. Forty Goths, the estimate had been. He had seen at least a hundred in the instant before he fell. Shivering, he thought of the twenty Gallus had promised to send out behind them – half of them recruits, too. Only Mithras could save them now.

The fighting slowed and stopped and then the Goths closed in on him. *Have to get back, to warn the legion.* The words echoed in his head as the Gothic warriors glowered down on him, their leader raising his sword over Brutus' chest. The centurion's roar of defiance came out only as a gurgling whimper as he slipped into the blackness of death.

The quiet farmlands surrounding the Moesian highway lay dotted with slaves and workers, tilling the soils, tending the crops. Occasionally, the clop, clop of carts echoed along the flagstoned roads as the estate owners surveyed their progress. The land seemed to be at peace in this pleasant spring afternoon. And then a feint murmur grew into a rumble of hobnailed boots on flagstones. The workers stopped, heads appearing above corn stalks like wildlife, darting to find the source of the noise. Their eyes fixed on the tight bunch of legionaries haring along the road. This could only mean one thing. Trouble.

Gallus jogged at the head of the twenty. Chin up, he ploughed on, eyes scouring the fields for the tell-tale signs; a flash of armour or a cloud of smoke. Deep inside, he knew the ten veterans behind him would be needed, and the ten recruits behind them; well they would be spear fodder at best.

The iron shutters had fallen over him as soon as the report came in. The report of the raiders was fuzzy at best, coming from a hysterical local wine merchant. The merchant expected a decisive show of force. In truth, the XI Claudia had seriously lacked manpower for over a year now, and a sizeable portion of the experienced legionaries who remained had been pulled to the scenes of various Gothic incursions all along the banks of the Danubius over the last few days. Indeed, the merchant's jaw had dropped in disbelief as he watched the straggle of twenty marching from the fort.

Some way down the road, Gallus' nostrils flared as the fresh country air took on a distinct smoky haze. He slowed to a walk, raising his hand, eyeing the now deserted fields. The monotonous crunch died to a gentle padding. The column looked around uneasily. To the north, sleepy tendrils of smoke crept up from a sea of blackened stumps. Gallus grimaced; one less villa for Dux Vergilius; just how would the fat, incompetent bastard cope? He flicked up a hand.

'Slow advance, ready shields.'

The corn crackled as they pushed through towards the smoky ruin, the stalks whipping them at face height. Every legionary footstep sounded foreign as they approached the grounds of the estate, until they broke clear into the villa grounds. Centurion Gallus raised his hand once more to indicate a full stop, and then proceeded alone.

The grass underfoot crunched, giving way to ash as he approached. Then his eyes fell on the carnage spread across the blackened earth. A scarlet tangle of bodies like a giant's entrails snaked across the dirt. In the centre lay Brutus, eyes gazing heavenward and his teeth clenched in grim determination. Gallus stared through the scene as an echo of the pain he used to feel raked at his heart, but the steely coldness prevailed. His head dropped and the emptiness of the afternoon whistled around him.

'Optio,' he called, his voice steady.

Felix padded up beside him, and then stopped dead at the sight.

'We're in way over our heads, Felix.'

'How do we play it, sir?' Felix replied, gulping.

'Cool, Felix. If those whelps over there see this, we don't stand a chance.'

With a grunt, Centurion Gallus pushed his shoulders back, and brought his head up. The gentle Moesian plain now felt like a predator's lair, the bones of its last meal strewn across the ground. He considered his stance and facial expression before turning back to the column of twenty that now looked so vulnerable. They had to be protected, yet at the same time they had to be steeled for the reality of the situation. He grimaced in frustration – there was no way of sweetening the truth. But he would have to play it in some manner or their already questionable morale would disintegrate.

'Centurion Brutus and his party have been slain by the invading Goths. They cannot be far from here. Before we return to honour the bodies of our dead, we must find them. Find them and *crush* them!' He punched a fist into his palm.

Gallus glared at the soldiers without emotion; the veterans reflected the stony expression, but the recruits stood wide-eyed and pale, some craning to see over the centurion's shoulder. Apart from Pavo; his face was wrinkled, eyes glassy and distant. The lad had indeed connected with the rough diamond Brutus, it seemed. The centurion's eyes narrowed; *that's what happens when you let personal feelings in.*

'Form a column. Proceed at double time!' He bellowed, burning with an itch for revenge.

A persistent, cool mist swirled across the ever-restless Danubius, blocking out the spring sunshine and encasing one tired old stone bridge in a damp chill. Two watchtowers stood on either side of the southern bridgehead, the wooden guardhouses on top splintered and rotten. One auxiliary manned each tower, cold and tired as they approached the end of their half-day stint. After their chat dried up, about two hours into the shift, only fear staved off the cold. The Gothic raids had spread along the frontier like wildfire, and the vastly depleted centuries of the V Macedonia legion had been pulled apart, century by century, to meet the threat. Thus, the fortlet fifty paces back into the mist lay absolutely empty apart from their two sleeping colleagues, when a fifty was the usual skeleton garrison. The four men stationed here were the wafer-thin link in the border system with the neighbouring XI Claudia.

Drusus, the auxiliary atop one of the towers glanced across at his equally isolated colleague, then busied himself poking the fire in the brazier, stamping his feet and blowing into his hands. Why in Hades was he out here? Then he remembered his little ones, at home with his wife, days away by cart. At least they were warm and safe and well fed every night. A job is a job, Drusus thought to himself, chuckling through chattering teeth.

The clatter of a plate falling from his colleague's tower jolted his senses back to the cold, cruel present. The other auxiliary grinned by way of apology. Drusus turned back to the bridge with a shake of the head. But this time the blood stilled in his veins.

He gripped the edge of the watchtower, his eyes scraping at the mist. Every hair on the back of his neck stretched and shivered as the unmistakable rattle of horse hooves – thousands of them – dulled the roar of the river. He swapped a glance of terror with his colleague. There were no friendly crossings scheduled today – surely this was the next raid. He darted a glance to the fortlet – no time to get there, and no point. He closed his eyes, mouthing a prayer to Mithras.

A gruff Gothic voice broke through the fog. '*Ave*, good Romans!'

Drusus blinked open an eye, then shared a glance of confusion with his colleague.

'Who goes there?' The first guard called, feebly disguising the primal fear coursing through his veins.

Slowly the mist twisted, rippled and parted. Through the ghostly curtain, emerged a bustling but ordered column of Gothic horsemen; ten wide, and what was beginning to look like infinitely long, they poured slowly from the nothingness and into the bounds of the empire. Helms tucked underarm, they were a sea of flowing blonde locks over leather armour.

The man at the head of the column, hair tumbling down from a classic topknot, a bristly blonde beard, a leather patch over his left eye and silver hoops hanging in number from his ears, raised a hand to salute the Roman guards. 'I am Horsa of the Thervingi. I come, as promised by Lord Fritigern, with my men in aid of Rome and her people.'

Drusus stared, speechless.

Horsa now raised both hands to his sides and flashed a grin at each of the towers. 'Do we have permission to enter the empire?'

Gallus raised his sword, instantly stopping his men. The dark figure that had risen from the corn stood stock still, topknot whipping in the wind, spear glinting in the sunlight.

'Ready yourselves, men!'

Then, like the teeth in a predator's jaws, equally towering figures rose up all around them – hundreds of them, like a foreign crop in the corn. The moment of calm that followed stretched intolerably; they were waiting on the Romans to make a move, to expose their jugular. On foot, he thought; not the mounted elite. Still enough to butcher his twenty with ease.

'Sir?' Felix whispered beside him.

'Athanaric's men! Only bloody politics could see us have one of his men in charge of the new legion while he sends his grunts pouring over our border to raid as they please!' He gritted his teeth together – this was the reality of it all. 'Shield wall,' he barked, his unflinching gaze on the central Goth.

His blood raged at the impotence of the situation, sickeningly similar to the Gothic ambush in Bosporus – forced into a shield wall again. But it was the only option – draw the buggers in and then hit them with ice-cold iron, for all it was worth. At least it would trim the Gothic numbers for the next detachment sent out to deal with them.

'Form a shield wall,' he barked, 'no gaps or you're dead!' He pulled the new recruits who dithered into the wall tightly. As he finished, the zipping noise of an arrow was followed by the sucking, gurgling noise of a recruit suffocating and drowning in his own blood. The small square of men collapsed in a clatter of shields and swearing into a tight square. The sharp rattle of arrowhead against shield filled the small box they had made. Gallus listened, furious. 'They're playing with us, but they'll come,' he grumbled, hand flexing on his sword hilt. Gradually, the frequency of the hail slowed. Gallus' ears pricked up at the sound of shuffling grass.

'On my call,' he growled, darting a concrete glare at each of the recruits. 'I want you to push out of this square with as much force as you can muster. We thin their number then we can fall back into a square. This is all we've got. Make it count.'

Pavo, crouching beside his Centurion, fumbled to dig his feet into the earth. A hairy set of knuckles grappled his arm; the face of Zosimus filled his view, forcing Pavo's arms through the handle of his shield, into a barging posture.

'If you want to live, do the same,' Zosimus spat to the nine other recruits. The recruits on either side of him scrambled into a similar poise.

Gallus rested the fingers of one hand on the earth. His call would see them live or die. A fraction too soon or too late...it didn't bear thinking about.

The tremble in the earth stopped. Gallus' eyes widened.

'Break!' He barked. Then, like a tormented lion bursting free from its cage, he pushed upwards and outwards, letting a hoarse roar of caged fury escape from his lungs.

Like an amphora shattering, the neatly formed testudo square burst apart into twenty iron fangs, sinking into the thick blanket of snarling Gothic infantry only paces from them.

For Pavo, time slowed as they broke from the square. The order was simple; kill or be killed. A low-pitched roar poured from Zosimus by his side and he felt the quivering limbs of Sura on the other side of him. Then, as they each sprang outward, he was alone. He thrust his shield arm forward, waiting on impact with the Gothic lines. Instead, he fell helplessly through them as two Goths parted in front of him then those behind converged on him as he fell to the ground. A blood-spattered blade swung right for his eyes.

Fire ran through his veins and he buckled himself under the swing – the flat of the blade clattering from his forehead. Ignoring the dull pain, he scrabbled backwards, rolling behind the second line of Goths. Their third line hared in on him as he stumbled to his feet – no escape.

*I'm not going out alone*, he growled, swiping his sword round the hamstrings of the first Gothic line. Two men fell, snarling, clutching their legs, blood adding to the already grotesque carpet of red mud and gristle. His gut lurched at the sight – blood spilled by his own hand; never had he hurt another person so brutally. Then a scream whipped his senses back to the here and now. Pavo saw the legionaries trying to fall back into a square, but the Goths had swarmed amongst them. Legionary recruits roared out in their death cries as the Goths scythed them down. Pavo stumbled back to fight alongside them, but then the second Gothic line cut him off.

The warrior at the centre thrust his sword point towards Pavo's gut, forcing him into a stumble, dropping his sword. The next Goth had swung his sword high and wide and was now bringing it scything at Pavo's head. Flat-footed and defenceless, Pavo braced for the strike that would end it all – only the pain and darkness never came. He heard the popping noise of the Goth's spinal cord being severed, and then a head, complete with stunned expression, rolled across the scarlet mire. He glanced up to see Centurion Gallus.

Gallus headbutted the second Goth, before turning to execute a saving parry on his own flank.

'No time to sit around and think about it, soldier. Get your sword and watch my back.'

Pavo shook the fog from his mind, snatched his sword from the slimy red muck, and thrust himself back-to-back with his centurion. Looking up, the hopelessness of the situation hit him like a hammer – hundreds of Goths jostled around them, eager for blood.

'Take him down, soldier!' Gallus roared beside him, nodding to a bloody and crazed Goth who raced in on them, screaming, with a sword raised above his head.

Pavo felt the phalera weigh heavily around his neck. He gripped his spatha, then lurched forward and thrust it up through the gut of the warrior before the man could execute a swing. The warrior's warm guts washed over his arms as he sunk down to the sodden earth, eyes bulging and then dimming, face sliding past Pavo's as the body dropped to kneeling. Pavo planted a foot on the man's shoulder and wrenched his sword free again, barely recognising the guttural war cry that rang out as his own.

Horsa sucked in the smoky tang that spiced the warm afternoon air. His horde of foederati remained at a halt as their leader examined the landscape with a frown. Then he locked on a feint plume staining the horizon.

The auxiliaries at the bridge had pleaded with the foederati to be swift to three different locations – all under heavy attack by rogue Gothic raiders. Horsa sent two detachments of five hundred riders to check on each of the reported disturbances to the west, while he and the remaining thousand had set off at haste to locate the site of a raid on a government villa. The blustering, dark column of smoke in the distance looked a likely candidate. He raised his spear, and pointed to the horizon.

'We have activity nearby. Be ready to engage hostile forces. Move out, half gallop.'

The swarm of horsemen hurtled forward. The smooth grassy plains slipped beneath the thunder of the foederati as they charged towards the activity on the horizon, which slowly grew clearer and closer, to reveal what looked like a pool of choppy water stained red in the sunlight. As they drew closer, the sparkling water became blood-stained armour, and the crash of waves became bitter screaming and iron upon iron.

Horsa's frown remained until he spotted a Roman plume billowing in the wind. He raised his spear to the swarm of raiders. 'It's Athanaric's men – treacherous bastards who don't deserve to call themselves our kin. Show no mercy, men. Ahead, full gallop!' He roared, straightening his eyepatch before lowering himself in his saddle. The foederati thundered forward.

The biting crowd of Goths were oblivious to the foederati until they were but seconds from their backs. They smashed into the Gothic rear, spilling around the circle with their far superior numbers. The Goths, stunned and packed in so tightly they could barely raise their weapons, began to panic.

Horsa powered into the Gothic mass, skewering man after man, careful to retain his spear. The roars of terror dropped off to be replaced by the grunts, gurgles and panting of exhausted warriors. Horsa glanced up after every kill – the billowing plume still stood, working its way closer to him, though surrounded by fewer and fewer intercisa helmets. Horsa hoisted his spear back to strike at the next Goth. Then the blade of another rider's sword came bursting through the front of his intended foe's throat.

The battle was won.

Dripping crimson from head to foot, the plumed centurion grimaced, panting and shaking. By his side stood five legionaries, one bore a smaller plume than the leader, next to him stood a towering man, a short man, and next to them two smaller, younger looking men, all sodden in the carnage. All around them, a soup of intestines, bone and flesh bubbled.

Horsa stumped the handle of his spear into the ground and used it to dismount. He walked over to face the centurion.

'*Ave*, good Roman. We come to serve the XI Claudia!'

# Chapter 28

The cobwebs of blackness drifted from his mind and Pavo winced. Every inch of his body screamed. He prised open an eye to survey the familiar ceiling of the barracks, and as a waft of chill air danced over him, he pulled up his hemp blanket and for once appreciated the warm comfort of the damp and scratchy straw mattress.

The weary journey back to the legion fort had been trance-like, with the remaining six Romans hitching a ride on the mounts of the foederati. Nobody spoke. Pavo had stumbled into the barracks and collapsed into a deep, thick sleep. That had been morning, and he had no idea how much time had passed. It was clearly night, going by the warm glow of torchlight from the courtyard. Shuffling his head around on the pillow, he could see the barracks were almost empty; just the shape of Sura in his bunk accompanied by steady, low snoring.

The voices in his mind squabbled with memories of the battle, and reluctantly, he allowed them to speak. He closed his eyes, squirming as the rhythmic scything of the bloody business still echoed in his ears. Every one of the recruits apart from him and Sura were now dead. His stomach tightened as he recalled them sitting in the mess hall that morning, laughing, relaxed and warm. Then he wondered if fate could have been kinder and had Spurius along on the mission, but he shook the dark thought from his head. Then he thought of Brutus.

He had not seen the remains of the centurion and his party, but the image of the red and white gore coating the field would never leave him. The man was a brutal sadist, no doubt, but absurdly he was one of the warmest people Pavo had ever known. Guilt traced his skin when he realised that he didn't even know if Brutus had a wife or a family. All he knew of the man was that his father was a slave. Pavo touched the phalera and vowed never to forget the centurion.

He prised himself from his bed, feeling the bite of the night chill on his legs as they touched the flagstoned floor. Managing a hint of a smile as he sidled past the snoring Sura's bunk, he threw on a heavy cloak and pushed open the barrack door. Outside was chilly; guards whistled as they strolled in the courtyard and the battlements, but otherwise all was still and silent. As he approached the mess hall, a muted rumble of banter escaped the cracks in the hefty timber door.

He pushed open the door to be hit with a welcome blast of hot air, then squinted at the deep orange glow pulsating from the hearth. All around the mess hall, recruits and legionaries were slumped in inebriation and muttered in muted tones. Men had been lost today and the usual raucous drunkenness was off the menu. The door swung shut, thumping, and all heads looked up at Pavo, their faces sombre and tired.

Pavo felt his throat turn to dust and his cheeks burn. Was he expected to say something? If so, what on earth could he say to comfort or inspire at a time like this? He gulped. Then Centurion Gallus stood up, opening a hand to the vacant stool at the table. He was dressed pristinely in full armour, the only one in the mess hall to wear more than a tunic and boots.

'Join us in having a drink to remember the comrades we have left behind,' Gallus spoke quietly, but it sounded stern, like an order. The scarred figure of Zosimus pushed the vacant stool out with a filth-encrusted leather boot.

Pavo moved to take the seat with a nod. Gallus eyed him sombrely as he did so. *Ice cold*, Pavo thought, *I've nearly died beside the man and he still looks at me like a leper.* His heart ached for poor Brutus.

The low murmur soon picked up once again and Pavo found a fresh jar of ale placed in front of him. He looked around the table as he gulped at the cool, bitter liquid. Any banter with the older, grumpier legionaries was hard at the best of times. *The ale will help with that*, he figured, taking another gulp.

Gallus rubbed his stomach and raised a hand to the kitchen staff.

'Bring on the food, whenever you're ready.'

Pavo suddenly realised how hungry he was. After the chaotic fight with Spurius the night before and the comfort-free night in the cells, he hadn't eaten since early that morning, and only the rush of the battle had kept him on his feet through the day. Now, his mouth watered as the kitchen door opened and the meaty tang of roast pheasant coiled out and around the tables. In the few months that he had been with the XI Claudia, the staple diet of beans and stew had gone past the stage of monotony and into sheer awfulness – this meal was going to be a good one. He was jolted from his gastronomic trance when Centurion Gallus clipped the edge of his cup with a follis, bringing all heads up.

'You all fought bravely today. Not just bravely, but effectively. We took out ten veterans and ten recruits this morning.'

Pavo's senses keened and he fixed on the centurion's words.

'Only a handful of my veterans made it out of that death trap of an ambush,' Gallus sighed. 'But that two recruits scraped through as well tells me that they are either damned good,' he paused, eyeing Pavo with that iron stare, 'or bloody lucky!'

Pavo blushed as a chorus of muted laughter filtered around the hall, along with a gentle slap on the back from Avitus. He took a swig of ale, begging its bitter wash to flush away his discomfort. Then, a steaming joint of pheasant was plonked in front of him, the skin roasted and glistening as the meaty juices trickled onto the bed of beans underneath.

'To our lost comrades!' Gallus boomed, lifting his ale cup.

'To our lost comrades,' the hall replied in unison.

*To Brutus*, Pavo echoed in his mind, sipping from his cup. He gazed into the swirling liquid, watching the bubbles rise up and disappear like a never ending tide, like legionaries charging into the field, he thought sourly.

'Our legion is severely depleted, soldier.' Gallus spoke. Pavo started – the centurion had sidled up next to him, unnoticed. 'Firstly from the harvesting of our second-line officers by the I Dacia and even more so by these Gothic raids in the last few days. We are looking to our recruit pool to reinforce our number – we need at least fifteen hundred infantry. You are going to be joining my century. The first century.' He paused for a moment, watching Pavo's face for a reaction. 'I'll have my eye on you, soldier, I have a feeling it's best to keep the troublemakers close.' He held Pavo's gaze. 'And one more thing; your sparring partners, Spurius and his big mate…'

Pavo craned forward.

Gallus' expression was like stonework, '...they're gone. Off with the I Dacia. Seems Tribunus Wulfric likes the fiery ones in his ranks.' The centurion shook his head, eyes distant for a moment. 'Anyway, as you were.' With that, he was gone.

Pavo stared into the space Gallus had been seated. At once shocked, embarrassed and euphoric, he knocked back another mouthful of ale. The punch of the golden liquid now swam like a delicious torrent through his mind as the words sank in. Nothing darkened his horizon now. Nothing. No Tarquitius, no Fronto, no Festus, no Spurius. He felt giddy at the sensation of relief.

'Anyway,' Felix cackled, having surreptitiously flanked him on the other side, 'that means I'm your optio, so you'd better not go drinking too much of that ale and making an arse of yourself in front of me now, lad.' He motioned towards the other veterans around the table. 'And over here are your brothers from today; Zosimus and Avitus. I don't think you've met Quadratus?' A blonde, moustachioed giant, rivalling Zosimus in stature, grunted over the rim of his ale cup. 'You'll be in our *contubernium*; so you'll march with us, drink and eat with us, and share a tent with us...so you'd better not be a farter.' The optio glared at Quadratus, who shot back an open-mouthed look of innocence.

Pavo had barely given the legionaries each a nod of greeting, when a bowl of swirling garum and dates was set down next to his pheasant. He followed the delicate hand that held the plate, all the way up the slender arms – and there was that fresh, milky white fresco-like face of Felicia, the barmaid from *The Boar and Hollybush*; bright blue eyes framed in amber locks tumbling down over her ample breasts. Did she remember him from the night he had compromised the integrity of Zosimus' balls?

'Er, thanks,' he simpered, 'you work here too?'

'Volunteer, actually,' she spoke briskly and then turned away.

'Leave it, Pavo,' Avitus whispered, 'her brother died in our ranks a few years back.'

Pavo looked back at her, eyes heavy. 'Goths?'

Avitus hissed back. 'Like I said, leave it!'

Felicia caught his gaze again as she worked her way around the table. 'Was there something else?'

'Eh…' Pavo stammered, 'Any chance of another ale?'

'Another ale? Don't know about that – I don't want you starting a fight again tonight,' she scowled. At this Zosimus cocked an eyebrow and examined Pavo's face again, then shook his head.

Pavo's face burned and his heart sank. 'No,' he offered, 'I'll be making sure we all behave tonight.'

A mock gasp of indignation from the legionaries was followed by a pitying shake of the head from the barmaid, her features melting into a sarcastic grin.

'You? But you're *only* a recruit,' she sighed.

As she turned and slinked away, Pavo's neck boiled with humiliation, yet his eyes hung on every swing of her broad hips. The stifled sniggering of Pavo's companions rumbled into harsh cackling. He turned on them, his teeth grinding. All the faces were wrinkled in hilarity. Then the barmaid drifted past behind Zosimus. She winked at him. His heart skipped a beat, his jaw fell open and the tension fell from him like a stone.

'I think she might have guessed that you like her,' Avitus sniggered.

Pavo, lost for words, raised his eyebrows in defeat.

Felix cast an arm round his shoulder. 'You'll get used to her tearing you to shreds. It means she likes you.'

Pavo grinned.

'Trust me, I would know,' Avitus added eagerly.

Pavo frowned.

# Chapter 29

Gallus watched the activity on the dockside pensively, sipping water from his cup. What he would gain from this he wasn't sure, but his gut told him to come here and see this new legion set sail. Sitting alone on a bench outside the dockside drinking hole he was, for the first time in months, dressed as a citizen, not a soldier. For a moment, his thoughts wandered; the absent weight of his scabbard and spatha felt like a missing limb. It felt strange, it let old memories back in.

He shook his head and turned back to the water's edge. So the I Dacia legion was almost ready to ship out, to begin their role as a roaming sentry legion, sailing the lower Danubius and the western Pontus Euxinus. Their fleet was supposed to complement the *Classis Moesica*, but in reality the rickety collection of *triremes* that the limitanei used to patrol these waters would be the mongrel herd hanging on to the stern of this immaculate new fleet.

Having ravaged the XI Claudia for officers, the ships of the fleet were already well-manned with legionaries, their armour as pristine as the trireme timbers were fresh. Now they would head upriver to collect Fritigern's mercenary hordes. It galled Gallus to think the Roman peasants in his ranks were being clad in rusting, ancient armour while the Goths they fought to protect the empire from were being dressed in the finest, freshly tempered scale-plate vests. He wondered just how strong the borders could be if the same investment was made into the limitanei ranks.

The sixty vessels cut their moorings and drifted free of the dock wall. At this, the gathered crowd roared in farewell. Once in the current of the mighty Danubius, the ships engaged their triple banks of oars, and then began to row upstream, with the power of the remiges winning against the current of the river. Gallus squinted, sure the fiery locked figure on the head trireme was glaring back at him. *Wulfric.*

The fleet gradually disappeared as it slipped upriver towards the late afternoon sun. The limitanei of the Danubius were well beyond cracking point now that the I Dacia initiative had begun. Once the Bosporus mission set sail, the empire was wide open. The thought chilled him to the bone.

*Wide open.*

# Chapter 30

A bitter gale rampaged across the vast Bosporan plains, torturing the fresh snow, never allowing it to settle for longer than a brief instant before whipping it back up in a never-ending cycle of blinding, stinging white. This absurdly late snowfall had coated the land just two nights previous, blotting out the spring sun.

Amalric shivered violently, pulling his furs tight, swishing his blonde locks around his neck and gripping his thighs firmly into his mount to draw in even a fraction more heat from the beast. His face was so cold it almost obscured the blue stigma spiralling across his jaw. Allfather *Wodin*, the great god, had deserted them; so was this the end for the Greuthingi Goths of Bosporus? He eyed his King, Tudoric, mounted next to him; the proud man wore the cold expression of a defiant leader – what more could he offer in these bitter circumstances? Then he surveyed the hastily assembled blizzard of infantry lined up in ranks behind them; men of all ages clad in the best leather and iron armour that the Gothic communities of the region could gather. The finest swords, shields and bows were on display and every one of them stretched proudly to their full height, topknots billowing in the icy gale. This was it, end of the line. All or nothing; to go for broke against the massive shadow staining the other end of the plain, or sit here and die. These demonic horsemen had poured in through the narrow neck of the peninsula, massacring, pillaging and desecrating everything in their path. The Gothic people had been brushed westwards like litter. Here it came to a head; Amalric and his army were now trapped in this icy waste. Nowhere left to run. The flat-faced yellow predators circled their stricken prey.

The Gothic women and children stood to the rear, armed with clubs and daggers, shivering and sobbing. The Gothic fleet, sent to rescue them, had never turned up. Thus, their only option had been to turn around and face their dark pursuers. But their tormentors did not take the bait. For days, they waited, watched as the Goths froze and starved. Gradually, the defiant morale of Tudoric, Amalric and the army had ebbed.

Amalric knew that their number could not hope to win this battle, and the war drums played by the Goths took on a dirge-like quality. At the last count, seven thousand stood in waiting behind him for inevitable death against the estimated twenty thousand baying, lasso and spear wielding cavalry and spear infantry.

As he scoured the shadow of his enemy one more time for any hint of hope, he noticed what looked like a mirage in the snow; a tiny black shape rippling towards him thought the raging blizzard. His senses keened.

'An emissary?' Tudoric suggested to Amalric.

'I implore you, my king – be wary of these dogs,' Amalric replied, 'they may not even know the meaning of the word emissary.'

'I don't think I've ever trusted anyone less,' Tudoric agreed, issuing a wry grin to his second-in-command. 'Unfortunately we have no option but to parley. Train the best archers on our guest. Should I not return – you are king.'

With that, Tudoric spurred his horse into a canter towards the approaching horseman.

Amalric was stunned for a moment and then cursed silently; his king was brash, too brash at times. He raised an arm to the line of chosen archers, the men who could kill accurately from the horizon, the front line of the Gothic forces. In unison, they picked arrows and nocked their bows, before arching their chests and raising their weapons to meet the required trajectory to perforate the approaching horseman.

Turning back, Amalric's heart thundered as Tudoric slowed to a trot, matching the actions of the Horseman. The pair circled each other tentatively, before settling to a standstill. Through stinging, driving snow, Amalric peered at the distinctive features of the rider – short in comparison with a Goth, but broad like a bull, and bearing three terrible, red, welted scars symmetrically on each cheek. Their reputation had started as raiders, but quickly word had spread of them as centaur-like demons such was their riding ability.

The rider nodded assertively as he spoke to Tudoric; the king sat with his back straight as usual, equanimity personified even at this; the darkest of hours. The conversation continued in a one-sided manner, and Amalric afforded a glance back along the Gothic lines. Towards the rear, where the families and the bulk of the army were formed up, Amalric grimaced at every spirit-sapping shuffle of a frozen kinsman falling, exposed and exhausted from the terrible conditions. Then he turned back to the meeting, Amalric felt his stomach turn over – a flash of steel glinted through the whipping winds.

The rider had somehow hooked his arm around King Tudoric's neck, holding a hound's-tooth dagger to his throat. Immediately, Amalric raised his hand to the chosen archers. At once, their taut bows slackened slightly. He knew that despite their extreme skill, the chance of killing their own leader was too great, especially with the turbulence of the blizzard.

An excruciating silence ensued, before the rider bellowed in an unknown jagged tongue. The aggressive rant rolled over the whistle of the blizzard until he finished his speech by drawing his dagger slowly across Tudoric's throat, letting a wave of dark blood jet forth, soaking the king and his horse. The Gothic people at once erupted into a torrent of moans and laments, some falling to their knees as Tudoric tumbled from his horse into the scarlet snow.

Amalric stared in horror, his heart hammering. The end had begun, and now he was king. The word to loose arrows lodged in his throat as he turned to his archers, his eyes widening as an ethereal dark mass emerged from the snow on the Gothic flank. His jaw simply hung open at the sight; an unchecked horde of a thousand or more demonic cavalry was charging directly for the exposed flank of his ranks. A cold certainty gripped his soul. Amalric drew his sword.

'Archers! Right flank, loose!' He roared. The archers stumbled and cried out as they saw their fate haring in on them. They let fly with a swarm of arrows, accurate as usual, bringing down several of the onrushing cavalry, but not nearly enough.

Amalric roared as Tudoric's killer trotted calmly back to his lines and the flanking riders poured into the side of the Gothic line. Up ahead, the full weight of the demon army now poured forward. The hiss of a thousand arrows filled the air, then a sharp pain ripped into his shoulder and his world was hurled upside down in chaos as the massacre began.

# Chapter 31

Bearing the pain of the blisters, scratches and bruises from the battle, Pavo and Sura hobbled up the dusty road into Durostorum. Dressed in clean tunics, belts and boots bearing purses modestly lined with a handful of folles – the legionary wage minus funeral club and kit replacement – they were ready for the night ahead, the last night before shipping out on the Bosporus mission.

The fresh air prickled their skins. Tonight the town promised every wonderment of debauched entertainment. Ale, wine, food, music, dancing and plenty of well-wishing local ladies were all the legionaries had talked of for the last two days. The pay had been issued that morning, and despite having less than half that of the legionaries, Pavo jingled his purse in pride; an honest wage earned entirely by him. He thought of Tarquitius for a moment, then let the anger drift away; *can't harm me now*, Pavo affirmed. And Spurius was gone too – he and Sura had been on the crest of a wave since the news. For once life was beginning to feel more than just tolerable. He shook his head – it was all temporary, for the lost Kingdom of Bosporus waited on them tomorrow, and rumours were rife that it was a treacherous land.

'Mithras! I can taste the ale from here,' Sura purred as a chorus of cheering spilled down the road to them from the town gates. The train of legionaries ambling up the road seemed to grow more animated and rowdy as they approached. 'You buying one for Brutus?'

'Eh?' Pavo was jolted from his thoughts at the mention of the dead centurion.

'Optio Felix was going on about it; you buy ale, leave it on the bar and say a prayer to Mithras – you know, to wish the person well.'

A half smile touched Pavo's lips. For all Brutus' bluster and delight in causing physical pain for the recruits, his loss had been felt keenly throughout the ranks. 'Aye, I think I owe him that at least.'

'Well, it'll be a busy one tonight; I just hope they've got the barrels stocked up to the ceiling!' Sura clapped his hands together and chuckled, his eyes sparkling at the activity in the town. 'Mind you, got to stay this side of bladdered.'

'Aye, shipping us out at dawn seems a bit cruel.' Pavo wondered how he would play it tonight. His mind was still plagued with memories of the skirmish, but his whole body felt taught, tired and in need of some relaxation. Maybe the presence of officers or lack of them would be the deciding factor on how much he would drink tonight. 'Bet that was Gallus' idea – to limit all enjoyment as far as possible. D'you reckon he will be there tonight?'

'Gallus?' Sura replied. 'Doubt it. He'd rather obsess over maps and plans than crack a smile with his troops. You needn't worry about him – d'you see big Zosimus and the like worrying about him?'

Pavo nodded. The cold wall Gallus had built between himself and the recruits made it hard to defend the man. Yet the centurion had a strong rapport with his veteran legionaries, Pavo mused, thinking of the way Gallus talked with Zosimus, Felix and the rest as if they were brothers.

'The veterans seem to have earned some kind of trust from him, but he makes me feel like I have no chance of getting that close to him. For Mithras' sake, I nearly died fighting by his side.'

'Seriously, forget it for one night at least. Anyway,' Sura continued, 'if you're looking for Gallus that'll leave me with a free run at your barmaid. Felicia, wasn't it?'

Pavo punched his friend on the arm. 'Watch it!'

'Look, you're better off not embarrassing yourself over her – she'll only be interested in the good-looking ones,' he chirped, jabbing a thumb into his chest.

'I don't know why they let a gem like you leave Adrianople,' Pavo sighed.

The thick stone walls of Durostorum towered above them as they approached the town, with guards on the watchtowers looking enviously down on the revellers pouring through the gate. Pavo sighed. 'It's hard to believe that I'm actually, very slightly, going to miss this place you know. That stinking hovel that they call the barracks has really grown on me.'

'Well, you'll soon be loving life in the lovely aroma of a legion tent. From what I've heard, mobilised legion life is about as grim as it gets when you're posted to some frozen wasteland where it's cold, wet and you're just waiting around to be gutted by some bearded, axe-wielding maniac. It'll be worse for you, though,' Sura grinned mischievously, 'now you're in Gallus' century, you'll be expected to set the example; drinking each other's piss; that kind of thing.'

Pavo cast a wry grin at his friend. 'Actually, I hear the first century gets dancing girls and roast dormice as standard. It's your lot who get the turd-shovelling jobs.'

Sura gasped in mock indignation, when, from out of nowhere, a pack of the mounted foederati thundered up behind them. The pair leapt clear of their path.

Sputtering dust from his lips, Pavo scrambled to his feet. 'What the...' he spat, and glared up the road at the plume of dust in the riders' wake. 'What's their hurry?'

Sura frowned. 'Don't know, but there's being in a hurry and there's being damned rude.'

Pavo helped Sura to his feet. 'I'm not so sure Gallus is happy with that lot being welded onto the Claudia, you know.'

Sura shrugged his shoulders. 'He might be an important bugger, Gallus, but he gets his orders from above, just like us.'

Another group of foederati trotted gently past the pair, paying due courtesy to the other users of the road this time. Pavo noted the distinctive eyepatch and blonde bunch of hair swinging behind the leader of the party, Captain Horsa, who led the pack. He had heard others talk of him – a real showman, but a man of honour too.

The gates of Durostorum lay wide open with a token auxiliary, standing atop the gatehouse, jealously eyeing the troops. As they strolled inside, Pavo marvelled at the soup of colours, the cacophony of voices and the questionable mix of odours packing the air. Ladies called to the legionaries, thrusting their cleavage out, traders waved silks and spices to their soon to be departed source of income. The town had thrived on legionary purses for years. Thousands of men with much time to spare and many folles to squander in between fending off Gothic raids had seen the lazy riverside town blossom into a bustling centre of activity in the years since the XI Claudia had been settled on its outskirts.

Ignoring the myriad of leathers, trinkets and charms thrust in front of them, they ploughed through the crowd. Pavo smiled dizzily back at the array of ladies, until a clip round the back of the head from Sura pulled him out of his trance.

'Oi, eyes front,' he beamed.

*The Boar and Hollybush* stood before them. The streets around it were heaving with drunken revellers. Legionaries swayed on table tops in an alcoholic hubris, cackling women hanging on their shoulders. The gruff laughter of the Goths and a sprinkling of jagged Germanian punctuated the Latin and Greek rabble and all were bathed in the orange glow of lamplight pouring from the windows and doors of the inn. The sun was setting and the going away party for the legion was already well underway.

Stumbling free of a particularly desperate trader, Pavo then scythed through the thick waft of perfume, ale and roasting meat to slap a hand on Sura's shoulder.

'I believe it's time to sample that ice-cold ale we talked about?'

In perfect timing, another hand came crashing down ungraciously on the shoulders of Pavo and Sura, accompanied by the reek of stale ale. They turned to see the far-beyond inebriated figure of Avitus.

'Showed up then…nice to drink,' he muttered whilst gazing lazily through them.

'Ah, Avitus, I see you got here nice and early then?' Pavo asked.

Avitus lifted his lolling head slightly, before erupting in a grumble of laughter, sharply punctuated with a hiccup.

'That'll be a yes,' Sura answered on his behalf. 'Gimme a hand, we'd better get him on his back or he'll never be ready at dawn.'

They helped Avitus to a soft spot of unsoiled hay and let him down. His head instantly dropped and he set off on a bout of violent snoring.

'Don't know about you, but I fancy catching up with him,' Pavo shouted above yet another chorus of raucous laughter. Heading inside with Sura in tow, he gasped at the sweltering heat; the cramped space inside was packed to the rafters with sweating bodies. Fighting his way to the bar, he dodged one swaying pack of legionaries after another. Then, like a ray of sunshine, Pavo saw her behind the bar; *Felicia!*

He made a dive between two legionaries acting as a crutch for one another. He popped up again at a preciously empty fraction of the bar. Even better, Felicia stood directly across from him, frantically drying cups. Her cheeks glowed scarlet and sweat dripped from her brow as the demand for drinks and food continued relentlessly. But to Pavo, she looked simply radiant.

Pavo thumped his elbows onto the bar, pulling a mischievous grin.

'What does a soldier have to do to get some service around here?' She would melt at those words, he chuckled to himself.

'Wait your turn!' she barked, her face crimson and pinched in fury. Her eyes burned holes in him for an instant, and then she softened a little, annoyed with herself. 'I'm sorry,' she offered as Pavo looked at his boots, 'I thought you were another one of…them,' she nodded briskly at the thrashing swell of foederati as another pewter cup crashed onto the flagstones.

'I'll have a couple of ales please,' Pavo mumbled. 'No hurry though. And get one for yourself, you must be parched,' he offered, pushing two folles across the bar towards her. She smiled at last and a grin curled over Pavo's features once more. They held the look until another crash of pewter on the floor was greeted with a gruff cheer. Felicia's face fell.

A rhythmic chanting and thumping of fists started up from the row of foederati craned over the bar. They rapaciously eyed the ale barrels and leered at Felicia. 'More Ale!' They roared.

She cast a nervous glance at them as she thumped two cups of ale in front of Pavo. As he pulled the cups closer, he realised that as soon as he turned away, she would be gone again. And this was it, his last night.

'You didn't get one for yourself,' he offered. She moved away, distracted. 'When d'you get to finish?' He asked, leaning over the bar, nervous tension rippling round his body.

'My father owns this place,' she replied over her shoulder, 'so I'm in for a long shift tonight – and every other night!'

'I think you're beautiful,' he blurted, at once frozen to the spot with embarrassment.

She spun round with a wicked grin on her face. 'Yes, I am, eh?' Then she leaned a little closer, looking up at him so her sparkling blue eyes danced across his face, circling his rounded eyes and beaky nose. 'And you, you remind me of...a little bird...'

Pavo reddened as she turned back to the barrels again – was she toying with him? His emotions hopping in confusion, he tried again. 'My name is Pavo. I'm part of the first century of the Claudia!' He shouted as she moved away.

She laughed out loud, 'I'm *sure* you are.' Then, she turned and stepped back to him, leaned over the bar and placed a hand on Pavo's arm. 'I think you're nice, a little bit different from the other soldiers who come in here. So don't go making me change my mind by saying things like that.' She winked at him and withdrew back over to the rabble of foederati.

Confused and elated at once, Pavo took up the two cups of cool ale and backed out of the crowded bar, spilling drops down backs and over heads, as he snaked through the terrain of writhing drunken bodies. He spotted Sura.

Standing near the door, his friend was poised, peacock-like and deep in conversation with a young blonde lady who shrieked at his every word. Pavo weaved up to the pair, lifting one of the cups behind the woman. At the sight of the cold ale, Sura's eyes lit up, he made his apologies and stepped forward to take it from Pavo. Turning back, he found an empty space where his ladyfriend had stood.

'What the...' he uttered. Then her shrieking laughter almost burst their eardrums as the bulk of Zosimus carried her, slung over his shoulder, out of the pub. 'Oh for...' he growled under his breath.

'Take it easy,' Pavo chuckled, 'there are no shortage of well-wishers to try your luck on.'

Sura hid his crimson features behind his ale cup, supping greedily. 'Don't know what you're laughing about, I don't see *you* getting anywhere?' He mumbled.

'Well, I tried being loud and brash, but she said she didn't want me to be like that...I think.'

'Well, there's always the next time...' Sura started and then trailed off, his eyes darting through the door back down to the distant hulk of the legionary fort. '...well, maybe not.'

'Aye, who knows when we'll be back here.'

Sura took a gulp of ale, and nodded. 'Or *if*.'

Pavo cocked an eyebrow, looked back to the bar and then his ale. *Shipping out at dawn*, the words made him hesitate. Then he glanced over at Felicia and took another generous swig of ale.

The lamplight outside *The Boar* glowed blurry and warm for Pavo, and the summer night had grown even warmer as each cup of ale went down. Resting against the wall where Avitus now lay slumped in thorough unconsciousness, he chuckled as he watched Sura, sitting with his arms around two girls, in what was probably a subconsciously protective manoeuvre after losing out to Zosimus earlier in the evening. He emptied his cup; his confidence bolstered, he eyed the door of the inn. It was now or never.

Laughter and singing washed around him as he pushed into the oven-like interior. But it seemed less intimidating for some reason, perhaps because his head seemed to swim with the ale. He scanned the room for Felicia, eager to lock eyes with her again, when like a clap of thunder, a table was flipped over onto the floor by the bar. A clay plate shattered, cups were spilled, and ale foamed across the grime underfoot. The rabble instantly died and all eyes turned to the foederati.

The tallest of them was seething. He let rip with a jagged verbal tirade at the short, lean barman, who was desperately trying to pacify the ox of a man, pleading with his hands. The giant Goth snarled, springing across the bar, his elbow smashing into the barman's face, the pair crashing into the casks behind him. Felicia rushed over to the injured barman, yelling. Her father, Pavo realised. Then the Goth rolled over on top of the man and started slamming fists into him over and over. Felicia leapt back with a scream.

It was like an arrow to his heart. He ducked past the first of the foederati, snatched at a barstool and sprang across the bar. His downward momentum brought him square on top of the barman's assailant and he swung the barstool straight down, crunching into the Goth's neck. His guttural roar filled the room.

The hubris drained from Pavo and the cold hand of fear then took a grip of his heart as the Goth looked up slowly, his face contorted in rage. The foederati began to encircle him like a noose as Felicia's father crawled round behind the bar and slipped out of the shutters. All focus was on Pavo and Pavo alone. One by one, they drew their swords, the iron screeches prompting a series of gasps from the stunned onlookers. Suddenly, a fist hammered into the face of one foederatus whose teeth sprayed across the bar.

'Draw a sword in my drinking hole?' Zosimus roared. Then Quadratus leapt on the back of the next-nearest foederatus. In a heartbeat, the inn erupted in a sea of fists, blood and roaring.

Pavo staggered back, mouthing silent disbelief. Then he felt a hand wrench at his tunic collar.

'What the...' he yelped.

'Just returning the favour,' Felicia yelled as she dragged him, stumbling through to the back room. Three foederati poured over the bar to pincer Pavo, crashing over each other in their haste. Felicia kicked at the oak plank underneath the pile of ale casks, sending them tumbling into disarray. The foederati disappeared from view with a chorus of roars behind the cask avalanche. Pavo winced and then glanced over to the back of the room to see Sura, fighting to get through to him. Wide eyed, his friend seemed to be mouthing the words, 'What the...?'

Pavo offered him a shoulder-shrug and a look of incredulity before a sharp jab to the ribs brought him spinning round.

'Want to stay and watch do you? Let's get out of here!' Felicia hissed.

'What about your father?' Pavo yelped.

'He's got some bloody big friends, see?' She nodded to the window and the posse of torch wielding giants marching towards the inn, her father at their head, patting a club on his palm, his eyes sparkling with intent. 'Now move or that lot will chop your balls off!'

Wide eyed and mute, Pavo simply followed her in a hurried crawl out of the back window. As he turned to close the shutters, a booming voice rang out from the inn. He caught just a glimpse of the eyepatch-wearing figure; Horsa.

'Order!' The Gothic commander roared. A brief moment of silence followed, and then all Hades broke loose once more; smashing clay, cracking timber, screams, punching, moaning.

Pavo closed the shutters gingerly, flashing a grimace to Felicia as if to say 'Woops!' Felicia narrowed her eyes, shook her head, issued a stinging slap across his cheek, then grabbed his hand and led him into the dark night.

# Chapter 32

The thickness of sleep dissolved, bringing the freshness of the early summer morning descending onto Pavo's naked body. That and the crushing pain of a headache. He cranked open an eyelid to see the ruined timber ceiling of a barn, stark daylight punching down through the gaping holes and into his eyes. The only source of heat came from his side. He glanced down to behold the delicate and naked figure of Felicia, curled around him. His headache evaporated and a grin the size of the Danubius shot across his face. He mouthed a silent thank you to Venus.

A gaggle of thoughts vied for attention in Pavo's foggy mind. *The Boar and Hollybush*, the ale, the Goths, the moment he thought he was about to be ripped limb from limb. Then the darkness of the night, running hand in hand with Felicia as she poured a torrent of abuse on him; language like he'd never heard, even from Zosimus. And then stumbling into the seclusion of the barn, where their lips met at last. Then after what seemed like an eternity of kissing, she slapped him again. Then they had undressed each other, and her warm, smooth skin glided against his as they came together in a tender and passionate embrace. He cupped her full, wide hips as she bounced, her breasts brushing against his chest as she moaned with every thrust, their lips locked together through it all, until the moment when she cried out and he buried his head in her neck.

'Morning,' he stroked the small of her back as she stirred, stretching her legs out and rolling her head with a contented sigh.

She shielded her eyes and afforded him a shy smile. 'Bugger me, it's cold!' she chattered, blowing away the illusion of feminine grace.

Pavo grinned, reaching for the pile of clothes and brought his tunic up and over them and they lay nose to nose, feeding on each other's warmth. But what to say to her? He remembered Optio Felix talking about her brother. Good honest chat about her family. What could possibly go wrong?

'Your brother...he used to fight in the Claudia, I hear?' He started, then choked on what to follow those words with as Felicia's eyes narrowed.

'He did,' she shrugged, pulling back from him just a little, her eyes wandering to the far corner of the barn. 'Got himself killed though.' Now she turned away from his gaze.

Pavo wished he could swallow the words. 'I'm sorry; I just thought you might want to talk about him...'

'Well I don't,' she bit back sharply, sitting up to pull her hair back into a tail, her hands working her locks vigorously. 'Who told you about him?'

Pavo could feel the frostiness in her voice. No wonder Felix had warned him off the subject. 'Just some of the lads. Well, the veterans really, the ones that have been there a few years, they must have served with him.'

'It's not *him*,' Felicia sighed, 'he's got a name. Curtius.'

'Was he much older than you?'

'Two years. That's all. Only served for six months or so before he died.'

'You must miss him terribly?'

She turned back to him, her eyes were red-rimmed and her face sad. 'Look, now's not the best time.'

'I'm sorry. I won't mention him again...'

'No!' She barked. 'I mean, not just now, but maybe later. I would be interested in hearing any of the old stories the legionaries have of him, really I would.' Her eyes were keen, hungry, all of a sudden. 'Anything you hear, you pass it on to me. Just between you and me though?'

'Sure?' Pavo replied, recoiling ever so slightly at her manic expression. He searched for another topic. 'I hope your father's okay,' he offered, 'and the inn. That's got to be some mess this morning.'

'Hmm?' she groaned, lying back and stretching. The tension seemed to have drained from her again. 'Probably is. That's what happens when a brawl breaks out. You really should just have left it with the Goths, you know. They always behave like that and my father can handle himself. Serves them pints of his piss after a few hours of drinking and they don't even notice.' She sat up, her nipples pointed in the cool air. 'Anyway, I think he'll be more worried about where his daughter is. Would you like to come and meet him over breakfast?'

'Er...' Pavo stammered, sitting up, 'Yes. I should take you home.'

She burst into a throaty howl of laughter, shoving him by the shoulder. 'You're such an easy target, Pavo. You want to get a thicker skin!' She pulled the tunic to cover her shoulders. 'Anyway, you won't get a chance to meet him, you're shipping out today, are you not?' she said, and then hatched a devious smile. 'You men are all the same, you get what you want and then you sail halfway around the world!'

Pavo's heart hammered. Dread poured across his skin.

'What's wrong?' Felicia's face wrinkled.

'Daylight,' he croaked, eyes bulging at the blue sky.

'Very perceptive,' she stretched, lying back.

'The legion!' He cried. 'We were supposed to be shipping out at dawn this morning.'

It was well past dawn, but by how long? They both scrambled out of the hay, pulling on clothes. Pavo darted from the barn. From what he could see, he was in the middle of one of the farming estates outside of Durostorum – a tell-tale trail of broken corn snaked through the field from their flight last night. Nearby, a group of horses grazed and the sun was still only new in the sky. As he hopped and tumbled time and again, trying to squeeze on his boots, the words of Gallus barked in his head. *Should there be a next time I will have no say in it, you will be executed.*

He hobbled to the nearest horse, a sturdy looking fawn creature. It eyed him with an equine distaste, then turned back to munch on the hay. His only previous and brief riding experience was as Tarquitius' stablehand at the city games, and all he could recall about that was the terror that sparked through his mind when the racehorse had set off at a gentle canter. He swallowed his fear, hoisted himself onto the mount's back, and squeezed his heels into her flanks. At last she jolted into life with a whinny.

'Felicia,' he yelled, trotting around to her.

She ran from the barn, tugging on her robe.

'Inciting a riot, now horse theft!' She spluttered.

Pavo shrugged, reached down and grasped Felicia's forearm, then in one deft flick, hoisted her into the saddle behind him. She squealed in surprise like a little girl and then coughed to disguise it.

'Watch it!' She growled, jabbing him in the ribs.

Pavo kicked the beast into a gallop, leaning forward in the saddle to focus on the sun-silhouetted outline of Durostorum. They burst clear of the cornfield and onto a rubble strewn dirt path leading to the town. The air grew as cold as iron as they sped faster and faster and the pit of his stomach shrivelled; one false move and they would both be dashed on the path. But Felicia gripped his waist, she trusted him. Then the town walls rolled into view.

'Pavo? What in Hades are you doing, the fort is that way?' She screamed above the rushing air, flapping a finger over to the distant glimmer of stonework on the plain.

'Just hold on,' he roared. They pelted on before slowing as the gates of Durostorum loomed above them. Pavo took a deep breath; hopefully, this might redeem his less than graceful naked scramble only moments ago. 'I wouldn't be the man you hoped I was if I left you stranded in the countryside, would I?' He purred, holding a calm expression while his mind screamed *run for the fort, run!*

'Very romantic,' she chided, 'but do one other thing for me, eh? Get your arse into the fort.'

Pavo nodded vigorously, his face dropping into panic.

'And come and see me…if you don't get executed.' With that, she set off at a run for *The Boar.*

The horse decided to add a little more drama to the occasion by rearing up on its hind legs. He turned to the fort and kicked the mount into a furious gallop.

The sun crept over the countryside, breathing the full light of morning over the hills and fields. Dawn was long gone. Pavo neared the fort, barely hearing the buccina blare such was the ferocity of the wind whipping at his ears. It meant the worst possible scenario for him. The legion would be forming up for the march. Forming up with one ominous space in the first century.

Just then, the main gates rolled into view, and began to swing open. 'Whoa!' he cried, reining in the horse. *I'm not running, stinking of ale, headfirst into Nerva and Gallus at the front of the legion*, he panicked. He pulled the horse right, towards the side gate. He slowed and slid from its back as it reached a canter, stumbling away from it and skidding onto his knees. Then he threw himself shoulder-first at the side gate. His shoulder smashed against its thick timbers and with a yelp, he slid to the ground as the gate remained stubbornly fixed.

'Bugger, bugger, bugger,' he panted. The shadow of execution cast itself across his mind again. No more Felicia, no more legion. Hades, even the turd-shovelling seemed like paradise now.

A clunking noise came from the side gate, freezing Pavo's breath in his lungs. His blood iced as the gate slowly creaked open. The unforgiving glare of Zosimus poked from the gap. He looked Pavo up and down, with a sneer of disgust and amusement.

'You're bloody lucky we were held up,' he mused, picking breakfast from his teeth. 'You'd better be getting your shit together, son,' he suggested.

# Chapter 33

Gallus stood with Nerva in the murky dawn light, surveying the arsenal of armoured infantry formed up in front of him. Eighteen hundred limitanei legionaries – the three full cohorts of the legion – standing in polished order in white, purple-trimmed tunics and mail shirts. The tips of their intercisa helmets and spears fanned along the muster yard like the teeth of a predator, and the wall of ruby and gold oval shields, freshly painted for the mission, coated their front like the scales of a dragon. It had been years since the legion had been mobilised as one unit, and to see them together stirred pride in the heart. Together with five hundred auxiliary troops – wearing little or no armour and bearing irregular weapons such as axes, long swords and composite bows, two hundred Cretan archers and the near two thousand foederati cavalry led by Horsa, the Bosporus invasion force stood at a number of nearly four and a half thousand fighting men. A healthy number for what was supposedly an impoverished border legion. Under the surface though, the tell-tale signs of imperfection and inexperience seeped through, especially from the recruit-heavy first and second cohorts; oversized armour on the slender frames of the raw whelps, most of whom had no battle experience. Added to that, the third cohort had been filled out with vexillationes from neighbouring legions to bring her up to her full complement, and Gallus feared for how cohesive these cobbled ranks might be.

'Feels good, eh?' Nerva spoke. 'We're entering the field, like a proper army.'

Gallus knew what the tribunus wanted to hear, so he buried his doubts. 'It's been a long time, sir. It feels like we have been peeking over the fort walls for a lifetime.'

'The cohorts are strong, just look at them. And the emperor has delivered with those archers, Gallus; those boys could hit a vole in the arse at a quarter of a mile.'

'More men – a welcome surprise indeed,' Gallus nodded. Nerva's face was bathed in sweat, jowls trembling, but his eyes were like torches, alert and darting. The tribunus was excited, but he had to be reined back to reality.

'Well we've got a *loan* of them at least until the mission is over,' Nerva added. 'Less than half of us will be true XI Claudia boys it seems!'

Gallus' eyes narrowed. 'And how does the foederati wing strike you, sir?'

'Horsa and his boys?' Nerva grinned. 'Typical bloody Goths,' he whispered, 'but by Mithras we need them.'

'Horsa's a good man, sir. It's just...the rest of them. They started some ruckus last night up at the inn.'

'It's in their nature, Gallus. In any case I'm sure our lads had some part in it,' he nodded to Quadratus on the front row; the big blonde Gaul sporting a bandaged hand and a black eye. 'I pity the bugger on the end of that fist,' the tribunus winced. 'Anyway, all units are formed up now?'

Gallus scanned the ranks quickly. All present and correct, save for one legionary still bustling into place in the first century. *Pavo*, he grimaced. 'It appears so, sir.'

Nerva nodded. 'Give the order to move out.'

Gallus turned and nodded to the aquilifer who held the legion's eagle standard. The man lifted the standard and the ruby-red banner bearing the bull effigy fluttered in the breeze. Gallus gazed across his men, who held their chins up higher at this.

Felix sidled up next to his commander.

'For the empire!' Gallus roared, punching his clenched fist into the air and turning to the first century, who exploded into an ear-bursting cheer.

The cheering rippled to the centuries surrounding the first. Even the initially bemused Captain Horsa took to beating his spear against his shield and whipping his men into a frenzy of cheering.

Then the buccinas sounded three times.

Gallus' blood raced. 'XI Claudia, move out!'

# Chapter 34

The docks of Durostorum heaved with the local populace, vying to wave off their loved-ones – and their main source of income. Gulls screeched, swooping down on the market stalls, and then flying clear with scraps of meat and bread. It was nearly midday before the Moesian Fleet was finally ready to embark on its voyage.

On board the *Aquila*, Pavo dropped his kit, hopped across the deck, dodging between surly legionaries and scampering dock workers and grasped the port side of the vessel. Taking a deep breath through his nostrils, he tasted the faint salty tang wafting from the nearby Pontus Euxinus. Despite the side-odour of foederati horse dung, he felt great; he had made it back to the fort just in time, and not a trace of a hangover left in him. Leaning eagerly over the side, he glanced around the docks, desperate to catch sight of Felicia. *What a woman.* She was as fiery inside as she looked on the outside. He frowned as he wondered for a moment about her brother – she wasn't just upset about his death, there was something else in the mix there too; despite her plea for stories about Curtius, he'd think twice about bringing the subject up when, or if he saw her next. Surely she would come to wave him off though? Then he realised his open-mouthed, wide-eyed expression as he scanned the docks again might not serve for the most noble and austere farewell, he forced his back straight, mimicking the stiff jaw of Gallus, standing by his side. Yet as the ship pulled free of its moorings, the sea of faces below cheered, but offered no Felicia. Pavo felt his anticipation ebbing as the docks slowly began to shrink before him.

The vessel drifted into the rush of the Danubius, joining the other forty triremes of the fleet in their voyage downriver to the sea. On this vessel, there was a mix of personnel – a spread of legionaries, auxiliaries and foederati along with the remiges on the oars and the mast, and the sole figure of the beneficiarius, clucking over every detail of the rigging. Durostorum drifted back into the horizon and the rhythmic lapping of the water and creaking of timber drowned out the cheering crowds. The ships of the fleet peppered the glistening waters under the morning sun. The expedition was underway.

Pushing back from the side, Pavo took a gulp of the cool air. His pride was intact, he assured himself. And no hangover. Now, where was Sura? So far, he had only been able to try to convey everything to his friend about the previous evening with a manic smile and roll of his eyes as they had passed each other during boarding, to which Sura had responded with a look of total confusion. No two ways about it, his friend had to hear of his misadventures.

Due to a shortage of remiges to man the oars, half of the soldiers on board the *Aquila* were posted below deck, ready to pick up the pace once they hit the open waters of the Pontus Euxinus. The other half were free to roam the ship – and avoid being assigned deck-scrubbing duty if possible.

Nerva was studying maps at the rear of the vessel, while Gallus strode around the deck as commanding officer. Pavo saw the centurion glare in distaste at a group of young legionaries, pulled from the V Macedonia for this mission, retching copiously over the side.

'Not got your sea legs today, lads?' He mused. 'Ah, that's right; you're from a landlocked legion, aren't you? Ah well, inhale that fresh scent of horse dung and think of home.' He winked at Felix, stood nearby, and moved on, oblivious to the glares of the nauseous legionaries behind him.

Pavo's lips curled wryly; the centurion was cold by nature, but at least he had something in common with Brutus - sadism. To Pavo it still felt like Brutus was still with the legion, just out of sight somewhere, and the grim truth of his death and the bloody skirmish now felt like a faded nightmare – the soldier's skin, Brutus himself had described it, a coping mechanism where the death of a comrade would seem absurdly trivial.

Avoiding Gallus' eyes as they swept past him, he moved on, milling past groups playing dice, laughing and joking despite the jealous curses of those on the oars. He passed a handful more who were sitting with a jade tinge to their features, gazing woefully skywards as the waves began to roll in the Danubius delta. Everyone's vomiting, but not me, Pavo thought, not even a hangover! Then one figure caught his eye; one of the foederati from the rowdy group of the previous night. Pavo stopped where he stood; how should he play it? He had only had time to throw on his kit and scramble out into line this morning – the outcome of the brawl at *The Boar and Hollybush* last night was still a total mystery to him. His heart hammered as the foederatus glanced up at him, their eyes locked. Then, to Pavo's relief, the Goth sensed Pavo's fear, laughed and breezed past him, no doubt satisfied with intimidation. 'Whoreson!' Pavo muttered under his breath. Then a hand slapped hard onto his back. Pavo's heart leapt.

'Oi! What in the world have you been up to, and more to the point, where did you get to last night?'

'Sura!' Pavo uttered. He looked annoyingly fresh; his blond hair combed neatly back off his face and a clean-shaven jaw to boot. Sura munched on a piece of bread. Pavo took a breath, eager to tell of his adventures, but Sura gulped his bread down and cut in.

'Well, I had a rather pleasant night – that big girl. She bought my story that I was an optio! Not long after you wreaked havoc at the bar. Didn't get much sleep last night, me,' Sura chirped, pulling another piece of bread from the chunk as Pavo made another failed attempt to interject, 'I bet you can't top that, eh? Where did you end up – out the back getting a kicking no doubt? I did have the good sense to make my way back to my bed in the fort afterwards, unlike some of us.' He let out a rattling laugh and then cocked an eyebrow; 'How did you make the line up this morning?'

Pavo sighed, time to tell the story. But a grey queasiness had crept into his system as Sura spoke and was now marching double time through his mind and his limbs. 'Well,' he started, when another hand clasped onto his shoulder. He turned to see the towering form of Captain Horsa.

'Pavo?' He questioned, his single eye fixed on Pavo's face.

Pavo nodded, confused. The ship bucked over a full wave and suddenly his stomach grumbled in a nauseous protest.

'Don't worry,' Horsa smiled. 'I just wanted to let you know that the ringleaders of the scuffle at the inn last night have been severely reprimanded. They'll not be part of this mission. Mind you, if we had jailed everyone who threw a punch, we'd have to build a new jail! I hope your woman's father recovers, and I trust that you will accept my apology on behalf of my men.'

'I…of course,' spluttered Pavo, somewhat taken aback by the politeness and dignity shown by Horsa, an officer, towards him, a mere recruit.

'If you need me to explain to your centurion...'

'No,' Pavo cut in. Gallus had no idea of his involvement; he was sure. 'No, thanks.'

'Fair enough,' Horsa then nodded to Sura. 'I see you know my newest recruit.'

Pavo turned 'Eh?' His head spun as Horsa grinned and wandered away.

Sura grinned. 'That's what I wanted to tell you, but you wouldn't let me get a word in edgeways. It all happened after you scuttled off from *The Boar* on your own last night.'

Pavo felt a burning wave of frustration that Sura had not even noticed the key presence of Felicia in his hasty departure from the inn. And what was Sura on about? And his stomach felt wrong.

Sura continued. 'Captain Horsa burst in to see what was happening, and then all Hades broke loose. Groups of foederati started piling into our lot, and the locals were only too happy to join in the ruckus.'

'Okay,' Pavo replied, putting a hand over his mouth, a cold sweat leaking from his skin.

'So me and Captain Horsa waded into the fray to prise the scuffling parties apart,' he stopped to give an officer-like nod to the Gothic captain even though the Goth's back was turned, 'and a few other Claudia who were actually trying to stop the chaos backed us up. So afterwards, Horsa gathered us round and suggested that he needed a Roman presence in the foederati wing of the Claudia. Zosimus and his mates turned it down – Gallus' chosen few, you know? But I reckon I'm the man for the job.'

'The foederati – are you mad?' Pavo croaked. 'Are you sure about this?'

Sura frowned in indignation. 'Gallus seems up for the idea – reckons it will calm everyone down, help them to mix a little.' Sura frowned, 'The pact still stands though, eh? You watch my arse and I watch yours.'

Pavo nodded, blinking as his head reeled. 'So, can you ride a horse like a foederatus then?' He asked through the fingers over his mouth.

Sura blinked a few times, as if shocked at being questioned. 'Rider for the imperial messenger service I was. Adrianople to Philippi in record time. Never seen a faster rider, they used to say.' He looked off to sea with a frown. 'Shame they couldn't see past a few missing coins – don't know what they lost the day they booted me out.'

'Okay,' Pavo groaned, swaying as the ship pitched over a swell. Every breath seemed to be on fire now.

Sura continued unperturbed. 'Anyway, I think the intention is for us to provide a bridge between the Romans and the Goths in the legion, so our riding skills will develop alongside our primary diplomatic and oratory skills,' he replied, holding his chin high and closing his eyes. 'Well, you could at least say *well done* or something. I managed to congratulate you on your move to the first century with dignity.' Sura cocked an eyebrow. 'Pavo? Are you okay? You're looking a tad green.'

Pavo moaned, pushed past his friend and grappled to side of the vessel just as a torrent of bitter orange bile exploded from his mouth, spattering the hull of the ship and splashing into the sea.

A sarcastic cheer broke out from a group of watching legionaries.

Sura sniggered.

# Chapter 35

The vastness of the imperial chamber dwarfed Valens, sitting in contemplation between the golden Chi-Rho cross and the old statue of Jupiter. Reports of the Gothic raids across the Danubius had been compiled. What had been a thinly spread but complete Roman border army was now effectively a fragmented militia. The departure of the XI Claudia legion to Bosporus, together with the new I Dacia legion's harvesting of the best troops from his Danubian legions had been the live or die toss of the dice. The remaining forces on the frontier, amounting to little over twenty thousand men scattered over the full length of the snaking river, was below the minimum operational strength for the first time in decades. Disjointed warbands they could cope with, but if the Goths pulled together and realised the state of the frontier, they would have the run of Greece and the new imperial capital. And if the Goths could do it, then what of the millions upon millions of tribesmen who pushed down on the empire behind them?

He looked out of the balcony to the sun-baked west. It was an option that often flitted across his thoughts – legions upon legions of fighting men, all supposedly under the banner of the same empire. But his nephew Gratian had been cold since ascending the Western throne in Rome, and the boy's attitude had seriously darkened since Valens had put in place Arian reforms in the East. Added to that, the borders of the Rhine were in an equally perilous state. No, Valens grasped reality; the answer did not lie with the West.

Equally, postponing the Bosporus reconquest was not an option. His reputation had been built on ever-greater glories. Indeed, the people had taken to calling him Valens 'the great'. While he was feared and respected, he could move the empire forward. The slightest whiff of fear or uncertainty would see the would-be usurpers snaking out from the shadows, daggers sharpened. The live or die call had been made; win, and you win greatness. Lose, he sighed, and you lose everything.

His head ached. How had he, *Valens the Great*, allowed himself to be drawn into this situation? Yes, the plan was his idea. Or was it? He groaned as he remembered the many nights spent, surrounded by the high and mighty of Constantinople. Politicians, holy men and so-called military masters, all desperate to offer their opinion on empire. 'Think, man, think!' He hissed under his breath.

The call for the reclaiming of the old province of Bosporus had arisen from the Holy See itself. 'Yes,' he grasped onto the hazy memory. Their argument being that the reestablishment of the kingdom as a Roman province would be another great tale in the emperor's legend. And for it to be achieved by the Christian armies of Rome would prove a decisive blow to the lingering pagan peoples of the empire and a victory for Arianism, the true faith. Even the soldiers, still clinging to the old deities, might unite under the Arian banner.

He looked again to the statue of Jupiter. Silent, steady Jupiter. Never dogged by a propensity for schism like Christianity was. His marbled and featureless eyes conveyed a sadness from an old and dying world. The Christian teachings of Arius held the candle of faith for him, but the old ways seemed so clear, so simple, no wonder the rank and file found comfort in them. But it wasn't faith that tore at the empire now, Valens chuckled bitterly as he thought; it was the men who purported to embody faith. Then there was the state, the rabble of the senate had become an insidious white noise. He issued a silent prayer to all the gods, fearing that he had made the biggest mistake of his life.

He clapped his hands and a slave slipped through the door. 'My emperor?'

'Call for my scribe,' Valens said, 'and prepare two messengers, with fresh stallions from the imperial stable.'

'Yes, Emperor,' the slave replied and then was gone.

Valens closed his eyes and massaged his temples. Was it already too late?

# Chapter 36

At the boatside, Pavo's stomach rumbled in protest at being left empty and in torment as his eyes followed another droplet of cold sweat falling into the swell below. He had spent the rest of the first day and night at sea by the boatside and now his body seemed to accept that there was nothing else to eject. The waters were choppy again as the sun dipped into the western horizon and the *Aquila* bucked and swelled, promising another night of no sleep whatsoever.

He slumped down, resting against the vessel side. He had replayed lovemaking with Felicia in his mind more times than he could count, and now it was just frustrating. While the veterans were snoring blissfully, most of the recruits of the first century had given up trying to sleep and had gathered in a circle in the centre of the deck. After a few deep lungfuls of cool air, he groaned as he pushed himself to his feet and then wandered over to join them. They were talking in hushed tones around a candle.

'The Goths up there are different. A trader in Durostorum told me; they ambushed a trade caravan and didn't spare a single one of them. Man, woman, child; slaughtered without mercy,' one of them said.

'It's the forests; they hide in the trees and sink arrows into you from above, so you don't even know you're dead till you find yourself wandering in the realm of Hades,' another said.

Pavo cocked an eyebrow, the hair on the back of his neck standing straight. He had fought against a small warband of Goths and that was it as far as battle experience went. That was in friendly territory, where enemy numbers were limited. Here this straggling band of border legionaries was wandering into the jaws of the unknown.

'…aye,' another legionary blurted out, a little too loud, 'but I heard there are these people who have moved into the peninsula, too. Dark riders. More fearsome than any of the Gothic warriors. They celebrate their victories by eating the dead children of their enemies.' Then, unnoticed until now, Gallus coughed and the group jumped as one and the young legionary emitted a high-pitched shriek.

Gallus surveyed the group. 'Choppy waters tonight isn't it, lads?'

Looking around at each other, they nodded and agreed. Pavo noted the stonier than usual look the centurion wore and stood back, keen to stay out of his glare.

'Usually I tire myself by walking the deck. If that doesn't do it then I find that a session on the oars helps.' The legionaries looked at one another again, agreeing this time less readily.

Gallus sighed and again looked round each of them. 'Whatever you do to get through this voyage, let's keep it light, eh? Now try to get some rest instead of winding yourselves up like this.'

But Pavo couldn't hold his words in. 'What is it like there, sir? Bosporus?' He asked, stepping forward. All heads turned to him. At once, his skin prickled with the dry heat of embarrassment.

Gallus turned to stare at Pavo, who braced for some form of rebuke, but there was none; instead, the centurion's eyes sparkled in interest.

'I just mean, perhaps if we knew some of the reality of the situation in the old kingdom, we might be able to focus, to set our minds at rest?'

Gallus nodded very slowly. 'It's a fair question,' he began. 'I'd like to tell you nice things about what happened to us when we carried out our reconnaissance of the peninsula, I really would.' Pavo watched as the centurion's eyes narrowed. He wished he had stayed in the shadows, as the centurion seemed to lose himself in some silent, dark memory. 'However, the reality of war is something that a soldier cannot afford to dwell on. We need to focus only on us, how good *we* are, how strong *we* are. Each of you might still be feeling like fish out of water,' he paused as the ship rolled again, 'if you pardon the expression, but the veterans think the same thoughts, feel the same fears. The only difference is that they've learned to deal with it.' He nodded to the slumbering heaps spread all over the deck.

Pavo watched keenly now as he saw the centurion's stare loosen. There was something there, a sadness. *He actually has feelings!*

Gallus' voice trailed off momentarily and the recruits shuffled in discomfort.

180

'Thank you, sir, I understand,' Pavo offered.

'Just remember, lads, no matter what this mission throws at us, every single one of us will be there by your side, sword in hand, ready to bleed for you,' he leaned forward, the candlelight flickering in his eyes, 'to die for you.'

The huddle of legionaries welcomed the statement with a unified roar of approval. Those who had been asleep in their beds groaned rather more disapprovingly. Gallus nodded to Pavo then turned and left them. It was a stony, cold nod, but Pavo's chest bristled with pride.

# Chapter 37

A vulture soared on a zephyr, high above the neck of the peninsula. The skies were clear, but so was the ground – not even a hint of blood or scraps anywhere. The vulture drifted on across the mountainous ridge, crossing over into Bosporus. At once, the ground turned from grey green to deep crimson. Circling below, thousands of fellow carrion birds eyed the growing pile of carcasses in growing impatience. The vulture swooped to join them.

'Pile them higher!' Apsikal barked at his soldiers. 'Noble Balamber will only be happy when the *Tengri* the sky god can taste their blood…and the Romans can see the tip from their cities!' He strolled amongst the gore-spattered troops, swiping at bloodspots on his own mail vest as he went. Seven thousand bodies, stripped of armour and jewels. These Goths were no match for Hun warfare. A victory won with only a few hundred casualties on their side. The Hun juggernaut was unstoppable, he enthused, turning to take in the sea of yurts filling the plain to the horizon. Horses whinnied at every remaining spot of open grass, feasting on the sparse pickings jealously. He strode over to his mount, stroking its ears as it munched. 'Not long now,' he whispered. 'Soon you will be feasting in the gardens of the Roman Emperor.'

Apsikal looked up at the tent of Balamber; a large enclosure, but certainly not embellished in any way – he was too wily to let his love for jewels and riches show. The Huns did not live under a king, but the strongest noble held power just as great as one. The men feared Balamber absolutely, but they loved him too. Being a horde leader, seeing Balamber's wrath first hand almost daily, Apsikal knew only of the fear, and it was time to report on the battle. He could not stall any longer. To lie and live, or tell the truth and die? His heart thundered.

He ducked as he entered the inviting warmth of the hide tent. The setup inside was simple; areas were sectioned off to make the entrance lobby he stood in, a room for his concubines and a council room. Oil lamps flickered in the gloom, casting dancing shadows across the stern figures of Balamber's personal guard. They parted without a sound as he approached.

Apsikal felt as though he was descending into an underground labyrinth as the curtains flapped behind him and a scent of burning meat curled around his nostrils; the council room was darker still and only a dim outline of Balamber was visible at the far end, slumped on his rudimentary throne – a simple timber bench on a raised platform. Apsikal approached gingerly, stopping at the foot of the platform. He looked up at the shadowy outline of the man; the man who had led their people through poverty and famine, moulding them into an army that nobody in the east could resist.

'Noble Balamber,' Apsikal spoke, his voice trembled. Moments passed with nothing but painful silence. Then Balamber shuffled to sit upright, to his full and towering height.

The first thing Apsikal noticed was the intensity in his leader's eyes. Was it fury? Like Apsikal and most of the Huns, Balamber wore a snaking moustache and kept his flowing, jet-black hair tied back into two knotted tails. His nose curled over the top of the moustache, the rising and lowering of which was usually a good indicator as to his mood. On his cheeks he wore the three distinctive childhood scars seared into his flesh by ritual-abiding parents many years ago – designed to introduce the young to pain and to discourage beard growth. Wrapped in a dark-red robe, Balamber simply rested his hands on the arms of the throne, and stared.

Apsikal gulped. 'Our business is complete with the rebel Goths, Noble Balamber. We have stripped their carcasses of useful materials, and desecrated their bodies, as you commanded.'

Balamber gave the merest of nods.

Apsikal unravelled a tattered scroll listing the inventory of bloody takings from the massacred Goths. Being one of only three literate members of the horde had sealed his rise to prominence. He drew a deep breath to ream off the highlights of the takings, but Balamber raised a hand.

'Are they dead?' He asked, his face devoid of emotion, all apart from his eyes, now almost burning holes in Apsikal. 'All of them?'

Apsikal cleared his throat. The question he was dreading. Genocide was the order he had been given by his leader, and he had failed to complete the order in full, albeit by the merest of fractions.

'They…' He cleared his throat again. *Lie and live, tell the truth and die.* 'They had a detachment of light cavalry, Noble Balamber. They managed to despatch a few of them before we shattered their lines.' Apsikal paused as his leader shifted forward on his seat, his moustache lifting as his lips pursed.

'Fewer than twenty of them escaped, Noble Balamber, and that was after several hundred fled. We brought them down in swathes with a single volley of arr…arrows…' Apsikal stuttered to a halt.

'Then those twenty will be dead and their skulls added to the pile before we move from the camp at the end of this week,' he asserted, his voice steady, fingering the gold cross hanging on a chain around his neck. 'And you will complete your orders this time. Gold piled higher than the corpses outside awaits us if we succeed here, along with the keys to the Roman Empire!'

Apsikal nodded and two beads of sweat coursed down his forehead.

'For if you do not fulfil my expectation this time, then the finest armour from the pile outside will be melted down and poured down your throat.' He pounded a fist on the arm of his throne.

Apsikal dropped his head and fell to one knee.

'I will not fail you this time, Noble Balamber.'

# Chapter 38

A stinging, torrential rain battered the fleet. Towering waves strove to raise each of the creaking hulks towards the sky and meet the full force of the storm. Then, an inevitable collapse back into the dark-blue abyss followed each of the ascensions. On board the *Aquila*, the crew lay scattered across the decks like twigs in a rainstorm, desperately clinging onto frayed rigging, shattered decking and crumbling masts. The storm had come from nowhere; one minute the sun baked their skins as the remiges rowed, the next, the sky had blackened and the fury of Poseidon was upon them.

Grasping a piece of worn rigging, Gallus blinked the frozen water from his eyes, willing his numb fingers to manipulate the loose end of the rope into a hoop. He staggered his attempts to save himself with barking orders to the flailing men on the deck. Every time the ship dropped into the trough of a titanic wave, he grasped the rope, praying that the other end was fastened securely enough, steeling himself against the screams of the less fortunate. Finally, the rope slipped into a loose knot. He braced himself as he waited for the next crashing impact, eyes shut tight, when a hand clamped itself around his ankle.

'Sir!' A desperate voice gasped.

Gallus blinked at the exhausted figure of Felix. 'Felix, thank Jupiter!' He roared above the noise, throwing down the remaining rope to his optio and grasping his wrist. 'Brace yourself…'

Again, a wall of salty, perishing water collapsed down on top of them for long enough to once again make them doubt whether their ship had went under or capsized – at least two other ships of the fleet had done exactly that.

Gallus coughed as the swell tumbled from the decks. 'Felix, what have you got for me?'

Felix spluttered, shivering violently. 'Sir, we only caught broken signals from the rest of the fleet in front before the storm hit us.' He stopped to retch, before lashing himself to the mast as Gallus had done. 'I don't know any more than anyone else – but it doesn't look good,' he chattered, nodding to the upturned hull nearby. 'We're being torn to pieces out here, sir.'

Gallus grimaced. 'Damn the senate, Felix, damn them!'

'*They* ordered us to set to sea yesterday?' Felix roared.

'All wrapped up in that deal between the dux, that fat cretin Tarquitius, the emperor and the Goths.'

Felix spluttered in incredulity. 'What in Hades does the senate know about navigating the Pontus Euxinus. Bloody idiots!' He raised his fists to the pitch-black sky as the next wave crashed down on them.

Gallus coughed. 'Whatever happens, just make sure we don't lose sight of the main body of the fleet!'

# Chapter 39

Valens waved away his candidati as they rushed to his side. They looked on anxiously as their emperor strode to the palace stables in non-ceremonial full battle gear.

'No, wait a few moments, then follow behind me,' he barked. He mounted his prize stallion, his functional if rather unbeautiful armour clanking as he did so. As he made to ride out of the palace grounds, he stopped in thought, before turning again to the candidati. 'Muster a fifty and bring them to the senate building, but give me a head start.'

Spurring his horse into a trot, the candidati hastily opened the front gates of the palace to reveal the Augusteum – the ornate square punctuating the heart of the city. A continuous roar rippled overhead from the nearby Hippodrome where the spring games had begun. The crowds swarming at the square-side markets outside parted. As he cantered through them, his people either stared up at him in awe or pumped a fist in the air, crying a salute. Valens had no business with the people of Rome today. Today the senate would be the focus of his attentions. By dusk they would know that one man alone ruled the empire.

He looked up as they approached the senate basilica on the eastern side of the Augusteum; one senator was lazily sipping wine by the marbled doorway, laughing as he watched two beggars fighting over scraps of bread. When the rabble of the citizens following Valens reached him, he glanced up. His eyes grew saucer-like as they locked with those of Valens and he hurled his half-empty cup to the floor and bolted off back into the senate chambers. Two urban guards shuffled quickly to their posts by the door, their chins and chests thrust out.

Valens chuckled, slowing as he approached the doorway. 'At ease, men,' he spoke gently, eyeing the cracks in the marbled arch of the doorway as he dismounted. Much to be repaired, he mused. His footsteps echoed in the cool entrance hall as he walked under the languid gaze of busts of emperors past. Then he set his eyes on the chapped and scarred timber door ahead – the senate hall. Valens stopped short of pushing the door open in his stride; he could hear the echoing babble of approval and disapproval. In a moment, they would be louder than a pack of carrion birds.

He shoved both huge doors and they boomed as they crashed open into the hall. Valens marched to the centre of the senate floor.

The hall still echoed with the current speaker's half-finished sentence. Valens scanned the rest of the room; he saw a sea of stunned faces, open mouths and bulging eyes.

The interrupted speaker felt the weight of obligation to speak first; 'Emperor,' he uttered. 'What brings your honourable presence to our floor today?'

Valens gazed into the stunned audience stonily. 'Today, my senate, I bring you an announcement which is overdue, and entirely necessary. For the good of the empire itself, I will afford no debate on the matter.' Valens allowed the ripple of murmuring to break before continuing. 'As of this moment, The Senate of Constantinople is suspended.'

Like a pack of vultures seeing their scraps disappear, the senators rose to their feet. The outraged roars rattled through the hall. The senator whom he had interrupted mid-speech dropped his veil of obedience and launched into a similar tirade, stepping backwards to merge himself into the advancing crowd of angry senators.

Valens stood motionless and completely alone in the centre of the floor, allowing his gaze to wander to the opening at the top of the hall where a disc of crisp blue sky peeked in. Far more emperors had been slain in hot and cold blood in the name of the senate than had died at the hands of the barbarians over the centuries. Nevertheless, Valens held his nerve until he heard the reassuring clatter of the candidati pouring into the room behind him. He breathed a disguised sigh of relief as the fifty filed in to form a circle around him. Then it all happened in a blur; one zealous senator lurched forward, unarmed, and three spears perforated his torso. Blood showered the rabble of toga-clad men and a tortured scream filled the hall. Valens closed his eyes. Why did it always come down to blood, he despaired. He waited for the chamber to fall back into silence.

'This measure will be in place until the empire has re-established firm control over its borders. This building is to be abandoned by sunset today. Any member of the senate who is found in political practice within the city,' he hesitated, this was where the hard line would be drawn, 'will be executed.'

The silence was intensified by the sea of gawping faces. With that, Valens turned on the spot and walked out as he had entered the chamber, head held high, and eyes set firmly forwards. The candidati poured out in reverse formation, the last two pulling the chamber doors shut. The members of the disbanded senate looked to one another for a voice, all the while the body on the floor cooled in its own blood. Moments passed like this before they erupted in a fit of anxious squabbling again. All except one.

Senator Tarquitius remained still amongst the mayhem, his eyes fixed on the blood-stained floor. Until now, the emperor had always had an air of malaise in his dealings with the senate. A soft touch, even. This, together with Tarquitius' senatorial status had been a fine foothold in the power ladder. In one motion, that had been torn from him, like a sandstorm stripping an oasis. His eyes narrowed as a bitter taste swirled in his mouth. His services were now on offer to the highest bidder. Sod the emperor, to Hades with the bishop; nothing would stop him from regaining power.

# Chapter 40

A rich orange dawn yawned over the still sea. Scattered across the placid surface, a shattered hulk of timber bobbed gently, punctuating the pepper of debris all around it. The *Aquila* bore at best a half of its original mast, and the hull bore small vertical fissures that drank in the seawater greedily regardless of their size. All across the deck, bodies lay sprawled, deep in an exhausted sleep or blue in the face, chattering and vomiting. A few bedraggled legionaries wandered around the deck waking their colleagues; dawn was upon them and sleep would have to wait.

Pavo rocked, holding his knees to his chest, shivering at the unshakeable cold that still dogged him. His frozen body had stopped him from falling asleep, and his brain raced over and over the chaotic events of the night before. They had fought like lions to pull down the sails and hold the rigging in place in order to ride out the worst of the storm, but the sheer muscle of the winds had broken the back of the fleet despite their efforts. On the horizon, Pavo made out the outline of one of the other ships. How much of the fleet had survived was unclear. Of the forty triremes that had been sailing in perfect formation the previous day, only that single one had been left in sight of the flagship by the end of the storm.

Gallus emerged from below deck, hauling a sack of wheat bread loaves with the help of the beneficiarius. The centurion's arms were scrawled with fresh cuts and encrusted in dry blood, and his eyes rimmed with the kohl of exhaustion. Then an aroma of broth drifted over the deck – broad bean and nettle he reckoned – not exactly the cuisine of emperors, but damn, Pavo thought, it did smell like it.

'Okay ladies, we've pulled together some eats. Line up, get your bread from me then back of the deck for some soup. We've got some serious repairs to do if we don't want to end up in the drink, so you need all the energy you can get – no excuses!' He directed his last statement to the group of vomiting legionaries.

Despite the centurion's tone, the soldiers merely looked around, contemplating the order, eyes shot with utter exhaustion. Pavo, all too aware of the precarious angle of the waterline on the hull, leapt up, disguising his burning joints and the nausea in his gut. He grabbed a loaf, nodding firmly to Gallus, before trotting over to the soup cauldron. The legionary 'manning' the soup bore an exhausted stare into the horizon and barely blinked as Pavo grabbed the ladle from him and muscled into his position. Clanging the ladle against the rim, he shot a glance around the deck.

'Soup's up!' he boomed. The metallic twang lifted the heads of the weary legionaries. As they began to converge on the welcome source of warm food, Pavo nodded sternly at Gallus. The centurion, emotionless as ever, gave him shrewd eyes and a faint nod in return.

Wiping his bread on the side of his iron food bowl, Pavo savoured the hot, peppery thickness as he dropped the last morsel into his mouth. He sighed, dropping his bowl and arms to his side to rest back against the side of the ship, then closed his eyes.

'What a lucky draw this was, eh?' Sura, murmured beside him. 'Torn to pieces overnight, then double stints on the oars.'

The oars. *Damn it*, he blinked his eyes open – the beneficiarius was readying to make a call, probably for the shift changeover. It only felt like a moment since he was last blistering his hands on them below deck. 'Makes you wonder, doesn't it? Why do we get the assignment from Hades when our friend Spurius and his monkey Festus get a plum role in the I Dacia? Comitatenses, my arse. I hear their legion is tasked with patrolling the Danubius – probably busy stopping in at every brothel and inn along the way.' He sighed.

Sura chuckled wryly. 'We're jinxed, friend. And the best is yet to come!' He swept a hand out towards the horizon.

Pavo groaned and closed his eyes, sighing. The broth had settled in his belly and he felt its warmth wrap around his body. Sleep began to curl through his mind and his head lolled to one side.

'Form for roll call,' the beneficiarius boomed. Pavo jolted upright, his precious instant of rest blown away and his head spinning. He stumbled to his feet with Sura and they joined the occupants of the *Aquila* shuffling to the centre of the deck. Then he noticed the dark look of Centurion Gallus up front. The crew looked far lighter than their full complement as they formed up. Even when everyone had gathered, heads still turned, expecting more, far more.

Tribunus Nerva hobbled over to stand next to Gallus. Captain Horsa flanked him on the other side, with Felix joining him. Quadratus, Zosimus, and Avitus stood on the front line. The officers had made it through okay, as had the veterans of the first century. But how many recruits had been washed away to an icy grave?

One by one, the beneficiarius read out each name on his roster, to which, the legionary in question would shout out in reply. Near the prow of the ship, a *capsarius* stood, holding bandages and salve, ready to reply for any of those too injured to form up. As the list went on, the first name went unanswered. Then another. Each one like a dagger in the guts. Too soon, Pavo lost count.

The crew of the *Vesta* had been fed almost enough to stop the men's stomachs roaring, and were now busy erecting a temporary mast. The large timber splinters and split deck boards would at least allow the sail to catch some of the gentle breeze blowing above the languid waters. That their hull was intact was something to thank angry Poseidon for.

Centurion Renatus, chief centurion of the third cohort, smeared in sweat and grime, wiped his forehead and gasped for air as he stood up. Backbreaking work was the order until they made contact with the rest of the fleet. Grasping a length of rigging, he hoisted himself onto the rim of the ship to survey the goings-on amongst the men of the fourth century of his cohort who were crewing this vessel.

All armour and arms had been shed, bundled below deck so they could work lighter and faster, in the effort to make the ship mobile again. They were sitting targets out here anyway, he thought, and had to find the fleet at all costs. First, a fire signal, then a flag from the distant *Aquila* had set his men to work. Safety in numbers beckoned and it had buoyed his men into action.

'Come on lads; let's show those pussies in the first century a bit of true Roman efficiency!' He roared. For the first time that morning, they roared back – the wind was in their sails once more, at least figuratively. Renatus mouthed a silent prayer of thanks as he leapt down onto the deck to aid the rigging work.

In lieu of a crow's nest, Porcus the legionary stood atop a precariously balanced tower of barrels and crates, he turned round from Renatus' rally, straining his neck and shielding his eyes from the glaring mid-morning sunshine. Still there was nothing on the horizon apart from the fleet's flagship – where were the other thirty-eight vessels, he wondered? Gingerly rotating on the shoddy platform, he scanned the blurred line where the shimmering sea met the brilliantly blue sky. As he turned, a piercing alien shriek sounded from what seemed like inside his head. The unimpressed, pointed features of a large gull stared at him calmly on his shoulder. Flailing his arms to shoo the creature, he felt the inevitable crumbling of his ill-advised viewing platform. The winged menace took off in flight, just as the legionary's legs whipped forwards and upwards. Instinctively, he made to let out a yell. But he caught the shout in his throat when he glimpsed the horizon on his way down.

Scrambling to his feet amidst tired laughter from his fellow legionaries, he scrambled back on top of the tallest freestanding crate, straining his eyes to the distance once more, his nails digging into the timber. His pupils narrowed, until they focused on two distinct dark shapes on the waves.

'Ships to starboard!' He roared in excitement. The legionaries dropped their tools and rushed to the edge of the ship, barging through each other to get a view of the mini fleet. A chorus of cheering rose from them, and Centurion Renatus laughed.

'They're coming straight for us - going to beat the *Aquila* to us by the looks of it,' he joked, comparing the complete sails of the group of fast-approaching ships with the many rags that the crew of the *Aquila* had patched together.

'Aye, we're more important than the flagship,' another legionary bellowed.

Renatus turned to his watchman to congratulate him, but stopped short when he saw the look of horror painted on the young man's face.

'Sir, they're not Roman,' he exclaimed, the colour draining from his face as his eyes grew like saucers. 'They're pirates.'

Renatus' jaw dropped as he turned back to see the black flags billowing on the approaching warships. His throat instantly felt like parchment; Renatus turned to the scene of his men, still in oblivious celebration, and glanced to the carelessly discarded armour and weapons piled below and scattered across the deck, as well as the crippled broadside ballistae, and felt his stomach knot. *Do something*, his mind screamed. Finally, he lurched forward, grasped the nearest pair of swords, and brought them together above his head, blade crashing against blade.

'Pirates! To arms!' He roared. It took a few moments for his call to sink in. By the time they were scrambling to pick up bits and pieces that they could fight and defend themselves with, the huge pirate vessels had cut over to them and now loomed large above – a massive quinquereme leading the charge. Renatus blinked at the sight of the snarling, bearded, sun-blackened faces of the scimitar-bearing crew who heaved along the side of their vessel. The pirates of the Pontus Euxinus left no soul alive – their reputations depended on it.

The pirate flagship boarding gangs slammed down onto the starboard deck of the *Vesta*, like an eagle's beak scything into its crippled prey. The legionaries backed into a huddle, loose armour clashing as they bunched up, losing formation. Renatus saw what was happening to his men and at once his iron will pushed ahead of the fear he felt.

'Pull yourselves together, form a square, enough room between each man to swing a sword. Don't make me come in there and sort you out!' The men stumbled out of the huddle and lined up in a proper square. Renatus whispered a prayer to Mithras as he pushed back into the front line – just in time as the pirates washed across the deck, heckling war cries as they closed in on their prey. 'Keep it steady, lads. Show them nothing but the boss of our shields and the tip of our swords.'

Then, like storm waves crashing onto a lone rock, the pirates rushed at and tumbled over the top of the Roman square, screaming. Their leader, standing at the edge of the main gangway roared them on. His long, knotted hair was dyed an unnaturally bright red and his teeth were filed down to fang points. The square now wobbled and swayed, and was hammered into a circle by the crush of the pirates.

'Hold them to the side of the ship,' Renatus cried hoarsely, gulping back a scream as the tip of a curved pirate blade sunk into his shoulder from above. Not too deep, but still enough that it would weaken him before long. He parried the strike then roared, butting the crazed pirate in the nose with his shield, and then pulling the shield to one side just long enough to gut the man. He ducked back and then out again to slash at one pirates exposed neck and then poke his sword neatly into the ribcage of another. Renatus felt the battle rage pump through him; all around the pirates tumbled to the ground as his men fought for their lives. But so many Romans had fallen too – less than half were still standing after only moments of fighting. His vision swam as the blood pumped from his shoulder wound, but he blinked it back. *It can be done*, he growled to himself, glancing back to see how far the *Aquila*, their only hope of salvation, was. Instead, he saw only the second pirate vessel sidling up to the portside.

The gut-wrenching clattering of another series of gangways filled the air, and Renatus felt despair tearing at his heart. The men of the second pirate ship coursed forward onto the *Vesta*, directly at the rear of the Roman contingent. Renatus ducked a sword swing and slapped a hand on the legionary to his side.

'Fight bravely, Minucius,' he barked. Then, he withdrew back through the square, ignoring the mush of blood and innards coating the deck as he moved, stooping to prise another sword from the clenched hand of a dead legionary. He burst out of the back of the square, threw his shield to the ground and glared at the new wave of pirates. With a snarl, he hurled himself into their midst in a hacking frenzy.

Renatus felt the many slashes of the scimitar only numbly, little realising the dull thuds he heard were the sound of his own limbs being sliced off and slapping onto the deck. His vision grew dark. But as he felt his life leave his torn body, he saw a blurry outline of figures pour onto the prow of the ship - Romans. 'They've made it,' he hissed.

Too late for him, but not for his men. The *Aquila* had arrived at last!

Pavo bit his lower lip, craning his neck and on his toes to see over the shoulder of Zosimus; the *Vesta* shuddered like a dying gazelle, devoured by the lion-like hulks of the pirate ships. The deck foamed with a froth of blood and metal and the screaming sent a chill across the waves and over the deck of the *Aquila* as its prow clunked into contact with the *Vesta*. He glanced at Sura, by his side.

'I've got your flank,' he spoke firmly.

Sura nodded, his teeth biting into his lower lip as he jostled on one foot and then another.

'Soldier's curse?' Pavo asked nervously. The full bladder and parched mouth had struck him as well.

Sura nodded vigorously through an anxious grin.

Gallus, perched on the beak of the vessel, bellowed for the advance and the ninety assembled legionaries let rip in kind.

'Let's show these squid-shaggers!' Sura yelled over the battle cry and at once, the group rushed forward, roaring, their intercisa crests rippling forward like a school of shark fins.

Pavo poured onto the deck of the *Vesta* with them as they hammered into the pirate sprawl. Having lost all shape in pursuit of victory, the pirates scrambled in confusion back to the starboard side. The pitiful, blood spattered remnant of the fourth century gasped in disbelief.

'Get into line!' Gallus barked at them.

Pavo almost retched at the reek of guts coming from the recruit of the fourth century who sidled up next to him. The boy was far younger than he was, probably only fifteen, and his head was gone; shaking, chattering, barely able to hold his sword. But they were still outnumbered and had to fight on.

The fang-toothed, fiery-haired pirate leader roared encouragement to his men, prompting an ever louder cry from Gallus; 'Take that bugger down!' he screamed, thrusting a plumbata at the fiery-locked figure. The dart skimmed the pirate leader's neck as he ducked to one side, not even drawing blood, and he emitted a howl of derision.

Pavo saw the centurion disappear into the pirate swarm at the head of the Roman wedge, his plume whipping around as he tirelessly felled the stunned pirates. The back half of the first century lagged, hesitant for the briefest of moments.

'You heard the centurion,' Felix snarled, waving them forward, 'Let's finish this!'

Pavo's heart thundered as the legionaries gave a rallying cry and followed the little Greek forward.

The remaining Roman number thumped into the compacting pirate crowd. Gallus' contingent had punched a hole through to the body of Centurion Renatus, and Pavo glanced down to his left to see the bloodied torso of the officer being passed back under the legs of the first century.

'Protect the bodies of our brothers,' Zosimus cried over his shoulder, 'or these pirate scum will scavenge every scrap from them.'

Pavo shuffled the body backwards, his shins sinking into the still warm stumps of limbs.

'Eyes forward, Pavo!' Avitus barked, shoving him around to face front.

A pair of pirates advanced on him, armed with spike shields and awful, ripping scimitars, already spattered in skin, hair and blood. He glanced to Sura and felt himself take a step backwards as the pirates stalked towards him, when Zosimus snarled in his ear.

'Lock shields. Barge them onto the floor, and then gut the beggars!' He growled.

Pavo nodded, his chest shuddering. He tensed his arms, and growled back at the two pirates. With a clank, Sura's shield was joined to his, then another shield joined, then another. The Roman wedge moved forward as one with Zosimus at its head, pummelling into the pirate line, their scimitar strikes useless against coordinated defence. The first line of pirates crumbled under the advance and fell to be skewered underfoot. Pavo felt the red rage of battle as he butted at his aggressors, hopping up to sink his sword tip into the throat of the spike shield bearing warrior, then another butt, then a slash at the gut of the scimitar man. His throat heaved as the man's last meal spilled onto the deck as the body collapsed. Within an instant, he was just another bundle of bones being crunched over by the advancing century.

On and on they pushed. Surely, the pirate number was thinning to the point of breaking, Pavo hoped, gasping as he stabbed through another open flank. Then, he felt a dull blow to his face and a flash of white light in his eyes. His helmet had been knocked off. No time to think about it, he grimaced. Then he caught sight of a crimson flash of iron hammering towards his face. A pirate, leaping from the boatside, careered through the air over the shield wall and towards him, scimitar not even an arm's length from his face. His arms pinned below shield level, Pavo waited for the shattering impact into his skull.

He grimaced at the popping and grinding of tearing flesh and shattering bone. But no pain. Just the flat edge of a scimitar, skimming harmlessly across the side of his face. He blinked to see the twisted face of his foe staggering backwards into his number, clutching the ragged stump that remained of his pruned arm. Blood washed from the wound and the man's face drained to white as he collapsed.

'There's another one you owe me, eh?' Sura growled, his eyes glimmering with a maniacal bloodlust.

'Duck!' Pavo yelled, swiping at the axe-bearing pirate who rushed at his friend. The spatha sliced through the man's jaw, which clattered to the deck before he did. 'Consider us even,' he grinned, wiping the hot gore from his eyes and feeling his chest burst with the rush of battle.

On the boatside of the *Vesta,* the pirate captain surveyed the scene, cursing. What had seemed like easy pickings had turned out to be a very costly affair, and they would probably lose twice in manpower what they would gain from looting. He turned to the crew on his other vessel, and gave a signal by drawing a line across his throat, and then he scampered around the side of the battle, heading for the gangplank back onto the quinquereme.

On board the *Aquila*, Captain Horsa stood, his leg shaking with an intolerable desire to fight. Gallus had been adamant – this was legionary work, the five surviving foederati on the *Aquila* were to remain on the Roman trireme. He gripped the ship's edge to view the battle, cursing every pirate, and striking every killer blow for himself. He spotted the pirate captain hauling himself back onto the retracting pirate flagship. Then he noticed its prow, and that of the second pirate vessel; it was moving, withdrawing. 'Is this victory?' he began to grin, the beginnings of a roar of joy swirled in his lungs. Then his blood froze as he saw the second pirate vessel lower its ramming spike.

'They're going to scuttle it!' He roared at the swell of legionaries on the deck of the *Vesta* again and again, but the shouts fell on battle-deafened ears. Seething with impotence, he then barked an order in Gothic to his five fellow foederati. As one they thundered to the hold of the *Aquila*.

Pavo now felt a sapping numbness pull his limbs groundwards, trying to prise his sword from his grip. The efficient, steady butchering that was played out along the Roman line now took on a rhythmic quality, entrancing the soldiers as they stepped over their dead enemies and fallen brothers, bodies churned into a bloody pulp, speckled with the sparkle of white bone. Then he heard the murmur and then the rabble of panic from the pirates. 'They're going to surrender,' he yelled.

'No they're not,' Sura gasped, staggering backwards, pointing to the fast approaching pirate vessel, growing like a Kraken rising from the waves, its sails dominating the sky above.

The ramming spike churned in the water as the second pirate vessel kicked back towards the *Vesta*. If the pirates sank the galley of the fourth and all the Roman troops on it, the barely-manned *Aquila* would be a sitting target, and the rest of the fleet were ready prey. Pavo leapt back from the front line, over to Gallus.

'Sir!' he yelled, spotting Gallus in the fray at the side. His voice drowned in the smash of weapons. 'Sir,' he roared again, managing to reach out and slap a hand on the centurion's shoulder. Gallus glanced back briefly, his features stony and dripping with blood.

'No time, Pavo!' He cried, turning back to skewer a pirate giant.

'We're going down, sir – they're going to scuttle us!'

Gallus shot a stare back this time, simultaneously hammering his shield boss into the face of a tenacious pirate midget who harried at him. Then he fell back from the line.

The centurion's gaze shot back and forth between the incoming ramming vessel and the pirate flagship, its gangplank now halfway raised from the deck of the *Vesta*. 'Pavo, drop your shield,' he spoke softly at first, then his eyes widened and he bellowed, pointing at the pirate flagship, 'and let's get onto that ship.' Gallus threw his helmet and shield down and lurched forward the gangplank; only paces away, but now surely too high to reach. He leapt and his fingers clawed at the edge before collapsing back onto the deck of the *Vesta*. 'Bugger! Pavo, you try, quickly!' With that, Gallus kneeled and cupped his hands as a foot lift. Pavo pushed the fear of what he was about to do aside, judged his stride and speed carefully, landing his stronger right foot in the centurion's hands to spring up. Now his fingertips grasped firmly on the frayed edge of the rising gangplank, and he scrabbled desperately to find the purchase to haul himself – still in full armour – over the edge and onto the pirate vessel.

'That's it, Pavo – get the plank back down!' Gallus cried from below. 'They won't scuttle us until their flagship's free – get it down!'

'How?' Pavo panicked, swinging from the almost vertical plank, the murky sea rippling below him. Then he felt hands push up against his soles – Zosimus and Quadratus, bless them! The giant legionaries pushed him up and over with a grunt and finally he was tumbling head over heels onto the pirate flagship. He stumbled forward, his hands slapping him to a halt on the deck where his eyes set upon a pair of salt-encrusted hide boots. He looked up – the gnarled pirate captain glowered back at him, a loaded bow on his wrist, pointed straight into Pavo's face.

'I could put you out of your misery with an arrow through your eye, Roman...'

Pavo winced, weaponless and pinned under a sharpened arrowhead.

'...but I would draw greater pleasure from watching you drown slowly with your kind.' Pavo gasped as the pirate captain sunk a boot into his chest. 'Over the side, boy!' he rasped. Pavo buckled over the timber lip of the vessel, flailing to catch hold of something, anything. A rope whipped at his palm and he grasped at it, falling until his weight swung him round to jolt his shoulder as he smashed his forehead into the outside of the hull. Dangling above the waves, he looked down on the deck of the *Vesta*; his ears rang as Gallus, Zosimus, Quadratus and Felix yelled at him silently, below.

'What?' he roared, as they grew redder in the face. Then he saw Zosimus draw a line across his throat, mouthing the words *cut it*. 'Cut it? Of course!' he looked up at the length of rope – taut, it was all that held the gangplank up. He grappled for the dagger in his belt. *Wait a minute*, he reasoned, glancing at the murky wash and smashing jaws of the two vessels waiting to swallow him below, then at the desperate looks on the faces of his fellow legionaries. *Oh bugger. Should've learned to swim, I suppose*. Then he swiped at the rope with the dagger.

With a twang, the rope above him sprung skywards, and the gangplank plummeted onto the deck with a crack as Pavo fell like a stone toward the water. Just then, the whinnying of horses signalled a charge of Horsa's foederati five, across the deck of the *Vesta* to leap onto the pirate flagship.

Pavo braced for the icy embrace of the waves, when his torso jolted violently in his mail vest. Croaking, he looked up to see the tree trunk fist of Zosimus holding his belt loop.

'No ducking out of battle that way, lad,' he grinned and then hoisted Pavo onto the deck of the *Vesta* with a grunt.

Gallus headed up the line of legionaries advancing carefully onto the deck of the pirate flagship. Horsa and his mounted men circled the pirate captain who stood alone but defiant.

'I thought I had given you orders, Captain?' Gallus spoke suspiciously.

'I thought you were done for – and us with you – if we didn't intervene, sir. Seems like young Pavo saved the day though,' he nodded to Pavo, who shrank at the praise.

'We'll discuss this later, Captain,' Gallus replied after a few moments of uncertain silence. 'Get our men on board here and get that gangplank up!'

Just then, all four vessels – the two pirate ships, the *Vesta* and the *Aquila* shuddered as a roar of metal crunching through timber filled the air. The pirate captain dropped his head in despair. Gallus spun round to see the second pirate vessel churning through the deck of the *Vesta*.

'In the name of Mithras,' he cried, 'we could have spared you, chained you and your men to the oars of our galleys,' he spat at the pirate captain, 'but it looks like we'll be a little short of deck space now. You didn't realise you were taking on the empire, did you. You didn't reckon on the resilience of the XI Claudia? Anything you'd like to say before I send you and your men on that ship for a bath?' He growled, jabbing a thumb over to the disintegrating deck of the *Vesta*, where the pirate warriors were now weaponless and restrained behind Roman sword point.

The pirate captain looked up, his dejection washed away by a sudden spark of realisation. Then, a terrible grin wrinkled across his face, his lips curling up to expose the sharpened yellow fangs. 'The legion? You truly are the legion they are waiting for?' Then he threw his head back and let out a demonic cackle.

The balance of power swung palpably as Gallus' brow furrowed, the centurion taken aback. Gallus then whipped his spatha from his scabbard and poked the point into the pirate captain's throat. 'No games, you dog. Talk or I'll drag you behind our ship alive for the sharks to tear at your flesh.'

The pirate captain almost foamed in fury as Zosimus and Quadratus wrenched his arms behind his back. 'We trade in these waters,' he snarled. 'This is our sea. We know what goes on in the lands you have long forgotten.'

'What did I say? No history lesson, no riddles,' Gallus barked, jabbing the point of his sword in to draw a droplet of blood. 'Talk!'

'You will not live to see the autumn, Roman dog. They will be waiting for you. Your cries for mercy will go unheard!' The pirate captain roared and took on the strength of a bull as he barged Zosimus and Quadratus from his sides. He lurched forward at Gallus, his hand whipping out a dagger concealed in his belt. As the blade jabbed out and towards the staggering centurion, Felix leapt out to hurl his spatha through the air, the blade punching into the pirate's chest, throwing him back to the deck. With a violent spasm, he let out a rattling cry and was dead.

Gallus gasped, righting himself, straightening his helmet.

'Good throw! I had it covered, though,' Zosimus growled, shoving at the corpse with his boot, his skin red with humiliation.

Gallus firmed his jaw and spun to see the *Vesta* disappearing under the waves, the pirates thrashing their last or scrambling for the sides of the ramming vessel as it struggled to pull its spike free of the sinking trireme. The centurion strode to the lip of the vessel and crashed his fist on the lip of the galley.

'Sir?' Felix offered.

'The old Kingdom of Bosporus must surely only be a day's rowing away. Scuttle the *Aquila* once we've got her supplies on board, and put a bloody big hole in the side of that boat,' he swept a hand derisively at the second pirate vessel, 'then pull the fleet together as a matter of urgency. Get Nerva and the centurions together. We've got to get on top of this mission before it overruns us.'

Gallus turned to look out from the prow over the serene blue infinity of sky and sea. He heard the shouts and scuffles of his men crewing the quinquereme, but his eyes lingered on the northern horizon. Empty, yet riddled with mystery. The pirate captain's words rang in his head.

*They will be waiting for you. Your cries for mercy will go unheard...*

# Chapter 41

Valens strolled beside the shuffling bishop, stooping to cup a flower from the honeysuckle bed, marvelling at their vivid colour and sweet scent while so much else in the palace garden struggled into bloom. The climate in Constantinople was turning very gradually away from the freshness of spring towards the all day long sweltering heat of the midsummer months. Now the sun glowed high in the sky, throwing down a pleasant heat, especially in the enclosed grounds. He stood straight again, letting the mellow trickle of the fountain and the lilting birdsong soothe his heart. The last few days had been so stressful, and he was only half way to completion of his plan.

His invite to the bishop had been open and friendly, and the Evagrius had accepted readily. They had shared a midday meal of eggs poached in red wine, boiled goat with yoghurt and then a thick apple patina with lashings of garum sauce. As usual, the palace slaves had kept their goblets topped up, but both men had been quick to refuse wine to drink – even watered down. They had talked all through the meal, but without substance or consequence; city development, ecclesiastical fund raising and the cleansing of the city docks. As they had strolled out into the sunlight to begin their tour of the gardens Valens had continued to play along, discussing the redevelopment of the area around the Hippodrome - the centrepiece of the new Rome, he had branded it. But now the preamble was over; it was time to broach the heart of the matter.

'The empire has a crisis on her hands,' he said calmly.

'A crisis? Doesn't she always?' Evagrius chuckled. 'Indeed the very nature of the empire seems to be a flux of crises.'

'You know what they used to do in Rome, Bishop, when the city was in danger?'

Evagrius' eyes narrowed, but he kept his benign veil in place.

Valens knew the bishop was well aware of the law of the dictator. How he would react to being told was the test. 'When Hannibal had Italy in his clutches. When the Samnites threatened the old city. When Caesar himself faced down danger from within in the shape of Pompey.' Valens halted his stroll and turned to face the bishop. 'In those dark times, for the good of Rome itself, one man directed her fate. All others stood to one side...or were forced there...for the benefit of everyone. A dictator they called it then. Now an emperor is required in the purest sense of the word. An emperor like the great men of the past; Trajan, Aurelius, Constantine.'

Evagrius nodded.

'Our empire is vast now, and one man cannot rule its expanse. So let our brothers in the West look after their affairs – God knows they don't have their troubles to seek. But the East,' he placed a hand on the bishop's shoulder, 'she needs direction or she will suffer. Like a lily in bloom at dusk and dead by dark, I fear for her future if I do not act.'

'You are referring to the recently defunct Senate of Constantinople, I presume?' Evagrius mused. Valens noticed the faintest tremble on the bishop's lips – maybe the beginnings of a sneer?

'Partially,' Valens corrected. 'For the time being, the senate are obsolete. A temporary measure, but until the empire is strong again, they will remain sidelined.'

Bishop Evagrius shook his head, cutting in before Valens could continue. 'Tread carefully, Emperor. The days of undiluted power enjoyed by men like Constantine are over. Your reputation is built upon meticulously nurtured relationships with bodies such as the senate. To alienate such entities could be a rash manoeuvre not easily righted.'

Valens kept his expression blank. The bishop could see what was coming at him and defence was his only card.

'It is not the senate that I wish to talk with you about today, bishop. Today the Holy See itself must also be removed from the sphere of political influence.' Valens watched as the bishop's jaw crunched between his pursed lips.

'I am dismayed, Emperor,' Evagrius uttered through his teeth. 'The church of Christ is your gift to the people of the empire. Take it away and you not only besmirch what it stands for but you pull the plug on the hard work of the last hundred years. Jupiter and the pagan deities are dying, Emperor, and it is the Arian Gospel, the word you put so much into supporting, which takes their place – your faith is winning!' Evagrius shook his head. 'To cripple it now could be to kill it altogether. What then? The West would sneer at us – tell us they were right all along, tell our people they are in the wrong half of the empire.'

Valens stifled a wry grin. Evagrius and his cronies had cursed the day Valens had announced Arianism over all other strands of belief, supporting the move only to stay in power. 'Bishop, as with the senate, your power will not be removed permanently. And it is only political power you will be denied; the religion does not need this to flourish.' Valens stood straighter as he sensed the thickening of the air between them. 'These are the rights of an emperor. I trust I have your full support, bishop?'

Finally, Evagrius spoke. 'Very well, Emperor. If this is your wish, then it is God's will.' He bowed his head momentarily. 'The Holy See will remain in place only to serve God and spread his word to our people. Call it politics if you will, but I would urge you to consider staying receptive to the carefully reasoned view of some of our most esteemed senators and, if I may be so bold, myself, as the bishop of God's city while you steer the empire back to greatness.'

'Advice is welcome, bishop. Interference is not.'

'Advice it is then,' Evagrius nodded.

Valens watched as the bishop smiled and then shuffled to the gates and onto the carriage that awaited him. His eyes narrowed. *Another snake in the grass.*

Evagrius grimaced at the beggars on the marketside gazing up at him as his carriage rumbled hastily back to his palace. 'Have your power, then, Emperor,' he muttered. 'It will last only until my new allies pour through the empire to lift me onto your throne.'

# Chapter 42

The hull of the huge vessel roared through the torrents of the Danube in the darkness. Wulfric remained in his favoured position at the prow, one leg up on the rim of the ship.

'We turn tomorrow at the delta and head back upriver,' he spoke to the beneficiarius.

'Perhaps we should wait here, Tribunus.'

Wulfric blinked and turned. The beneficiarius had not spoken. Instead, the slender, short, shaven headed Egyptian with the smooth dark skin by his other side had spoken out again. Menes. Wulfric turned back to the river.

'Wait? We have been waiting for days, Menes. I trust your master actually *has* a plan?' He asked, directing his question into the darkness of the river.

'You do not need to know all that my master has planned. That is why he sent me, his most trusted emissary, to accompany you.' He spoke with an African twang, eyeing the tribunus furtively through narrowed and kohl-stained eyes.

'An emissary for the bishop eh?' Wulfric mused. 'Well I doubt very much that's what you are, Menes. Just as long as you remember that I'm your master from now on. Any questionable advice you give me, any strange goings-on, even if you're not involved directly, it will be *your* throat that is cut,' he stated in a matter-of-fact voice. This was power, he thought.

Menes remained perfectly calm. 'By serving you, I also serve my master.'

'Don't test me, Menes,' Wulfric growled. Then a cry from the crow's nest cut him short.

'Ship to port!'

Wulfric craned over the stern. The darkness betrayed the dim outline of a white sail. A Chi-Rho symbol emblazoned on the linen.

'You see, tribunus?' Menes spoke softly. 'My master has all matters in hand.'

# Chapter 43

Throughout the afternoon, the newly acquired pirate vessel looped around the sea, picking up the remains of the Classis Moesica fleet along the way. They stopped every time they came across a stricken vessel to rig up those that were still vaguely seaworthy, and to take on board the crew of the vessels that were fatally crippled.

By evening, the sun dipped lazily into the water, casting a tired red glow across the surface; the remains of the Classis Moesica were reformed. Tribunus Nerva stood with Gallus, surveying the rag-tag collection of ships trailing in their wake. Thirty-four of the forty had been found and only twelve were anywhere close to full working order. A quick roll call on all ships had been taken; nearly four hundred men missing, most of them auxiliaries and legionaries. One in ten lost before they had even landed.

Pavo and Sura were sitting near the prow of the vessel. Still blackened and bruised, the two watched their commanding officers muttering; Nerva groaned and shook his head wearily over and again as they despaired over the remaining capabilities of the legion.

'Makes me nervous to see him like that,' Pavo muttered.

'Nerva?' Sura replied. 'They say he's a bulldog on the battlefield, but he's hardly the role model off it, eh? Mind you, I think Mithras himself would be shitting himself about now. Look at the state of us!'

'But it's rubbing off on the others,' he nodded to the huddle of recruits, their heads down, firing glances at the tribunus. Anxiety had gripped them all after the pirate captain's last words had spread around the centuries, but this was embarrassing. 'Gallus has kept his cool, at least.'

'The ice king? Course he has. I don't think he's ever felt emotion.'

They fell quiet and Pavo picked at his cold, hard salted meat ration as he spoke, flicking a string of gristle over the side. A bird swooped, catching the morsel before it hit the water. Sura and Pavo looked up, and then at each other.

'Was that a…' Sura started.

'A falcon!' Pavo yelped.

'Land ho!' the legionary in the crow's nest cried.

Night had well and truly fallen. Amalric and his men threw themselves through the undergrowth, blind and desperate. Having disposed of their exhausted horses the previous day, the eight men that remained of King Tudoric's Gothic army were now soaked in cold sweat and caked in filth as they fled like rabbits.

Barbed plants whipped across Amalric's face and his bare and flayed feet stung on the coarse rubble as the exhausted scramble continued after two days. Over a hundred of the dark riders raced up and down the hilly terrain, combing the area relentlessly. Of the original twenty Goths who had escaped the massacre in the blizzard, the dark riders had picked off five of them. Then, the Gothic mounts had tired and the fifteen had continued on foot, and the dark riders had slain seven more since then. The leader of the dark riders, who appeared frantic in his desire to exterminate what was surely an insignificant number of stragglers, wore the severed heads of each man caught around a loop in his belt – their stunned expressions staring out at the world they had just left.

Amalric heard yet another chorus of thundering hooves behind him. He dropped to his belly, into the freezing mud, and gritted his chattering teeth. The rider galloped past him. He was safe once more, for at least another few moments. Then he heard it – the feint crashing of waves, distant but unmistakable. This was it then, the coast – nowhere left to run. Death would have him soon enough.

Another bloodcurdling scream split the air. He spun onto his back to see the dull shape of one of his men impaled on the end of a spear like a fish, hoisted up from his hiding place by the stocky rider who cried in delight at his kill.

To the south it was, then. He made out the form of a grassy ridge through the blackness. Over there would be the clear, open beaches of Bosporus. He vowed to kiss the sands of his beloved homeland before they skewered him, and then leapt from prone to break into a sprint. He roared in defiance as he heard the Hun riders sweep round to lock onto him as he bolted for the ridge.

'Come on then, you dogs!' He boomed, turning to face them while still stepping backwards up to the lip of the ridge. 'Valhalla awaits me!'

Then he spun to continue his run, but stopped dead in his tracks at the sight on the beach that spread out before him.

Gallus again set his eyes on the dark and murky coastline, trying desperately to distinguish the shore from the water. Only the moon and the generous sprinkling of stars betrayed gloomy outcrops of rock and shimmering grass. Then something on the almost ethereal caught Gallus' eye; movement, he was sure of it!

Clamping his arm onto Nerva's shoulder, he pointed to the movement. He strived to catch anything at all that would indicate their position, when suddenly, below the area of movement, he saw it, the unmistakable froth of a lapping wave.

'Fire arrows!' He bellowed. The Cretan archers on the sibling galley, standing by crackling braziers, lifted their bows and let loose a volley. The sky glowed. And the smooth beach was revealed. 'Shore ahead! Prepare for landing,' he roared.

The calm of the night was rudely interrupted by the grinding arrival of the Classis Moesica as first the pirate flagship and then over thirty more vessels crunched onto the shingle.

When the ship finally ground to a halt, Nerva strode to the prow again, over to Gallus, who instantly stood to attention and saluted his tribunus, awaiting orders.

'First century, form a perimeter for disembarking,' Nerva boomed.

Despite their exhaustion, the bruised, dirtied and damp legionaries scrambled to collect their equipment before thudding, one by one, onto the wet sand, forming a line a short distance up the beach. This seemed a lot easier than the recon, Gallus mused. Maybe it was the presence of the tribunus, or maybe it was because they were all desperate to get off this creaking hulk.

'Excellent. You've got them well drilled.' Nerva said quietly to Gallus. Then, reverting to the booming tone of a tribunus, he cried over to Horsa; 'Captain, form up with a hundred of your riders and perform close proximity reconnaissance.' He turned back to Gallus. 'Let's see what we find out there before we get our heads down,' he grinned.

Gallus returned a stern nod. The tribunus was back to his enthusiastic best. Gallus wanted to believe they were in control, but his gut screamed danger.

Pavo straightened himself as the first century formed up. He eyed the line either side of him; Zosimus bore the expression of a confused animal growing steadily angrier as he fidgeted in a tiny mail vest which would be lucky to fit Avitus. Coincidentally, Avitus held the end of the line wearing what looked like a mail tent on his diminutive frame. He looked ahead to see Sura with the clutch of foederati who stood around Horsa; the captain led his detachment into a gallop and then disappeared over the grassy ridge at the top of the beach.

One by one, the ships of the fleet fanned out across the beach and the legion formed up on dry land. The auxiliaries, severely thinned from the storm, took their place on the wings, with the foederati outside them again. Nerva strode to the front to address them. He stopped and took a breath to speak out, when a spine-chilling cry pierced the air from behind the grassy ridge at the top of the beach.

The clomping sound of a solitary set of hooves raced towards the Roman line. The darkness worked its icy magic on the imaginations of the Romans, who instinctively braced in the direction of the noise. Pavo watched the shape emerge from the pitch. *Horsa!* But the Goth's face was wrinkled.

'Riders! Hundreds of them, we're engaged and we need infantry backup!' he cried. With that, he wheeled around and disappeared back into the darkness like a ghost.

Nerva's brow furrowed and he glanced to his left, where the archer auxiliaries stood. 'I want light on the field. Now!' He yelled. Then turning back to the centre of the Roman line, he continued. 'First cohort, advance – double line. Second and third, keep our perimeter around the ships.'

Pavo tightened his grip on his shield as Gallus underlined the order with a cry to advance. The first and second centuries formed the first line, with the third, fourth and fifth making up a generous second line. As they set forward, a rush of flaming arrows flew over their heads, and at last their surroundings were apparent. The crest of a small rolling hillock lay ahead where the sand and shingle petered out, and at its foot a mass of foederati were locked in battle with a large band of horsemen. The foederati were being pulled in every direction as their enemies swooped around and through them like birds of prey. They hacked and moved, never stopping to fight in one place. Pavo was transfixed on the shadowy riders as the century jogged forward. Soon the technique of their foes became clear. They made battle by sweeping into a victim with a large, curved slashing blade, only to continue on to safety before drawing an unusual composite bow, and firing off several arrows, on the move, hands free of the reins, while turning their horses to prepare for the next sweep into the fray. They would alternate this with lassoing their foes with a loop of rope, bringing them down and dragging them away from their group. Pavo felt a powerful chill as he watched another body being trundled through the brush like this, screaming and helpless, only to be encircled by the riders and butchered. He saw the dim glimmer of Sura's mail vest, fighting by Horsa, and mouthed a prayer to Mithras for his friend.

'Foederati, take the wings!' Gallus bellowed over his shoulder, seeing the number of riders they had to contend with.

When they were only paces from engagement, Pavo saw the rest of the foederati emerge from the wings like pincers to wrap around the battle. The foreign riders saw the jaws of the trap just as they snapped shut, but it was too late, the Roman circle advanced for the kill.

The riders fell back from the foederati, instinctively nocking their bows at the advance. In the split second before they fired, Gallus barked. 'Shields!'

Pavo ducked with the approaching line of the first century as they rippled into a wall of iron, and a chorus of rattling followed as the hail of arrows clattered against the shields, a peppering of gurgling cries and thuds marked out the handful that were too slow. As the first volley fell silent, Gallus, wary of the more eager men who may not have expected a double or triple volley of arrows immediately barked; 'Stay down!' Again, the arrows rained on the shields of the first – no cries this time, though. After the third volley, Gallus held his breath to the count of three to be sure, before screaming the advance. As one, the first century bristled up from its shield wall, and rolled forward in a perfect line. In the meantime, the foederati were powering into the flanks and rear of the riders.

The riders dropped their bows, whipping their swords free. They gathered into a pack and their momentum soared as they fell away from the foederati and towards the Roman line. Their leader urged them on, motioning to break through the infantry ahead of them.

Pavo gawped at the grimacing rider who galloped for him. Only his eyes sparkled in his shadowy frame, and then the raging symmetric scars on his cheeks flashed in the latest illumination of arrows. His straggly black hair and moustache whipped up as he cried, lifting his sword. Pavo was sure he could feel the horse's breath on his face when the order finally came.

'Split!' Gallus cried.

Like a trap door, the century drifted into widespread files, dampening the impact of the riders and sending them into the depth of the ranks. Pavo ducked from the sword swing of the rider, the tip of the blade glancing from his helmet. As the rider shot past, he crouched and hacked at the horse's legs. With a whinny of agony, the beast crumpled to the ground. Pavo shivered as the creature thrashed in pain, the rider crushed under its weight.

'Close!' Gallus roared.

As quickly as they had opened, the files closed in again like a flytrap, snaring the riders with their weapons. The few who broke free at the other end ran straight into the wall of the second line. They wheeled round, racing for the narrowing corridor of escape between the first and second centuries and the rest.

'Take them down!' Nerva cried, bringing the line of the legion forward with a swipe of his sword overhead. With a smash, the Roman lines crashed

214

into the flanks of the fleeing riders. Such was the impact that some horses leapt up and over the crush, leaping free altogether to gallop into the night. Those trapped in the pincers were quickly despatched, and in moments, the smash of iron on iron was replaced with a growing roar of victory. Pavo noticed Gallus still wore a frown.

'Prisoners?' Gallus bawled to Horsa.

'No prisoners,' Horsa gasped, gulping down the cool night air. His skin glistened with sweat and blood. 'A group of them at their front escaped, less than ten of them.' Wincing, and clutching a gash in his midriff, he paused for a moment. 'I've sent a detachment of fifty after them.'

'Again!' Nerva muttered. 'We're being starved of intelligence.'

'Those riders,' Gallus started, turning to Nerva, who wore the same dark look. 'They are the same dogs who shadowed us on the reconnaissance, sir.'

'I assumed so,' Nerva replied coolly. 'We need more information; we need to understand our situation. Our fleet is not even close to being seaworthy, if we are attacked, we cannot retreat to sea, and we don't know of anything other than our immediate surroundings on land...' Nerva screwed his eyes up and sighed, rubbing the furrows on his brow.

Gallus sensed his tribunus spiralling into panic. 'I'll order a double watch while the men set up camp for the night. I'll put the word out that we need any information going. But these men need rest – *we* need to rest – before we can tackle this situation,' Gallus offered.

'Agreed,' Nerva nodded wearily.

# Chapter 44

It was a balmy night. In the torchlight, the outline of a standard legion marching camp was now visible in the dry sand on the large, flat area to the right of the grassy hillock. Legionaries and auxiliaries sweated as they piled up mounds of sand and earth behind the rectangular ditch and rampart of the camp's outer perimeter. Other parties worked on stripping the terminally damaged ships to prepare a timber palisade perimeter to line the lip of the rampart, and to piece together basic watchtowers so the other men could work to complete the camp in the knowledge that their backs were covered.

Pavo winced as another blister burst on his palm. The red, stinging flesh left behind scraped against the pick axe handle mercilessly. He stopped to wipe his palm over his growing-in crop of dark hair, yelping as the bristles further aggravated the wound.

'Enough moaning, Pavo,' Quadratus muttered, flicking sand over Pavo with his boot with an evil chuckle. 'Quicker we finish, quicker we get some kip!'

He hadn't spent the night in a tent with his contubernium yet, but he had had the misfortune to sleep near Quadratus on the boat. 'Sleeping? In our tent? Depends if you're farting like there's no tomorrow,' he replied, scooping a basketful of dirt and sand and hurling it over his shoulder.

'Watch it!' Sura yelped as the sand tumbled over him.

'The big foederatus can't handle a lump of sand...' Pavo trailed off, his eyes widening. In the brush, just below the ridge at the top of the beach, a shape moved – like a huge snake, slithering on its belly. 'What the? Back me up,' he hissed, slapping Sura on the shoulder before leaping out of the ditch.

'Oi! Get your arse back here,' Quadratus howled behind them.

Ignoring Quadratus, the pair stalked forward. Crouching as he approached, Pavo was both repulsed and intrigued by the glistening form; it was a man, sparkling in wet blood and gore, but black with filth, too. Pavo whipped his fingers out and round, mimicking Gallus' pincer movement signal.

'What *is* that? I thought all casualties had been rounded up,' Sura hissed back. But Pavo was already off and running. 'Oh for...' he spat, setting off at pace to form the second pincer. The pair converged on the figure, leaping to land on an end each.

The entire camp dropped their tools at the roar produced by the filthy, bedraggled figure as they pinned him down.

'Easy!' Pavo yelled as the man thrashed below him. 'You're surrounded.'

At the sound of his voice, the man slackened. 'Roman?' he croaked.

'Too right, the empire's finest,' Sura barked, shoving the man's face into the dirt. 'Now on your feet!'

Pavo looked to his friend as he bound the man's hands. 'At last, a prisoner!'

Gallus frowned. The man was a Goth, not one of those riders. Even in his muddied and bruised state, the long blonde locks, the blue stigma on his jaw, the long, narrow features and towering height screamed Goth through and through. He eyed Pavo and Sura. They had broken from orders to apprehend the man, but there was no way he would reprehend them for doing so.

'Sir, he's playing dumb, but we reckon he was with the party of riders,' Sura offered enthusiastically. 'He might be able to talk for us and tell us a bit more about them?'

'Don't assume anything yet, soldier,' Gallus replied. 'Take a shoulder each and get him to the *tribunus'* tent. Zosimus, you back them up, he's a big bugger.'

Nerva's tent glowed a sleepy orange inside as the lanterns flickered. The sensation of shelter and warmth hit Pavo like a punch between the eyes;

instantly he blinked to stay awake, digging his dirt-packed nails into his palms at the same time. The tribunus stood over a table with a pile of soaked but legible maps together with the surviving senior centurions of the second and third cohorts. Each of them jabbered, eagerly advising the tribunus of their suspected location, both seemingly equivocal in their opinion.

'Tribunus,' Gallus announced firmly as he pushed back the tent flap to enter.

Nerva glanced up at first before slowly raising his head. He surveyed the captive with keen eyes. 'What have you brought me Centurion?' He asked, his voice tight with anticipation.

'He's a Goth sir,' Gallus spoke, 'Couple of our more alert recruits caught him sneaking across our lines.'

Pavo tried not to react, but felt himself stretch a few inches taller at the praise. Cold and indirect praise, but praise indeed from the centurion.

'Probably some local peasant lowlife,' Gallus continued. Pavo noticed Gallus' eyes dart to the Goth – the centurion was provoking him.

Until now, the Goth had watched, with his brow wrinkling as he tried to follow the Greek dialogue. At this slur, he started and glared at Gallus, his pupils dilating. He opened his mouth to say something, when Zosimus hammered his fist onto the man's jaw, spinning him into a dazed silence. Pavo stumbled backwards a step as the power of the blow went through him.

'Easy, we don't want to kill him,' Gallus hissed. 'The idea is to get him talking?'

Nerva cocked an eyebrow. 'A Goth? Those riders were no Goths.'

Gallus sighed. 'Exactly. And if these riders are on the peninsula, then we need to know what the situation is with them and the Goths. Remember what we saw, sir, on the reconnaissance? The mass Gothic migration, the war graves. There's a conflict here on a scale we never imagined.'

Nerva punched the desk, setting the lantern jumping. 'Pitched headlong into chaos, you mean. Does the senate ever do it any other way?' The tent fell silent as Nerva rubbed his raw eyelids and then pointed into the face of the Goth. 'Get him to talk, if it's the last thing he does!'

'Oh, he'll tell us how things stand here, sir. They've had years to familiarise themselves with the landscape,' Gallus grumbled. At this, a flash of anger rippled across the Goth's face.

'This place was only ever yours through conquest,' the Goth spat, his massive frame bristling. 'You must accept that we won these lands when you could no longer govern them.'

The tent fell silent and the tension swelled. Nerva stared stonily into the eyes of the Goth, who held the gaze and returned it with venom.

'A civilised tongue on a Goth this far into the barbarian wilderness?'

The Goth relaxed the furrows in his brow and sighed deeply, closing his eyes. 'We are not a people too proud to adapt and change when the world is obviously changing around us. Your culture still echoes in these lands. Or at least it did.'

Nerva seemed mesmerised by the Goth's words. 'What do you mean? What was happening out there tonight before we landed?'

'A people were dying,' the Goth winced, his head dropping into his chest.

'What people? Give me the facts and I'll give you a quick death!' Nerva snarled.

The Goth raised his head again – tears were streaming down his filthy and bruised face, trickling into the stubble that flecked his jaw and masked the blue stigma. 'My name is Amalric, prince and heir to the great King Tudoric...and probably the last living soul of the Greuthingi Kingdom of Bosporus, a kingdom that now lies cold and dead like its king.'

Nerva and Gallus shot a frown at each other. 'This land is overrun with your kin!' Nerva protested. 'Your Gothic hordes were plentiful not half a year ago.'

The Goth looked up again with an expression of incredulity. 'Since then they came like a plague. This land is defenceless now.'

Nerva finally let his frustration boil over. 'Do you expect us to stroll into a trap?' He spat, striding forward, nose to nose with Amalric. 'Do you think we will take the word of some beggar – claiming to be a prince – that the Goths are gone and the armies of Rome should abandon caution and march happily to claim this land?' His eyes bulged, red veins throbbing in their whites.

Gallus drew a sharp breath through his nose. 'That's not quite it – I think he's telling the truth, sir.'

Nerva stopped his rant on the spot, and fired a searing glare at his chief centurion. 'Gallus?'

'As I said, sir. The Gothic hordes we sighted. They were undoubtedly fleeing these lands…'

Nerva jumped in to cut him off. 'That's in their nature, Gallus! They roam; they don't take pride in cities and civilisation like the empire. But you don't seriously believe that they upped sticks and buggered off into the sunset, leaving this place for Rome to come and reclaim her?'

Gallus held his face firm and expressionless, biting back the temptation to snap back at his tribunus. For all he the qualities he admired in Nerva, the tribunus' stubbornness was challenging to say the least.

'Sir,' Gallus spoke gently. 'He's talking of a plague that has wiped his people out.'

'Disease?' Nerva eyed the filthy Gothic prisoner with a sneer.

'No, not disease. A plague of *conquerors*, sir. The dark riders tonight. We were assured there were handfuls of them, scattered raiders from Scythia maybe. But I feel it, I know it…' Gallus composed himself, '…I think that advice was so far off the mark. An army of conquest has scattered the Gothic Kingdom that thrived here just six months ago.'

'Gallus,' Nerva cut him off, 'You'd have to be talking about a force large enough to wipe out the Gothic armies. Do you know how preposterous that sounds? An army that size couldn't possibly hide from our intelligence.'

The Goth raised his head once more. This time his eyes had dried, and he wore a wretched smile across his face. His head tilted right back, and his mouth fell open as he let out an exhausted belly laugh.

'*Hunnoi*,' he called aloud, before laughing to himself once more. Pavo felt his ears prick up. The Goth continued. 'Mighty Rome does not know of the Hunnoi! I look forward to meeting you in the afterlife.'

Nerva scowled, then gave Zosimus the nod. The Thracian brought his tree trunk fists crashing down into the side of the Goth's head. Pavo staggered backwards again, shuddering at the crack of the Goth's cheekbone shattering. As the Goth fell into unconsciousness, the laughter stopped dead. Gallus sighed in frustration, glaring at the satisfied legionary.

Nerva growled under his breath. 'Put him in a tent and put a guard of three on him tonight. He's got plenty more talking to do.'

Gallus turned to Sura and Pavo. 'Take him outside and arrange a watch for him.' He nodded to the flap of the tent.

Pavo heaved at the dead weight of the man, his mind turning to the welcome prospect of bed and a solid, uninterrupted sleep, but something buzzed in his mind, nagging him. Then, as he pulled open the tent flap, a blast of cool air rushed over him. As if splashed with cold water his mind clicked into clarity, and he released his grip on the Goth, turning back into the tent; Gallus and Nerva, who had only begun a private conversation, stopped and turned to Pavo in confusion.

'Pavo!' Sura hissed behind him.

'Soldier?' Questioned Gallus.

'What are you doing, you've been given an order?' Quizzed Nerva.

'Hunnoi,' he whispered. Nerva and Gallus looked at each other with matching cocked eyebrows. Pavo shook his head. 'Hunnoi. The Goth spoke of the Hunnoi.'

'And?' Nerva replied wearily. At the tent flap, Zosimus swore and hoisted the Goth's unconscious body over his shoulder.

Pavo continued. 'Have you ever read Ptolamaeus sir?'

'The *strategos?*' Gallus replied.

'No. Claudius Ptolamaeus, the Geographer.' Still blank looks from Nerva and Gallus. 'The libraries of Constantinople are packed with his scrolls – I read a lot of them when I was a…when I was a bit younger,' he blushed. A brisk sigh from Nerva spurred him on. 'Ptolamaeus wrote of a people, nomadic horsemen, to the northeast of the Scythians, always moving southwest, called the Hunnoi, or the Hun. He spoke of them being intent on conquest…' He paused to consider his next statement, his eyes drifting into the lantern-light. '…and driven by a love of destruction. He said they lived to drink the blood of all who stood in their way.'

Nerva's eyes narrowed as a wind rippled around the tent. The lantern flickered in the momentary silence and then the tribunus nodded as if pulling himself from a trance. 'Report to my tent tomorrow after first roll-call. Despite your poor disciplinary record, you can be of some value, it seems.'

Pavo squirmed.

Nerva continued; 'And as we are in no fit state to continue talking tonight, I suggest we leave it at that. On your way, soldiers.'

They pushed out of the tent and trudged back to the neat lines of contubernia tents, now almost all pitched.

'Nice one,' Sura shook his head. 'I hope you know what you're doing?'

*Me, too*, Pavo prayed, glancing up at the crisp starlight above.

# Chapter 45

A mild breeze swirled around the campsite of the XI Claudia. Memories of the carnage and chaos of the night before had softened a little in the morning light as the refreshed legionaries milled around the tents and campfires, their eyes puffy from a precious but short spell of sleep. The night watchmen were now staggering to their tents to catch up on that precious commodity.

While the other seven of his contubernium bantered and ate outside, Pavo sat cross-legged inside the tent. After returning from Nerva's tent, he had collapsed into his cot and fell into the thick fog of sleep instantly, only for the dark dream of his father to wake him after only moments. This time, his father had beckoned him from the sandstorm, as before, until the empty wells of his eye sockets were fixed on him again. This time though, Father's lips had moved weakly. He had mouthed something…then grasped Pavo's forearm.

He had woken, bathed in a clammy sweat with a yelp, only for Zosimus to voice his disapproval in a string of muttered obscenities. After that, the morning meeting with the tribunus had played on his mind all night, and despite his body crying out for a long, thick sleep, he had lain, open-eyed, while the other seven of his contubernium snored incessantly, or in Quadratus' case, farted violently. But as he was in with the veterans, he dared not complain.

He brushed at the mail vest frantically – still the rust clung to it like shield glue. 'This is hopeless!' He hissed, throwing the weighty vest to the floor to begin on his dull, battered helmet again. He only had a few more moments to attempt to bring his gear up to a presentable state – then he would be standing in front of the tribunus of the legion, expected to talk and to advise. His stomach shrivelled. Ignoring the latest hoot of laughter from outside, he spat on the cloth and rubbed vigorously at the crown of the helmet. Yet all his work that morning had managed to bring up was a dull shine at best – even the tip of the iron intercisa crest was bashed into a smooth curve instead of the sturdy sharp fin it was supposed to be. He eyed the muddy heap that was his tunic and sighed, hanging his head and letting his aching hands drop to his sides. It was hopeless. He leant back, resting his head on the foot of his cot. His mind buzzed with the fog of three days awake. So tired, he thought. Calm settled over him and his mind swam with the memory of Felicia's warm body wrapped around him.

His eyelids fell shut.

Outside the tents of the first century, Optio Felix gulped at his broad bean stew, chuckling to the 'most-debauched-tale' contest that had been struck up on a whim between Zosimus and Avitus. Quadratus and two younger legionaries alternated grimaces and chuckles as each man put dignity to one side in front of their colleagues purely in the name of one-upmanship.

'…and then her grandmother joined in as well!' Zosimus offered, his face wrinkled in determination that his unsavoury story would beat anything Avitus could conjure up.

Gallus strolled towards the contubernium, refreshed and fed. His face dropped as he picked up on the details of the conversation, and he veered towards Felix. 'Sorry to draw you away from the hilarity, Felix.'

'On the contrary, sir, thanks. I think I might be about to hurl up my stew if I listen to any more of that! Honestly, have they no shame?' The optio winced.

Gallus chuckled. 'Where's young Pavo? Is all this soldier's talk too much for his guts? He's got a big meeting this morning – Nerva's tent.'

Felix nodded. 'Yes, he's in the tent, thinks he can spruce up his legionary gear so the tribunus will promote him to emperor.'

'Aye,' Quadratus chortled through a mouthful of stew, 'I told him you can't polish a turd!'

'Well he can turn up in silver armour if he wants, but if he isn't at the tribunus' tent before Nerva turns up then he's dead meat.' Gallus surveyed the camp, his eyes locking on to Nerva, making his way back to his own tent from the canteen area. 'Well he's late as it is. I'll sort him out,' he muttered, striding towards the contubernium tent. He grabbed the leather flap, and whipped it back to release a pungent cloud of sweat and farts. Coughing sharply, he pulled his head back, '*Mithras!* You boys need to see the capsarius – smells like a dead rat in there – you want pulled through with a spruce tree!' He spluttered to Felix and the rest. Quadratus stared back in a wide-eyed protest of innocence.

Ducking inside the tent, Gallus eyed the setup; all of the cots were empty and made up apart from one at the far end. The slumbering figure of Pavo, slung half on the cot and half off, snoring like a boar, brought Gallus' blood to boiling point.

Gallus gritted his teeth and booted the side of the cot. Nothing stirred. Again he booted the cot so the bundle of blankets flapped up in the air. Yet still nothing. Pavo's mouth hung open, his face a picture of total serenity.

Gallus crouched down next to Pavo's ear and rested his elbows on the side of the cot. 'Pavo,' he called in a honeyed tone. 'Breakfast has been served – care to join us?' At this Pavo's face curled into a full smile, and he grunted happily. Gallus' face twisted.

'Now wake up you little turd before I have you stoned to bloody death!' He roared at full centurion volume, whipping the cot up and over. Pavo tumbled onto the dirt floor, flapping at the edges of his blanket as he sprang to standing position in a flash. Gallus stepped backwards, his face pointed in rage.

'Reporting sir...duty calls!' The bewildered Pavo stammered.

'Duty calls? We've been here before, soldier. What in Hades kind of way is that to address your centurion, your primus pilus?' Gallus retorted, his voice laced with fury.

Pavo's eyes rolled as he adjusted to his surroundings and he blinked at the thick matter that had collected in them. Gallus allowed a deliberate silence to pass.

'Sir...I...oh, bugger,' Pavo grumbled as he shook his head clear. 'I'm sorry, sir I was only trying to...it will never happen again.'

'Too bloody right. We all had a long wait for sleep before last night, and you're no better than any of us,' growled Gallus. 'I'll tell Nerva you were waiting on me. So be outside the tribunus' tent by the time I've had my morning turd, Pavo,' he snapped. 'If you're late for that, the tribunus gets to hear about your performance.' Gallus whipped around to leave, and then barked back over his shoulder with the slightest hint of mischief, 'And sort your kit out – it's a bloody disgrace!'

As Gallus disappeared through the flap, Optio Felix came in before Pavo could take a breath.

'Get moving, Pavo!' He roared.

As Pavo stumbled around the tent to gather up his gear, his mind reeled – he burned with shame but felt an odd spark of...elation; the ice-cold centurion had torn strips from him, but the way he done it was almost human – like the way he would talk to the veterans. He grasped his kit in both arms and hopped through the tent flap into the brilliant blue morning. He just had time to note the circle of grinning legionaries awaiting him before torrents of icy cold water crashed into either side of his head and for a moment he felt as though he was underwater. His ears cleared and the sound of roaring laughter filled the void, and he blinked away to see the grinning faces of the legionaries of his contubernium. Spotting the buckets behind the backs of Avitus and several others, he pointed and opened his mouth, but before he could protest, Felix butted in.

'Pavo. Tribunus' tent. Remember what the centurion said – he's probably wiping by now.'

'I've got an appointment with the tribunus, let me through,' Pavo stuttered.

The larger guard of the two looked at his colleague with a raised eyebrow. 'Got an appointment, apparently.'

The smaller guard replied. 'Getting his teeth checked is he?' Before bursting into a snigger, shared by the other guard, who added.

'Aye, bog off, son, the tribunus is busy.'

Pavo felt his blood boil. The delayed rage from his rude awakening and subsequent humiliation now came steaming to the surface. 'The primus pilus sent me, and he's in a foul mood. So let me through or you'll have him to deal with!'

Suddenly, the first guard stood at attention, his face rigid, stepping to one side. 'Sorry, sir!' Pavo grinned – *that had shown him* – then moved one foot forward to enter the tent, when a hand slapped onto his shoulder.

'As you were, soldier,' Gallus nodded to the stiffened guard. 'So you made it,' Gallus observed coolly without looking at Pavo, beckoning him on through the tent flap.

Inside the tent was pleasantly warm, with a small fire smouldering in a brazier. Nerva's cot lay dishevelled, the blankets lay knotted across the floor - maybe the tribunus had had a restless night too? However, Nerva sat at his table in an incongruously crisp, white tunic, his jowls quivering as he muttered to himself, staring at the map. His hair was still wet and combed neatly back from washing, and despite a slight bagging under his eyes he looked a different man from the tired, irritable figure he had cut late into the previous night. Pavo glanced down at his own filthy kit – a stark contrast to the tribunus. At Nerva's side, the equally transformed figure of Amalric sat, free of chains, and wearing his cleaned blonde hair tied back from his narrow features. He too wore a clean legionary tunic and apart from the cuts and bruises on his face and arms, he looked alert and fresh. His expression was one of keen interest in the maps and papers that Nerva had spread across the table.

Pavo's sense of unease grew for a few moments, as the tribunus and the Goth remained engrossed. Then Gallus shuffled impatiently, before offering a polite cough to announce their presence.

'Gallus,' Nerva smiled. 'Come in, draw up a stool.' He beckoned with his hands before lowering his head into the maps again. Gallus drew a timber stool from the side of the tent and sat across from Amalric. Pavo stood still, realising his name had not yet been mentioned. He was not keen on committing another foolish mistake today.

Nerva traced a finger over the map and Amalric nodded in agreement and Gallus craned over the parchment for a better view. Looking up, Nerva began; 'We have some vital new information about our surroundings from…' he stopped, staring up at Pavo. 'What are you doing, boy? I told you to draw yourself a stool!'

Flustered, Pavo dropped his starchy legionary pose and stumbled over to the table, swiping at the remaining stool. *A boy*, he repeated over in his head, *they think I'm just a boy!* Then, pulling his seat in, he bashed the edge of the table, sending a goblet of water near the edge of the map spinning precariously on its base. Gallus quickly wrapped a hand around the stem of the goblet, and shot Pavo a look of wide-eyed disbelief, before turning back to Nerva, who took the goblet and placed it on the ground with a shake of his head.

'As I was saying, we have some vital new information about our whereabouts and the local populace now. Last night was fraught and some things were said which should not have been said.' Amalric looked both Gallus and Pavo in the eye in turn. 'Amalric has sworn loyalty to the empire. As long as we are an enemy of these...*Hunnoi*.'

'Can he prove his loyalty, sir?' Gallus spoke firmly, holding the Goth's gaze. 'I mean, the Goths have a history of backstabbing us. And remember Brutus, sir? We are already relying on them for nearly half our manpower – maybe we should be more cautious in allowing them to influence our strategy?'

Pavo's mind flashed with the gritty images of the battle in the countryside – Brutus would be with them now around this table were it not for the Goths.

'Amalric has made his intentions clear, Gallus. A common enemy has wiped out his people, and he offers us his knowledge of their abilities and weaknesses. And remember that the Goths who raid over the Danubius are of the Thervingi – pawns of that belligerent whoreson Athanaric.'

'But his very people,' Gallus continued regardless, stabbing an accusing finger at the Gothic prince, 'the ones on this land, the Greuthingi, slaughtered half my first century on the reconnaissance...'

'We were fighting for our lives!' Amalric barked – his tone was of frustration rather than rage. Gallus braced and the air grew thick with tension. 'I do not know of what happened to your century, but my people – and remember all of them are dead now – were being hunted like animals. Is it any wonder they attacked a unit of foreign soldiers on their land?' A silence ensued, Gallus and Amalric holding each other's gaze. Finally, Amalric continued; 'Turn your mind from distrust, Roman. Your people will be ground into the dust like mine if you cannot.'

Gallus raised his eyebrows and turned to Nerva.

'We are in no position to bargain, Gallus. Last night made it clear how thin our intelligence is on this sortie – we need him and he's offered to help. Bear with me on this one.'

Amalric spoke at Gallus across the table. 'Centurion – my race consists of heroes, dogs and nobodies, just like yours. I don't presume to justify the actions of the Goths you talk of who attacked your men. All I care about is finding and finishing those who slaughtered my wife – slaughtered her in front of my eyes.' The Gothic prince punched a fist into his palm, his words fizzing through clenched teeth.

Pavo watched as Gallus and Amalric stared at each other and something changed in the atmosphere around the table. The Goth's eyes were glassy, his lips trembled, and Gallus wore a wrinkle of pain on his face – a rare insight through the centurion's wall of iron. Another silence ensued.

'Then I'll go with that,' Gallus spoke at last. Then his face fell expressionless again as he leaned over the map. 'Let's see what we can thrash out.'

Nerva visibly relaxed and pulled his stool in closer to the map. 'Amalric has told me more than we would ever have worked out in months of roaming this peninsula aimlessly.'

Pavo and Gallus pulled in closer.

'First of all, and most importantly, we know where we are. Well you might have guessed we are on the Bosporus peninsula, but now we know we are here,' Nerva jabbed a finger into the map, at the right-most tip of the diamond-shaped peninsula, 'around halfway up the eastern coast. That storm must have been a mighty one – pushed us right past the headland!' he flicked his eyebrows up, eyeing the distance the fleet had been blown from the planned landing point at the southern tip. 'Furthermore, Amalric has gone into detail about the Hunnoi that we spoke of last night.' He glanced at Pavo, who nodded a little too enthusiastically. 'They are known more commonly in Scythia and beyond as the Hun.' Pavo felt the hairs on the back of his neck prickle. 'They came here just over six months ago, and since then they have stopped only to rape the settlements in their path. The Goths haven't been chased from this land...' Nerva looked each of them in the eye, his expression grave, '...they never left.'

An icy finger traced Pavo's spine, he touched the disc of the phalera medallion through his mail vest. This was life on the edge of a blade; the life Father had known until the last. He closed his eyes momentarily and imagined Father beside him.

'We've got our work cut out here, gentlemen,' Nerva continued. 'Clearly, the Huns primarily make use of the mounted unit, and they ride with a skill and dexterity that is simply...' Nerva shook his head in silence as he searched for the words.

Gallus puffed out a breath. '...it's impressive, sir. They ride as if they were born on the saddle.'

Nerva glanced at him, his eyes distant, before continuing. 'This is the key; they number over fifteen legions, some twenty thousand riders and infantry.'

'Twenty thousand?' Pavo gasped, unable to bite back the exclamation from his lips. 'They outnumber us five to one!'

Nerva, Gallus and Amalric turned to him in distaste.

'Perhaps a sentiment you should not share,' Nerva spoke firmly. 'It's not numbers that win battles. Roman military skill and bravery has seen the imperial armies over taller hurdles than this, boy.' Pavo felt the skin on the back of his neck burn. 'In any case, whether we should face them or not is a moot point as things stand. We have no means of retreat – the fleet is crippled. In any case, I'd rather not attempt to cross the sea again only to arrive in Constantinople with our tails between our legs, with a shattered navy and a hugely expensive failure of a mission as our only gifts to the emperor.'

Pavo felt smaller than a mouse. The tribunus was still pent-up with frustration inside and he had simply lit the fuse. Gallus cut in to spare him a thorough bollocking.

'So the question is – how do we make best use of our numbers? It has to be strategic engagement. We surely cannot afford a pitched battle against their number of cavalry on the open terrain inland.'

Nerva firmed his jaw.

Gallus had said it perfectly, Pavo thought – the same sentiment as his own but put tactfully. But the tribunus wanted the moment as his own; 'We will move inland, at a quick march, via a series of strategic points that Amalric has highlighted on our maps. We may be able to make use of the towns and ruined forts that are dotted around the landscape. This will allow us to do three things; measure the true size of our opponent's forces, collect the resources needed to repair our ships and finally,' he turned to Amalric, 'round up any Gothic survivors – Amalric has promised me they will fight alongside us on this. Ultimately, our goal is to reach the old citadel of Chersonesos as originally planned,' he drew his finger from the landing site to the bottom of the diamond, 'just to the west of the southern tip of the peninsula. It will take us about two to three days to get there. We have no idea of the state of the place – it's been off the trade routes for years because of pirates. It remains our best chance though – Amalric tells me that the citadel remains standing, with crumbling but functional walls. The place was a large Gothic trading centre until the Huns fell upon it three months ago – they tore everything of value from the place and moved on. Crucially though, the citadel has a dock. If we can establish a bridgehead there, we can repair our ships without fear of attack.' Nerva leaned in, drawing the other three closer to him. 'This is the crux – If we can get our fleet operational then we are no longer limited to infantry mobility. With our ships we can land anywhere around the peninsula and put these Huns on the back foot. Moreover, we can send for reinforcements should we need to.'

Gallus shuffled in his seat. 'I like the end result, sir, but it's getting there that worries me. How will we protect ourselves while mobile? If we get caught in the open by the Huns, a marching infantry column of just over two thousand – three hundred of those injured and sick – we would not stand a chance.' He glanced to Pavo.

'I can't disagree with you on that, Gallus, they'd cut us to ribbons.' Now Nerva glanced at Pavo, the merest hint of forgiveness traced his features. 'This is where we need to use the foederati wisely. They number at fifteen hundred going by this morning's count,' Nerva paused to double-check this on his notes, then he frowned, 'although that includes the Roman recruits who joined them, who will need to take some swift training in the arts of husbandry. They *cannot* slow down Horsa and his men. Between us, I expect

Horsa and his men will be the first to land on Hun spears, and any recruits lagging near the back...' Nerva trailed off with a shake of the head.

*Sura*, Pavo's skin prickled.

Nerva composed himself and continued; 'The foederati will split into several smaller detachments, each of which will perform a swift reconnaissance in each of the alternative routes to our next waypoint. The infantry will then proceed swiftly to the waypoint deemed safest, all the time covered by the foederati detachments. As for the fleet, well, all of our ships are crippled apart from the captured pirate quinquereme, yet we cannot abandon them. So the crew will rig them up as best as they can and make a series of short trips along the coast to stay as close to us inland as possible. One century of infantry from the third cohort will move up the coast to track the fleet's movement, to protect the landing point of each trip. When we reach Chersonesos, we should be able to bed ourselves in and find a supply of timber to repair the fleet, and then all of our options are open again. I realise this means that we are spreading ourselves even more thinly. Though frankly, I don't see that we've got any other options.'

'Then we must go with it,' Gallus nodded.

'I'm with you,' Amalric asserted.

All three nodded in conclusion and Nerva made to roll up the map. Pavo felt the familiar burn of words dancing on his tongue.

'What if the fleet doesn't make it to Chersonesos?' He croaked, gulping. The three scrutinised him – almost as if they didn't understand. 'I just mean – if the Huns are so mobile and so numerous, and they obviously have the jump on us in terms of our positioning and...'

'Get to the point,' Gallus cut in firmly.

Pavo stammered. 'The Huns could engage our fleet at any of the landing points along the coast. If they do – we're stranded.'

Nerva nodded, his jowls hanging in a stern sincerity, but the glint of panic was there, too. 'Problem noted, soldier. Do you have a solution?'

Pavo shook his head silently.

Nerva turned back to Amalric and Gallus. 'Once we have an accurate operational count, we can balance the centuries, and plan our order of movement.' He nodded as he eyed his plans one more time. 'By dawn tomorrow, we need to be on the move. The Huns know our position, so until then, we need a triple watch.'

Pavo was the last of the visitors to leave the tent. As he did so, Nerva grappled his arm. Pavo recoiled at the etching of barely disguised terror on the tribunus' sweat-soaked scalp and face.

'We all fear the same twists of fate, soldier. We can only ride the mount the gods provide us.'

# Chapter 46

A crowd gathered round the entrance to the sprawling Hun camp as a dozen weary riders trotted in. Sipping cups of tepid horse blood, chewing on raw meat, they searched for a sign from the lead rider, who rode with a motley collection of staring, severed heads hanging from his mount.

Apsikal kept his broad yellow face expressionless, lifted his head high and raised a clenched fist in the air. Roars of delight then erupted from the warriors and their families, greeting the sign of victory – a Hun could never be defeated.

Apsikal glanced down and watched the ground roll past, but couldn't hear the cheers. His head felt hollow as he contemplated his plan. *Lie and live, tell the truth and die.* He had told the truth the last time, and had barely escaped with the promise of death should he fail again. Only one Goth had slipped from their grasp, and he and his men's lives now rested on a ruse to disguise that fact. The crowd parted as they moved on through the seas of yurts, towards that of Balamber.

Balamber was sitting on the timber platform erected on the clearing at the tent entrance, basking in the warm morning sunshine. His eyes were drawn to the approaching commotion, narrowing to identify the source. When Apsikal's form shuffled humbly before him, Balamber's expression hardened. Apsikal slowed to a halt and dismounted, his men following suit. Silence fell over the thousands who crowded round to view the meeting.

'I have succeeded, Noble Balamber,' Apsikal gasped, his head still bowed. An excruciating silence ensued, and Apsikal shivered as he felt the invisible dagger plunging for his neck as he stared into the earth below, but no, that would be too quick. Still nothing – he risked a glance upwards. The silhouette of Balamber craned above him with the sun casting a glaring halo around his form.

'What happened?' Balamber spoke softly.

Again, Apsikal looked up to address his leader, squinting his eyes at the blinding sunlight. 'We hunted down the Goths, and we exterminated *all* of them...' He pointed to the flank of his horse and that of his second-in-command – both bore rope lassos with twenty rotting, gaping heads strung together, misted eyeballs staring out at the world they had once known. '...every single one.' His voice trailed off as Balamber stepped slightly towards the front edge of his platform and rose up to his full height. His form seemed to fill the sky. The noble eyed the grotesque specimens, and Apsikal felt his stomach lurch as he did so. He followed his leader's eyes over each one; nineteen blonde and white-skinned expressions of horror, and one last one – features mutilated beyond recognition. Balamber's eyes stopped on this one. Apsikal shot a glance at the head and then his leader – Balamber's fists gradually balled and then his moustache twitched ever so slightly. Apsikal gulped.

'To fail is one thing,' Balamber mused with a quizzical tone, 'but to lie to your noble leader?'

Apsikal felt a distant spark of realization – the most horrible end was coming for him at the speed of the fastest mount. He fell to his knees. 'No, we have them, all of them...' his words tailed off.

Balamber leapt down from his platform, thumping into the dirt to tower over the cringing Apsikal. He stalked over to the mutilated head, grasped it by the tufts of hair remaining on the bloodied scalp, and wrenched it up so the crowd could see. 'Fine skin for a Goth, is it not?' He roared, stretching the one remaining untouched patch of skin on the neck – a dark-yellow complexion.

Apsikal felt fear thunder through him, 'We may have recovered the wrong head – there were many bodies. It was...' he stopped short as a stone smashed against his forehead.

'Die like a warrior, you grovelling fool!' The thrower cried from the crowd. Apsikal tasted the metal wash of blood coursing from his nostrils.

Balamber's face was swept over with a black expression. 'Enough!' He roared to the crowd. 'Apsikal will not be harmed...'

Apsikal looked up, his heart slowing to a controlled thunder. There was a chance he could survive! His mind scrambled as he searched for something to build on. 'The Romans have landed! It was pitch-black when we clashed, however, we estimate a number of some three thousand and...' Apsikal looked up again and tried to gauge his chances of being spared. '...and we can't be sure about this, but their fleet looked crippled.'

Balamber's face curled into a mean smile. 'Wrecked?' From deep in his belly, a terrible grumble erupted into a cackle. 'The Roman Senate send their fleet out into a storm and then the pirate dogs honour their word to thin their remaining number. The gold of Rome shapes this world – and soon it will be in our hands! A sweet victory will be ours!' He lifted his arms aloft and the assembled thousands roared in approval. He glared down at Apsikal. '*Tengri*, the mighty sky god, is about to open many doors for us. Doors to power and riches that will see us as unequalled masters of the world.'

Apsikal's heart slowed further at Balamber's words – he made to stand once more. As he rose on one knee, Balamber cocked his head to one side, with a calm expression settling on his face. 'No, you should not be harmed, Apsikal. You should be rewarded...'

Balamber wheeled away to ascend his platform again. Apsikal stood up and felt elation course through his veins. Then Balamber clicked his fingers.

Apsikal's eyes bulged at the clunk of the metalworking urn behind him and his stomach leapt and turned. Two pairs of hands clamped onto his shoulders and forced him back onto his knees, and the crowd roared in expectation. Grinning faces were mixed with horror and intrigue all around him. Apsikal glanced behind him – the remainder of his riders were systematically having their throats cut, toppling to the ground one by one. Those who were lucky enough to have their spinal cord severed in the process remained motionless. The rest suffered the indignity of scrabbling, haemorrhaging blood into the dirt as they asphyxiated. Apsikal felt his stomach heave again and his bowels loosen, then his attentions were unceremoniously ripped back to his own fate when a pair of hands wrenched at his hair, yanking his head backwards. He felt a bone in his neck snap; such was the ferocity of the movement. Another fist rammed a knife into his clenched bite, and prised his jaws apart, sending teeth and blood arcing out like some vile fountain. Then, like the rising of a terrible sun, a ladle of glowing molten metal rose into view and the bloodthirsty howls of the crowd simmered down into silent expectation.

'You have earned your reward, Apsikal,' Balamber purred, 'savour every last drop.'

Apsikal stared hopelessly into the cobalt sky, pleading to *Tengri* the sky god, as unearthly pain coursed into his chest. He felt the blackness of death rush in as his body disintegrated from within.

# Chapter 47

The outline of the now deconstructed beach camp was still etched on the sand and shingle, but now the XI Claudia were formed up on the plain across the grassy ridge. The afternoon sky was azure streaked with grey, a mild breeze flitted across the tall grass and further inland and the forests hugged jagged peaks still snow-capped from the winter.

The five divisions of the foederati had thundered off into the distance shortly after roll call, diverging along the five suggested routes of passage supplied to Tribunus Nerva by Amalric – valleys, plains and hill-tracks. Having deconstructed the camp, the three cohorts of the legion, the auxiliaries and the train of pack mules waited, ready to move off as soon as the foederati divisions returned and the best route was decided. Meanwhile, the eighth century of the third cohort had been detached and waited by the shore, ready to shadow the movements of the hastily patched-up fleet.

Front and centre, Pavo was standing with the veterans of his contubernium. He watched the cloud of dust from Sura's departing foederati division gradually settle.

'Your friend – good rider is he?' Zosimus nudged him.

'So he says…'

'Aye,' Zosimus chuckled, '…but he's full of horse shit, eh?'

Pavo grinned. But inside he prayed to Mithras that Sura hadn't bitten off more than he could chew.

'No way that I'd ride with them,' the big veteran scowled, tearing a piece of dry meat to chew, 'I don't trust those buggers as far as I could throw a plumbata.'

Pavo looked up to him. He thought of the brawl at *The Boar*. The Goths were mixed bag allright. If only they were all as personable, as warm as Horsa. 'They've got a good man for a leader.'

'Aye, good lad, that one,' Avitus butted in. 'Still a Goth, though.'

'I don't envy him; imagine having to control that lot – two thousand of them. Even the ones under him, the *officers*,' Quadratus chuckled. 'I thought Zosimus was a thug, but they're something else.'

'A thug? Watch it or I'll rip your moustache off!' Zosimus grunted, shuffling nervously.

'They've been gone for a long time, eh?' Pavo noted before Quadratus could deliver an equally witty riposte.

'Aye, what's bloody keeping them?' Avitus moaned.

'Hold on,' Zosimus batted an arm across them, nodding to the front of the legion. Gallus stood with Amalric while Nerva strode across the front ranks. 'Here comes the speech!'

'Beautiful isn't it?' The tribunus boomed, sweeping his hand back over the land. A coordinated ripple of armour filled the air as the men straightened to attention. Nerva grinned and nodded.

'That's more like it!' He continued. 'Straighten up, and look to the horizon. They might call us limitanei, men, but we are at the furthest frontier any Roman troop has seen for hundreds of years. The comitatenses can patrol their zones safely within the empire's borders, but today it is we – each and every single one of us – who are lions!'

Zosimus cocked an eyebrow and nodded. Pavo couldn't hold back a smile as the soldiers rumbled in agreement. Nerva had never come across as the most tactful of speakers, he thought, but the man was working the crowd here, for sure.

'Your commanding officers will have told you about the threat we face. These Huns are strong horsemen. You saw them when we landed. They are skilful fighters, yes.' He nodded, sweeping his eyes across the front line. 'And they are exactly what we specialise in. Like the Gauls, like the Carthaginians, like the Goths…' His voice trailed off as he set his eyes on Amalric.

Avitus groaned. Zosimus sighed. Pavo cringed – thank the gods the foederati were off on reconnaissance.

'…and the Goths will join us on our glorious march…' Nerva's eyes darted around; all but the front ranks seemed to have missed the slip. 'So let's stride forward like the lions we are! Let's take the fight to these Huns and make sure they don't die before they know of Rome!' With this, Nerva brought his sword up above his head and belted out a thundering cry. The air exploded as the legionaries brought the hilts of their swords crashing down on their shields and roared in joyous appreciation. Pavo breathed a sigh of relief for his tribunus.

Timed to perfection, a foederati division appeared on the horizon, and with no signal of danger. In just a few moments the mood of the legion had been catapulted into optimism and hope, the grey smears of cloud had cleared and the sun's warmth bathed them.

Pavo scoured the approaching division until he recognised the dark-red leather armour and eyepatch of Horsa, then he quickly checked for Sura. Sure enough, the chubby, red-cheeked face showed up, clearly exhilarated at his sortie, and true to form, he was racing neck and neck with his commanding officer.

'Clear!' Horsa barked to the waiting legion as his horse drew up near Nerva, Gallus and Amalric. On the horizon, the four other scouting parties appeared and, one by one, they drew up to announce the safety of the routes they had inspected.

Nerva rolled up his map and turned again to face the legion. 'XI Claudia, move out!' He roared, motioning in the direction Horsa's unit had come from. The chief centurions of each century barked in echo to their men. The silver eagle carrying the fluttering ruby-red bull standard of the XI Claudia rose from the front line of the first century and another roar met its ascension.

Pavo took a deep breath, and marched.

# Chapter 48

Constantinople baked as the sun dipped towards the west. The land walls caught the best of the late afternoon heat. The stone bulwark, running across the peninsula neck, raised a stony palm to all and sundry that approached the city along the magnificent *Via Egnatia*, the highway that snaked all the way from distant Illyricum to this, the magnificent Saturninus Gate. Lavishly corniced in gold, studded with gemstones, and watched over by gilded statues of emperors and the old gods, this portal into the city was truly 'The Golden Gate' as they had taken to calling it. And this was just the first of the titanic markers of empire the city presented, giving this *Nova Roma* her might and beauty.

Bishop Evagrius strolled out of the stairwell and onto the battlements, basking in the warmth as he surveyed the countryside. Trading posts and inns dotted the sides of the highway as travellers stopped to lighten their purses and slake their thirst. Further back from the road, farming settlements poked from the wheat fields, with slaves swarming through the crops, toiling to finish their quotas before the dusk arrived. All this splendour, he mused, all that lay over every horizon was in the hands of only one man, a man who no longer played the dice of politics. The *Imperator*, as he called himself, an echo from the days of the pagan weakness, when they could not rule by democracy, and eventually proved they could not rule by despotism. Added to this, Evagrius gritted his teeth, the fool chose to defy the church and lean to the Arian preachings. So sad, he shook his head, so much shared wealth could have been had if the emperor had just towed the line like some of his predecessors. Evagrius rested his hands on the battlements to gaze over a group of farmers driving their carts towards the gate below. These people could be ruled with the power of faith. Fear of God and fear of the afterlife would control them. More importantly, he grinned, faith in God's sole representative…no, not faith, but complete obedience, would bring these sheep to their knees.

He spotted the solitary figure of the wall guard captain and wiped the grin from his face as he strolled over to him. The minions of the wretched army still clung to Jupiter, Mars and damned Mithras, but the fearful citizen inside these soldiers feared the new God as much as anyone else.

The captain shot a furtive glance at the bishop as he approached, but pulled his eyes front again quickly. Evagrius stopped behind him and sighed. The captain turned, his face creased with panic.

'Your Eminence,' he mumbled.

Evagrius smiled. The presence of the bishop or even more lowly members of the Holy See struck fear into most citizens.

'Can you feel the warmth in the air?' He asked gently. The captain looked puzzled.

'Your Eminence, it certainly is a fine evening.'

'Yes, the sun is warm, but it's more than that you know,' Evagrius mused.

The captain nodded, but a tell-tale wrinkle on his brow betrayed his continuing unease.

'It's the favour of God that sheds such a warm light on this city. You and your men are guardians of the city of God.'

The captain smiled. 'And we're honoured to be in such a position, sir…I beg your pardon, Your Eminence.'

Evagrius laughed heartily. 'It doesn't matter what you call me, Captain, just as long as I know you are with me, with God, when called upon. And as God's representative here in his good city, you should feel free to talk with me.'

'Absolutely, Your Eminence. And equally, anything we can do to be of service to you or to please God, we will be delighted to do so.'

Evagrius smiled. 'Simply by protecting his city you and your men provide an invaluable service to God. I would appreciate it greatly if you could continue to do so.'

'Certainly, Your Eminence. Consider it our highest priority.'

'And if you could spread the word amongst the wall's guard centuries, and to the docks also. I will know of your good work, captain – you must believe that.' The captain looked worried again. 'So I would be most pleased if you could distribute this amongst your men.' Evagrius produced a bulging canvas purse from his robe.

'Your Eminence?' The captain frowned.

'Obviously, you would do your duty in any case. But should the situation arise,' Evagrius' eyes narrowed as he dropped the purse into the captain's hand – the gold coins inside clinking on impact, 'I trust I can count on your support when called upon?'

A bead of sweat escaped the captain's brow and he licked his lips, feeling the weight of the bribe. 'Your Eminence, I...' his eyes darted around the battlements.

'Fear not, captain, you are doing the right thing.' Evagrius rested a hand on the captain's shoulder. 'How can it be wrong to serve God?'

'Consider it done, Your Eminence,' he gulped, tucking the purse into his belt.

Evagrius smiled and turned away towards the stairwell. The time would come, and soon, where the city would be at his mercy. An army of God was forming beyond the empire's borders, and he alone controlled them.

# Chapter 49

Every season seemed to have touched the valleys of Bosporus at once. A summer heat swirled in the air over the spring green grass carpeting the valley floor that the legion marched upon; lush pine forest coated the horizon inland to the right of the column, punctuated by towering grey mountains, capped in pure white and a tang of pine danced on the gentle breeze.

Pavo eyed the peaks and then looked to his left to see the shimmering waters of the Pontus Euxinus, slipping gradually between the green slopes as the legion moved inland. He tapped his fingers onto the disc of the phalera briefly, wondering if he would see the waters again.

'Pavo,' Zosimus grunted. 'I hear you know your onions about these Huns? Felix says you've been brown-nosing Nerva about it.'

'Eh?' Pavo shook his head, glowering ahead at the optio. 'Just stuff I've read.'

Zosimus looked entirely unimpressed. 'Well, let's hear it then?'

Avitus and Quadratus marched a fraction closer to get within earshot.

Pavo sighed, remembering the recruits swapping horror stories about the Huns on the deck of the *Aquila*. *Keep it down-to-earth*, he thought. 'Well, there is a section in the library in Constantinople that's stuffed full of scrolls from old writers. There's a bundle from a geographer, an Egyptian called Ptolamaeus, who knew a lot about the people outside of the empire. And just by chance, he'd been in contact with them – the Huns. He wrote about how they lived; always on horseback, sleeping on their horses even! They don't settle either; he wrote about them being far to the north and east of here, but he reckoned that because of some power struggle way to the east, it was only a matter of time before the Huns came west and arrived at the empire. Anyway, that's really all I know.'

'I think it's a safe bet that that is a latrine-load more than we know put together and doubled, Pavo,' Avitus mused less than subtly.

'Aye, but what about their armies – do they have legions, what do they do with prisoners, all that stuff?' Zosimus quizzed.

Pavo's mind flashed with the memory of one scroll. Etched on it was a scene of a battlefield; the Huns had fought, won, and left behind a curious and massive dark heap in the centre of the plain, circled by carrion birds. He looked straight ahead. 'They don't take prisoners.' The three listening in fell back in an uncomfortable silence.

Finally, Zosimus shot back. 'Well, they'll be tasting iron soon enough.'

Quadratus and Avitus replied with a throaty chuckle.

Just then a murmur of excitement rippled through the column. The foederati scout up ahead waved frantically.

'Theodosia, dead ahead!' Gallus boomed over his shoulder, raising a hand. 'Full halt!'

Pavo craned his neck to examine the plain below; a squat stone wall ringed a collection of thatched and tiled roofs – once a Roman town, now Gothic. But something wasn't right – the place was still, lifeless. The buzz of excitement had died as the rest of the column saw the tell-tale signs; the walkway on the wall was deserted, no smoke rose from the chimneys and no flag or banner flapped on the pole in what looked like the town centre. Amalric had talked of his people having been exterminated – but this looked as if they had simply vanished. Something was terribly wrong. Then he spotted the dark circle of vultures spinning in the grey sky above.

Gallus turned to the column and eyed the front line of the first century. 'Pavo, Avitus, Zosimus, Quadratus. You're going ahead to scout for any danger – stealth is the key here. I don't want the legion stumbling into a trap, so keep your heads down and let's see what the story is in there. Avitus, you have the lead.'

'Sir!' Avitus barked stepping forward. 'Right, ladies, drop your packs and spears – swords and shields only for this. Move!'

The three leapt forward at the diminutive Avitus' incongruous roar.

'Thinks he's a bloody centurion,' Zosimus grumbled.

'Pipe down, Zosimus,' Avitus snapped over his shoulder as they jogged ahead, doubled over while flitting through the tall grass.

Pavo longed to see a trader, a child, a guard, anyone as they thudded down to the dirt trail approaching the main gate. But nothing. The gate itself lay ajar, but not far enough to see inside.

'Sir?' He gasped.

'Pavo – keep your voice down.'

'Sir,' he whispered, 'Should we look for an alternative entrance?'

'Gate's open – why should we? You reckon it's a trap?'

'It just seems…too easy?'

Avitus continued his jog, gritting his teeth. The other three kept with him until eventually he relented and stopped. 'Fair point. You don't just leave the town gate open, eh? All right, what are our options?'

'We could chuck a rope up the wall?' Quadratus suggested, stroking his moustache.

'There's got to be a guard entrance. And if the main gate's open that might be too?' Pavo offered.

'Yep,' Avitus scanned the stonework. To the left edge of the town, a small, arched timber panel presented itself. 'Okay, Pavo. Your idea so you're up – get in there and give us the thumbs up from the wall. Then we'll come in the main gate. If we don't see you, we know you've had it.'

Pavo gulped as a pang of cool terror grasped his heart. 'Me?'

'Don't be a fairy about it,' Zosimus growled. 'Look on the positive side – there could be nobody in there and we could all be sitting down eating roast boar and supping ale before sunset. Now get a move on!'

'Oi! I'm in charge,' Avitus hissed.

'I should've been put in charge over you two clowns,' Quadratus sighed.

'You? You couldn't organise a hangover in a wine cellar,' Avitus snapped.

Pavo stepped away from the quarrelling three. *Sod it*, he thought, stalking forward in a crouch towards the guard door.

'Attaboy, Pavo,' Zosimus hissed after him.

The wall was the height of three men and the mortar was flaked in disrepair, but there were no signs of siege damage – if it had fallen to the riders then it had not been taken by force. He slowed as he reached the guard door. Nudging the timbers with his shield boss, the door creaked back on its hinges, sending a shiver up his spine. The gloom before him offered up only the first few stone stairs of a staircase, no doubt leading to the battlements above, then darkness prevailed. *Next time, I keep my mouth shut.*

He stepped into the shadows. Looking up, a tiny square of white light presented itself as the doorway onto the battlements. *Here we go.* He stalked up each stair carefully, tapping his sword flat ahead of him like a blind man. The staircase wound upwards squarely and he broke into a hop as his confidence grew along with the white light above. *A wave or the middle finger,* he wondered, *what should I give them as the signal?* He chuckled as he sprang the last few steps. Then the breath stopped in his lungs and his heart lurched. A glint of iron appeared and disappeared just above him.

Time stopped as he stood frozen in the darkness, his thundering heartbeat filled his head. Then a scream filled the stony enclosure, echoing from the walls like a thousand warriors, and Pavo ducked behind his shield instinctively – just as a sword hammered into its rim, sending a shower of sparks through the air. In the instant of illumination, the twisted features of a scar-faced warrior appeared.

'What the,' Pavo gasped, steadying himself. Then, from behind him, footsteps thudded up the stairs and another war cry pierced the air. 'Oh bugger!' He cried, swinging his sword into the blackness behind him and butting his shield out above him. Then a sword whipped past his chest, scraping his armour and another hacked into the stair by his ankle. Pavo threw down his sword and shield and leapt from the stairwell –clawing out at the blackness, his fingers whipping through the air in the brief moment of weightlessness. Just as he braced himself for the plummet onto hard stone below, his fingers snapped onto something and his body slapped against the stonework – the other side of the stairwell. His attackers roared as they smashed swords with each other.

Pavo pounced on the instant of confusion, pulling himself up, feeling around the floor for the stairs. Sprinting upwards, the square of white light was just above. He lurched up until it grew and enveloped him as he burst out onto the battlements, gasping. *The signal!* He panicked, rushing for the edge of the wall, but there was nothing; just grass where he had left them. Just then, his two attackers bundled out into the walkway too. They stalked towards him, flat yellow faces grinning as they noted his lack of weapons. Pavo whipped out his dagger, backing off. The warriors were both built like bulls – short and stocky, with flowing dark locks and wispy moustaches. They wore layers of skins and leggings, with crude linen armour over their chests and held long, straight swords in their hands. Filling the width of the battlement, they forced him backwards. Pavo craned to see over the parapet. He whipped his hands up, waving, and roared – surely Avitus and the lads would be watching, but still the plain lay empty. The Huns barked at each other in their jagged tongue, agitated, and then one relented, turning to roar out across the town. From the streets, the clopping of horses' hooves rattled out, a Hun rider raced towards the main gate, lowered in his saddle – then burst from the gate and thundered across the plain.

*Bugger!* Pavo hissed to himself as the rider shot for the horizon. Then he turned to his two attackers, raised his dagger, and remembered his own words to Zosimus only moments ago. *They don't take prisoners.* His legs wobbled as he staggered back. Then he thumped into the end wall of the battlement – the breath lurched from his lungs. The Huns smirked and ran for him.

Pavo slid to the ground, kicking out towards the nearest Hun's gut. He felt the man's ribs crack as he fell backwards. Then the glistening sword of the other Hun arced down for his neck. Pavo, penned in at the corner, could only brace himself and tear his dagger across the path of the blow. A metallic screech sent sparks flying as his dagger caught the blow and sheared in half. The shard of dagger blade sclaffed up and across his knuckles, gouging deep into the skin and chafing the bone.

Roaring in agony, instinct took over and he sprang up to headbutt the momentarily vulnerable Hun, catching him right on the nose. A sickening crack rang out and the Hun moaned, dropping his sword. Pavo dipped to take the weapon, bringing it up to rip it across the Hun's midriff – but the linen armour rendered the blow harmless and the sword flew from his hand into the town below. Jumping backwards the Hun reached for the bow slung on his back, wrenching back the shaft and the razor-sharp bone tip. Pavo's eyes widened – it was now or never.

As the Hun's fingers slackened on the arrow, Pavo leapt, punching upwards to knock the bow offline. The arrow rocketed upwards and he brought the stump of his dagger ripping into the Hun's throat. With a gurgling scream, the warrior toppled from the battlement into the town below. Pavo's limbs felt leaden as he staggered back from the edge, then he heard a dull growl behind him. His stomach lurched as he spun to face the noise; the sweating, pinched features of the first winded Hun stared back at him, teeth gritted as he pointed his sword into Pavo's face.

'Your life is over, Roman. Just like the Goths,' he nodded towards the town centre.

Pavo glanced over, but could see nothing behind the taller buildings in the way.

'They opened their gates, expecting mercy – they thought we might let them live as slaves. They were wrong! Now you will join them. *Tengri* wills it...'

A distant whirring caught Pavo's ear; iron...coming his way.

'Duck!' he heard behind him.

Dropping to his knees in lieu of any other strategy, Pavo felt a spatha zip over his head from behind, then plunge into the Hun's neck, sending a torrent of dark blood into the air. The warrior tumbled into the town below, lying broken next to his comrade in the bloodwashed packed-earth street. Pavo turned to see Avitus at the end of the battlement.

'What kept you?' He stammered.

Pavo stood well back as the legion filtered into the town centre. Zosimus, to his immediate right, was still pale at the sight of the mountainous feast that awaited the vultures.

All around the flagpole. Pink limbs and shards of white bone projected from the grotesque pile. Severed heads of men, women and children, locked in spasms of pain and gaping emptily into the distance. All this was coated in a dark-crimson sheath.

Amalric looked at the scene with the cold expression of a man who had seen the same – and worse – many times over. He stood with Nerva in a solemn silence.

'We're always one step behind, eh?'

'Sir?' Pavo blinked, turning to Gallus beside him. However, the centurion's gaze was lost in the mountain of gore.

Then a lilting harmony rose up, a soft voice gliding through a foreign lament. Amalric. Horsa came to stand beside him, placing an arm on his shoulder.

Pavo looked around the circle. He thought of Tarquitius' grim prophecy.

*You will be dead within the year, boy, I can guarantee it...*

# Chapter 50

Night fell on the coast of Bosporus as the eighth century of the XI Claudia bedded into their regulation ditch and stake encampment – a miniature of the standard legion camp. Centurion Aquinius had chosen the site carefully. The features offered by the location, on the side of a plain, were a sheer cliff face to the immediate west, a clear view to the beach, the sea and the disembarking fleet to the south and an open vista of the inland horizon to the north and east.

He had been happy to be trusted with the coast watch task – a relatively plum sortie; far less likely to run into riders on the beach, and the boats were a handy option should they find themselves in trouble. Nothing could take them by surprise here; he smiled in satisfaction, lifting his water skin to take a cooling swig, eyeing the setting sun.

Twenty sentries stood watch at regular intervals along the palisade, while the other sixty huddled around the braziers at each tent, gratefully munching boiled goat stew. It had been a stroke of luck to come across a deserted farmstead, still populated with fat livestock. Now after their day of quick march across boggy terrain, this was the perfect tonic. The fleet had cruised smoothly, with a gentle wind providing the perfect pace to stay level with their land escort. Now, like a train of ants, the crew from the fleet filed up from the beach towards the camp to eat and to gather salted beef, pulses and fresh water for the following day. Only the skeleton crew of the giant pirate quinquereme remained at sea, as a contingency measure against a naval attack. So far, so good, Aquinius thought as he tore a piece of bread from his ration.

The sentries at the gate of the camp shuffled in agitation as the aroma of cooking meat wafted past them. They examined the inland horizons, keen to find any distraction until their shift finished. A small cloud of dust puffed up from the eastern plain. Both men jumped to attention in alarm.

'What is it?' The first sentry hissed, bringing his spear forward.

'Will you take it easy? Wait a moment and let's see what it is before you declare war...' his companion spat. Then he, too, screwed his eyes up. After a moment his shoulders dropped, and he relaxed his grip on his shield. 'Look, red leather armour - it's the *foederati* messenger,' he chuckled, 'what are you like?'

A lone *foederatus* was tasked with keeping the shore century in communication with the main body of the legion. A heartbeat between the two parties, and it had worked well. The billowing blonde hair of the rider settled as he slowed on approaching the camp entrance. Then he saluted the sentries dutifully.

The sentries looked at each other in mischief. 'What's the password?' The first sentry called.

'You've let me in twice already, don't be ridiculous!' He moaned in a Gothic twang.

The sentries simply grinned and stood firm.

'Teutoberg!' The *foederatus* sighed.

Aquinius wandered among the legionaries, offering conversation and encouragement to the fresh and unfamiliar faces of the recruits who had flooded his century only days ago. He supped at his second course; an urn of broad bean broth, allowing the salty aroma to curl into his nostrils as his eyes passed over the fleet crew trudging back to the beach to board their vessels again. He felt his eyelids leaden at the final traces of sunlight slipping from the horizon above the cliffs. He sipped and then stopped, his brow furrowed – a rather frantic figure was waving from the deck of the quinquereme. Then he noticed the train of crew. Suddenly they broke into a run, dropping their supplies. Every hair on the back of Aquinius' neck rippled as he heard the dark rumble of hooves from behind him. Surely not...from the cliffs?

He turned numbly to see a dark wash of riders pour over the cliff edge. He rubbed his eyes in disbelief as the Hun riders strafed their animals down the treacherous and impossible terrain unharmed. Like a dark avalanche, thousands of them hurtled towards the western stake palisade – sparse and poorly fixed as it was, the riders would be upon them in an instant. Aquinius dropped his urn of broth, the scalding liquid leapt up in protest, coating his bare shins, yet he felt nothing. The legionaries, too, were completely stunned, only being able to stand in disbelief and watch the wave of destruction as it roared over them.

'To arms!' Aquinius roared. Those who managed to grab some form of weapon or protection managed at best a few parries before being swept to their death by the merciless torrent, the Huns cutting down the century like tall grass. Aquinius stumbled backwards, flailing, before he fell to his knees. A lasso wrenched around his neck and with a dull crack, he was lifted from the spot and trailed like a broken doll behind the rider who had snared him.

Within a handful of heartbeats it was over, the camp was carpeted in black-blooded remains. The Huns circled the centre of the camp, whooping a piercing high-pitched victory cry, while their majority thundered down to the shore to butcher the crew.

The celebrations settled, and the Huns milled towards the front gate of the camp. As they approached, two petrified sentries stared back at their certain death. The first sentry glanced briefly over his shoulder to see the shocked figure of the still-mounted foederatus, barely through the gates – frozen like an ice-statue.

'Ride! Get out of here and get word to the legion!' The sentry screamed. The foederatus quickly snapped out of his trance and spurred his horse round into a full gallop. Almost instinctively, the Horde of Huns swarmed towards the gate to pursue the Goth. The sentry stood with his hands wrapped around an unused palisade stake, and waited until the thundering horde were almost upon him before he dropped the post across the gate just as the first handful of riders made to pass through. With a crack of horse limbs, the riders were thrown from their mounts.

A precious few moments had been bought for the foederatus to make it back to the legion, the sentry gulped. Then he felt his bowels loosen at the scream of his fellow sentry being butchered. Glancing skywards, he searched for Mithras, then a thundercloud of arrows tore through his torso, and a glistening blade scythed through his neck.

The foederatus horseman dug his heels into the sides of his mount without mercy, and felt the beast straining at the breakneck pace they gathered. He did not allow any let up until he was almost into the forest to the northeast. He began to slow as his beast tired, turning eventually at the terrible victory whoop from the shore.

In the distance, the Classis Moesica fleet was ablaze, fire arrows raining down on the inferno. Without those ships, the legion was in dire trouble. Without news of this, the legion was truly doomed.

He jumped as something caught his eye from the trees.

'Time to die, Roman lover!' A Hun horseman trotted towards him, an arrow nocked in his bow. Two others appeared silently to encircle him.

Fear hammered at his heart as he raised his hands, shaking his head. 'No,' he stammered, dropping his sword and reaching into his purse.

'So the Roman lover thinks he can buy his life?' The three Huns sneered.

The foederatus very slowly raised a small gold Christian Chi-Rho cross hanging from a chain, then slipped it on over his head and held it to show them.

'I'm no Roman lover,' he grinned. 'I'm with you!'

# Chapter 51

The ground quaked as the Hun horde moved off. Balamber rode in their midst, gleaming in his iron Sassanian armour and surrounded by his loyal horde leaders – the nobles who would share the largest spoils of his winnings. He scanned the seas of mounted troops that surrounded him; no neat formations or tidy units – this army fought like a pack and devoured all who stood in their way. The swell of spears, caps, arrowheads and bows filled the land to the horizon in every direction, riders and the poor wretches who begged for the honour of serving as his infantry, bobbing gently as they moved southwards.

*Destroy all before you*, the mantra rang in his head. For the briefest of moments, he allowed the distant memory to run free in his mind, the one that he had fought to keep back for so long, since he was a boy on that very night. His stomach shrivelled as he recalled the scene; the thousands upon thousands of his kin, wailing, bloodied and maimed on the plains. The *Qin* regiments had cut the throats of his people in a night raid on the tribes. The stragglers, those who had fought their way free, staggered across the deserts and plains, always following the setting sun, numb from such brutal loss, in hope of finding a new home. Something touched his heart for an instant; a misty shade of the stinging sorrow behind his eyes he had felt on those long past days. Meekness brings defeat and dishonour, he gritted his teeth, recalling yet again the pain on his father's face when he grappled young Balamber by the shoulders on one of those long, dark nights; *with this slaughter, the mighty Tengri has spoken to our people these simple words; destroy all before you.*

Balamber blinked the harrowing echo from his mind. He checked his horde leaders around him. They feared him more than they feared any foe, be they this ever-less distant empire of Rome or the proud dynasties of the Far East. He spoke gently. 'A legion of Rome awaits us to the south. Their reputations do them a great service, but keep this in mind when we face them: they are not what they once were. Lambs ripe for the slaughter, if you will. Spill their blood and we open the gates to our destiny. Their empire is a land of bounty stretching to the far end of the world where the sun rests at night. And it will be ours!' The horde leaders' eyes glistened in longing and wonderment at his words. 'You, as my most trusted men, will share in the cream of this bounty. Fight well for me, men, and share my honour!'

'Rest assured, we will shed our own blood for you, Noble Balamber,' one replied. The others rumbled in agreement.

He smiled, trotting forward. These men would cut their mother's throats at the sight of gold. And only the promise of gold would tame them.

Balamber nodded to his personal bodyguard – a giant of a man who wore a huge ox-horn bound around his neck by a ragged leather strap. The bodyguard lifted the horn and filled his lungs. The deep, ominous moan that poured from it echoed across the landscape and was greeted with an animal-like guttural roar of over twenty-thousand Huns.

The horde marched to war.

# Chapter 52

A roaring fire punctuated the black of night as the grotesque pile of corpses was reduced to ash. All legionaries were posted to the empty houses and halls of the town, and only a few topknotted figures stood around the inferno in silence.

Pavo rested his spear on the battlements and let his eyes rest on the crackling blaze – some brief respite from the monotony of sentry duty and staring out into the blackness of the plains. Amalric the Gothic prince had demanded for the gore-pile to be set alight as a pyre in some last attempt to regain the dignity of the dead. At first, Nerva had steadfastly refused, insisting the thing would be like a beacon to the Huns. Gallus had winced as he stood between the two while the whole legion watched. Pavo replayed the nerve shredding moment when he had been called up from the ranks to explain to Amalric that the Huns had left spies in the town, and that their position was compromised in any case due to the rider who escaped.

Pavo sighed, turning to look out over the blackness in front of him. With only a tiny lantern tucked into the corner of the battlement, the Hun army could be assembled right out there, yet he couldn't even see the ground from up here. He glanced down at his mail shirt, picking at the gore cladding it had taken on. A tiny piece of matted blood crumbled away, leaving a beautifully unblemished sliver of iron behind it. He pulled the thong with the bronze phalera free of his vest and eyed the writing longingly as always. His mind drifted to the heat wave summer of his childhood in Constantinople.

Sitting on the doorstep facing onto the dusty lane of the slums surrounding the Gate of Saint Aemilianus, Father pummelled the scale vest relentlessly despite the blistering sun beating down on his back. Meanwhile, Pavo had cartwheeled back and forth across the lane from house to house, giggling with his playmates. 'My father's going to fight in the legions!' He had cried, his chest puffed out. 'My father will be emperor!' His friends had eagerly joined his child-legion of six – armed with broom handles and wearing caps and bowls on their heads, they had marched on the forum. Or at least as far as the end of the lane.

Pavo smiled, momentarily transported from the cool, dark battlement in this alien land. Then the cold hands of reality traced his spine as the dark memory returned; the gaunt, dead-eyed soldier who dropped the pitiful purse of coins in his hand – announcing the death of his father without a word of solace.

Pavo shivered as a chill breeze washed over him. *Enough*, he chided himself with a chuckle, *stay alert or you'll be the legion idiot again!* He blinked to stare out into the dark plains again, when a pair of hands stabbed into his sides. His heart leapt and his eyes bulged.

'Allright?' Sura sniffed.

'In the name of…what d'you call that? Did you actually get any sentry training?'

'Relax! Nobody can see diddly squat – we could be over in that inn there – Zosimus claims they found seven unopened casks of ale in the cellar,' Sura frowned.

'Aye, a cup of ale and the lash from Nerva – sounds lovely. Have you seen anything…' Pavo's voice trailed off as he saw the darkness swim on the ground below. 'Sura, look!'

The pair clamped their hands on the battlement, peering into the night. There it was; a rider.

'Who goes there!' Pavo yelled, grappling his spear. At once, the sentries all along the battlement jumped to attention and the call was echoed.

'Foederati scout, let me in!'

'Password?' A cry came from above the gate.

'Teutoberg!' he hissed back.

'Allright lads, let him in!' One sentry bawled.

Pavo and Sura craned towards the gate for a better look.

'Could be Julius Caesar for all we can see,' Sura tutted as they strayed from their sentry points, screwing their eyes up.

'He's a bit late isn't he?' Pavo reasoned. Sura nodded with a frown. The sun had set a long time ago –the scout had been due back just after dark.

'Sura, Pavo!' a voice barked. Both spun round to see Felix fuming back at them, with Quadratus glaring likewise a few paces back. 'Is that what Brutus taught you? To be distracted by every coming and going, every little detail? Eyes forward, and stay at your post.'

Pavo jumped to stand upright and stared fastidiously out into the blackness again. Sura scurried fifty paces along the wall to his post to do the same.

Felix sighed. 'Anyway, you couple of morons, shift's over; we're here to relieve you.'

Flitting down the steps, Pavo caught a muffled mumbling from the gate – the jagged twang of the *foederati*. 'Move,' he hissed over his shoulder to Sura, 'we might get an ear in on the report.'

The pair burst out from the stairwell and into the gatehouse enclosure.

A pair of *foederati* huddled with the scout rider and they talked in hushed tones in their native tongue. As soon as they noticed the entrance of the pair, they stopped, breaking apart. Two glared stonily at Pavo and Sura.

'Move on!' One barked.

'Wait a moment, you're in my wing, aren't you?' Sura ignored the two and spoke to the rider.

The scout rider's face was stern at first, and then he broke into a grin. 'Sura, isn't it? They've got you back on foot duty have they?' He nodded up to the battlement. 'Hah, we'll make a rider of you yet!'

As the rider spoke, Pavo let his eyes drift. Then something caught his eye, a glint of metal on a chain around the rider's neck. His eyes keened.

'Did you see me this morning?' Sura roared. 'I was ahead of Captain Horsa. You lot were well behind.'

The rider laughed. A warm laugh. But as he did so the chain lifted, and the edge of a dull yellow cross peeked from his breastplate. Something was etched on its surface. The breath froze in Pavo's lungs.

'I'll show you tomorrow, eh?' Sura concluded, turning to Pavo. The rider roared in laughter again.

'Come on!' Pavo hissed.

'Eh?' Sura frowned. 'What about getting a listen in on the report?'

'Screw the report. *Come on!*' He tugged Sura by the elbow and together they stalked away from the gate. At the first corner, Pavo turned in sharply.

Sura glared at him. 'Well?'

'That cross,' Pavo's eyes darted as he rifled through memory.

Sura frowned. 'What cross? What are you on about?'

Pavo gripped him by the shoulders 'There's no time. We need to speak to the officers. We could be in bigger trouble than we ever imagined.'

# Chapter 53

Dawn had arrived. The legion stood on the plain outside the town's main gate formed up and ready to march. Nerva and Gallus stood to the fore, looking to the dim horizon for any sign of movement. The foederati scouts had set out before dawn in their five divisions to reconnoitre the second hop of their trek to Chersonesos.

'That's too long already, damn it!' Gallus grunted.

'If they don't come back...' Nerva trailed off.

'Sir?' Gallus frowned.

'I'm just thinking aloud. If they don't come back - for whatever reason - we still have to move, Gallus. The Huns know we're here. I won't let us hole-up here as a sitting target. This town simply won't hold out against the numbers reported.'

'The fleet is always there, sir. It might not be in any sort of shape to sail, but it could take us offshore. There have been no reports of a Hun navy.'

'Then what – sit off the shore and starve? With no means of repairing the ships?'

Gallus looked to the coast, far in the distance. He never thought it would be him who suggested it, but needs must. 'Sir, may I suggest we call on the I Dacia.' Gallus expected Nerva's grimacing reaction. 'As much as I hate to say it, sir,' he checked to make sure that no legionaries were in earshot before continuing. 'But as things stand we are positively buggered. Maybe we should put pride and reputation to one side?'

Nerva chuckled – but his expression remained cold.

'I hear you, Gallus. The pragmatist would admit we need help here; one legion was supposed to be enough to tackle a disorganised society of Gothic farmers and warbands, but instead we are being fed to the wolves.' He dropped his distant gaze to his boots, shaking his head.

Gallus glanced around nervously – body language like this would percolate through the troops. The Nerva he aspired to seemed locked away inside this cage of jangling nerves.

'Sir?'

Nerva looked up, his eyes red-rimmed and ringed with tiredness. 'You are right. Despatch a messenger...no, two, send them on different routes, to the fleet. Whatever state the fleet is in, get that quinquereme sailing for Durostorum. We must put pride to one side and call for the services of ...Wulfric,' he spat the name like a troublesome sinew of meat. 'But they will not get to us for days, so we *must* attempt the hop to Chersonesos – we can bed in if we get to the citadel, but we cannot stay here.'

Gallus felt a weight lifting from his shoulders – not exactly as he would have played it had he been in charge, but at least the tribunus had offered some compromise. One more hop to Chersonesos it would be, then; all money on the next throw of the dice. But the dark cloud in his mind remained. What if? Then he thought back to last night. Pavo and his friend Sura had turned up at his billet, babbling. It all sounded so outlandish – Horsa and the foederati had been bought by the Holy See? Pavo had been right before, he mused reluctantly. The lad seemed to attract trouble but was one of the sharper recruits in the legion.

After issuing orders to two mounted auxiliaries, Gallus turned back to his tribunus. 'Sir,' Gallus started, fighting to keep the uncertainty from his voice, 'do you have any concerns over the foederati?'

'Concerns?'

'Apart from the obvious. Yes they put their backs into the rowing, but they sneer at our boys, they don't tow the line like Romans. I just mean...do you trust them?'

'As far as I could throw them, yes!' Nerva chuckled. 'We've got to accept it, Gallus, they are not fighting for the empire. They're after gold and gold alone – it's a fact we have to live with.'

'Whose gold?' Gallus cut in.

'I beg your pardon?'

'The emperor paid Fritigern for his allegiance I presume?'

'Gallus, I don't know where you're going with this,' Nerva quizzed.

'But he did pay them?' Gallus persisted.

'Well, yes. Standard policy these days – if you can't beat them, buy them. Sadly. Look, Gallus, spit it out. I don't want surprises later on.'

Gallus watched his tribunus grimace in frustration; Nerva was brash, wanted it all out on a plate up front. 'Okay, it's a long shot, but it adds up, albeit roughly.' Gallus glanced around to ensure nobody was within earshot. 'Our foederati have been seen carrying marked gold. Nothing special there, but one of my lads – Pavo – recognised the marking.' He leant in to the tribunus. 'From the Holy See of Constantinople, sir.'

Nerva's eyes narrowed. 'Interesting. That lad Pavo, he has a chequered history to say the least, no? In any case, it could be nothing – they might trade currency with the imperial coffers?'

'I hope so, sir. I don't know why the See would pay them on top of the emperor, and I'm not sure I want to know either.'

Nerva's eyes grew distant momentarily and then he grinned wryly. 'Bishop Evagrius…'

'Slippery as a snake in oil,' Gallus nodded. 'I doubt he would release a bent nummus unless there was something sweet in it for him.'

'Well, I'd love to quiz them about it, Gallus, but they're gone and we're here,' he sighed, casting a hand to the horizon over which the five divisions had slipped too long ago.

'Maybe we should bed in here after all?' Gallus nodded back to Theodosia.

Nerva hesitated, then shook his head. 'No, we move on. We're almost there. The detachment shadowing the fleet is almost there. Stay focused, centurion, you're made of stern stuff and I know you'll see us through this.' With that the tribunus wheeled away to address the legion, who rippled to attention.

'Men, hold steady in your hearts, for we have arranged for reinforcements to bolster our mission. But the time to move is almost upon us – we head for Chersonesos. Our scouts will return soon. Prepare to march!'

Gallus' mind raced. If only he had pieced the theory together earlier. Perhaps he should have insisted on a Roman rider going on the next heartbeat run to check on the fleet. He watched the legion ripple into perfect ranks again, and then glanced to the horizon. What lay over those hills? A terrible apprehension gripped him.

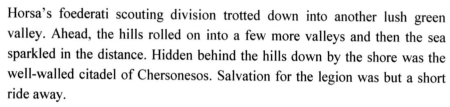

Horsa's foederati scouting division trotted down into another lush green valley. Ahead, the hills rolled on into a few more valleys and then the sea sparkled in the distance. Hidden behind the hills down by the shore was the well-walled citadel of Chersonesos. Salvation for the legion was but a short ride away.

Sura eyed the sides of the valley sleepily. The thick, dew-coated grass shimmered and swayed to the rhythm of the babbling meltwater brooks trickling down from the hills to the north. He sucked a breath in through his nostrils – sweet and fresh. The distance to Chersonesos had been a good many miles further than anticipated, and they had had no option but to slow the pace so as not to wear out their mounts. Really though, the scouting today had been quiet, just like yesterday. Only the stop to watch a fox-fight had disturbed the hypnotic gallop from Theodosia. *Sharpen up!* He muttered to himself, digging his nails into his palm. Pavo's theory from last night seemed ethereal now after a night's sleep and his initial fears had quelled somewhat. These riders were mercenaries all right, gruff buggers, but no more, he concluded.

He checked his riding position – good, he was a comfortable distance away from the Goths around him. They had been none too appreciative of him the first day – too close, they claimed, kicking out at him and swearing in Gothic. Horsa had chided them and dropped back to ride with him, but the riders were never going to accept a Roman in their midst. He probably hadn't helped matters by cheating at dice the previous evening, he mused. He glanced round at the riders again and their typical Gothic cavalry gear; leggings and leather boots, thick red leather tunics or chain mail vests, and then some who owned conical helmets. He felt suddenly all the more alien in his intercisa helmet and white, purple-edged tunic under his mail vest – stood out like a Roman from a hundred miles away, he surmised.

Then, Horsa twisted on his saddle to address the men. 'Okay, pick up the pace – we can take in some water and meat when we round on this city. But the legion will be expecting us by now so we need to be speedy and make a quick return.'

Sura heard the order and made to spur his mount on, but he was snapped out of his daydream as he realised the column was slowing down rather than speeding up. Looking up, he saw Horsa – still twisted in his saddle. But something was wrong. The Gothic captain looked as though he had been struck by lightning. Sura traced the captain's line of sight; there, right up on the lip of the valley to their left, an endless line of dark shapes rose with a chorus of thundering hooves. Huns, countless in number, swept towards them.

Suddenly, right behind Sura, came a guttural roar of pain. Icy fear ripped through him. He spun his mount round; two foederati were in file behind him, the closest with a pallid face, blood rushing from his mouth and down over his tunic and over the spear tip bursting through his chest. The man behind him grimaced, ripping his spear back. In the same instant, cries of pain rang out all around him; in a blur, the foederati started slaughtering one another. Sura spurred and bucked his horse in a panic at the sudden chaos, only instinct brought his shield around his flanks – rebuffing two spear-jabs. His limbs like wet sand, he glanced around for Horsa, hacking at the two swords focused on him.

'Treacherous dogs!' Horsa roared.

Sura's wide-eyed gaze flicked to Horsa, and then to the closing jaws of the Hun attack, now only paces away and with lassos spinning and spears and bows raised, poised to fire.

'Ambush! Return to the legion!' Horsa screamed, hacking his way around the edge of the chaos.

Sura locked eyes with Horsa, who gritted his teeth and roared, pointing his spear back in the direction of Theodosia. A handful of loyal riders gathered around their leader, fending off blows. Horsa roared, but whatever he said was drowned out in the thundering of the Huns, and he swept past Sura. But Horsa was being driven away from the path to Theodosia, the Huns herding him and his party back up the valley. A hissing shower of arrows spat past Sura and without another thought, he too was off at full pelt behind the Gothic captain.

The sun now stretched high into the blue, birds raced across the plains around Theodosia and the cicadas chattered incessantly. But while the wildlife hunted and played, the legion shuffled uncomfortably in both the heat and the non-appearance of their foederati scouting parties. Even the pack mules brayed in thirst at the rear. On the front line of the first century, just behind the officers, three figures baked in the sunlight.

'Bleeding joke, this is,' Zosimus huffed, pulling his helmet off to scratch his dark stubbled scalp and wipe at the waterfall of sweat on his forehead.

'Come on, come on,' Avitus grumbled, 'give the order to go back into the town!'

Pavo felt sweat race down his back, matting the rough fibre of his scratchy tunic under his oven-like mail shirt. They had been standing outside for far too long now. Surely, something had to give. Legionaries had strolled around, chatting after a while. Gallus had quickly whipped them back into line though. But now even the primus pilus was shifting his weight from one foot to the other. Shielding his eyes with his hand, Pavo looked to the south again for any sign of movement; just lush green rolling hills, pines rippling in the lofty zephyrs and the occasional darting deer. His eyes flicked back – something had moved. Red leather and iron. The foederati had returned.

First one division, then another emerged from the heat haze. More poured into view behind them. They trotted rather than galloped, and Pavo counted them – only four divisions.

'Do they think we've got all day?' Spat Avitus.

'We'll make them walk from now on in, see how they cope with it, lazy buggers! I'd happily sit on my backside on one of their horses all day,' Zosimus chipped in.

As the foederati approached, Pavo strained to see which of the five was missing. Going by the directions they approached from it was the one he dreaded. Sure enough, Horsa and his men were the ones. The four divisions fanned out in front of the legion. Pavo's brow knitted as he watched the approach.

'Foederati!' Nerva bawled. 'Proceed to check-in.'

The foederati practically ignored the tribunus' orders and continued their lazy amble up to the officers. A grumble of insults and moans grew from the assembled legion.

'Silence!' Gallus snapped.

Pavo watched as one foederatus nudged another, who finally broke into a trot forward. He respectfully dismounted, but then strode past the officers, ignoring them to address the entire legion.

'I bring sad news. Captain Horsa has been slain.'

Gallus stepped forward to reprimand the Goth's disregard for protocol, but it was too late; a wave of groans swept across the legion.

'His path to Chersonesos was clear, but he attempted to cross onto our path on his return. Just as he sighted us, the Huns descended on him – he and his men didn't stand a chance.'

'All of them, dead?' Nerva stammered.

The Goth nodded, his lips tight and thin.

Pavo felt a cool ripple of dread wash through his limbs. All of them? Then Sura would not be returning from this far-flung land. None of them would be at this rate. The phalera weighed heavily on the thong around his neck.

'How many?' Gallus quizzed.

'Three, maybe four thousand.' The Goth's face remained expressionless.

*Then where are the other sixteen thousand?* The question screamed in Pavo's head.

'And how did your men return intact?' Nerva replied to the Goth. 'If the Huns intercepted Horsa on your path then surely you would have been caught up in it too?'

The Goth nodded in agreement. 'He saved us; his men absorbed the impact of the Hun charge while we sped to their aid, but Horsa waved us back – roared at us, demanded we escape and get back to the legion.'

Nerva nodded. 'A good man till the end.'

Gallus remained steely faced. 'You weren't in too much of a hurry. Did you lose them?'

The Goth looked up, his face betraying indignation. 'Of course we lost them; do you think we would lead the Huns right onto the legion? We slowed only because our mounts are exhausted from the flight.'

'Very well. Let's hope you shook them off well enough,' Gallus replied icily, eyeing the foederati horses for signs of fatigue.

Pavo noticed as the centurion's eyes narrowed at the Goth.

'But you must make haste. Our route was clear. Round the last valley by the coast,' the Goth barked, swerving past Gallus and Nerva, now addressing the legion again. 'If we move quickly, we can slip past the Huns.'

The legionaries rumbled into a chorus of agreement.

'Enough!' Nerva roared. 'And you'll not speak over me again or I'll have you in chains!' He spat at the Goth. Then he turned to his primus pilus. 'What do you think, Gallus?'

Pavo watched the centurion – their eyes met briefly.

Gallus' eyes darted momentarily across the ground by his feet, and then a grimace spread across his lips. 'We have no other option, sir. In lieu of better intelligence, we have to move. Again we must go with what little we have.'

Nerva nodded briskly and without hesitation looked to the Goth. 'Form up your men on the wings.' The tribunus then turned to face the legion. 'Form column, move out!' He bawled. With that, the tribunus leapt onto his mount.

Pavo turned over the facts in his head; Sura was dead. His friend was dead. A sickness hovered in his stomach, not at the loss, but at the lack of emotion to go with his thoughts – the soldier's skin. Ashamed, he tried to visualise Sura's face, gritting his teeth as the legion bristled for the march. In front of him, just as the Gothic riders had ridden clear of earshot, Gallus leaned in to Nerva and whispered something. The tribunus looked unsure, but Gallus persisted. Eventually, Nerva nodded and turned back to the men.

'Double line. Foederati on the wings and narrow on the front!' The tribunus called.

Pavo's ears picked up as he visualised the formation. His mind spun back to the formations drill with Brutus on the training ground; a double line would mean abandoning the column they had marched in so far for a slower but more defensible shape. The infantry rustled into the formation as he thought it through – the second and third cohorts would make up the wider back line, with the auxiliaries joining the first cohort on the front line, with the foederati close on either flank of the front. Then he noticed Gallus flick a hand signal, four fingers extended and fanning out, to the leader of the pack mule train; carrying the tents, palisade stakes and artillery kit, the mules would come along at the rear. The meaning of the hand signal wasn't clear to Pavo – but the primus pilus would know what he was doing. He looked to Gallus, but the centurion faced forward now, cold and still. This new shape meant the foederati were pinned in with the legion – no more free roaming on the flanks of the column for them. At once, fear and pride gripped him. Gallus was buying into his theory of the previous evening. He prayed he hadn't got it wrong.

A shield boss rammed into his back, knocking his breath out and tipping his helmet over his eyes.

'Move it!' a voice barked as the cohort advanced.

Stumbling forward, Pavo muttered an apology, pulling his chin straps tight. He glimpsed round at the formation. No doubt about it, this was an insurance policy. Maybe his theory wasn't altogether correct, but if there was some seam of truth in there, this move might give them half a chance.

Then he thought of Sura and tightened the grip on his spear.

# Chapter 54

Balamber roared the horde onwards, who cheered in reply like an innumerable pack of starved wolves. They had formed now into two loose wings, numbering nearly ten thousand each, and the ground rumbled violently as they made their way towards the network of hills and valleys. Balamber rode beside the turncoat foederati captain, who was explaining the situation with the legion as he fingered the gold cross hanging around his neck.

'The valley is steep and narrow, but flat at its bottom. At either end you will have a plain large enough to swamp them and block their escape,' he purred, pointing to the hills by the coast. 'Their column is perfect for a flanking strike – we will cut through them like a knife through oil.'

'This tribunus, Nerva, he will not suspect?' Balamber asked.

'Absolutely not,' the foederati captain affirmed. Then his eyes dropped from the stern gaze of Balamber. 'Nerva is a spent commander. Good in years past, but now he relies too much on those outdated glories. His keenness of instinct is gone and he'll lead them blindly into your hands…and onto your spear tips!'

Balamber continued to stare at the foederatus after he fell quiet. 'Something else you want to tell me?' He asked quietly.

The Goth's eyes widened and he licked his lips. 'The rider, Horsa,' the foederati captain answered grudgingly, 'he presumed to lead us. But he's an excellent rider. If your men don't catch him and he returns to the legion first to warn them…'

'You've seen the skills of my riders. Do you think any man could outrun them, or avoid their arrows for that matter?' Balamber growled inside as he remembered the blubbering excuses from Apsikal.

'Of course not, Noble Balamber,' he replied sheepishly.

'And in any case, the final piece of the jigsaw is nearly in place, is it not?'

The foederatus looked puzzled momentarily, then a grin curled across his features. 'Indeed, Noble Balamber. Contact has been made. They will be in place at the allotted time.'

'Excellent. This XI Claudia will be crushed from every direction.' Balamber turned to face the rolling landscape in front of them. 'When this Roman legion is destroyed, we will descend onto the great River Danubius. There they have left themselves stretched and vulnerable. We will flood into their proud cities, bearing their precious standards with their tribunus' heads upon them. Their walls will tumble and their blood will stain the streets. Before the winter falls twice more, I will sit on the throne of the empire. *Tengri* wills it from his realm of the sky.' He pulled a handful of the gold crosses from his purse. 'Some in this scheme believe they are the puppet master when they are in fact the puppet.' The foederati captain nodded, his eyes glimmering at the treasure. 'Don't concern yourself over the whole affair, rider. All you need to know is that when I have achieved this, you and your warriors will form a new wing in my armies.' He traced a finger along the edge of one cross. 'Who can stop me,' he grinned, 'when I have a path into the Roman heartlands paved with gold from God himself?'

# Chapter 55

The pace was relentless. Sweat lashed from every brow and throats rasped like sand in an urn. The sun pushed against them, growing hotter and hotter until now, just after midday, soldiers began to lag and only the officers croaking out to rally them punctuated the rumble of their march.

Pavo winced as his mail vest scythed into his shoulders with every stride. The scrap of cloth stuffed in there to relieve the pressure had slipped out, sweat-sodden and bloody, miles back. His water skin sloshed mockingly – full but no time to stop and take a swig from it. The apprehension of earlier had been consumed by the brutal labour of the march – probably an army trick to distract the ranks from falling morale, Pavo thought. Then he realised he had dropped back a pace. A harmony of curses rang out as a boot caught on his heel and the disruption rippled back behind him.

'Come on, Pavo,' Avitus hissed, looping an arm round his to pull him level. 'Centurion'll boot your balls if you show up his first century.'

'Any idea how far now?' He panted.

'I reckon we're over halfway,' Zosimus groaned, his face red as beetroot.

Halfway sounded like there was still a marathon ahead of them, Pavo winced. Every stride felt like a sack of lead was being added to his belt, and his vision began to shrink to contain just the heels of the legionary in front of him. In the periphery, yet another yawning valley rolled up ahead of them. Maybe it was his fading grip on reality, Pavo wondered, but this one seemed steeper and narrower than the rest. He noticed the two foederati wing leaders had sidled over to converse with Nerva. Eventually, the tribunus nodded.

'Foederati, over the hilltops!' Nerva barked from his mount, firing fingers in either direction up the sides of the valley. At once, the two wings shot free of the legion and up a side of the valley each.

'What the…' Pavo spluttered as he saw Gallus' head dart left and right in shock at the unplanned move.

'Not to your refined tactical manoeuvring taste is it, Pavo?' Avitus gasped.

'No, it's just that, this formation,' he panted, 'we wanted the foederati close and in front for a reason.'

'Oh did we – and how do you know?' Zosimus mumbled.

Pavo opened his mouth to reply, but a cry from the front cut him dead.

'Full halt!' Gallus had both hands raised and stuttered to a stop. The legion bunched up clumsily, but within moments they were still.

'What in Hades?' Nerva cursed at his primus pilus, wheeling back round, stood out on his own at the front of the entire legion. 'What's going on, Gallus? Fall in behind me,' he hissed.

'Get back in line, sir. Trust me…' Gallus held his stance, his eyes darting around the tips of the valley on either side. '…sir!'

Nerva stayed motionless, twenty paces ahead of the legion.

Pavo's skin crept as he glanced up – the foederati wings had disappeared over the lips of the valley. 'This is it,' he shuddered.

'Eh?' Avitus and Zosimus grunted in unison.

Pavo stiffened. 'Get ready.'

'Gallus,' Nerva bawled. 'Get the legion moving at once.'

Then, the hum of the breeze and the chatter of the cicadas died, and a dreadful whirring replaced and swamped it. At once the sky darkened, shafts rained toward the legion from the valley top in their thousands, like a storm cloud from the underworld.

'Shields!' Gallus cried.

The legion broke out into a chorus of cries, and then rippled into a roof of ruby-red as they turned their shields up as the deadly rain battered down on them. Screams pierced the air – hundreds of them, where soldiers were too slow. Then the rain slowed, and Pavo sneaked a glance out from under his shield. His eyes locked on the solitary figure of Tribunus Nerva up front; he and his mount took on the appearance of some grotesque effigy, peppered with arrow shafts, his jowls limp and his eyes shocked and staring at the legion. Silently, the Roman tribunus slid from his mount, crashing to the earth like wet sand.

Pavo blinked in disbelief. Paranoia was gone. The nightmare was upon them.

The sky lightened momentarily and then again was black. Every wave of arrows tore more screams from the ranks. He looked to Gallus, crouched under his shield next to Felix. This was the life-or-death moment.

'It's the recon ambush all over again, Felix; we need a way out of this.' Gallus cried over the rattle of the lethal hail.

'We're going to be picked off if we sit here, sir.'

'Well then it's pull back or push ahead. We need to get out of the low ground and out of bloody archer range.' A shaft ripped across the centurion's shoulder, spraying blood on his optio's face. Neither man flinched.

'It's just more open terrain back there,' Felix shouted.

'Death or the unknown,' Gallus spat bitterly.

Then Pavo saw it; bursting along the valley side, swerving through the arrow storm, three riders sped. The bouncing blonde topknot – it was Horsa!

'Ahead!' Horsa roared, 'Get to the other end!' He waved his spear frantically back over his shoulder towards a flat near the far end of the valley.

'Decision made,' Gallus growled, then stood, turning to face the legion with his shield over his back and boomed to the ranks; 'Legion, fast as you can – get to the end of the valley.'

Pavo rose with the ranks as they raced forward, formations stretched like spilled grain. The screams of the stricken tripled without the shield roof, and every stride felt like a lottery of death as arrows zipped past his ear, thudded into the earth before him and sclaffed across his mail vest. Horsa and the two riders up ahead had slowed, out of archer range; they waved frantically, encouraging the legion on.

'Get to that flat ground!' Gallus cried, waving his arm again and again to the end of the valley. 'Then form up – five ranks deep. We must hold the flanks!'

They spilled forward and the arrow rain slowed. The bedraggled cohorts poured onto the flat to about face and form up. Pavo snatched a glance along the new Roman front line at the two riders with Horsa. One was Roman. Blonde. *Sura was alive!*

Pavo's mind reeled, euphoria mixed with the dread in his veins.

Then Gallus rallied the legion with a roar, battering his sword on his shield as he faced their still invisible enemy. 'Steady, men. Let's see what these dogs fight like when they meet us face to face. Let them taste our iron!'

An ill-fitting silence settled on the scene. The panting, rasping and groaning legionaries stared back along the valley floor at the crimson carpet of their fallen brothers. Yet, curiously, the hillsides lay green and empty, the breeze rippling through the grass. The shades that had attacked them nowhere to be seen.

'Cowards!' One legionary roared.

'Come face us!' Another added.

The legion broke out into a rabble of insults at the emptiness before them, as if beckoning an army of shades from the realm of Pluto.

Pavo looked along the lines; desperation painted on every face. These men were at their limit. Wounded and starved of revenge. So many had fallen, but it would take a ferocious enemy to overcome them still. Suddenly, the ground began to shake.

'They're coming,' Pavo whispered.

'What is it with you?' Zosimus muttered. 'Got a sixth sense or something?'

Then the valley tops darkened; from each side, the horizon boiled over with a mass of steel and thunder. First the Hun spearmen, clad in linen armour with leather skullcaps and wooden shields, thousands of them, tumbled down the valley's end to converge at the bottom in a crescent. Behind them came wave after wave of Hun cavalry – spear tips jostling as they poured incessantly until the lonely valley was nearly full. Then the foederati came, the turncoat horsemen adding only a small wing to the Hun horde.

Dead in the centre of the enemy number, one warrior stood out; on a tall black stallion and clad in shimmering Sassanian iron armour, he barked out at his men through the bone and fur standards held by his surrounding guards.

'What the…there must be ten thousand of them,' Avitus gasped, his eyes darting back and forth over the sea of fluttering banners and spear points.

'Twenty thousand. Plus the two thousand turncoat foederati,' Pavo added reluctantly. Suddenly a figure bustled into place next to him – *Sura!*

'You lead a charmed existence,' Pavo welcomed him, clasping his forearm.

Sura, gaunt and sweating, grabbed at his water skin and poured the entire contents down his throat. 'My foederati days are over,' Balamber asserted, burping then throwing the skin to the ground and steadying his feet into a soldier's brace.

'Glad to hear it,' Avitus grinned, 'welcome back to the ranks.'

Horsa stood just in front of them with Gallus. 'They came at us in the next valley,' he nodded to the east. 'We tried to return. They couldn't catch us, but they herded us, driving us north, away from the legion.' Horsa punched a fist into his palm. 'Let me and my last rider loose, sir. I'll take down as many of those treacherous dogs as the gods will let me. The gold they were bought with will not serve them in the afterlife.'

'Save your energy, captain, we've got no cavalry wing now; keep your mounts safe to the rear – if we need speed they'll be priceless.'

'But what's our next move, sir?' Felix interjected.

Gallus hesitated, scanning the Hun horde – they had formed into a crescent shape, curling around the valley's end like pincers, their front ranks boasting huge packs of cavalry punctuated with small units of spearmen like the teeth of a predator. The horde crept forward towards the Roman line – less than two thousand strong now. At last, the primus pilus responded. 'Horsa, Chersonesos – how far?'

'Through the next pass and downhill. Too far, for sure.'

'It'll have to do,' Gallus snapped. 'Legion, prepare for a fighting retreat'

'Sir,' Felix cut in, 'We've got no clear reconnaissance on that place. The city is probably packed with Huns.'

'Horsa?' Gallus asked.

'It's as your optio says, sir, we never even sighted the place.'

Pavo's breath shortened as the Huns tightened around them like a hungry snake. The need to act overcame his fear and he spoke out; 'Is there anything else defensible nearby? A natural choke point...or something we could use to at least cover our flanks?'

Gallus, Horsa and Felix turned, faces wrinkled in frustration. Gallus relaxed his expression first. 'Amalric, you know this land – is there anywhere we can retreat to?'

The Gothic prince was pale and streaked with dirt and sweat as he watched the murderers of his people encircle them.

'Amalric!' Gallus persisted.

He jumped to attention. 'Near Chersonesos?' His eyes flickered and he turned to survey the hills, pinpointing his location mentally. 'Yes! There is a small fort – Greek mercenaries built it during our civil war. It's on the hilltop, overlooking the coast.' He pointed up to the next valley. 'It was used as a watch station for the shipping lanes off the coast.'

'How far?'

'About half that to Chersonesos, but it's a whole lot rougher. There's a steep rocky path we'd have to climb to get there.'

Gallus eyed the Goth – the look of despair wringing his features said it all. The question hung in his throat – what if the Huns were already there too? But the men needed to believe, and the Hun horde was now only a handful of paces from missile range. Another arrow storm would wreck the legion. 'Fine, beats this hands down,' Gallus snapped. 'You lead the retreat from the rear – we'll cut these whoresons down if they dare to come any closer.'

'Sir!' a voice piped up from the rear of the formation, 'We've been saved!'

Gallus spun round in disbelief, together with every head in the legion.

Pavo blinked. Surely, some kind of dream lay behind them; a shimmering patchwork of iron squares crunched up over the southern horizon. A legion – a full and fresh legion of some three thousand men; scale armoured legionaries, archers, auxiliaries and a fresh cavalry vexillatio.

'Comitatenses!' One legionary roared. Gallus pushed his way through the ranks to face the new arrivals.

'It's the I Dacia!' another added.

Gallus frowned. He had sent for the I Dacia, hundreds of miles away, only a short time ago. An impossibly short time.

Tribunus Wulfric grinned at the head of the legion.

'*Ave!*' Wulfric called.

'*Ave...*' replied Gallus. The Gothic tribunus simply stared at him, while the air hung silent bar the fluttering of banners; the torn and soiled ruby bull of the XI Claudia and the pristine emerald boar of the I Dacia. Even the Huns were stilled. 'From whom did you receive the call to come here?' He ventured.

'What kind of way is that to address your relief force?' Wulfric chuckled. 'These men have sailed the Pontus Euxinus and marched from the neck of this peninsula at full speed to save you – and from certain death. Pull back, Centurion, fall behind our lines and we will see you safely to our fleet.'

Gallus eyed Wulfric carefully, 'When did you arrive, and I ask again, by whose orders?'

'Compliance is not optional. Fall back, Centurion.'

Gallus glanced over their ranks; Mainly Goths clad in legionary armour, but there were also Romans, surely eager to pitch in and help their brothers. He grimaced; what choice did he have in any case? 'Stand down, men. Fall back behind the I Dacia lines.'

The Huns, momentarily halted by the appearance of the legion, now waited on the order from their leader. Gallus noticed how the Hun leader remained silent and motionless. As the XI Claudia rumbled backwards towards the I Dacia, he turned back to lead the retreat, when something caught his eye. A small thing that meant everything: dangling from the neck of Wulfric was a small, gold, Chi-Rho cross.

Time seemed to slow as he looked up and locked onto Wulfric's eyes. As he did so, the Goth grew a terrible grin, and all around him, the I Dacia lifted their plumbatae as Wulfric raised his arm. The unknowing troops of the XI Claudia were marching backwards right into the range of the darts.

'Treachery!' Gallus roared. 'Back ranks, about face!'

Confusion reigned as the ranks stumbled to a halt, some turning, and some continuing their backwards march. As the plumbata hail was loosed, Gallus cried out again; 'Shields!' The thick and heavy iron rain smashed into the crippled legion, catching hundreds of legionaries unawares, and then the I Dacia armed with the next volley.

'Come on then, you dogs!' Gallus spat.

Then he heard a jagged cry from what was now the rear of his army. The earth began to shake. The Huns were advancing; the noose was snapping shut.

The world shook. Pavo lifted his shield to add to the Roman wall as they instinctively bunched together. Chaos reigned; cries of saviour had rang out at first but had been quickly cut off with a hail of I Dacia plumbatae from behind, now the Huns thundered for them on their confused front. Now the XI Claudia stood like a lame gazelle in the centre of a pack of ravenous lions.

'Hold the line!' Felix boomed, barely audible over the thundering of hooves. 'Hold it or we're done for!' With that, iron armour screeched and wooden shields groaned even tighter as the Hun mass raced to within paces of them. 'Here they come!'

A strange calm touched Pavo. When only one outcome was possible, what was there to fear? He envisioned his father standing beside him, resplendent in his old legionary armour. Then it happened; all around, the tsunami of spear tips and swords bit into the Romans like a thick noose snapping tight on a neck. The head of the Hun infantry battered into the Roman front line, spears jabbing past his face and snarling Huns inches from him. Pavo felt his feet lifting from the earth as the full weight of their number told. His chest felt like a grape in a press as from behind, the I Dacia smashed into the unprepared Roman rear. Pavo wondered just how long it would be before Spurius and Festus fought their way through to him, and even if he could cling onto life long enough for that to happen.

He wrenched at his sword arm, wedged between his side and that of Sura. A spear tip flashed forward at his face, but he could not even lift his shield in defence. Dipping his head to one side, the spear smashed into the face of the legionary behind him with a crunch of bone and an animal scream. The Hun pulled his blood and gristle coated spear back, and with a vicious snarl, he thrust it forward again, this time at Pavo's neck. Pure instinct kicked in, and Pavo used the surge of strength to rip his sword arm clear, and grunted as the blade parried the spear thrust. Then, with a swift jerk of his arm, he pulled the blade over his shield and ripped it through the throat of the Hun, who collapsed under the push of his comrades. Another stepped forward from the endless sea, ramming his spear forward before the first had even hit the ground. Then the sky darkened. The arrow storm had returned.

His shield was compressed against his body, and he could only tilt his head forward in hope – a handful of arrows danced off the iron intercisa but behind him, screams rang out in their hundreds, as the crushed legionaries fell like defenceless flies to the arrow storm. Glancing up, he saw the massive swell of Hun riders taking aim again as they moved to add to the push on the Claudia. His heart thundered as he lost sight of the end of their lines, such was their number.

'We're dead!' He grunted.

'Maybe so, but I'm not going out without at least a hundred of these buggers coming with me!' Zosimus snarled.

'Been good knowing you, Pavo,' Sura stammered, the battle fury racing through him, 'now let's end this like soldiers!'

Pavo gritted his teeth, ramming his sword point forward again and again, in between ducking and parrying. Dealing out death like Hades, his face ran with warm blood and gristle, his mind hot with fury and flashes of his father, of Brutus. From the side of his eye, he saw his brothers fall. Only a precious few moments remained. Would this be a proud end? But then, who would there be to grieve for him as he had done for Father?

Then, from the rear of the Hun ranks, a terrible moan rose as something ripped right through them like an invisible serpent, throwing men up into the air like toys and sending jets of blood skywards. Then again and again. Pavo felt the pressure on his chest drop and he gasped for air as the Hun numbers fell back in confusion. Then he heard it; the twang of ballistae.

Up in the valley, the four ballistae snapped one after the other. The twenty or so auxiliaries operating them looked like gods. *Gallus*, Pavo thought, remembering the four fingered hand signal – the centurion had pulled a masterstroke, having the pack mule train assemble artillery and follow up the legion a good mile behind. Although not in the line of sight of the ballistae, the I Dacia had fallen back just a little in confusion at the twist, and the XI Claudia had their precious and fragile window of opportunity.

'Pull back, to the hills!' Gallus' voice rattled over the eerie lull in battle. Like a wounded animal, the legion scrambled to life and moved as one, still bearing a shield wall, pushing through the join in the encircling noose between the I Dacia and the Huns. The ballistae fired another volley before the Hun leader roared and with a sweep of his hand, sent a block of some five hundred riders off to despatch the artillery.

'Move fast, men. We can't get encircled again or we're dead!' Gallus cried as they rumbled up the hillside. The I Dacia rallied their number and the Hun riders rallied likewise. As they tumbled up to the top of the hillside, a taller hill became visible, its sides strewn with rocky passes and sheer cliffs, presenting a snaking canyon in between, rising to the summit. But at the top, salvation presented itself – the tip of a stone wall. 'To the fort!' The centurion roared. 'Get into that canyon – we can defend the mouth!'

The straggle of exhausted legionaries, smeared crimson and silver, hobbled for the narrow gap. The Hun riders hared in on one flank of the legion, and the I Dacia on the other just as the XI Claudia spilled into the pass. Their flanks secured, all the legionaries turned to face front and the wave of Huns and I Dacia smashed against their lines.

Pavo felt the breath rattle through him and realised he was shaking violently. Life had been snatched from the jaws of death, but for how long? Now at least he could fight without restriction, he thought, as the legion formed up with a thin front to fill the neck of the pass. He thought of the heroics of the Spartans at the hot gates; he had read of it in the library, now he was to live it and probably die for the experience. His blood pumped even harder.

'Come on!' Zosimus spat, smashing his gore splashed sword against his shield boss.

'Fire plumbatae at will. Archers, fire at will!' Gallus roared.

The legionaries launched their darts with relish, each man holding three of the deadly missiles, and the front lines of the fast approaching Hun and I Dacia army crumbled.

'See how you like it, eh?' Avitus growled, wiping at the bloody gash on his arm after releasing the last of his darts. 'Get the archers firing!' He yelled to the auxiliary units.

Overhead a thin cloud of arrows arched up and dropped onto the heads of the enemy. The I Dacia lines were well drilled and lifted their shields to deflect the danger, but the Huns, clearly unused to pitched battles and close formations, soaked up almost every arrow, swathes of them dropping with a scream, but still barely a drop in the ocean compared with their overall number.

Over in the valley, the ballista twang ceased as the artillery division were crushed under the five hundred riders sent to despatch them. Now the I Dacia and the Huns advanced on the rocky pass at full speed. Gallus forced his way into the centre of the front line.

'We're not beaten yet, men. Let's make every sword count.'

# Chapter 56

'The right is about to collapse!'

The front line of the first century looked up to see the legionary standing on top of the left-hand cliff of the rocky pass, waving his banner. 'Strengthen the right or they'll break us!' He repeated before the thud of an arrow punching into his throat and a gurgle signalled his end and he toppled into the sea of Huns. Below, the distinctive caps and black locks of the Huns jostled well within what should have been the retreating line of the Claudia.

'If they break we're all buggered,' growled Zosimus as he butted out his shield and slipped his spatha forward to skewer a I Dacia legionary.

'Agreed,' Gallus bellowed to Zosimus, pointing further up the pass where pile of heavy rockfall lay. 'You and Pavo get yourselves up to that pass, it's our only chance.'

'Do what now?' Zosimus replied, dropping back from the front line as Quadratus took his place. He squinted up at the rock pile and then grinned. 'Ah, I'm with you, sir.'

A Hun raised his spear to strike at Sura and Pavo swished his spatha into the exposed flank. The Hun's ribs shattered and he crumpled to the ground. Pavo turned to face his next foe in the tide, only to be wrenched back from the front line by his collar.

'You're needed,' Zosimus yelled.

Righting himself, Pavo followed Zosimus' gore spattered boots as he hopped up the scree-strewn climb. His own boots slipped in the dust and at the steepness of the path – close to vertical at points, and his quivering limbs begged for an end to this relentless torment. At last, Zosimus came to a halt by a pile of rockfall. Three other legionaries stood there, eyeing the veteran expectantly.

'We need to buy some time if we want to get our boys up this path,' Zosimus barked, jabbing a finger towards the swell of the legion plugging the pass – tiny in comparison to the black and silver sea of Huns and I Dacia swarming at the mouth of the pass – and then up at the hilltop, where the fort wall and gate were now visible. Two figures were already almost at the hilltop, having been despatched by Gallus to do a swift reconnaissance on the fort. 'So get yourself behind one of these bad boys,' he grinned, sidling up to the rockfall; a number of jagged boulders, sized just larger than a man, sitting precariously on the lip of one of the near vertical sections of the pass. Down below, the right flank was now bent in almost past the safety of the cliffside protecting them. 'Come on, no time to waste!'

Zosimus and the other three pressed their shoulders to the rocks with a chorus of grunting. Pavo flicked his eyebrows up, took a deep breath and hurled himself into the side of the smallest boulder. Its surface gouged at him and took the breath from his lungs as he pressed into it. The boulder didn't even shake. 'In the name of…how am I supposed to shift one of these?'

'Put your back into it, lad!' Zosimus scowled.

Pavo dug his spear into the dirt under the massive rock and threw all his weight on the shaft. 'Come on!' he snarled, sweat pouring into his eyes. Slowly, ever so slowly, it rocked and then slid forward. He heaved at his boulder until, in tandem, his and Zosimus' boulders crashed forward down the pass together with the three heaved by the other legionaries.

'Have that!' Zosimus screamed. And in unison, the five fell back, panting.

'Hope that one fits you, Spurius!' Pavo spat as his boulder thundered downhill.

Gallus, watching their progress, turned to yell across the lines; 'Break!' His voice echoed through the pass and over the iron clatter of battle and as one, the ranks of the Claudia broke apart at the centre, like floodgates. The Huns and the I Dacia poured into the gap, their momentum throwing their front ranks to their knees as those behind powered forward, lusting for blood. Then an almighty rumble stopped them dead in their tracks.

The five ragged stone juggernauts ripped right through the gap in the Roman line, crunching over the Hun and I Dacia swell like a herd of rhinos charging over ants. Bodies exploded under the masses, limbs were ripped off and blood jetted skywards. The ranks staggered in confusion as five broad crimson paths lay in their wake. The unstoppable tide that had threatened to drown the XI Claudia just moments before now drained away in panic. The sea of Huns swarmed backwards at last, and the I Dacia turned and fled in their wake. Right on cue, another three boulders careened down the mountainside, shattering the ranks that remained in the gap. A hoarse cheer erupted from the Roman lines. Then as soon as the boulders were through the breach in the Claudia, the two halves of the legion closed up, quickly hacking down the stragglers in their way, before Gallus cried out.

'Quick retreat!'

Without hesitation, the legion beat a fast march up the rocky slope, covered by the remainder of the Cretan archer auxiliaries who lined the higher portions of the path.

Pavo watched as the legionaries streamed past him, unable to tear his eyes from the carnage. He felt only numb.

Sura bounded up to him, slapping him on the back. 'Nice move with the boulders. I thought we were dead meat there! Now come on, they're coming up after us!'

'What're you standing around for? The fort's over the next ridge,' Gallus barked on his way past.

Pavo looked up to see the two legionaries up top, waving the standard – the fort was safe. He set off at the tail of the retreating legion, his boots scraping and slipping in the ever steeper climb. A blood-spattered legionary beside him laughed deliriously, holding a hand out to help him. He took it and wrenched himself level with the man.

'You saved our bacon there, lad. That's an ale I owe you,' he grinned and then set off uphill, but his boot slid.

'Whoa!' Pavo gasped, swinging out a hand to catch him.

'Better make that two ales, eh?' the legionary chirped.

Pavo smiled and made to reply, when two arrows thudded into the legionary's chest. Blood sprayed Pavo's face. Recoiling in horror, he shot a glance down to the regrouped Hun and I Dacia ranks, they were advancing again – and fast. As another wave of arrows leapt up into the air he dropped the still form of the legionary and turned to scuffle through the rubble, his legs felt like lead and the ground like ice as he struggled to make any headway.

Felix urged him on from above, reaching out to clasp his forearm and haul him up – just as a pack of arrows thudded into the spot he had been standing. 'Come on, Pavo!' They turned to hobble on, when Gallus skidded down the slope next to them.

'Felix!' He gasped, holding out a stuffed ration pack. 'Take this. It should be enough to sustain three men for six days.'

'Okay...' Felix raised an eyebrow. Ducking as arrows thudded just behind him.

'We have a chance to bed ourselves in this fort. But once we are in there, we are completely cut off from any route of escape. Take two men and get round the hill and down to the coast.' He pointed to the snaking rubble tracks wrapping around the girth of the hill. 'I don't care how you do it, but get yourself seaborne and get back to Constantinople. Time is of the essence, Felix, before they encircle us.' Arrows began to patter down only paces below them, and all three cast nervous glances at the rising tide of Huns. Pavo spotted the snarl of Festus at the front line of the accompanying I Dacia.

Felix stood a little straighter. 'Allright, Pavo, you're with me.' The optio glanced around for another man, but Gallus cut him off.

'No, he's needed here.'

Felix hesitated, 'Hold on – you're from the capital, aren't you?'

'Constantinople? The place runs through my blood,' Pavo panted. His mind coloured with memories of his time before slavery.

'So you know the streets?'

'A little too well,' he panted, 'kind of why I wound up in the legions!'

Gallus looked Pavo in the eye and then nodded. 'You're a good soldier, Pavo. Do us proud.'

Pavo felt his heart was close to bursting under his mail vest. Months of pain and dejection just for one line of praise. It felt like the sweetest honey. 'Yes, sir!'

'He's yours,' Gallus nodded to Felix. 'But remember, you must enter Constantinople as a civilian – no armour or anything that would give you away as a legionary. Treat the place like the snakepit it is!'

'Sir, what...'

'Just listen, Felix. You must only speak to the emperor and nobody else. You must tell him of our situation and the treachery that has taken place. Don't trust anyone else except the emperor in person. I've met him once, and if I'm any judge of character then I believe he has no part in this. He will see justice done for this treachery, I'm sure of it.'

'Consider it done, sir. But even if I make it through to Valens, it'll be days at least before I return.'

Another arrow zipped past them and the roar of the climbing enemy shook the ground the stood on. 'Felix, this is our only hope, you must leave...now!'

Pavo could almost feel the desperation in the centurion's voice.

'As you command,' Felix barked. 'Sura! You're coming with me, too.'

Sura, ten paces further uphill, spun round. 'Eh?'

'We're going to Constantinople,' Pavo yelled.

The legs of the Claudia were beyond leaden as they plodded in exhaustion up the ever steeper climb. Even the Hun pursuit had slowed and the arrow hail nipping at Roman heels had thinned as the afternoon sun set its rays on their backs. A red dust cloud hung over the mountainside marking the path of the climb – the coarse powder lining the throats of every legionary. Finally though, the ridge above them rolled level to reveal the small, sturdy stone fortress.

'Sanctuary!' Amalric cried.

The walls were the height of two men, crenellated and punctuated with squat but solid looking towers, one on each corner and one at the midpoint of each wall. The place looked like a reasonably sized auxiliary fort – it would be cramped, but they were in no position to quibble. Abandoned for years, nature had been hard at work reclaiming the stonework; tendrils of ivy laced the walls and thick grass sprouted from the mortar.

Gallus stumbled up onto the plateau where most of the legionaries had collapsed in exhaustion. 'First cohort, line the lip of this plateau – no bugger gets up here without a sword in their face! Get the second and third cohorts inside the fort.'

The men stumbled to their feet, cajoled by their equally shattered centurions. Gallus pulled his helmet off, scraping his fingers through his matted charcoal crop of hair, and hobbled to the far edge of the plateau to take in their surroundings; the plateau encompassed an area of probably one to one and a half stadia, with the fort perched on the sea-facing edge, covering maybe a third of that area. Behind the fort was a sheer cliff drop of some five storeys, and below, the shingle of the coast met with the shimmering blue sea, filling the horizon to the south and east. To the west, Chersonesos presented itself. The city was a patchwork of red tiled roofs, marble and stone structures and an impressive fortified wall, stretching many times higher than a man, tantalisingly close. Then he rubbed his eyes; tiny shapes moved through the streets like ants – thousands of them. Huns. 'They're everywhere,' he gasped, his throat rasping. He rested his hands on his burning knees and gulped hungrily at the thin hilltop air. Hobbling back to the other edge of the plateau, he helped a straggling legionary up to safety, then the breath stuck in his lungs as he took in the horde that swarmed below them. They covered almost the entire floor of the vast valley and the face of the hill. Near the right of their front lines, a relatively ordered silver square marched – the treacherous I Dacia. Then he noticed their movement, they were climbing back down the hill. 'They're pulling back!' He cried.

Avitus sprinted over. 'Starving us out, then? We're royally screwed. I'd prefer a fight.'

'It may not come to either, Avitus,' Gallus chirped, pulling the legionary with him into a jog over to the southern edge of the plateau. He wrapped an arm around Avitus and pointed out over the deserted blue sea behind the fort. 'Salvation lies that to the south.' Then his eyes narrowed and he whispered; 'May the gods be with you, Felix.'

'Centurion,' Amalric called from the northern edge. 'This fort is well built. But we cannot hope to hold out here for long.'

Gallus nodded. He kept a sincere expression, but his mind jabbered with a thousand voices. The loudest being Nerva's last words – berating Gallus' decision to overrule an order – was it the right thing to do? Would the tribunus be standing next to him now if they had moved forward through the valley as one unit? He cursed to himself and shook his head. Nerva was gone and he had to lead these men through this. Primarily, food supply was a

288

concern – having lost the pack mule train meant they had soldier ration packs alone for sustenance. 'Can we forage for anything up here?'

'Nothing substantial, berries and a few roots and pulses,' Amalric replied, 'although we have plenty of fresh water,' he nodded to the trickling brook, snaking out from the calm pool of water sitting in a natural reservoir. 'There's probably enough in there to last a week, maybe a little more. And then we're in the lap of the gods,' he flicked his hands up at the cloudless sky.

Gallus looked to the first cohort – still lining the northern lip of the plateau, waiting on the order to stand down. 'Fine. Zosimus, Avitus – in lieu of Felix, you are promoted to be my optios. Zosimus, you're in charge of keeping a cistern inside the fort – I don't care what you use as long as it's clean and it's full. Avitus, you're in charge of food. Collect all the men's rations and set up a store. We're going on half rations, so your next job is to tear every edible morsel from this hill and bolster what we have. Take ten men each.' The rest of the cohort looked to their centurion expectantly, faces lashed with sweat and either pale with weakness or crimson with overheating. So many had been lost, he realised, only four hundred or so of the eight hundred full complement of the first cohort were present. He glanced briefly down the rocky slope they had just ascended – dead legionaries and auxiliaries lay still and silent in their armour like scattered scrap metal. Gallus shook his head wryly; 'Keep a twenty on each face of this plateau. Three shifts a day. The rest of the first cohort – fall out!'

The cohort breathed a collective sigh of relief, moving as one to the fort gates, now being prised open fully by the second cohort.

'Quadratus – hold on,' he caught the big Gaul by the arm as he trudged past. 'I've got two optios, so why not make it three. You're in charge of the watch. I don't care how tired these men are - they stay awake or they get their balls cut off!'

'Heh! My pleasure, sir,' Quadratus chuckled. The big Gaul's eyes were red and bagged, but he was a man who would never relent to fatigue.

'Right,' Gallus cried, 'let's investigate this fort, get some food in our bellies and get our heads together – we need a plan!' He stopped a moment, letting the wind catch his hair. He hadn't thought of Olivia today until now. Not once. Guilt dug at him from all sides. He pulled his helmet back on and fastened the chin strap so tight that it dug into his skin and his mind cleared again. They had all seen too many of their comrades die today.

# Chapter 57

A cool wind blew in Pavo's eyes, welcome but barely offsetting the heat of exhaustion. He watched Sura and Felix's boots slap rhythmically in front of him, kicking up the chalky red dust into his parched throat and stinging eyes. A salty tang speckled the air as they rounded the eastern path towards the coast. The call of gulls had led them round until the marine blue of the Pontus Euxinus had replaced the green of the hills. Once the hill was between them and the battle and the clash of iron and screaming had stopped, it felt to Pavo as though they could have been a million miles away from danger. But a glance to the ground below was enough to shatter the moment of calm; a thick dark belt of Hun riders poured around the base of the hill like a serpent. If they could not get round and down from the hill before the jaws of the enemy closed around them then all was doomed. The walls of Chersonesos then peeked out from the edge of the hill – the battlements also writhed with Hun soldiers.

'Whoa!' Felix skidded to a halt. Pavo and Sura stumbled up next to the diminutive optio and followed his line of sight. Down below the stream of Huns coming round the mountain from the east and west had met. They were encircled in a noose of ferocious riders. 'Get down – we need to think of a backup plan – and quickly!'

The sun was falling. Only a few hours of daylight left. Pavo crouched with Felix and Sura behind a rock pile near the southern base of the hill. Ahead, a thin strip of brush ran between them and the beach, which shimmered in the long orange late afternoon rays. Beyond that lay the waters – the way home.

They had scrambled down the hillside in between each Hun patrol. Packs of roughly fifty riders were sweeping around the mountain base, giving almost blanket coverage to the area. The three had used the few moments in between where the patrols had been a little sloppy, throwing themselves down the rough terrain, and now wore the cuts and bruises to prove it.

'No boats,' Sura muttered.

'Thanks, Sura,' Felix hissed, 'I think we established that some time ago.'

Pavo gazed into the dock of Chersonesos – about a mile to the west – and counted the number of triremes bobbing gently in the harbour area. Wulfric and the I Dacia were in this up to their eyes. 'There's got to be a way that we can get into the city and get one of those ships.'

'This isn't nicking fruit from a street stall, Pavo,' Felix chided him, 'We're XI Claudia all over, and we're talking about getting inside that bitch of a wall, strolling through some twenty thousand of those stocky little buggers, plus the small matter of a couple of thousand cutthroat traitors who call themselves legionaries. Then,' he gasped, running out of breath, 'then we have to man a trireme – three of us? Come on, think again.'

Pavo scowled. 'Maybe it's not going to be that difficult, sir.'

Now even Sura looked at him in incredulity. 'I've pulled off some spectacular heists in my time, Pavo, but come on...'

'Hear me out,' he insisted, 'We want to get a boat, right?'

Felix shot him a glare.

'I'll take that as a yes...sir,' he added quickly. 'So why not go the direct route? If we want a boat, we go in by sea. We swim it!'

Felix cocked an eyebrow. 'Aye, thought so. You are mental.'

'Sir!' He gasped. 'That sandbank that would cover us, so we would be able to slip right up to the harbour. Time is not on our side and,' he held his arms out, 'I can't see how else we are getting in there.'

'Allright, Pavo,' Felix nodded, casting an eye to the sun, 'I'm entertaining you here. But tell me – how do we take control of a trireme from water level – we couldn't take our armour or anything if we were to swim it?'

'Well I don't know, but at least it gets us closer to our goal,' he blurted. He felt his heart race as he tried to salvage his argument.

Sura shrugged his shoulders. 'Aye, but still, how do we pilot a trireme with three people?'

'There might be a small cog in there somewhere – we'll never know unless we get closer. Look – do either of you have a better plan?'

Felix and Sura stared back blankly, and then shook their heads in resignation.

'Pavo, I can't believe I'm saying this, but you win. Armour off, chaps, just a dagger and some rope or we'll be fish food.'

Another pack of Huns thundered past, just on the other side of the rock pile. 'Don't they ever lose any time?' Felix hissed in frustration as the first pack slipped around the hillside and yet another pack rolled into view covering the line of sight.

'What if one of us acts as a decoy, sir?' Sura chirped. 'To distract the riders for long enough so the other two can get in the drink?'

'There are only three of us, Sura. It's a good idea, but it's risky. If the decoy gets caught, then we'd all be stuffed…and I dread to think what would happen to the decoy should these whoresons get their hands on him.' Silence descended on the trio for a few moments as the Hun party rumbled past.

'I'll be the decoy, sir,' Sura spoke in a low voice. Felix turned to argue once more, but Sura cut him off before he could begin. 'I'm a fast runner. Long legs and all – no offence, sir.' The diminutive optio barely suppressed a grimace. 'And although he's built like a gazelle, Pavo is more like a pregnant cow when he tries to run. So it's got to be me. Come on, it's now or never.' Again, a silence descended onto them.

Felix was clearly flustered, and he hesitated for a few moments too long.

'See you on the boat,' Sura chirped, before leaping over the rock pile just behind the Hun patrol.

'Sura…' Pavo swallowed his words and ducked as the Hun pack snapped round at the sound of his friend's boots scraping on the rocks.

'Come on then!' Sura cried at the riders, then cupped his hands to emit a shrill whistle.

'I thought you were a scatterbrain, Pavo, but that boy is a bloody idiot!' Felix was scarlet with rage.

Pavo felt his blood run cold as he watched the Huns close in on his friend, lassos spinning and spears dipped. 'No disrespect, sir, but I made a pact with Sura. I'm not having him die for nothing.' With that he leapt up and over the rock pile, landing gently in the grass.

'Pav...' Felix spat behind him, 'Oh for...' he finished, hauling himself up and over too.

They scudded stealthily past behind the crescent of Huns who closed in on Sura, then flitted over the sand and onto the sandbank, then into the shallows.

'They're going to see us,' Pavo hissed as he glanced over his shoulder to see Sura jinking from a lasso throw, and then breaking into a sprint. But the Huns were on him, it was only a matter of moments before he was a goner.

'No they're not!' Felix grunted, thrusting a hand into Pavo's back. With a splash, the pair were underwater.

The icy water, a stark contrast to the baking dryness of the last few days, stabbed at every inch of Pavo's skin, but he pulled himself down. He had to hold his breath and wait until the Huns were out of the line of sight of the water. Finally, his lungs burned like coals. He lost control and burst clear of the surface.

'In the name of...will you get down?' Felix yanked at his sopping tunic and he sank back to have only his eyes peeking from the water. They watched as a dust cloud kicked up behind a detachment of five Hun riders who galloped off at speed to Chersonesos – dragging something in their lasso. 'Don't think about it, Pavo, we can't let anything stop us. Now let's get our arses over to that harbour.'

His skin burned as he realised his most basic of mistakes. 'Sir, there's something I forgot to mention,' he winced.

Felix gave him a look that he could only surmise as one of utter disbelief. 'Let's hear it.'

'I,' Pavo stammered, 'I can't swim.'

Felix made to roar with disgust and just swallowed the urge in time. 'I get sent on the most important mission of my life, and I get two bloody clowns for sidekicks. What in Hades d'you mean you can't swim?'

'I just got carried away and forgot that I couldn't...' Pavo started

'Bollocks! Come on!' Felix wrenched him by the scruff of his tunic, dragging him through the shallows until he felt his feet kicking only at water. 'Only one way to learn,' the optio grunted.

Pavo felt the cool water lick at his face as he flailed, the depths striving to pull him under. His limbs searched furiously for purchase, his fingers clawing at the wake of Felix's paddling feet. Another wash of salty water filled his mouth and he hacked it out, sucking in the next breath that was half spray anyway.

'For Mithras' sake, Pavo,' Felix hissed, 'keep it to a gentle racket or we're dead!'

His mind screamed at him. *You're going under, you're going to drown.* His lungs burned and his heart raced like a drum. Then a long-forgotten voice echoed, quietly at first, and then it grew. It was Father, standing with him in the warm summer shallows of the Propontus, coaching him to paddle. *Fill your lungs and you'll shoot to the surface, Pavo. That's it, now it's you that's in control, not the water! Now pull your arms out and around, imagine you are as light as a feather. That's it – keep moving!* The waves began to part in front of him and he gasped in another lungful of air.

'What the? Are you taking the piss? I thought you said you couldn't...' Felix spluttered as Pavo drew up next to him.

'Seems I could after all,' he replied, frowning.

They paddled on in silence, and the harbour walls of Chersonesos began to peek over their covering sandbank before long. Pavo glanced up, counting a handful of spear tips bobbing behind the crenellations. 'Stay in close to the bank,' he whispered to Felix.

'No need,' the optio hissed, lifting a seaweed and slime coated length of rope from the water. The rope caused a shiver in the surface of the water, betraying its lie all the way up to the hull of the second trireme. 'This'll take us in between those two ships. Out of sight and with our pick of the vessels!' They pulled forward on the rope, cutting through the grimy harbour water until they touched the Hull.

'You first,' Felix nodded.

The rope waved up above them, looping onto the deck of the vessel. Pavo shimmied up only a few times and then slithered back into the water.

He tried again under a fiery glare from Felix, only to come crashing down again. 'Too wet and slimy – we need another way up.'

'Bugger!'

Pavo examined the side of the vessel; the oar holes punctuated the hull every few paces about halfway from the waterline. 'If we can get up to the oar holes?'

'You'd need to be tiny to get in one of those...oh, I see. *I'll* do it, shall I?'

'Needs must, sir.' Pavo smiled innocently. 'Here, I can give you a foot up.' He cupped his hands and the optio used the momentary fraction of extra height he gained before Pavo sunk down underwater to launch himself up and grapple the edge of the oar hole. Pavo saw the optio's legs squirm inside. Alone, Pavo felt suddenly cold and alone as the scummy water lapped at him. He rallied himself with his father's words as he paddled gracefully to stay afloat and wondered what else might be lurking in the shadows of his mind. Then he jolted to attention as a Hun Lasso dropped around him and wrenched tightly around his arms and midriff.

'By Mithras, you're heavy for such a skinny bugger,' Felix grunted from above, his face straining red and his boots anchored on the lip of the vessel.

The rope lurched upwards in fits and starts, and Pavo felt like some kind of prize catch as he flapped the bottoms of his pinned arms uselessly. Finally, he tumbled over the edge and onto the deck with a wet slap. Felix fell back next to him.

'Right, we've done the first impossible step. Now how in Hades do we sail one of these things?'

Pavo sat up, wiping the water from his eyes. His entire body froze as he looked up the deck. Twenty legionaries stood, grinning, swords drawn, I Dacia colours emblazoned on their shields.

'That's the least of our worries, sir.'

Sura cried out as the horsemen dragging him rounded the gatehouse of Chersonesos. His knees, already stripped of skin, scraped onto the flagstones, leaving a scarlet trail. Flitting glances up at the roadside, he saw the baying faces of Hun soldiers, women and even children, all bearing angry scarring on their cheeks. Stones rained down around him, and only the speed of the riders saved his bones being crushed under the hail. Only when his eyes began to slide shut from the pain did they finally slow.

A dagger glinted in the sun, but it barely registered as he waited on the blade to sink into him. He was numb now. Instead, the thick chop of rope snapping was all he heard.

'Roman!' A jagged voice boomed. 'We are not finished with you yet. We will cut your throat soon enough, but first you will serve us. You will be the downfall of your pathetic legion.'

A spear shaft smashed into his jaw, sending a white light through his brain, and then another shaft ground in underneath him and propped him up, limbs dangling uselessly at his side. Then an icy wash of water crashed down on him and he gasped. His eyes flickered open; he was in the town square. Before him, a wooden platform had been erected. A Hun was sitting on a timber bench, affixing him with a glare that bit at his soul. All around him, the town square was bordered with Hun warriors, cheering as their leader settled to speak.

Then a voice called out. 'All hail the great and noble Balamber!' At once, the square fell silent to a man. The man on the platform smoothed his wispy moustache. His hooked nose and dead eyes seemed to judge Sura like a piece of rotten meat. A pile of iron armour lay by the side of the bench, but the man was dressed no differently from his kin; a red tunic and goatskin leggings, with a necklace of animal teeth. Sura trembled, the man had a terrible aura around him, and the thousands surrounding him seemed cowed into silence by his presence.

'Do you know who I am?' Sura grumbled belying the terror in his veins.

The Hun leader wrinkled his lips and a smirk hung on his face.

'I do, you are one of the many who will die before me. My mercy is rare and sparing. Your life is...'

'...Unofficial King of Adrianople...' Sura muttered, cutting Balamber short.

Balamber's eyes flared. 'Silence him!' He roared.

At once a sword hilt smashed into Sura's cheekbone and he fell back to the ground, head lolling limply to one side.

'Throw him in the cells. And cook up some metals!'

Pavo circled back to back with Felix, dagger in hand, near the centre of the deck by the mast.

'You dirty whoresons are going to make a fine kill,' Felix spat at the twenty as they formed a circle around them. 'Call yourselves Roman?'

'Roman?' The largest called back. 'No, I call myself a Goth – a proud follower of Athanaric. Good of your emperor to foot the bill for all this kit though, eh?'

'So you're whoring yourselves to Rome one minute and to these vicious, ignoble buggers the next? I wouldn't be too proud of that,' Pavo threw back. 'Do you know how many of your kin they have slaughtered?'

The legionary chuckled, tucking his sword away. 'Not as many as Rome has over the years,' he patted his purse, 'and besides, it pays handsomely. Now if you want to die then keep waving those toothpicks at us, otherwise, drop them; Noble Balamber wants to meet you.'

Pavo shot a glance over his shoulder to Felix.

'Don't look at me, lad. Only way this dagger comes out of my hand is when I'm cold and stiff.'

Pavo eyed the mast; a rope billowed in the breeze from the crow's nest high above. 'Hold on!' Pavo gasped and then swiped at one half of the rope with his dagger, grasping the other half with his free hand. With a ripple, the sail tumbled down, yanking Pavo upwards. 'Grab my legs!' Felix spun round just as the rope zipped up, carrying Pavo with it.

'Whoa!' Felix cried as he grabbed on and the pair shot up, wind roaring in their ears all the way up until Pavo's shoulder smashed into the foot of the crow's nest.

He winced at the searing pain - blood dripped from the gash in his shoulder. Then down below a posse of Hun footmen thundered onto the deck, pulling composite bows from their backs.

'Take them down,' the I Dacia trooper snarled. 'Hit them in the arms and legs – your Noble Balamber wants them alive – but not for long!' Their bowstrings strained and Felix kicked out violently into the air.

'Come on, stop dallying and get me in the nest!' Arrows zipped past them, thwacking into the timber of the mast. 'Bloody...argh!' He barked as an arrow scythed past his cheek, spraying blood.

Pavo's mind swam, his lungs still burning from the swim and his gushing arm numbing as they hung. He pulled with everything he had, but Felix was like a dead weight.

'Right,' the optio snarled.

Suddenly, Pavo felt as if he was under a stampede. Felix's boots and hands dug into his thighs, then his stomach and then his neck as the optio clambered over him. With a thud, Felix was gone, over into the crow's nest, leaving Pavo dangling in the hail of arrows. Then he felt an arm wrestle him up and over into the tiny safe haven.

'Wake up you dozy bugger,' Felix roared, slapping Pavo across the face. 'This was your great idea – what now?'

Pavo rubbed the top of his shoulder. 'Didn't think that far ahead...' He looked around the tiny bucket shaped enclosure – empty apart from a bundle of canvas rolls and some cloth covered pewter jars.

'For Mithras' sake,' Felix gasped, gripping the edge of the nest and peeking over the edge, 'we'll have to jump into the drink again. Even then, they'll skewer us before we land!'

Pavo unravelled one canvas, and the acrid stench of paraffin curled up his nostrils. Thick bundles of arrows, their heads wrapped in dirty cloth tumbled to the floor. 'Fire arrows!' Behind the rolls, a pair of bows lay conspicuously, together with urns. Pavo popped the top off one and recoiled at the stench – more paraffin. 'Let's start a fire!'

'Burn the ships? Heh, like it, but how do we get back to Constantinople then?'

'Well maybe we don't, but at least we cripple these buggers as much as possible – it's all we've got.'

'I'm with you,' Felix replied, unscrewing the top of one of the urns.

Pavo fumbled in his purse – two flint chips, still dry, worked their way into his hand and he pulled them out and set to work, chapping them together until they began to spark. 'You ready, sir?'

'Hold me back,' Felix growled, holding his prepared arrow over.

One more strike of the stones and the arrow burst into an orange blaze.

'And this one,' Felix held the second bow over the flame.

Just then, a voice roared out from below. 'You're trapped! Stay up there and you'll just make things worse for yourself!'

Backs pressed against the nest wall, Pavo and Felix shot each other a glance. 'Ready? Ready!' They nodded in unison, before leaping up to hold their nocked bows high.

'Back off, or your fleet will light up the seas!' Felix yelled as his blazing arrow roared in the lofty breeze.

The I Dacia legionary's face dropped, eyes wide. 'You'll die in the flames too,' he stammered.

'Worth it to see your face when you realise you're trapped here – then when our reinforcements come you'll be powerless to stop them landing!'

'There are no reinforcements! You and your legion are already dead!'

'Bollocks to you!' Felix roared, stretching his bowstring.

Pavo followed suit, tilting his bow to the bank of triremes further up the harbour. 'Sir, are we really going through with this?'

Felix shot him a now all too familiar glare, but before he could reply, the voice from below boomed out.

'Perhaps you'll see sense now?' A patter of footsteps was accompanied by the swearing of an all too familiar Thracian voice.

'Sura!' Pavo gasped, glancing down to see his friend thrashing in between two Hun spearmen.

'We'll gut this one here and now. You've got till I count to three.'

'Sir?' Pavo fretted.

'One...'

'Er...stay strong, Pavo,' Felix mumbled.

'Two...'

'Oh, bugger,' the optio moaned as he lowered his bow. 'This isn't going to save anyone.' He turned to Pavo with a tired look. 'Any other ideas?'

Pavo sighed, his limbs slackening as he smothered his flaming arrow. 'Suppose we've got to face their leader then? It buys us some time, at least. I don't know how much, but while we stay alive, there's always a chance.'

Like starving wolves, Hun warriors scrambled up the mast and were upon them in moments. Pavo's eyes widened as the first sent a crunching blow with both of his fists into the back of Felix's neck, dropping the optio like a stone. The second smiled a cavernous yellow-tombstone grin before thrusting his spear shaft into Pavo's face.

# Chapter 58

The gentle bleating of a distant mountain goat filtered into the stone hall where the bulk of the legion had set up their beds for the previous night – a cramped but sheltered dorm. An amber sliver of sunlight explored the hall through the cracks in the rotting shutters as the morning sun began to peek over the hills to the east. The men of the legion lay in a thick sleep, and the morning buccina call roused barely half of them. What precious sleep they had managed had been rudely interrupted by the briefly terrifying and coarse braying of a straggle of pack mules, the few who had lagged behind before the Huns fell on the main mule train and had subsequently wandered to the hilltop. After much swearing and grasping for weapons, the legionaries managed to forgive the petrified animals, who brought with them a pair of prefabricated ballista parts and bolts, a handful of tents and a pack of salted meat.

Gallus rolled his legs out of his hastily arranged cot – a pile of foliage and his cloak. His body screamed of the previous day's battle. He hobbled to his tunic and threw it on along with his boots, which burned into his raw, blistered feet. As the rest of the legion rose, he shuffled to the barrel of grimy water in the centre of the hall and scooped a double handful of it, lashing it across his face. It jolted him as if it had washed over his heart and he gasped, running the remaining liquid through his hair. He slipped on his mail vest – stinking of dried blood – and then looked around at the still slumbering numbers and grimaced.

'Make haste, ladies! Have you forgotten the situation we are in?' He boomed. 'I want you out there and alert right bloody now!' The centurion's voice worked like a thousand buccinas and suddenly the shuffling legionaries became sprightlier and those asleep were jolted from their cots.

He fastened his sword belt and then slid on his horsehair crest helmet. Buckling his cloak he visualised the iron shutters closing in again. *These men need you to lead them*, he repeated to himself as he strode out into the courtyard of the fort. Already, those that remained of the first cohort were all present as far as he could tell. He gave them nothing but a firm nod. Zosimus, Avitus and Quadratus waited on him at the front, the trio looked haggard and even grumpier than usual for an early morning, but they were there for him, and that was what mattered. He gathered them into a small circle.

'We are safe from the south side,' he nodded to the edge of the fort overhanging the sheer drop, 'so that's in our favour at least. Harvest whatever timber we can find – get us set up with ballistae on the walls,' he pointed to the northeast and northwest corners of the mossy bulwark penning them in. 'Catapults, rocks, anything we can cobble together and fire down their throats, we do it.'

'Sounds good, sir.' Zosimus grunted.

'Quadratus – how did the watch go?' Gallus turned to the Gaul.

'Quiet – too quiet. They're all around us down there and they've men to spare, to say the least.'

Gallus thought of Felix. Defeat crawled across his mind, but he pushed it firmly to the side. 'Then there'll be all the more for us before reinforcements come!' The three optios smiled, and Gallus allowed his eyes to sparkle wryly.

Finally, the three cohorts and the auxiliaries were formed up. Gallus eyed the ranks and suddenly felt more alone than he ever had. Barely a thousand men stood before him. Many of those hobbled on crutches and those who stood freely wore bandages or coughed roughly, spitting blood into the dirt.

'I hope you're all feeling refreshed, because last night may well have been your last rest for quite some time. We are safe for the very short term up here, but if you haven't noticed, there are no cattle or olive groves up here for us to feast on. In short, we've got to make what we have last.' Gallus paused for a moment. 'As you all well know, we lost a lot of our brothers yesterday.' A solemn silence hung in the air as the wind whipped up dust around the legion. 'We're short on men and we're short on food, but when it comes to Roman endurance and cold, hard skill with sharpened iron – we are kings!' Gallus paced evenly in front of the legion. 'A detachment has been sent out to call for a relief force. I'm talking of true Romans here, not of the

treacherous whoresons down there, willing to sell their honour to animals.'
The legion rumbled in exhausted agreement. 'But let these animals come,'
Gallus whipped his hands up to either side. 'Let them come, for we will be
waiting, like a lion waits on its prey. For the empire, men...for the empire!'

Suddenly, the air was alive with the hoarse cries of the thousand.
Punching the air, rattling swords on shields.

'Cut down what timber you can find, we need artillery, we need arrows
and bolts. Pile rocks on the battlements, find urns that we can heat sand in
and pour from the walls. I want you to busy yourselves today by building this
place into a real Roman fort – to be a testudo for us to defend until a relief
force comes.' Gallus heard the words *if a relief force comes* echo in his head
as he spoke, but simply acknowledged it and showed his stiff jaw to the
legion as they broke up to set about their tasks.

'Is this really all there are left?' Avitus sighed when the cohorts were
out of earshot. 'A thousand men against twenty times that. Sir, you know we
don't stand a chance, don't you?'

'We can't win, Avitus, fair enough. But we don't have to. The relief
force is our lucky dice.' Gallus saw the unconvinced gurn the three new
optios wore, and dropped the rhetoric. 'Okay, it's looking bleak, but those
men need to believe,' he swept a hand back over the tattered legion. 'Stay
with me, men, I need you.'

# Chapter 59

Pavo sat up with a start, chains clanking and biting at his wrists. Dank didn't even begin to describe the filthy dungeon he found himself in. Illuminated in a semi-gloom from a portcullis entrance, high above, a stench of mould and rotting meat insistently clawed at his nostrils. With a retch, he realised he had been lying semi-submerged in a green-brown pool of *something*. He ignored the thundering pain marching through his head and tried to focus on the shapes on the floor around him

'Welcome to my lair,' a voice croaked from the darkness.

'Sura! What happened?'

'Seems like they want to get a bit of inside information on the XI Claudia.'

'What in Hades…' another voice croaked as a shape beside him sat up. The gloom outlined the short form of Felix. 'Feels like I've been sleeping in a bath of turds? Oh bloody heck…I have,' he yelped, wiping the murky slime from his face. 'Well, we've got the time you were after, Pavo. Let's start thinking.'

Pavo held up his shackles, as thick as his wrists and nearly rust-free.

'Forget it,' Sura cut in. 'Believe me, I've tried – nearly broke my wrist in the process.'

'How long have you been in here – how long have *we* been in here?' Felix snapped.

'You've been out cold for the best part of a day – as best as I can tell.'

'A day?' Pavo yelped.

Felix dropped his head into his hands. 'We've screwed it up.'

'What are they waiting on out there? Why don't they torture us or kill us – what use are we to them in here?' Pavo muttered.

'What use are we to anyone in here?' Sura mumbled in agreement.

'Right, how's about we start shouting?' Felix offered.

'What, to get attention? That'll work, but it'll likely be in the form of a spear shaft in the face...again!' Sura mused, rubbing his fingertips on the angry red welt around his eye.

'Sod it, we've got to do something,' Pavo reasoned.

All three fell silent for a moment, and then in unison, they filled their lungs.

'Come on then!' They cried. 'What are you waiting for?'

Their echoes bounced from wall to wall until they were breathless. Pavo's head thumped in protest as they fell silent, slumping back down in despair.

Then a roar of iron grating filled the stairwell above.

Four shapes filled the dim light at the top of the stairs and then thundered down to the dungeon floor.

'All right you pigs – you want what's coming to you?' Festus sneered, his three I Dacia legionaries grinning in unison. 'Ah, Pavo,' he cocked an eyebrow, 'it's going to be doubly painful for you, I can assure you.'

# Chapter 60

Gallus padded the battlements, wringing his fingers as he clasped them behind his back. Night had fallen, but the legionaries still swarmed around the walls. Probably more to give themselves less time to think of their predicament than anything else, he mused. Certainly, the day just past had stretched on forever for him as he supervised the proceedings. He examined the blistered, raw patches between his fingers. All the men, officers and ranks had mucked in and made a fine job of it though. Rudimentary ballistae had been hewn from every scrap of timber which they could harvest from the fort. Mounted every twenty paces along the wall were catapults; two of them had been put together and were now being bolted onto the courtyard, one facing northeast and one northwest. Spears, plumbatae and bows were piled at every second crenellation. A fragile but lofty timber watchtower had been erected in the middle of the courtyard, giving them an eagle-eye view of every area of the wall. Zosimus and Avitus had filled the designated supply rooms and cistern to their limits. How effective all this would be remained to be seen. In his mind, Gallus saw it as a dam of twigs waiting on a tidal wave.

He blinked and gritted his teeth. The injuries and shock from the initial battle with the Huns had settled. Eight hundred and seven fighting fit men remained. Just over seven hundred legionaries – enough to line the walls with a few hundred in reserve should the gate collapse.

'Quadratus,' he yelled across the courtyard, seeing the hulking Gaul about to set off on his inspection of the guard. 'What's the latest?'

'No change, sir. Think they're happy to sit in and starve us out.'

Gallus felt the slightest tinge of satisfaction. In a sustained siege, they would survive in the short term, but it was effectively a stay of execution. His only hope remained as fragile as his army – Felix, Pavo and Sura; if they could slip away undetected, the Huns might fancy waiting it out and letting the Romans starve. He scanned the sea of torches swimming around the base of the hill below and sighed as the balance of play grated on his exhausted mind.

'Give the current watch full rations. If a mosquito farts, I want to know about it.'

'Yes, sir!' Quadratus saluted.

# Chapter 61

Pavo stumbled to his skinned knees again as Festus rammed a sword hilt into his back, driving the breath from his lungs. He spat a mouthful of steely blood onto the floor.

'On your feet, you little turd!' Festus chuckled. 'You'll be wishing that pussy Spurius had finished you back in Durostorum, because you've got a whole world of pain to live through now.' He raised his sword flat and made to swing it down on Pavo's face.

'Hey Festus, I hear your mother is giving the troops in Constantinople a bargain two for one?' Sura croaked from the darkness behind him.

Festus stilled and then turned, striding across and swinging his boot full force into the shadows with a crack. Sura could only whimper.

'Think you're a big shot, do you, Festus?' Felix snarled. 'You're just a runt recruit – one of the poorer ones if I remember rightly. Enjoy your moment of power, because it'll be short, and after that…you'll be executed for this!'

'You'll not be around long enough to worry about that,' Festus snarled, then turned to his three legionaries. 'Get them moving!' At once, the three tumbled out into stark morning sunlight, staggering forward into the flagstones of the town square. The light burned at Pavo's eyes, reflecting from the pale flagstoned square and limestone of the surrounding buildings. All four sides of the square were packed with jeering Hun warriors, women and children. His eyes swept around their snarling, baying features until he spotted the sneering face of Tribunus Wulfric. Bile rose inside his chest.

'You treacherous whoreson!' He cried, lurching forward from his captors only for a sword-flat to smash into his shoulder. He tumbled onto his knees and gazed up at the sky as another thick chorus of jeers rained down on the three. Then stones began to smack down around them. Pavo felt one skate from his crown but he barely blinked. Then all at once, the crowd was silent.

Up front, a tall Hun, laden with animal teeth trinkets and wearing mottled animal skins, stepped up onto the wooden platform in front of them, and then settled down on a simple carved bench. Resting his bearded chin on his wrist, he burned holes into Pavo's heart with his stare.

'I didn't tell you about this bit,' Sura wavered. 'Balamber, he's their leader.'

Pavo looked his friend in the eye – fear danced there. Never before had Sura showed anything but foolish bravado in the face of danger. He glanced at Felix. 'What's the plan, sir?'

'Buggered if I know…defiance to the last,' Felix grumbled.

Balamber raised a hand and clicked his fingers. At once four Hun warriors shuffled from one side of the square, heaving a steaming cauldron with them. Festus roared with laughter and the crowd of Huns erupted again in excitement.

'Is that…bronze?' Felix stammered.

Pavo gulped at the optio's face – pale and wet with perspiration, and then he turned to his friend. 'Sura, what's going on?'

But then the cauldron was slapped down in front of them. Glowing red like the depths of Hades, metal swirled as liquid. Black char formed on the surface as the air tried in vain to cool its rage. A thick iron ladle hung from its side.

'Now, my Roman guests,' Balamber spoke smoothly, 'your brothers of the I Dacia have cooperated with me – look at them now; they have more gold than a lifetime as a soldier would pay. I hope you will be as cooperative?'

Pavo glanced up at the Hun's eyes and then down at the hand of the warrior by the cauldron as he lifted the ladle clear of the molten metal. The warrior held out a petrified vole. The creature pulled and tugged with all its strength at the warrior's leather glove, but to no avail. The ladle moved over the poor creature's head, and tilted.

Pavo whipped his head back in disgust as a stench of burning flesh clawed at his face and the screaming of the animal slowed and stopped. Sura wretched beside him and Felix growled in disgust.

'As a little twist,' Balamber continued, 'I will be rewarding you with precious metal, not if you cooperate, but if you fail to!'

The crowd roared and Balamber stood, reaching down to an urn by his throne. He grappled at something and lifted it up by black strands attached to it. Pavo blinked as he tried to put a shape to the glistening ball of metal and hair dangling there. Then it spun around and a grotesque meld of eyeball and cooled bronze hung out of what was once an eye socket.

'Apsikal displeased me, and now his head is an ornament. Now you will talk, or your heads will form a new set of ornaments for my throne room when we take your precious empire from you!'

Pavo felt his stomach weaken as he watched Sura being wrenched forward, his head tilted to one side and the ladle held over his ear. A pair of filthy hands grappled with Pavo's jaw and twisted his neck, forcing him to watch the spectacle. Beside him, Felix stifled a roar of frustration as he too received the same treatment.

'See, Pavo – that's going to happen to you, too! I'm going to enjoy this,' Festus roared from the sidelines.

'Now talk, or feel my wrath!' Balamber cried. The crowd roared on his every word.

Pavo felt his vision close in. Then Sura thumped forward onto the ground - unconscious from fear. The crowd began to jeer in disgust.

'Enough,' Balamber roared over them. 'It seems that these Romans don't have the heart to die like men. Yet they have not talked!'

'Die!' Roared the crowd in unison.

Pavo winched open one eye just enough to examine Balamber's face; the Hun leader stroked his beard, eyes darting from the cauldron to the three of them. A wicked grin split his face and he raised his hand and pointed a bony finger right at Pavo.

'Let this one *taste* the precious metal...'

Pavo's heart thumped in terror and the crowd erupted in cheers as his head was wrenched back and his mouth prised open. A grinning Hun lifted the growing ladle to Pavo's mouth and the stinging heat of the liquid metal singed the hair in his nose. His limbs trembled and terror raced in his blood and Pavo desperately sought the words of the soldier's prayer to Mithras.

Then a shout came from the harbour walls.

'Fire!'

Balamber dropped his hand, his mouth falling open as he turned to the disturbance. Two Hun warriors tumbled forward into the square. 'One of the ships of the fleet has been set alight – we must hurry or they will all catch!' Panic rippled around the watching thousands, and the jeers for death stopped.

'To the dock!' Balamber cried, sweeping his hands at his people as if they were toy soldiers. 'Keep the wall guard full strength though – this smells of treachery to me!'

Pavo fell forward, panting in disbelief. He shot a glance up at Felix, whose face was wrinkled in befuddlement as smoke billowed from the harbour.

Balamber strode over to Pavo, Felix and the prone form of Sura. He leaned in next to them, the reek of animal blood wafted from his teeth as he whispered, 'You will die and die horribly – but only once you have talked!' He stood tall again. 'Guards, take them back to the cells!'

Three I Dacia legionaries bundled them forward. Pavo caught flitting glimpses of the dock and the fleet through each passing alleyway; an angry black smoke snaked up around the masts and an orangey glare tinged the air above the decks. His head spun – he was sure they had doused their fire arrows.

'Stop!' A voice grunted.

Pavo's blood curdled in his veins. That voice. He looked up slowly, and their eyes met. Spurius. The contorted spasm of anger that was his face hadn't changed a bit.

'Hand them over to us,' Spurius barked, motioning to the two I Dacia legionaries by his side. 'We're taking them to the cells – you lot are needed at the docks!'

'Lucky us!' Sura gasped.

The legionaries grappling them looked at each other.

'What are you waiting for? Get moving!' Spurius roared.

The legionaries scuttled off and Spurius stepped round to wrench Pavo forward. Felix and Sura cursed as his two helpers grabbed them. They were bundled roughly along the main street and then sharply into a narrow alley between two dilapidated Roman style tenements, dim and shielded from the pandemonium nearby.

Sura fell to his knees and spat at Spurius' feet. 'I should've known. Festus is a traitor but at least he obeys his new Hun master. Go on, stick a dagger in our throats then – but you'll be the ones who end up getting liquid metal in your head when your master, Balamber, finds out.' His voice bounced off the alley walls and up and over the buildings.

Pavo winced as Spurius lurched forward and swept his fist into Sura's jaw. With a crack of bone, his friend's head fell forward and he was silent.

'Any more loudmouths?' Spurius hissed.

'What are you playing at?' Pavo spoke, eyeing the face of his old tormentor. Spurius wore a look of agitation, sweat drenched his v-shaped brow, trickling over his nose, and his eyes darted again and again to the alley mouth.

'No time to explain.' Spurius whipped his spatha free with a rasp of iron and hoisted it aloft. 'Stay still,' he croaked before bringing it hammering down.

Pavo clenched his eyes and waited on the iron to split his skull. The pain would be short lived, and then blackness would overcome him. He felt his arms being jolted forwards at the shoulders and a thunk of iron cutting iron. Blinking, he looked to his wrists to see the severed chain of his manacle swinging. Felix and Sura had been freed likewise. He looked up at Spurius, mouth agape.

'No time - I mean it! Come with me.' Spurius wafted his hand and stalked towards the mouth of the alley. He leant out, then ducked back and hugged the wall as a crowd of Huns tumbled past, laden with buckets and urns. Then with another quick glance both ways, he flipped his hand again to wave them forward.

Pavo went first, stopping just short of the shaven-headed hulk of a man he had strived to stay well away from until now. Suddenly, Spurius was off across the flagstoned main street and he dived into the opposite alley – between two more crumbling Roman tenements patched up with mud and roofed with rotting thatch. Pavo had a look both ways, ducking back as another ten of the I Dacia raced past. Then he, too, scudded across the road.

'What now?' He panted to Spurius as he pushed his back against the cold stone wall, the reek of smoke from the docks stinging his eyes.

'Give me a foot up,' Spurius whispered, jabbing a stumpy finger upwards.

Above them was a drop in the roof of the tenement where the mortar had crumbled, leaving a v-shaped hole just a few feet above them. Pavo cupped his hands, just as the rest of their party stumbled into the alley. Spurius wasted not a second, springing up from Pavo's hands and clutching at the wall's edge. Despite his considerable bulk, he managed to squirm up and over. The thud of his hobnailed boots on timber from within the building caused them all to start. Then Spurius poked his head over.

'What are you waiting for? Move!'

Pavo caught Felix and Sura's suspicious looks and then shrugged his shoulders. 'You got any other ideas?' Felix shook his head, then stepped forward and cupped his hands, nodding to Pavo in distaste.

Soon the six of them were up and inside the exposed attic of the tenement, creeping along the dry and rotting timber floorboards, squatting and rising to keep their eyes just above the dilapidated brickwork. The building was empty, but they all held their breath as they watched squads of hundreds racing back and forth to the docks, where now they could see the nearest trireme – black underneath the curtain of orange flame that enveloped it.

'Not a bad job, even if I do say so myself?' Spurius mused.

'You what? I want some answers – what in Hades is going on here?' Pavo hissed.

'Time for that later, suffice to know I'm on your side, now you see that boat?' Spurius extended a sausage-like digit to the bireme at the far end, bobbing innocently far from the blaze. 'Well that's our route out of here.'

'We've been here,' Felix hissed, poking his head in between the two. 'Six men cannot pilot a bireme – think again.'

'Already have,' Spurius cut in, 'there are forty men on that ship, ready to do anything to clear their names. They're due to do a patrol of the coast for the next few days, but they're well up for getting back to Constantinople. Yes, they took the gold, but like me, they had no choice; take a lump of gold in your hand or a blade of iron in your throat – which would you go for?'

'I don't bloody believe it...we've got a chance!' Pavo gasped to Felix and Sura.

'So all we have to do is get through the thousands of Huns out there?' Sura sighed. 'You chaps will be okay, but we're a little conspicuous?' He eyed the filthy, soaking and bloodstained tunics they wore.

'Lads,' Spurius whispered, clicking his fingers, 'get the gear!' His two colleagues scuttled over to the corner of the attic, pulling away a dusty canvas to reveal three sets of I Dacia armour. Spurius grinned. 'Get kitted up, we've only got so long before people start asking the lads on the bireme questions.'

Pavo clipped on the scale vest – light in comparison to his old mail one; the comitatenses armour was leagues ahead of the limitanei armour in terms of quality – scales of iron, much lighter and offering more complete protection, and it was still silver in colour, not a hint of brown rust. And the intercisa helmets were mirror-like, such was their perfection. He tightened his sword belt; it felt good to be armed again. They tightened up their chin straps and looked each other over.

'Bloody affront to the Claudia this is!' Felix chuckled, cricking his neck and rubbing his hands.

Without comment, Spurius hopped over the edge of the wall and slid down to the alley again. Pavo followed suit and they edged warily through the shadows to the opening. The cry of gulls grew and tang of saltwater and black woodsmoke thickened in the air as they approached. Spurius gave them all a stony look.

'Chins up and chests out, lads. We've only got one shot at this.'

# Chapter 62

The fire roared, the night sky glowing orange from its light. *No point in hiding now*, Gallus mused wryly as he stared into the flames. Fifty more had died of their wounds since the previous day and now, as darkness fell upon them again, he looked over his tired and hungry bunch. Numbering seven hundred and eighty three, only a few hundred more than a single cohort, they had still worked like a full legion. Now the place was armed to the hilt with every form of projectile, incendiary and obstacle they could harvest from the plateau. The bushes had been stripped of berries and a precious pair of wild mountain goats had been herded inside the fort. The cistern brimmed with fresh water. They were ready in so many ways. However, Gallus sighed, he knew they could never be truly ready for what waited on them down below.

Anxiety had settled in once the fort modifications had been completed. Too much time to think was never a good thing for a legionary, Gallus knew, and he had set them to the task of piling up this fire; a reward of roast goat waited at the end of the task. He pulled the meagre scrap of goat meat from the rib he held – the sweet fatty juice running down his wrist. Starvation wouldn't be an issue for a few days yet, but by then it would be too late; tomorrow, the Huns would climb the hill and come at the fort with all they had.

The scouts had moved expertly – like snakes in the grass – to observe the activities in the Hun command camp. Until now, the Huns had ringed the base of the hill, content to starve the XI Claudia into submission. Then, at dusk, one scout had stumbled into the fort, rasping foamy blood with every breath before he collapsed from the arrow lodged in his lung. His dying words had sent the fear of the gods around them all; some report had come into the Hun camp, not long after the curious blaze in the docks, something which stirred the dark Hun leader into a rage and to at once issue the order to prepare battle lines.

Only one thing could have stirred such a reaction, Gallus mused as he chewed down on another mouthful of goat meat. Somehow, Felix and his men must have escaped the peninsula. He lifted an eyebrow wryly as he imagined what sort of ploy the group must have conjured to pull off the impossible. But they must have been spotted, or somehow the Huns now knew about it. At least the initiative had been seized back, even if it was meaningless. For now the Huns would move in on them and they would be pulverised long before the days passed that it would take for any kind of meaningful relief force to be mustered and then to arrive.

He perked up as a legionary on the far side of the fire struck up a lilting tune on the strings of a kithara. Then his gaze fell into the fire again as he chewed on the meat. Olivia's face danced in the flames.

'Who are you thinking about, sir?' Zosimus asked quietly beside him.

Gallus blinked, turning to his new optio. 'It's a long story, I wouldn't know where to start,' he sighed.

'My little daughter's going to be four this year,' Zosimus continued. 'Lupia was talking of having a family feast to celebrate. On the fields to the north of Adrianople. The sun stays bright and warm all day long there. Just the chattering of the insects. Only place I can relax these days.' He fell silent for a moment as the fire crackled. 'Don't suppose I'll be going there again.'

The bluntness of his statement caused no visible reaction, but Gallus felt an empathy with Zosimus and the other men around him. Acceptance was no bad thing, but one thing was for sure; if they were to be annihilated by this black swarm from the wilderness, they would fight with the fire of wronged men.

# Chapter 63

The stolen bireme bobbed on the Pontus Euxinus, cutting a path through the darkness. Almost all of its crew of forty-six scrambled up and down the rigging like spiders, tweaking the mast so the sails could catch the best of the strong wind. Two figures were seated near the prow, panting, as they took a well-earned break.

'They'll kill her – make no bones about it. Cutthroats to a man. She gave me this the last time I saw her.' Spurius shook his head, rubbing tirelessly at the bronze trinket hanging from his neck. 'You'll never understand what I've risked for you, Pavo. The Blues…if we don't get back before…'

Pavo thought of his own mother – the empty space in his heart where she should have been. He ached, not for her, but for the pain Father must have been through in losing her. He reached forward, clamping a hand on Spurius' shoulder; the Blues were ruthless, mindless animals – just like the Reds and the Greens. 'I'll do everything I can to help you. Your mother won't be hurt, I promise you that. If you hadn't made this move, the Claudia would be slaughtered for sure.' He eyed the sky – still pitch. It was morning when they set off from the docks of Chersonesos and they had no accurate measure of their position or the time they had been at sea. It had felt like a long time, for sure. 'We're not far from Constantinople now.'

'Less words, more action!' Spurius snarled, shaking Pavo's hand free, and then lurching over to the mast, where he shimmied up to the soaked rigging and started bawling at the exhausted legionaries. 'Faster, you buggers!'

Pavo's legs wobbled as he tried to stand – just a few more minutes, he afforded himself, slumping back down again. He touched a finger to the phalera around his neck. So different yet so similar, he mused. His thoughts whirled like the wind around him as his mind tried to settle the state of affairs. Spurius, the bullying bane of his life for months at Durostorum, had been unveiled as a victim; in masses of debt with the Blues of Constantinople and with no means of paying it off, the thugs had sworn to kill his mother if he did not complete a contract on Pavo's head. Allied to this, it was surely only a matter of time – if it had not already happened – until the Huns realised their prisoners, and a patrol boat, had went missing. As soon as that coin dropped, Pavo shivered, the Huns would know a relief army was a possibility and the remains of the XI Claudia would be crushed. Every instant was precious from here, yet time seemed to be dancing away from him, taunting him with catastrophic failure. He prised himself to his feet and hobbled towards the mast.

'There she is,' Felix cried as the faint band of orange glowed on the horizon of the night sky.

Constantinople. Pavo felt warmth and bitterness wash through his veins at once; childhood with his father and then slavery under Tarquitius.

The silhouette of the great capital emerged gradually; domes and towers became distinguishable as they approached. Then, like the beacon of imperial majesty and faith that it claimed to be, the emblem of the cross pierced the glow from the tips of the highest buildings. The capital dominated the horizon and a choir of gulls congregated around the vessel to welcome them.

'Right, lads,' Felix called, dropping down from the mast onto the deck, 'into the rags, as we discussed!' The optio slipped off his sword belt and kicked off his legionary boots. Now, dressed only in a torn and shabby grey wool cloak, he looked more like a tired beggar than a legionary. The crew around him followed suit, while some set about rolling up the eagle-emblazoned sails and hacking tell-tale parts of the boat's structure away. 'A bireme passing itself off as a trade vessel?' Felix chuckled. 'If we pull that one off, we're charmed!'

'I wouldn't even take time to think about it, sir. We've got to just go for it,' Pavo sighed. 'One other thing though, sir. It's Spurius.'

'What about him? He'll be lucky not to be executed.'

'He's risked everything to get us out of there and come back here.' Pavo's eyes darted across the optio's face. 'We should give him some men.'

'Is this to do with all that blubbering about his mother?'

'He's talking about facing a gang all by himself – we've got to help.'

'Dunno,' Felix grumbled, 'like you say, we've got to stay focused. Anyway, chin up, lad, we've done so well to get this far.' The optio then addressed the men once more. 'Get all the shit in the hold up here, scatter some tools on the deck, break stuff - make this ship look like a floating turd!'

Pavo frowned as he set about pulling the ropes from their tightly coiled spindles and spreading them across the deck and then scattering tools on top of them – a mess any trade cog would be proud of. Then he leapt just in time as Sura hurled the latrine bucket across his path.

'No need to go that far,' Felix chided him, 'bloody moron!'

Other cogs and light vessels bobbed past as they approached the city – the hub of trade in the empire. Pavo tried to keep his eyes on his business, just as a trader crewman would. But Spurius haunted his thoughts. He looked up to see the bull of a legionary hauling at the fur boxes with Sura.

'Allright, Pavo,' Felix grunted from behind him. 'You've earned the benefit of the doubt. We'll send ten along with him. But if this goes wrong...' the optio stuck out his lower jaw and widened his eyes.

'Fine by me, sir,' he beamed.

Then a cry erupted from the crow's nest. 'Prepare for boarding!'

Felix bristled and he instinctively reached for his missing scabbard, checking himself just in time. 'Bugger!'

Pavo spun to find the approaching vessel; in the darkness, the form of another bireme drifted into view. Its sides were lined with twenty eager looking legionaries. 'Urban guard!' Pavo hissed. 'The worst kind of money grabbing, corrupt buggers in all the empire.' He rubbed the old scar on his temple – courtesy of the urban guard's sword hilt that day back in the Palace of the Holy See.

The ship slid up to their starboard and the gangplank dropped into place, thudding on the deck of the bireme. The twenty thundered across it and onto the deck, fanning out to either side as they did so. The captain strutted to the fore like a peacock, dressed in an immaculate moulded breastplate and a highly polished and scarlet-plumed helmet.

'Here we go,' Felix whispered to Pavo. 'Looks like we've got a would-be Caesar to deal with.'

Pavo bit back the words of his reply, dropping his gaze to the timbers of the deck when he realised that the captain had heard Felix and was glaring right at them. Act humble and we might slip through this, he reasoned. The captain strode towards them, stopping barely a pace from Felix. Pavo noted with a sly grin how the captain had chosen to stand toe to toe with the smallest man on board.

'What's your business?' He barked.

'Trade,' Felix replied matter-of-factly.

'In this thing - trading what? Where did you steal this piece of driftwood from?' He snorted, eyeing the setup on deck. 'And you'll address me as an officer, you dog.' He brought the top of his hand cracking across Felix's cheek. The crew braced for a fight, the boarding party grabbed for their sword hilts.

'I'm sorry, sir. Textiles and furs,' Felix yelled, leaping up in between his men and the captain's. Tentatively, the two parties relaxed, swords sliding back into scabbards. He pointed to the carefully cut up pile of sail they had strapped up to look like batches of rough linen.

'Tat! Where are the furs?' The captain snapped.

'Furs?' Felix stammered.

The captain brought his knuckles raking across Felix's mouth again. Dark blobs of blood spilled down the optio's chin and onto his tunic.

'Are you going to make me repeat myself, you scumbag?'

Pavo's mind raced. They had not been prepared to be boarded, never mind for their handiwork on the ship to be scrutinised like this. Was this the point where they had to act, before their disguise was rumbled? He reached for his sword hilt, concealed beneath his cloak. The others by his side did likewise. But Felix shot them a glare, quickly pushing himself in between the crew and the captain once more.

'Again, I'm sorry, sir,' Felix offered humbly, wiping his mouth with his cloak. 'We don't collect the furs until we dock in the city. The Germanians bring them in to trade, so we ship this rubbish in from Pontus and they lap it up,' he chuckled, nodding vigorously.

Pavo sensed the captain's intentions as he brought his hand up again – another punch might be more than Felix could laugh off. 'Sir, the samples?' He offered to Felix. The captain's hand froze. 'The fur pieces below deck?' He repeated, widening his eyes at the optio. Three furs lay down there – probably left-behind bedding from the soldiers of the I Dacia.

'Eh?' Felix cocked an eyebrow, glaring back over his shoulder. Then his face relaxed into a grin. 'Ah, right. I can give you a few samples if you like, sir? Keep you warm in the colder months.'

'Will the pockets be full?' The captain grinned rapaciously.

Felix sighed, 'How much for safe passage back to the docks?'

'Fifty *sestertii* and we might not put a hole in the side of this pigsty you call a boat,' the captain grinned.

'Fifty? You're robbing us blind,' Felix grumbled.

The captain leaned forward again, towering over the optio. Pavo gritted his teeth as Felix played the cowardly trader and cringed under his shadow. In the real world, the bully of a captain would have been beaten senseless by now. The captain snapped his fingers to one of his legionaries who followed Felix below deck to collect the furs. If they had to sleep rough, they would be doing it in their tunics and shabby woollen cloaks now. A small price to pay, he mused as the legionary returned from below deck, peering over the top of the pile of furs. Felix grimaced as he dropped a purse on top of the pile.

'Escort them into the docks,' the grinning captain barked, before striding back onto his own boat. 'Then we can hand these dogs over to the dock watch.'

Pavo shot Felix a glance; the optio's eyes were burning like hot coals.

# Chapter 64

Dawn shot its orangey tendrils out over the rugged landscape of Bosporus, grasping at the penumbra enveloping the hilltop fort. Gallus rested a leg on the crenellated battlements that now bristled with iron intent. His breath clouded in the dewy morning freshness and his stomach swirled as he observed the shadowed horde in the valley below. For now they were growing, rising like a flood towards the fort, causing the earth to shake. He glanced along the wall at the thin but determined line of legionaries.

At the crack of dawn they had been woken not by the legion buccina, but by the awful moan of the horns carried by the Huns – thousands of them at once wailed out, filling the land below, to be accompanied by a guttural roaring and gnashing like that from a pack of preying wolves. The wailing had tailed off only as the terrible rumble of thousands of hooves and boots packed the air. The ground trembled, even up on the hilltop, and a thick shroud of dust rose up to encircle them.

'So the scouts got it right,' Avitus observed in resignation. 'They know there is the slightest chance of a Roman relief force, so they are ending it, snuffing us out.'

Gallus nodded and sighed. The sea of Huns disappeared below the lip of the upper plateau upon which the fort was situated, and their terrible cacophony dulled too. In moments, they would reappear over the lip to fall upon the fort.

'You reckon they actually did it though, sir…made it to Constantinople?' Avitus' words were laced thick with doubt.

Gallus knew the answer. Getting to the capital was the first towering hurdle of many. And they could not hope to beat time itself. He studied the look on Avitus' face; defeat was swallowing the tinge of hope on the little legionary's features. 'Avitus,' the centurion started. The men did not need to know that they had no chance of salvation.

'Yes, sir?' Avitus queried at his centurion's hesitation.

'You make sure every man knows he's fighting for survival,' Gallus grinned. 'Let's make sure Felix, Pavo and Sura's efforts are not in vein, eh?'

'Yes, sir!' Avitus grinned, then turned to pass on the news.

Cries broke out all along the walls, piercing the rumble of the Hun advance. 'For Felix and the lads!'

Then they fell silent as the plateau flooded with a dark mass. The Huns poured onto the hilltop, their cries bursting out like a wall of noise as they thundered across the short stretch between the lip and the fort wall. The infantry led the charge, swathes of them lifting hastily hewn timber ladders, lassos and all with their trademark bows. Behind them, the shimmering pack of the I Dacia filled the hilltop, buccinas keening out in a spine-chilling discord with the Hun horns.

He gripped the hilt of his sword and swept it above him. The ground seemed to be shaking so violently that his vision blurred, but he filled his lungs. This would be the last line he could deliver before the two sides clashed. His eyes widened as he saw the spit frothing from the mouths of the front line Hun spear infantry – inebriated on the promise of blood.

'XI Claudia! You are the proud survivors of devious treachery. Our numbers may be thin, but our hearts burst with the fullness of our honour. All of you, each and every one of you, are now part of the first cohort. Fight like lions, men, let's show them what a mistake they have made in coming at us!'

He smashed his sword hilt on his shield and roared. The legionaries lining the wall, faces wrinkled in bitter determination – some tear-streaked and snarling – all cried out in reply. Then they bristled, ready for the Hun tide.

The ladders were now being passed forward as the tide of Hun infantry closed in on the wall. Gallus felt the coldness descend on him. *That's right,* he growled, *just a little closer.* Then the first of the Huns tumbled through the earth – a square black hole opening below him. His screams were not heard and only a jet of red told of his fate in the spike pit below. All across their front line holes crumbled below them and the charge faltered as the following ranks continued to charge full pelt. Chaos ensued across their lines as they tangled, fell and fought each other to avoid being barged into the deadly pits.

The charge had slowed almost to a standstill. Gallus' face curled into a determined grimace.

'Ballistae - let them have it, everything we've got!'

The array of some twenty ballistae, waiting on tenterhooks on the walls of the fort, finally spat forth iron in a crushing hail. The bolts ripped through the densely packed Hun ranks, skewering and snapping handfuls of men with each strike. Gallus felt his spine tingle as the XI Claudia roared above the sudden lull in the Hun war cry.

'Archers, loose!' He bellowed next. The platform in the centre of the courtyard bristled like a porcupine as the remaining ninety Cretan archer auxiliaries presented their bows and with a whoosh, their hail scattered over the confusion outside.

'Mithras! This feels good, sir,' Zosimus grinned with an insane sparkle in his eyes.

'You're telling me,' Gallus growled. He turned back to the carnage. The Hun infantry were being shepherded back into order by a contingent of their cavalry. And thin bands were being ushered carefully forward through the thin lanes between the pits, despite the ballistae rain.

'Take them down!' Gallus roared. The archers picked off a few men at a time, but their paltry number could not halt the tide. Soon the Huns were flooding past the pits and the charge was on once more. Thousands were barely twenty paces from the wall now, while those to the rear had been ordered to tip earth into the pits.

Gallus felt the joy at his booby-trap evaporate. He handled his spatha firmly and braced as he watched the Huns nearest to him race forward with their ladders. 'Ballistae, fire off every last bolt before they reach the walls! Men, brace yourselves and stay strong - this is going to get bloody ugly!'

# Chapter 65

A fine rain whipped down on the minor wharf of Constantinople as Pavo shuffled humbly from the deck behind Felix, unloading crates under the gaze of the urban guards. He glanced up at the shiny cobbles and the algae and weed coated dock walls, all illuminated grudgingly by a single filthy lantern swinging in the spray. The place was dead; so different from the daytime when you would barely be able to move for cheeky traders and vendors. But the eastern horizon behind was now bursting into an orange splendour – they had to shake off this leech-like captain and his men before the daily chaos ensued again. The high stone wall in front of them had stairs cut into them leading up to the city, and Pavo could just make out the intercisa peaks of a pair of guard's helmets at the top. They were obscured, but only just.

'Get a move on,' the captain of the urban guards growled. 'And make sure you leave out enough furs for another piece for each of us. But I want three pieces.'

Pavo felt his heart skip a beat. They had successfully bluffed their way past the boarding and inspection, but they had clearly been brought to this dark corner of the city to be robbed of everything they had.

Pavo heaved at the next of the empty crates on the deck.

'What in Hades do we do next?' Sura hissed under his breath, picking up the other crate. 'We've got nothing else to give them!'

'Hold on, we can stall them,' Pavo whispered, then turned back to Felix. 'The small stock of sample furs we have will come out last,' he offered. Felix turned to the urban captain and shrugged apologetically.

The captain jabbed a finger into his chest. 'Just make sure they come out soon! We've got other business to attend to.'

The disguised crew shuffled uncertainly, darting glances to one another. Blank looks all round as they moved each of the empty crates with painstaking care and attention.

'Am I going to have to slit one of your miserable throats to get you off your ship with my bounty?' The captain hissed at Felix, hammering another finger into his chest.

'Sir, I...' Felix stuttered, rolling his eyes over their surroundings. '...I...oh sod this!' He barked, bringing the hilt of his sword up from under his cloak in a clean swipe, straight into the captain's gut. The urban troopers leapt back in alarm as their leader spluttered a mouthful of bile onto the cobbles. Before he could regain his senses, Felix spun round to his men.

'Take 'em out! They haven't drawn a sword in anger in their lives,' he hissed, wary of the presence of the guards above them. 'Didn't mind bullying a handful of manky traders did you? Well you picked the wrong ones!'

The legionaries dropped their cloaks to reveal their sword belts and clamped onto the urban troops like wolves, dropping them swiftly with a series of headbutts, sword flats across the neck and solid punches. Pavo smashed his elbow up and into the chin of his opponent, who collapsed like a bag of wet sand. As he turned, there was only XI Claudia and I Dacia left standing. But someone was missing. Felix.

'Argh! Bloody...' The optio lay on the ground, clutching at his grotesquely dangling shin. The lower half of his leg was bent like a twig, with a shard of pure white bone pushing at the skin behind the wound. 'The bugger got me,' he cast an accusing finger at the prone guard captain.

'What do we do now?' Sura gasped. The I Dacia contingent looked to Spurius, while Sura and Pavo looked to Felix. A murmur grew into a rabble.

'Shut it, you idiots! Keep it down or we're dead meat,' Felix snarled through his pain. 'Here's what's going to happen; Pavo, you're in charge!'

'Him?' one of the I Dacia legionaries beside Spurius spat. Spurius shot him a cold glare.

'You'll address him as sir from now on or you'll be flogged, you fat turd!' Felix growled. The legionary dropped his gaze to his boots.

'What about me?' Sura moaned.

'You're bloody mental, son. Pavo is slightly less likely to get us all killed than you are,' Felix hissed.

'Sir?' Pavo felt his mouth shrivel like parchment as all eyes fell on him.

'Just listen! I'm knackered, so you'll have to take the men through the city, and keep your heads down. Get to the emperor, Pavo, I don't care how you do it. But deal with that swine first!'

Pavo followed the optio's gaze to the crouching, gagging figure of the urban captain, and then glanced up at the guards high above at the top of the steps. They had not heard anything from the scuffle. He took a deep breath, glanced around the group gathered around him – catching the eye of each one, just as Gallus would do. Then he tipped the end of his sword down to tilt up the captain's head. He stared into the panic-filled pupils of the man, before ramming his foot square into his face, sending him crumpling backwards into deep unconsciousness. 'Right, he's out of the picture for some time!' He whispered. 'But we can't have them wake up and raise the alarm.'

'What do we do with them then, sir? Are we going to kill them?' One of the legionaries asked Pavo in a hushed tone.

Pavo looked to Felix. Felix nodded to the ship.

Pavo turned back to the legionary. 'As much as I'd love to, no. I think we should send them for a little voyage. A ten should go back out to sea with Officer Felix, splint his leg and keep this lot bound and gagged – and sail as far away from imperial shipping lanes as possible.'

Nobody stepped forward. Pavo looked to Spurius, whom the I Dacia legionaries gathered around. Spurius nodded nudged ten forward. 'Move it, we've got business to attend to here,' he hissed.

Pavo gave a firm appreciative nod in return, and then addressed the ten. 'Good. Now take her out and just circle for a few days. Keep them below deck and stay out as long as you can. Remember, a missing watch won't go unnoticed for long, so expect patrols.' He watched them shuffle around Felix, each waiting on the next to lift the optio. 'Move it, you sods!' He barked.

'You tell 'em Pavo,' Felix cackled, and then stifled a howl as the ten hoisted him unceremoniously from the cobbles.

Then a gruff voice uttered from behind him; 'Pavo, you know I'm going my own way from here?'

Pavo turned to Spurius. His granite features remained in the usual grimace, but his fingers rattled on the top of his sword hilt. 'Think that's the least we owe you. Let's divide the men down the middle, eh? Ten for you, ten for me – how's about that?'

'Steady on,' Sura whispered at his shoulder.

'Don't worry, Sura,' Spurius grumbled, 'I know you need the muscle more than me – you scrawny runt.'

'Right, that's it!' Sura lurched forward; Pavo threw up an arm just in time to catch him.

Spurius dropped his cold stare and let a chiselled, broken grin creep over his face. 'I only need five men.' He nodded to five who jogged over to him.

'Was that his idea of a joke?' Sura mumbled.

'Take it easy, keep your cool,' Pavo whispered back.

'Be seeing you,' Spurius grunted, offering a hand to Pavo.

The wind whipped up, cooling the sweat bathing Pavo's sweat and saltwater soaked scalp. Dawn pierced the sky at last and he took his old enemy's hand. 'Hope you get things sorted out,' he nodded.

Spurius nodded in return, then turned and whirled his hand over his head, pointing two closed fingers to the shadows at the end of the wharf. In a dull rumble of hobnailed boots, they were gone.

'You trust him? Because I don't,' Sura muttered.

'He got us here. Whether I trust him or not doesn't matter anymore, we've got too many other things to think about.'

'Aye, we do. Don't expect me to call you sir, by the way,' Sura chirped.

Pavo shot him a grin and then turned to the remaining fifteen I Dacia legionaries. His skin burned at the thought of having to issue orders to them. He bit back the uncertainty, reassuring himself that they were all a good couple of years younger than him.

'Right, this is the crux of it. We're all in this together – we must save the legion, and in doing so you can save yourselves from execution, clear your names. And believe me, you'll be heroes if you pull this one off – the empire is at stake here! We can't have any more incidents like this one, so from now on we need caution and stealth all the way. You're civilians from here on in, not soldiers, no matter what happens. Keep your daggers on you, but leave the spathas – anyone spots them and we'll be rumbled.'

They all nodded and murmured in agreement, tossing their swords into one of the empty crates. Pavo felt his chest swell – they were listening to him, their eyes keen just as he had seen when men listened to officers.

'The key is to get to the Imperial Palace. I don't know how we're going to get on once we get there, but let's cross that bridge when we come to it. We're already low in number, but I propose that we split into two groups. Sura, you take eight and I'll take the other seven. Use your instinct and see what our options are. Keep a low profile but ask around – there's got to be a way of getting in there. We should meet up at The Eagle, a shithole of an inn near the Hippodrome, a few hours before dusk tonight.'

'Yes,' Sura nodded, before adding begrudgingly; '...sir.'

'Good. Let's make this quick and we could be on our way to save our brothers before dawn,' he said optimistically, then glanced at the I Dacia legionaries, 'and remember, you lot could be heroes.' The men gave a murmur of agreement.

Sura waved his half of the party on behind him and made his way along the dock wall in search of a safe place to ascend into the city streets in search of the emperor. Pavo looked up the opposite stretch of the dock and turned to his men.

'Let's go!'

Above the scene of the landing, the two guards looked down on the events, then glanced at each other nervously. One pulled the small purse from his belt, fingering the thick gold cross.

'We accepted this, so we should tell the bishop.'

'This stinks – but aye, let's go.'

With a nod of agreement, they scuttled off into the streets.

# Chapter 66

'Come on then, you whoresons!' Gallus snarled as hot blood sprayed across his face. He ripped his spatha back from the chest of the Hun infantryman and kicked at his gut, sending the body toppling like a log onto the thick carpet of gore below the walls. His vision was sharp in the centre and blurred at the edges, his joints ached and his muscles felt numb from the relentless hacking and stabbing. But the delicate line of Roman defence had managed to hold on desperately; no Huns had established a bridgehead at the top of the thirty or so ladders that clawed at the battlements. 'Don't let a single one of these buggers breach us. Use every dirty trick in the book to keep 'em out!'

He smashed his sword hilt into the nose of the next Hun who tried to head charge him in the gut. With a howl, the soldier stumbled onto the battlement and straight off the edge to plummet onto the flagstones inside the fort, where he was quickly despatched by the thin pocket of reserve auxiliaries. Gallus turned back to face his next opponent, his teeth grinding like rocks. But there was nobody there. The next Hun was only halfway up the ladder. He glanced around the foot of the wall – the Huns were thinning. 'We're doing it lads, keep it up!' He squinted at the I Dacia who had withdrawn and waited near the edge of the plateau. 'Don't be shy,' Gallus roared, wiping the blood from his sword flat then holding it up to catch the sun, 'there's plenty iron waiting for you over here!' The legionaries of the XI Claudia, gasping and crimson coated, roared in appreciation. Then the ground started to rumble.

First, it was like a distant thunder clap, then like a storm directly overhead as all across the lip of the plateau the Hun cavalry washed forward.

'We've not even dented 'em,' Zosimus moaned.

'Stay firm, Zosimus,' Gallus cut in. But his own heart plummeted; a few thousand infantry – the weakest Hun soldiers – had been mown down, but the legion were close to spent, just as the Huns were sending in the first wave of some seventeen thousand cavalry.

In a flash, the Hun cavalry had swept past the front of the fort to circle at the sides. At the same time, a fresh wave of a thousand infantry thundered towards the front walls. From the left of the fort, the twang of countless arrows being loosed rang out.

'Shields!' Gallus roared. The walls became a thin testudo, the legionaries crouching behind the parapet to protect their front. As he ducked down, he breathed a sigh of relief that the tinny rattle of arrowheads on shields far outweighed the gurgles of pain from those caught out. But almost immediately after the first volley had landed, the cavalry on the right unleashed another even thicker volley. This time the cries of pain were numerous.

'Sir, their infantry – they're almost at the walls!' Zosimus yelled over the arrow hail as he lifted his shield to peek over the front parapet.

'Covering fire, Zosimus, their cavalry are pinning us down, nullifying what little we have. How long do we have before their spearmen are on the ladders?'

Zosimus snatched another glance. He turned to Gallus, his face fallen. 'Half a stadia, sir. And the I Dacia are coming too.'

'If we stay pinned down like this we're dead meat!' Gallus could only feel the vibration of his chest as he growled, such was the din. He waited for the lull between arrow storms then punched up from the shield roof of the legionaries on the wall. He hammered his sword against his shield boss. 'Clear those flanks!' He roared across the din of battle. At the same time, the front ranks of Huns parted to allow the I Dacia a clear run at the walls with more ladders. Gallus turned to the auxiliary units; they were pinned near the back of the fort by the arrow hail and the catapults lay unmanned. He waited for the brief pause in the bombardment and then bellowed; 'Catapults, blind fire to both sides of the fort – now!' The auxiliaries lunged forward, scurrying around the three catapults, winding the ropes, turning the devices on their bases to face flank; two to the right and one to the left. Gallus ducked under his shield for the next rain of arrows, then darted up again as they slowed – the I Dacia ladders were resting on the walls. He glanced over the edge to see a swarm of Wulfric's men scuttling up the ladders for the battlements. They had but an instant. 'Come on, come on!' Gallus cried, but the auxiliaries were faltering, several slain with the last bout of arrow fire. One skinny auxiliary, no more than a boy, heaved at the east-facing catapult all alone, until a wounded soldier came to his aid. It was finally shunted around to face the swarm of Huns on the eastern flank. The first of the I Dacia were only rungs from the wall tops. Gallus could hear their fingers scrabbling on the parapet when finally a voice cried out from the courtyard. 'Ready, fire!'

'To your feet,' Gallus cried, 'to your feet!'

With the twang of rope and bending timber, three heaving catapult volleys lurched over the fort walls and troughed their way through the packed Hun cavalry swarms, smashing men and horses alike like kindling. At the same time, the walls rippled to life with a battle cry, the squat testudo suddenly bristling into a solid line of sword points. They hacked into the first line of I Dacia as they attempted to hop onto the battlements. The next line was only a rung behind.

'Fire plumbatae at will!' Gallus cried. 'Thin them out at the ground!'

A volley of plumbatae spat forth, toppling the I Dacia around the ladder bases. Then rocks were toppled onto them. It was a soup of iron and gore, but still the I Dacia were but dented, and the Hun cavalry were reforming for another pass.

'And keep the catapults spitting!'

Gallus smashed his spatha into the face of the I Dacia legionary who dared raise his head over the ladder top. Hot blood sprayed the centurion, soaking him in a fresh layer of gore. 'For the empire, men, for the empire!' He gasped.

# Chapter 67

The Augusteum was thriving as usual. The blistering summer afternoon heat prickled on Pavo's skin as he pretended to look at the Hippodrome up ahead, sneaking darting glances to the palace gates as often as he dared; two urban guards stood like marble sentinels either side of the gate – their build and ugliness surely a key factor in being chosen to guard the emperor himself. *Great for the emperor*, he thought, *not so good for us*. He realised that one pass of the palace walls was normal, two passes suspicious, but now in their third they must look bloody stupid. He held a hand to his moist brow to block out the glare of the sun and his eyes relaxed at the moment of respite. Eyeing the wall tops discreetly, he felt his heart fall again; dotted along the walkways, at every ten paces or so, stood a member of the candidati, pristine in a white tunic and wearing the same stiff-jawed expression of sincerity. The urban cohorts were buggers, he thought, touching his thumb to the tender pink scar on his temple, but these guys were utterly ruthless. The cream of the loyal palatini, they were brute-strong, nimble and skilled beyond anything in the legions. Most of all they would gladly die for the emperor.

Beside him walked a soldier of the I Dacia named Cato. He was at least four years younger than Pavo and was a bag of nerves. Despite that he was a good lad at heart, clearly given no option but to take the bribe of gold along with the rest of the I Dacia and he was now eager to restore his honour.

'There's no way we're getting in there,' Cato murmured.

Pavo rolled his eyes, and then chuckled dryly – this lad was him just a few months ago. 'Yep,' he sighed, 'and the side gates are guarded just as heavily.'

'We could wait for the emperor to come out?' Cato offered.

'Nah, been there, the emperor travels with more protection around him than he has on those walls,' Pavo reasoned, his mind flitting with images of the legionary shield boss being whumped into his face as he tried to gatecrash the imperial procession two summers ago, 'we'd be skewered if we got within a hundred paces. And I've been given the strictest of orders to speak with the emperor only, so it's got to be inside the palace.'

Cato sighed, his shoulders slumping.

Pavo nudged him with his elbow. 'Let's see what Sura and his lads have come up with.' The Eagle rolled into view as they left the outer palace grounds behind them. Washed in white paint and hiding behind the shade of a palm thicket, the building strived to look somewhere close to clean, but the stench of stale urine and vomit wafted out to greet the pair as they approached.

'Urgh!' Cato wretched.

'Wait till you taste the ale...' Pavo cocked an eyebrow.

Another of his party of seven leaned against the wall next to the entrance. Upon recognizing the approaching two, the legionary straightened up and gave them a nod, before strolling inside.

The belly of the inn seemed to contain the afternoon heat rather than provide respite from it. The faded timbers were plastered with dubious stains, coated in layers of dust, and the battered oak tables were dotted with handfuls of toothless and lame veterans and filthy street dwellers. At a table near the back, the rag-tag group of disguised legionaries were devouring platters of cooked meat and sinking foamy, pale ale in gulps.

'By Mithras, you must be desperate?' Pavo mocked in a low voice as he pulled over a free stool to join them.

Sura was at the head of the table – his fingers pressed to his temples. 'We need something to keep us going – the cooked rat, or whatever it is, isn't bad with a bit of garum.'

'I'll pass,' Pavo replied quickly. 'Any ideas? Because all we saw was a wall of stone brimming with candidati just desperate to gut the first chancer who wants to take them on.'

'Bollocks,' Sura spat, 'same with us. We're waiting on some divine inspiration then?'

Pavo sighed, rolling a piece of the meat in his fingers, pressing at the fatty rind until it came away. 'There is another option.' At once, all fifteen hunched in to get within earshot. He kept his eyes on the scarred surface of the table. 'Scum like us won't get near the palace. But I know someone who

335

might be able to.' He paused for a moment, feeling sick at the thought; the despicable character that had used him like a dog – Tarquitius' disgusting buttery features crept into his mind. *Show your face in this city again...and you will die horribly.* The words rasped in his thoughts. But something else dawned on him; he was not afraid. He took a deep breath and looked up.

'I know a senator.'

A muted gasp rippled round the table as the fifteen leant back. Sura looked at him, astonishment curling into a grin. 'Well that changes things!' He chirped.

'It's not that easy,' Pavo cut in. 'He used to be my master.'

The rest of the table fell silent, turning to him, eyebrows raised.

Pavo pulled a wry grin at the utter lack of shame he would once have felt. 'Aye, aye, I was a slave; get over it – it's not like I buggered a camel, eh?' The legionaries dropped their stunned expressions. 'This senator is a...he's a nasty piece of work. There are no guarantees, but it's a possibility, okay? We might have to convince him that this won't damage his career, but...'

'What career?' another legionary butted in. 'Didn't you hear? The senate's been disbanded! The emperor's pulled the plug. Rumour was that he thought they were getting too much power – corruption or something.'

'Well thanks for sharing that with us, Kyros, only we've been sitting here for ages and you've not said a word – too busy stuffing your bloody face!' Another legionary moaned.

'Well how was I to know we had a senator's bum boy amongst us?' Kyros grumbled.

'Enough!' Pavo hissed. Kyros looked apologetic – and he certainly would if only he knew the pain Tarquitius had inflicted on his slaves. 'Look, we don't have any choice – whether the senate is shut or not, we've only got that dice to throw. So here's what we're going to do...'

The fifteen gathered around again, listening intently.

Pavo felt his mouth dry again as expectation rested heavily on his shoulders; to engineer a break-in to the Imperial Palace. Well, he thought, this is where experience will come in handy. He eyed each of the men.

'Okay, this is going to be as rough as a badger's arse...'

The summer sun drooped towards the west and a grey-purple haze hung in the air. Constantinople was at its busiest at this time of day. Exhausted traders shifted their stock mercilessly, coins rattling into their purses as the spices and fruit vanished from their stalls. The throng of the crowd had thickened all afternoon and was now a sea of exhausted, sweaty and dusty faces.

Cutting sharply into a side street to avoid the crush, Tarquitius, dressed defiantly in his senatorial purple trimmed white toga, eyed the narrow passage. He wiped the thick sweat from his buttery pate with a rag; tenements on one side, shrub lined aqueduct struts on the other, but brightly lit and open, there might be a chance that he wouldn't have to part with his purse by taking a shortcut through here. 'Fronto, how I miss your big, dumb presence,' he cursed under his breath. He had been too wary of hiring a cutthroat replacement for his slain bodyguard, and had chosen to spend most of his time in the villa anyway. Since the senate had been effectively abolished, he had no purpose to be out and about. Fear of the bishop's hired blades lurking in every street corner had penned him in, but weeks of constant introspection had driven him to the edge of madness. Now, as he trod the flagstones of the alley gingerly, he channelled his fear into bitterness; his life had been a black void since the emperor had destroyed one of the oldest institutions of the empire, of the republic. *The fool!* And the bishop, he seethed, that most unholy of creatures had used him like a pawn. *Damn him to Hades!* All he stood for had been taken from him, with only the empty shell of his life left. One chance, any chance to claw back power and respect was all he needed, but had so far proved elusive. Better to die on the streets, he pouted stubbornly, jutting his wobbling chins up. Nothing could scare him anymore. Then, five hooded figures dropped from the aqueduct channel above and landed like rocks in front of him.

'Oh, by the gods!' Tarquitius trilled, throwing up his hands to shield his face. He dropped to his knees and clawed at his belt, feeling for his purse. 'Take it, take it! Just leave me unharmed!' He waited on the sensation of a dagger plunging through his skin – what would it feel like?

'Shhhh, For Jupiter's sake!' A familiar voice hissed.

Tarquitius cracked open one eye; the shadowed face of one of the hooded thugs loomed over him.

'Stand up, will you?'

Tarquitius felt his fear melt into confusion as the hooded figure reached for his forearms and hoisted him to his feet, and then pulled the hood back slightly. In the dusty haze, a bruised and battered, sunken, hawk-like face was revealed. Tarquitius yelped with joy.

'Pavo!' He whooped before a hand was quickly clamped over his mouth.

'One more word, you fat pig, and I'll have to knock you out,' Pavo hissed.

'But why…' his words trailed off as the four other hooded figures converged on him.

'We need to talk – in private.'

Tarquitius opened his mouth to speak, and then stopped again, feeling the glares of the five. He nodded, turned to leave the alley and beckoned the five with a flick of the hand.

The sun straddled the skyline in the late Constantinople afternoon, casting yawning shadows of the Imperial Palace walls across the streets, silhouetting the buildings and colouring the sky a pink-orange.

At the palace gates, the imperial guard eyed Tarquitius with disdain, glancing down at a piece of parchment. Tarquitius shuffled uncomfortably; he should have insisted the five standing beside him stayed at the villa. Despite a wash and shave, they still smelled like vagrants. A jug of iced fruit juice had pacified the runts and they had planned quickly and carefully. A plan that would suit all parties, he mused smugly. Insisting on an audience with the emperor might well ruin him if he did not possess such scandalous information. So the XI Claudia had formed suspicions of the bishop's treachery – while the quiet senator had remained anonymous so far in the whole affair. Yet today would see him hailed as the saviour of the empire, and Bishop Evagrius would be doomed to a public execution. Yes, the bishop would protest his innocence, and then he would doubtless point the finger at his co-conspirators, but before such stories could be heard, a hired assassin could easily slip into the jail and sink a blade into the holy man's ribs. How ironic, he thought, that his own slave should come stumbling back from the lost lands to the north to present him with salvation?

'Senator Tarquitius, you don't have an appointment to speak with the emperor, and you turn up with these sacks of garbage who could be anyone...and you expect me to let you in?' The urban guardsman scratched at his side in distraction. 'The senate is dead anyway – what business could you possibly have?'

'Well I appreciate that. But think for a minute what harm could be done if you don't let me through. When what I have to say comes out, you could be lauded as a hero for trusting in me.'

'Aye, or end up being stoned for being the whoreson that let an assassin into the palace.'

'Fine then, escort us in – six unarmed men can easily be contained by, what, a few urban guards? Or do you think this would be a job better suited to the candidati?'

The urban guard took the bait, his top lip stiffening. 'Watch your tongue, Senator.' He eyed the party carefully, then spat a thick glob of phlegm onto the sand. 'Okay, you can come in, but these five scoundrels wait outside.'

Tarquitius looked to Pavo. His ex-slave nodded. The boy was clearly desperate to save the rabble of dogs he called his legion. But once inside, he alone was the one who could word the message to the emperor. It just kept getting better and better. Tarquitius turned back to the guard. 'Very well, lead the way.'

The guard grunted and flicked his head to beckon Tarquitius and then yelled in through the guard gate. 'Open up!'

As Tarquitius stepped through into the palace grounds, he felt empowered and proud once more.

Then a voice screeched out over the rooftops.

'He is an assassin. Slay him!'

He spun around. That white cloak and the snow-white hair, but the face was curled into a fury. *The Bishop!* Evagrius' eyes were burning on Tarquitius' skin and his outstretched hand pointed a gnarled finger at the senator. A twenty of urban guards surrounding him poured forward, swords drawn and teeth bared.

Pavo's heart hammered as their hopes and lives wavered before his eyes.

'Protect the senator!' He barked. The five, unarmed and wearing only grubby tunics, hesitated for only an instant, before lurching forward to shove Tarquitius into the palace ground and block the entrance to the guard gate. 'Get this gate closed,' he spat to the urban guard behind him. Confused, the guard stuck with protocol and moved to slam the gate shut.

'Keep that gate open!' The bishop roared to his twenty. Before the gate could be locked, a plumbata plunged into the guard's heart and he fell back, eyes wide, mouth spewing blood. 'Now finish these dogs and take down the senator!'

As the wall of twenty lunged for them, Pavo kicked out, crudely parrying a spear thrust with his boot. In the same breath, he called out; 'Claudia!' From the bushes across the flagstoned walkway, ten more filthy subjects popped up, bearing spathas and shields, and raced towards the melee. A bundle of spathas were hurled forward, and Pavo leapt to catch one.

Pavo ducked as a spear ripped past him and plunged into Cato's chest. The young lad slithered to the ground, rasping blood. Pavo snarled; '*Whoresons!* Let's see how you fight against real soldiers!' He barely recognised his own growl as he smashed forward, hacking one spear tip clear of its shaft before ramming his sword point through the mouth of one of the guards, whose eyes and nose erupted in a volcano of blood. The ten XI Claudia reinforcements clattered into the back of the urban unit, and soon the two sides were tangled in a storm of crimson and iron.

'We're barely holding them!' Sura yelped as he ducked a sword cut.

Pavo stepped over the fallen Kyros to stand back to back with his friend. 'Doesn't matter what happens to us, so long as we hold out long enough for Tarquitius to get to the emperor.' He jinked to his left as a spear jabbed at him, roaring as the blade ripped open his shoulder.

'More company!' Sura wailed.

Pavo looked up over his shoulder; another urban twenty hared in on them, being swept forward by the snarling bishop. 'To the last, Sura,' he barked. Then the twenty hit them and enveloped them. The vice-like crush intensified; there were only seven of his party left against roughly thirty of the urban guard. He roared in fury as another XI Claudia legionary was hacked down in front of him. As the body of the legionary fell, He looked up at the three bloodied and grinning faces that closed in on him.

'You're dead, sunshine, an' you know it,' the central guard shrieked. But then three thuds stopped them in their tracks, their faces dropped in confusion and blood rocketed from their mouths and nostrils. They tumbled to their knees and then collapsed forward almost in unison, the arrows lodged in their necks still quivering.

'Don't hang about, knock the shit out of 'em!' a familiar voice growled, his bow still raised.

*Spurius!* The stocky legionary was poise with his bow still raised, at the head of the five he had taken with him, together with a band of filthy and gnarled characters – *the Greens!* Armed with swords, daggers, slings, bows and rocks, they were every bit as dangerous as soldiers. The remainder of the urban guard turned to face the mob that now outnumbered them.

Spurius barged through to Pavo. 'I've sorted out my business,' he grunted with a typically ferocious grimace, 'thought you could do with a hand!' With that, he plunged into the melee.

'*Spurius?*' Sura gasped, spitting blood and shards of tooth onto the flagstones. 'Never in a million…'

'It only counts if Tarquitius gets to the emperor – come on, you're with me!' He yelled, pulling Sura by the wrist through the guard gate.

They slipped out of the rabble on the streets and down a long colonnaded path before bursting into an expanse of greenery; lawns, hedgerows, foliage and flower beds, studded with explosions of coloured blooms and gilded figurines. A marble fountain babbled without a care in the world in the centre of the garden, and the palace dominated the vast walled enclosure at the far end. Slaves bobbed in amongst the foliage, trimming, seeding and watering the lush beds, completely oblivious to the melee on the other side of the gate. *Too easy*, he wondered, slowing to a crouch behind the fountain, pulling Sura down with him. Then he spotted the pristine white tunics and froze; two pairs of candidati patrolled either side of the garden, and where in Hades was Tarquitius?

'I see him,' Sura hissed, jabbing a finger towards a hedgerow maze that zigzagged across the western half of the gardens, waist height at first and then expertly pruned to slope up to be tall as a man. There, behind one of the strolling candidati pair, the first bank of waist-height hedging ruffled a little, and the shiny pate of Tarquitius gleamed in the sunlight. A most imperfect hiding place.

'In the name of...he'll get skewered in a heartbeat – those guards are nearly on him,' Pavo growled. 'We need him – he dies then we've got nothing. We'll be executed – no questions asked.'

'Aye, I'm hearing you. But I'm not so keen on taking on those two.' Sura nodded towards the candidati.

Pavo watched their path as the pair strolled up to the front of the garden, and then back down towards the maze. He noted the alternating path of the two on the other side, and the fact that the wall guard faced out towards the city. 'When they walk behind the high hedgerows, then we slip round behind them, grab Tarquitius, duck down, wait for them to do another circuit of the garden, then...'

'Then have breakfast and a game of dice?' Sura cocked an eyebrow. '*Come on*, we need to move!' As if to underline his point, the bishop's roar filled the gardens and the ground shook with the trampling of boots. The pair spun; urban guards, at least forty of them, thundered for them, armour clanking, barely forty paces away, swords drawn. The bishop hobbled in their midst, roaring them on.

They glanced at each other for a heartbeat, faces pale, and then they were up, floundering mercilessly through flower gardens, churning up a multi-coloured glory in their wake. They hurled their spathas back at the advancing soldiers, then sprinted on.

'Tarquitius! Get up! Get into the maze!' Pavo rasped. But the senator's sweating pate simply raised a little to present his piggy eyes which quickly grew in shock. 'Get up!' The pair thundered to the hedge, stammered to a halt and then dipped down to scoop the senator up.

Tarquitius squealed, kicking out, his eyes screwed shut. 'They kidnapped me, they made me come here!'

Pavo acted without thought, bringing his fist crashing into the senator's cheek. 'It's us, you fat fool!' At once Tarquitius was silent, stunned. The urban detachment was almost upon them and the candidati raced for them too.

'Pavo, how dare you?'

'You want to see tomorrow? Move!' Pavo and Sura hauled him forward and the trio stumbled into the hedgerow maze. The hedges grew taller and taller as they took each turn blindly. Every corner felt like running blind onto a sword point and all the while, the clatter of urban guards seemed to swirl around them as the detachment spilled into the labyrinth. Pavo grunted as Tarquitius slowed, panting, his face a raging scarlet. 'Come on, we can't carry you!' Then he set off again, bursting round another corner. A dead end.

'Oh bugger!' Sura spat.

'We're dead!' Pavo added.

Then a foreign voice sneered behind them. 'Aye, you are now!'

The pair turned to face the sunken-eyed urban guard who beheld them, flicking his spatha nimbly on one hand and clutching his spear on the other.

'In the gut or through the throat?' He growled, eyes sparkling. 'Ah, what do you care?' With that, the guard's eyes bulged and he hoisted his spear forward at Sura. Pavo leapt to parry the thrust with his forearm. But the weapon simply lunged weakly between the pair and there was a sinewy rasp.

The urban guard stood stock still, still holding his sword, but his eyes were distant. Then blood erupted from his mouth. The guard's body toppled forward, revealing the quivering and sweat soaked figure of Tarquitius, still holding the crimson coated dagger in his hand. 'I...I want immunity over this...' Tarquitius stammered.

'There 'e is!' Another voice cut through the air. Behind Tarquitius, a trio of guards stood at the far end of the maze corridor, and then bundled forward with a cry.

'Spare us!' Tarquitius warbled.

'This is it,' Pavo gulped, backing against the dead-end hedgerow.

'Not yet,' Sura rasped, 'This way!' He yanked Pavo and Tarquitius with him as he pushed back through the hedge. The branches tore at them and they roared, blinded and bleeding until they stumbled out into another green-walled corridor. From the other side of the hedge, swearing broke out along with the thudding of men running into the back of each other.

'Nice one,' Pavo gasped, wincing at the stinging array of cuts. Then his eyes widened; more guards haring in on them – this time from both sides. 'Let's stick to the quick route!'

One after another, the three leapt into the defiant hedge wall, bursting through one, then another, then another. 'Are we even going in the right direction?' Sura moaned as they delved into another razor-like growth. Tumbling out onto the grass at the other side, they spluttered out leaves, and stood up to delve forward once more. But a set of ten sword points hovered at their noses. Ten pristine candidati glowered over them, standing on a set of marble steps leading up into a side entrance of the palace. Buccinas blared across the walls. The game was up.

To their right, Bishop Evagrius and his party burst free of the maze exit, thundering over to them, swords drawn. 'Strike the intruders down!' Evagrius roared.

Surrounded by iron, Pavo clenched his eyes tight and his stomach turned over. Suddenly, a voice boomed across the great hall.

'The candidati take orders from the emperor and the emperor only!'

Emperor Valens was standing in the palace doorway, flanked by ten candidati, his face wrinkled with doubt. 'What is the meaning of this? Who are these men?' He whipped his purple toga clear of his feet as he moved down the steps and his face fell. 'Bishop Evagrius? What business have you on palace grounds? Why do you have an armed escort?' As he spoke, a twenty of candidati rounded on the urban guards and disarmed them. Then Valens pushed his line of ten candidati apart, his eyes falling on the bedraggled trio of Tarquitius, Pavo and Sura.

'I remember you – Senator Tarquitius, isn't it?' Valens spoke quietly, eyeing the bedraggled, bleeding and sweating Tarquitius.

'Well, technically…I was, my m…magnificent emperor,' Tarquitius gushed. 'I truly do not deserve to be in your presence, and I offer you my most sincere gratitude…'

'Enough!' Valens barked. 'Give me answers, what is going on here?'

Pavo longed to unburden himself with the whole sorry tale, but he remembered Gallus' words; *you must only speak to the emperor and nobody else.*

'Assassins, Emperor,' Evagrius barked.

'No!' Pavo and Sura gasped in unison.

'They murdered many of your gate guards.' Evagrius continued in an even, matter-of-fact tone.

'He's lying!' Pavo roared.

Tarquitius' mouth opened and then, with a glance at the bishop, closed again.

Pavo held the emperor's gaze. For once, his nerves were stilled and his heart steady. 'Emperor, we request a private audience with you.'

At this Evagrius roared with a rasping laughter, then his face snapped back to a pointed rage. 'Do not hesitate, Emperor. They mean to end your reign. Slay them!'

A trio of candidati moved their sword points to hover by each of Pavo, Sura and Tarquitius' jugulars, and then looked to their master for the order.

Valens eyed the kneeling three with an austere distaste. 'You come to my palace, the heart of the empire, like *this!*' He muttered, his nose wrinkled as he stared at each of them in turn. 'You reek of treachery!'

Pavo's spirit plunged into blackness. It was to end here.

'Execute them, but imprison the senator,' then he hesitated, 'but take them outside, slice off their heads in the Augusteum – a fine lesson to any who would dare follow their example.' With that, the emperor turned to ascend the steps back into the palace.

Pavo's ribs cracked as the candidati hauled him up. He caught the resignation in Sura's eyes. Then he thought of Father – the legionary, the hero. Now his son was to die as a traitor. The XI Claudia was doomed and Gallus and the rest were dead. 'I'm sorry, Gallus,' he rasped up to the darkening sky as the candidati butted him forward, blinking back tears. Then he stopped abruptly as the candidati on either side of him suddenly halted to stand bolt upright. He blinked. Valens now stood in front of him, cobalt eyes piercing.

'Gallus?' Valens spoke in a murmur, his eyes searching.

Pavo fixed his gaze on the emperor's eyes.

'The centurion of the XI Claudia?'

Pavo's lips trembled. He felt the bishop's eyes rake his features. 'No. He's now acting tribunus. Nerva has been slain.'

Valens' face tightened, his lips almost white. He looked to the bishop, then to the senator. A moment of stillness passed, before he spoke, his voice ice cool. 'Senator, bishop...and you two,' he pointed to Pavo and Sura, 'come to my strategy room.'

The candidati surrounded them, glowering.

# Chapter 68

Gallus spat a curdled lump of blood and phlegm into the gore-coated battlement. His lungs rattled as he clasped his hands to his knees and sank back against the wall as thick, black smoke snaked across his face from the smouldering remains of the catapults in the courtyard, below. The Huns had withdrawn with the sun, leaving behind a shattered trickle of legionaries still standing amongst a carpet of dead. Less than two hundred men remained; not nearly enough to man the walls against the next wave of attack. Outside the fort, Horsa led a detachment of legionaries through the field of corpses – four deep in places, warrior and horse limbs entangled like weeds – in the grizzly task of collecting spears and arrows to bolster their own scant supply. Throughout the day the Huns had swamped the battlements twice; somehow, Gallus thought, somehow his men had dug in and managed to repel them. But to what end? The fort had been stripped back to what it was when the XI Claudia had found it – all traps used and all heavy weaponry shattered. The Hun retreat for the night served as little more than a taunt.

'They should've just come and bloody well finished us,' Zosimus growled, smashing his shield boss into a crippled ballista. The soldier's face was black with dirt and smoke.

'Easy, soldier. They'll not get our blood cheaply tomorrow – they'll have to die in their thousands to see a drop of it.' Gallus slapped his flayed and stinging hand on Zosimus' shoulder.

'Don't worry, sir, they'll be feeling my sword all right,' Zosimus nodded firmly.

Avitus and Quadratus hobbled over to stand beside them. These men were his limbs in the legion. They had stepped in strongly where Felix had served. It meant that those left alive had the benefit of facing an organised end the following day.

347

The bobbing torches down on the valley floor, below, still stretched impossibly like an infinite colony of fireflies. They had taken down maybe six thousand of their number, more than ten for every one of the XI Claudia fallen. Commendable but meaningless at the same time. The treacherous I Dacia had taken their share of the damage too, Wulfric barking them forward throughout the day while remaining back out of catapult range. Gallus balled his fists and gritted his teeth; if the man was as bold as he made out back in Durostorum, then he would be on the front line, dying with his men. But no, the I Dacia, while backed with the resources only afforded to a comitatenses legion, lacked the cohesion and spirit of the long-standing XI Claudia. He shook his head – pride was of little value now.

He turned, startled, as the tap-tapping of hammers on wood rang out; the legionaries had finished their rations – salted beef and biscuit – and were now busying themselves around the shattered artillery.

'What's this?' Gallus called out. 'I ordered you to fall out – we need fresh men for tomorrow.'

One filthy faced, gaunt trooper stepped forward, hammer and nails in his hands. 'Beg your forgiveness, sir, but we want to work on the fort – there's plenty of time for rest.'

Avitus leant in to his centurion's ear. 'They've got a point, sir – nobody will sleep tonight anyway. Let 'em make tomorrow count?'

Gallus sighed – his body ached and his mind spun – rest could wait a while longer. 'Go for it, soldier. Good on you, men, save a spot for me!' He pushed off the battlement, his legs groaning under the strain, blistered soles roaring in protest. 'Are my optios game for this, too?'

All three nodded with a grin, but Avitus added; 'I have an idea sir – might buy us some time?'

Gallus, Quadratus and Zosimus all looked to the little optio.

'We're fixing the artillery – but we don't have enough men to work the devices, let alone man the walls – the fort is too big.'

'You call that an idea?' Zosimus grunted.

'Bear with me. If we can fix the catapults, then we can use them to make the fort smaller!'

'What - knock the walls down? Have you been on the sauce?' Quadratus spluttered.

'Aye, why don't we open the gates as well?' Zosimus chuckled dryly.

Avitus turned to Gallus, exasperated. 'Sir, you remember when we were in Dacia. That Gothic cavalry charge was coming right at us...'

'...But they wouldn't charge our spear line,' Gallus' eyes glinted, 'because they won't run onto a blade!'

'Exactly, sir. And that lot out there, they've hoisted cartloads of missiles in here at us,' Avitus waved a hand across the carpet of bent arrowheads, spears and I Dacia plumbatae, 'So rather than sitting, waiting on them to swamp the walls tomorrow, how's about we take the initiative. We can bring the side walls down into a steep pile of rubble and embed every bit of sharp iron we've got into it – their mounts won't come near it. And it'll take them Mithras knows how long to have what infantry they've got left to pick through it – at least longer than it would take for them to walk up to an undefended side wall with a ladder.'

Gallus nodded. 'And we only have the front wall left to defend. Just like the rocky pass on the way up here.'

Avitus nodded briskly, shooting a frown at the unconvinced figures of Zosimus and Quadratus. 'We can fashion caltrops out of any spears or arrow heads that are too mangled and sprinkle them on the rubble, just to be sure – it'll cut them to ribbons.'

Zosimus and Quadratus looked at each other, wrinkling their brows.

'Avitus is right; it'll buy us time, albeit a precious sliver of the stuff.' Gallus patted their shoulders and then nodded to the legionaries who busied themselves around the fort, 'if nothing else let's do it for them.'

As the three shuffled down the stairs to the courtyard, Gallus took another look over the wall to the foot of the hillside, grimacing at the storm that would smash them tomorrow. His momentary optimism evaporated.

# Chapter 69

Pavo felt like a rodent in the ornate and cavernous room, Sura sat to his left, while Tarquitius and Evagrius flanked them and a ring of fifteen stony faced candidati ringed the four, leaving only a gap to the emperor, sitting behind his map table. The tall open shutters allowed a cool night breeze to waft in, but the darkness only reminded him of how long they had been away from the legion – more than two full days, plenty of time for the Huns to have crushed the XI Claudia twice over.

Valens burned his intense gaze onto the map, his hands forming a triangle under his chin. The emperor had remained straight-faced throughout Tarquitius' report, his arching brows giving him the appearance of a man who never quite believed anything he was told. *Why*, Pavo cursed inside, *why had Tarquitius omitted the bit about the bishop from his story?* The holy man, sitting right here next to him, smiling? Tarquitius had pulled on his tunic sleeve halfway up the marble staircase and hissed in his ear; 'Your suspicions about Evagrius – not a word, for the greater good!' He eyed his old tormentor – soaked in perspiration and looking an entirely wrong shade of green.

Valens finally broke the silence with a heavy sigh. 'My worst fears have been realised.'

Pavo sensed the bishop and Tarquitius brace slightly in their chairs.

'The Danubius frontier has been stripped bare. Without the XI Claudia there to patrol it, we were relying on the quick response time of the I Dacia to protect us until the Claudia returned, triumphant, from Bosporus,' he snorted, his upper lip shrivelled in distaste. 'Yet now I find that the expensively constructed I Dacia have betrayed the empire?' Valens curled his fist into a ball and hammered it down on the map.

Another lengthy silence ensued. Pavo felt his brow dampen and his mouth dry out. *Every moment is precious.* Before he could check himself, he felt the words tumbling from his throat. 'Emperor, we promised Gallus, we promised the legion. We must return to them.'

Valens screwed his eyes tight and burned his glare into Pavo's skin. 'Do not test me any more than you already have, *boy!*' The candidati touched their scabbards in warning.

Pavo's spirit sunk again.

Valens scoured the map one more time. 'But our borders *are* wide open, by God.' His eyes keened on the small diamond shaped peninsula of Bosporus. 'If this force, these Huns, descend on us in our current state…God help us.' He lifted his hands and clapped them twice.

An aide rushed through the door to be by his side. 'Emperor?'

Valens eyed each of the four as he spoke. 'Rouse Tribunus Vitus. It is time to utilise our insurance policy.'

'Tribunus Vitus. Insurance?' Evagrius spoke, his voice soft. He sounded every inch the harmless snow-white mopped old man. 'Emperor, if we could discuss this terrible misunderstanding; we were informed that these two were assassins…'

'Enough!' Valens cut him short. 'The comitatenses of Asia and Greece have been on standby for some time. They have been mobilised under Tribunus Vitus, and will be ready to embark for Bosporus before dawn.'

Evagrius leaned forward, his eyes now narrowed and his face creased. 'When was this order given?' The bishop snapped.

Valens turned to him slowly, allowing a moment of silence to pass before replying; 'Your emperor should not be questioned.' Two candidati moved a step forward. Valens lifted a hand to halt them. 'Do you think me a fool, bishop? You will be accompanying the relief force.' Valens' ice-cold glare curled into a menacing sneer. 'You will be on the front line, bishop, front and centre. You will be expected to inspire our legions to victory.' The emperor was fixed on Evagrius with a dark glare.

The bishop dropped his gaze first and slumped back in his chair with a throaty rattle.

Valens then turned to Pavo and Sura, arching one eyebrow even higher; 'You two, you came from the wilderness outside of the empire, across the sea, infiltrated my city, then broke into my home?'

Pavo gulped his heart back down as the candidati keenly gripped their sword hilts again. He opened his mouth to speak, but his voice was gone and his tongue as dry as a dead toad.

Valens' glare remained, but his words softened. 'I want to flay you and exalt you at once. You are a credit to your empire, soldiers. But time is short as you say. Head immediately for the docks where you can eat, wash and then take arms once more – you are to march with the relief force.'

# Chapter 70

A man-sized rock came hammering down on the front wall of the fort, renting a jagged fissure up the wall and sending the legionaries at the top flailing as the force knocked them back into the courtyard.

'Artillery - damn them!' Gallus spat, watching the five dark wooden hulks at the edge of the plateau. Before the orange of dawn had fully spread across the land, the Hun hordes had spilled once more over the lip of the hilltop. But upon seeing the huge rubble mounds hugging the sides of the fort spiked with caltrops, bent spears, ballista bolts and timber shards like a pair of massive porcupines – they had backed off, not taking the bait of the narrow front left open for attack. They now waited like baying, bloodthirsty hounds, tethered behind their artillery line while the I Dacia loaded the catapults one by one. The second device fired; another rock smashed into the base of the wall – just left of the first one, and the sturdy bulwark shifted inwards. 'They'll be in here before the sun's fully up at this rate. That artillery needs taking down!'

'We can't get to them, sir,' Avitus snarled, punching his fist into his palm. 'We'd need our cats up on the walls to reach them. We only need a few more paces to come into range and I promise you, they'd be firewood in no time!'

'We can't open the gates to push the cats out, their cavalry would be on us in a heartbeat,' Zosimus grumbled, pulling at the thick stubble carpeting his chin.

'The speed of cavalry is your answer,' a voice piped up from behind them. 'Just as you suggest.'

Gallus turned to see Horsa; the Goth had cut a subdued figure since they had holed up in the fort. Spurned by his treacherous unit, he and one other rider were all that remained of the loyal foederati now. But his good eye sparkled with an inner fire and his face was firm with determination as he straightened his eyepatch.

'We've got two healthy mounts; fast ones too. Get me close enough to that artillery and I can take it down.'

'One man to take out five catapults?' Gallus asked.

'No, he'll have a man on the wing,' another voice added. Amalric strode over to stand beside Horsa.

# Chapter 71

Pavo leant over the prow of the imperial flagship as it cut its way, full sail, through the waters of the Pontus Euxinus. The salt spray stung his eyes, but he could not tear himself from this unblemished view of the northern horizon. Gallus had been right to send them to the emperor and the emperor alone.

Valens had proved to be a shrewd thinker. He had played along with the bishop's plan for the Bosporus mission, but a seemingly costly insurance policy of having two legions on standby had proved a cheap premium given the turn of events. Before dawn had broken, the fleets had set sail; Pavo and his party along with the contingent of some two thousand men from the garrison of Constantinople itself had set off from the city docks. Then before sun up they had rendezvoused with the fleets of the I Italica and the XII Fulminata. Some seven thousand legionaries had been tasked with racing to the wilderness of Bosporus to slam the gates to the empire firmly shut. Yet they were still massively outnumbered, and time ticked against them.

'You and Sura did a top job, Pavo,' Felix said, resting on a crutch beside him. 'Don't punish yourself for what happens next. It's a miracle we've made it this far.'

'It all counts for nothing though, doesn't it? If we get back there to find another pile of corpses and the Huns have gone, then what? They'll fall upon our borders before long while we're scratching our heads, hundreds of miles away.'

'The papyrus-thin frontiers? Yep, I'm with you,' the optio sighed. 'But take heart, Centurion Gallus is no mug, and he trusts in us. So he'll have held out...*will* be holding out till the very last.' Felix rested a hand on his shoulder before hobbling off.

Pavo turned away from the spray at last, his eyes red and his nose running. The boat was packed with idle legionaries while the oars remained retracted and the crew scrambled up and down the rigging. His gaze fell on Spurius, sitting on the deck, throwing dice with the seven of the I Dacia contingent who had survived the mission to the emperor. Spurius had been quiet since his last-minute intervention at the palace gates, quiet but contented. Maybe this was the real Spurius, he mused?

'Funny how things turn out, eh?' Sura spoke quietly having sidled up next to him.

'Makes you wonder who you can really trust in the end. Nothing is as it seems.'

'Think you could be friends?'

'I don't think Spurius ever really has friends – he's a loner. I think he tolerates people rather than likes them.'

'Well I'm glad he tolerates us now – no more looking over our shoulders.'

'When one problem is solved, Sura, I usually find another one pretty quickly,' Pavo sighed. 'And we've got a pretty big one to deal with when we land.'

'Aye, and there's another one,' Sura nodded to the solitary white-cloaked figure of Bishop Evagrius, sentinel-like at the stern. 'You think he's really tangled in this?'

'It stinks, Sura. But Valens knew what he was doing in sending him here. Either he'll inspire the legions with divine inspiration, or he'll destroy himself. You know the saying *give 'em enough rope?*'

Tribunus Vitus of the XII Fulminata stalked towards them. 'Not long now, lads,' he mused, craning his neck at the sun overhead.

'We'll be there by mid-afternoon – if the gods are smiling upon us.'

Pavo shot another glance at the bishop and smirked wryly at the tribunus' choice of words.

# Chapter 72

Gallus wheezed through the dust coating him and the men on the wall. Each gargantuan boulder now ground the shattered battlements into a spray of rubble, and crimson smears along its length told of those caught under a direct hit.

'They're prising us open like a shellfish!' Gallus hissed as another rock crunched down. Barely any defensible battlement remained, and only a few more hits would surely rent open a clear path into the fort. Of the defiant two hundred who had filed up onto the battlements this morning, a further seventy had been slain, and morale had dropped like one of those rocks.

'Horsa's nearly at 'em, sir!' Quadratus yelled from the timber watchtower. 'Amalric's just a few strides behind.'

'Ride like the gods,' Gallus whispered under his breath. Horsa would he would be the decoy while Amalric, weaving behind him, would hope to slip in close enough to the catapults to spring his surprise attack. They had slipped out of the side gate of the fort and dropped into a dip running around the eastern edge of the plateau. From there they had rode around the dip, obscured from Hun eyes, taking them almost up to the flank of the Hun line on the north edge of the plateau. They would be bursting into the enemy line of sight in moments. The centurion gripped the cracked crenellation in front of him, willing them on.

'Amalric's nearly in behind 'em, sir!' Quadratus cried again.

The straggle of the XI Claudia roared in support all at once as Horsa burst up to be level with the enemy. Like a porcupine, the Hun line bristled in surprise. Horsa whooped, spun his sword over his head, and galloped across the Hun front. The Huns, seeing a single rider, visibly relaxed, a detachment being sent out to slay him while the rest turned back to the fort. Just as they dropped their guard, Amalric burst out onto the plateau behind their front line, strides from the artillery.

'He's there!' Avitus yelled.

The I Dacia artillerymen scrambled back in shock, crying out to the Hun spearmen, standing oblivious only paces away. But Amalric thundered forward, bringing a glowing ball of flames spinning above his head in a sling. The blazing pitch sack roared until he released it to zip across the air like a comet towards the rightmost catapult. The sack exploded in a fury of flames against the timber device. The Hun cavalry pitched forward to meet the solitary threat, but not before Amalric had unleashed the second, third and fourth sacks onto the remaining catapults.

'They've done it!' Gallus roared as the fifth catapult exploded in orange. 'Now get our artillery trained on those riders!' he pointed at the wave of nearly a thousand haring after Horsa and Amalric like a swarm of wasps – now in range. 'This is the last free shot we get at them, lads. Fire at will! Take 'em down!'

The men roared as a stone zipped through the air and ploughed right through the flank of the swarm. Gallus joined them, roaring until his lungs were spent, smashing his sword against his shield.

The roar subsided, and then died. Horsa and Amalric weaved across the plateau only to be blocked as they approached the fort by a detachment of Hun riders. Gallus watched as they wheeled round and then slipped towards the northeastern edge of the plateau and out of sight, down the hillside. *Gods be with you*, he mouthed.

The rest of the Huns, realizing they now had only one option left – to crush the pathetic remnant of the XI Claudia under weight of numbers – rumbled forward towards the shattered fort. He turned to the thin smattering of filthy and exhausted men.

'This is it, lads. This is it!'

# Chapter 73

The two *equites* heeled their mounts into a gallop back over the lush grassy ridge, waving the all clear vigorously. Pavo's heart pounded with anticipation.

'We're almost there!' Sura cried, slapping his friend across the back. 'One more ridge and we're there!' He yelled to Tribunus Vitus.

'Forward!' Vitus yelled in turn over his shoulder, waving the thick, shimmering column forward. He jabbed a hand at the aquilifer, who waved the purple flag on the end of the silver standard of the XII Fulminata. The equites read it at once and wheeled round to join the legionary column.

'Well, we've not encountered any of their scouts yet. You said they were wrapped around the hill?' Vitus quizzed.

'Well, they were two days ago,' Pavo frowned.

'Excellent,' Vitus rubbed his hands together. 'A nice narrow line to smash into the back of!'

Pavo thought better of reminding the tribunus over the Hun number. A narrow line it was most definitely not. Then something flashed on the horizon – his eyes locked onto it, something dancing just above the ridge top. A topknot, then an eyepatch.

'Horsa!' He yelled. 'And Amalric?' The prince bobbed into view, dust billowing behind them.

'They're in a bloody hurry?' Vitus mused. Then his eyes widened. 'Form up to repel a cavalry charge!'

The XII Fulminata, leading the relief column, rippled into a wall of shields and plumbatae. Pavo fell back in line, realisation dawning on him as he watched; Horsa and Amalric bounded from the ridge top, thumping down onto the grass as a dark wave of arrows arced over them. 'Sir, send the cavalry out to the flanks – I know what's going to happen here.'

Vitus rubbed his chin momentarily. 'Parthian shot? Hit and run.'

Pavo nodded vigorously.

'Equites, out wide,' Vitus cried, 'ready to pinch anything that comes over that hill!'

The cavalry raced out as he ordered, just as a wall of dark riders exploded over the ridge, only twenty paces at most behind the fleeing Horsa and Amalric.

Pavo gulped as the riders came and came – his mind flitted with flashbacks of their descent onto the ill-prepared XI Claudia just days before.

'It's just a detachment,' Sura gasped, reading his thoughts. 'Look, they're tailing off!'

'Then we've got to cut them off,' Vitus barked, then turned to the legionary holding the silver eagle standard and the trio carrying bronze horns. 'Aquilifer, buccinators – get my cavalry round the back of them – pen them in and destroy them. I don't want a single one of them getting back to their main force – let's keep surprise in our armoury.'

'I'm trying, sir!' The aquilifer roared as the Hun detachment wheeled around fully, breaking from the pursuit of Horsa and haring back in the direction they had come from.

'Damn it! If they bring their full cavalry force onto us on open ground…this could be a disaster!'

Pavo felt his spirit crash. If the Huns slipped away they would be chasing shadows again. Then, on the horizon, something rippled, just ahead of the Hun detachment. 'Sir – look!'

All across the grassy ridge, a harvest of spears rose up, held firm by blonde-haired warriors. The Hun riders reared up, throwing their flight into chaos, as the equites thundered into their rear.

'What in the name of – who are they?' Vitus spluttered, straining his eyes in the cloudy gloom at the spectre-like line of spearmen. Horsa and Amalric rode to the rear of the newcomers, exchanged some barked words and then wheeled around, whooping, punching the air in delight.

'Goths, sir? I think they're Goths?' Pavo gasped.

Amalric leant from the saddle as Horsa galloped up to the Roman front line and Vitus. 'My brothers are here, under Fritigern's banner – here to avenge their kin!' He pointed to the flapping orange flag they held.

'One of our boats escaped, fishermen of my people, they crossed the sea to get word to our cousins! We thought them lost to the Huns!' Amalric blurted, his eyes sparkled with tears.

As one, the Roman lines erupted in a roar of delight, while at the ridge, the Hun thousand were crushed in the Roman-Goth vice, speartips and plumbatae felling them swiftly.

'Who'd have thought it, lads?' Vitus mused, gazing at Horsa as he wheeled back to enter the fray. 'Saved by Goths!' His laughter filled the plain.

In the murmur of excitement, nobody noticed the white cloaked and hooded figure of Bishop Evagrius pushing through the crowd, past the flank of the army and up to the ridge.

# Chapter 74

Gallus waved the remaining clutch – barely thirty – of the XI Claudia back from the walls, screaming through the thick smog of battle. The auxiliaries loosed one final volley of rubble onto the Huns as they washed over the crippled battlements and into the courtyard like a black torrent.

'Fall back – now!' He rasped again, knocking a rock from the hand of one young legionary and shoving him towards the tiny bunker-room they had set up in the sleeping area.

Arrows spattered against his mail vest, one punctured his shoulder and another ripped across his neck in the tiny unprotected sliver between his intercisa helmet and his vest. The last to leave the rubble-heap of the walls, his skin crawled at the whirring of lassos that grew like a giant swarm of dragonflies behind him. One legionary scudded along the ground, away from the bunker, his ankles trussed in a lasso and his face contorted in a pained scream. Gallus grappled the soldier's wrist as he slipped past and clung on, but the Hun at the other end used his mount's power to yank the lad back, before another rode up and speared the legionary in the face. Gallus staggered back on his palms, eyes wide at the sea of riders all now thundering towards him. He turned, scrambled to his feet and ran.

He ducked under a spear thrust from his left and leapt over a sword swipe at his knees, before hammering his fist out to his right, delivering a crunching jab into the nose of another would-be killer. He swivelled, dodging another swoosh of a spear tip, all the time trying to keep one eye on the tiny doorway to the bunker.

'Cover me!' He roared.

'Sir – duck!' A familiar voice cried in reply. Gallus leapt forward and down underneath the plumbata volley from the men at the bunker entrance, his palms skinning as he skidded forward and into the bunker doorway, pulling himself round and into the corridor inside just in time to miss a volley of spears, which clattered on the doorframe, sending a cloud of mortar up in his wake.

Wincing at the grinding from a broken rib, Gallus scrambled to his feet. 'Get that doorway sealed!'

Inside the hall, Zosimus and Quadratus leapt to action as he ran past them; grappling on two hefty timber stakes supporting the ceiling they had weakened earlier, the two legionaries heaved them backwards, tearing the support away. Three Hun horsemen had bolted inside, eyes red with the promise of blood, when the corridor roared with collapsing masonry like a furious earthquake, filling up the entrance with solid rock and burying the Huns.

The noise died, and the hall was thick with dust and a shattered group of Legionaries. Gallus made a quick head count; nineteen men left. Zosimus, Quadratus and Avitus still stood – brothers to the last.

An eerie quiet rippled around them, while from outside, the dull roar of the Huns continued unabated. Gallus' heart slowed. He saw the face of Olivia in his mind's eye. 'How long?' He asked his optios. As he finished, a metallic clank shook the building, and the rubble blockade shifted visibly. A ram. The Romans eyed one another as the noise came again, and again.

Avitus, shining with sweat, looked to his centurion. 'Moments, sir. If we're lucky.'

# Chapter 75

All around the foot of the hill, tents lay empty and fires doused, as the full force of the Hun horde coursed up the hillside, crushing in on the doomed fort. Outside the command tent, Balamber stood in dialogue with Wulfric, surrounded by a handful of Hun nobles and I Dacia centurions.

Balamber glared upon the Gothic tribunus. 'A sea of blood has been let from my horde! Crushing this legion was supposed to be easy. A two day siege on a hill fort was not part of the plan, tribunus.'

Wulfric grimaced at the Hun noble's tone, before replying. 'And the blood of the I Dacia has been spilled equally freely. It is both of our armies who failed to stop their retreat to this fortress.'

'And it was your precious soldiers who dishonoured themselves and decided to turn back to the empire they had betrayed in the first place,' Balamber snarled. 'But what more could I expect from traitors?'

Wulfric gritted his teeth together. 'A handful of impressionable recruits lacked faith in our master plan and saw a chance to save their necks.' He waved a hand dismissively. 'In any case, a rabble of inexperienced legionaries would never have made it back to the heart of the empire – our sponsor in this affair has gilded our path to victory.'

'Ah, yes, your holy bishop? Well, when this legion is ground into the dust and we descend upon the empire, I shall have to have an audience with the man. Well, we still number, what, some twelve thousand – plenty to finish the job in hand. But we will need to raise further manpower after this – maybe the bishop will spend more generously this time to guarantee our success.'

'Perhaps. And I trust you will be able to raise more manpower from your homelands, Noble Balamber? Your people will still be happy to let their sons march under your command?' Wulfric replied.

Balamber stepped forward, toe to toe with the Gothic tribunus. 'You speak with hidden venom, Tribunus Wulfric,' Balamber sneered, his moustache twitching, teeth bared.

Wulfric shot him a stony gaze. 'You are but a pawn in this game, cheap manpower for the slaughter.'

With a roar, Balamber lunged at him, clawing for his throat. Wulfric leapt back, whipping his spatha free. Wulfric's centurions followed suit while Balamber's nobles stretched their bows at point blank range. He held the Hun leader's stare. Both men's eyes sparkled with fury. The air around them seemed to crackle with tension, until something caught Wulfric's attention from the corner of his eye. Something that didn't look right. Not right at all.

He turned round to the hillside; the vast throng of the Hun and I Dacia army swelled up its sides, focusing on the tiny heap of rubble at the top; then he glanced to the opposite valley-side and froze: there stood a white-cloaked figure, fervently waving a purple rag on a staff.

'What do we have here?' Balamber cooed in curiosity. The nobles relaxed their bowstrings and the centurions lowered their swords.

The purple rag fluttered in the breeze, displaying a grubby Chi-Rho emblem. Wulfric's jaw fell. 'You wanted an audience with the bishop?' He scooped a hand to the figure.

'Your bishop, here?' Balamber's face wrinkled. 'He's signalling us?'

Wulfric stared at the Hun leader, sharing his confusion. Then his heart thundered as he pieced it all together. 'Noble Balamber, we must turn the army around!'

# Chapter 76

The Hun detachment lay broken, still and silent in the grass. The Gothic spearmen had finally stopped cheering, and let Amalric down from their shoulders. The Gothic prince had then roared the warriors into the Roman line – now formed in a wide crescent, six hundred men wide. Auxiliary archers hovered in front of them and the equites circled on the flanks, eager for the push over the ridge. Eight thousand they now numbered with these reinforcements.

Pavo stood with Sura on the front line, quickly gulping at cool water and tearing at their bread rations. No matter how much water he swigged, his mouth remained dry as sand, and he jigged on the balls of his feet as his bladder seemed to have filled up again.

'Ha - the old soldier's curse!' Vitus grinned down at him.

'It's becoming all too familiar, sir,' Pavo cocked an eyebrow.

The standards rippled across the line, lifted by a growing wind which seemed to be scudding dark storm clouds across the afternoon sky.

Vitus raised his arm to indicate to the I Italica Legion; the men of the XII Fulminata were ready. Only a murmur of voices and ripple of armour being adjusted could be heard, until Vitus grabbed the legionary standard and pumped it into the air.

'Soldiers, advance!'

Pavo felt his blood race at the roar of the army. As one, they thundered forward. The ridge hovered ever closer.

Destiny lay on the other side.

# Chapter 77

The wind whipped and howled in the valley and the sky was now a foreboding grey. Outside the Hun command tent, Balamber remonstrated with his nobles, who scrambled around the rear of their army, roaring, desperately trying to control the horde. He threw a pewter cup against the hearth as the swarm continued to push on at the fort, blinded to the orders by their bloodlust.

'Turning round when we're on the cusp of victory? You'd better be right about this, Wulfric, or there'll be a price to pay for making me look foolish.'

'I think we have confirmation, Noble Balamber,' Wulfric barked, pointing to the ridge again.

There, like an iron sunrise, two shimmering eagle standards sparkled even in the gloomy grey. As true as day follows night, a thick blanket of armed men rose beneath the standards, pouring over the lip of the ridge, dressed in white tunics, scale armour and intercisa helmets. The bishop was unceremoniously swallowed by the march.

A fine whipped rain descended and Balamber's eyes widened, his hands wringing at his sword pommel.

'Bring my horse,' he snarled at his bodyguard. 'I want a thousand left to finish the stragglers in the fort. The rest – they must prove their worth to me now. Muster the garrison in Chersonesos – the Romans will die under our hail.' With that, he leapt onto his horse and spurred her into a gallop, roaring above all of his nobles, whacking his sword flat into the backs of those bringing up the rear of the horde. Like a forest fire, the horde turned, gradually at first, then in a fluid motion. Their cries filled the air and they began to spill back down the hillside, Balamber marshalling them like a war-god.

Wulfric thundered towards the I Dacia ranks. Having recognised the coming attack far sooner, they were already formed up on the right flank of the Huns, facing into the base of the valley. 'Refuse the flank!' Wulfric boomed at his men and they dropped back to present a diagonal front to the Roman advance. With their numerical advantage, they could anchor one flank and let the Huns do the dirty work of fighting forward and encircling the Romans. As they settled into position, the massive Hun horde formed by their side.

As the Roman relief force thundered down the hill, now less than a stadia away, the assembled dark riders waited on their leader's word.

'Forward!' Balamber cried, barging through to the front line, sword raised high.

The valley trembled as the two massive forces careered down the opposing sides. The sky roared with thunder as the gods gathered to watch.

'What in Hades was our bishop doing trying to signal the enemy?' Vitus growled over the whipping wind, blinking rain from his eyes as he trotted forward.

Pavo panted as he jogged to keep pace with the tribunus. 'He bribed the foederati, he bribed the I Dacia, and he's in league with the Huns!'

'Let's give him his reward then, Pavo. Eternal damnation for him and his gold-loving dogs!'

Vitus threw a guttural roar forward, Pavo and Sura echoed him and the noise erupted along the Roman line, augmented by a chorus of buccinas. The Hun lines raised their horns and threw a terrible wail in return. The stretch of land between the two sides vanished with every stride and Pavo focused on the front ranks of the opposing line; the I Dacia.

'Looks like it's time to settle some scores, Sura,' he trilled as the earth shook.

'I'm with you!' Sura roared.

'Stop!' Vitus bellowed as they closed to within twenty paces. The command was echoed along the Roman line and like a single organism, the Roman army halted. 'Plumbatae, loose!'

The Roman army bristled with the first of their standard three darts poised. Then Pavo hoisted his into the sky with a grunt. Together with thousands more, they arced and then dipped, crashing down on the Hun front line. The I Dacia sent their reply, along with the first sky-darkening volley of Hun arrows. Blood leapt from the ranks of both sides and bodies fell in their hundreds. Then the Hun cavalry wheeled to the left, churning out volley after volley of arrows, pinning in the Roman flank and effectively halting the Roman advance. Hundreds more legionaries fell under this hail, impotent to reply under the relentless bombardment.

'Ballistae!' Vitus roared, his voice rasping. From the ridge top behind the roman lines, fifty metal shafts were powered forward from the trailing line of ballistae. The bolts soared over the Roman lines, then dipped and hammered into the Hun horsemen just as they turned their backs – wreaking fissures of crimson with every hit. The Roman lines rose to loose their remaining plumbatae and The Hun infantry and the I Dacia lines stuttered at the onslaught.

'That's it – fire at will!' Vitus roared as the twang and thud of the ballista hail continued. 'Now, on my mark, engage them!'

The Hun cavalry, wheeling in disarray, had formed into an oval; bent back behind their infantry lines as the sky turned black and the rain came in torrents.

'Cease fire!' Vitus cried to the ballista crew. 'Legionaries – advance!'

A moment of silence hung in the spray, and then the sky let loose another clap of thunder and the Roman line poured forward in a clatter of iron and a chorus of legionary roars. The Huns bristled back into formation, rallied by their leader, and washed forward to meet the Roman charge.

'Gods be with you!' Sura yelled to Pavo, his voice drowned by the argentine crash of the two armies colliding. Men skidded over the shield lines from the momentum of the clash. Mud and blood arced high in the rainstorm and horses reared up in panic as lightning streaked the sky.

'Pin them in – surround them!' Vitus barked from his horse, his voice barely audible over the cacophony. He circled his hands as if throttling an invisible foe, urging the units of the legion to the flanks of the Hun cavalry. 'Don't let them loose again!'

Pavo staggered forward, drowning in a sea of blood and iron, soldiers crushing past him, a riot of snapping bones, ripping flesh and screaming all around him. A curious numbness filled his mind as the grimacing faces of the I Dacia merged with those of his own men as he was battered backwards and forwards, both armies losing the integrity of their front lines, but so tightly packed they were barely able to lift their swords. He saw Vitus plough through the throng, stabbing down into the masses, kicking attackers away from his mount. *Focus, Pavo*, he screamed inside. He imagined Father beside him, and Brutus on his other flank. Nobody would be taking him down lightly. Another spatha shuddered against his shield. He blinked rainwater from his eyes and peered at the snarling I Dacia legionary over the rim of his shield. Then with an iron cool, he butted forward and rammed his sword into the soldier's guts. As soon as the soldier fell, his place was taken by the next – fresh and ready for a kill. He ducked under the sword jab at his face and swiped at the soldier's shins. He only felt the vibration of his foe's screams as the man toppled and was swallowed up by the march of the I Dacia. Pavo glanced to both sides – something wasn't right; the allies were losing ground and the swell of battle was turning on them.

'They've got reinforcements,' Sura gasped, grappling his shoulder from a rank back, 'from Chersonesos. We're being outmuscled!'

Stepping backwards, butting away the flurry of sword blows, Pavo looked down – he was tramping through the grey and red mush of another legionary's split head. His stomach lurched as he tried to jump back from it, but instead he fell backwards into the gore-bath.

Booted feet of the backtracking legionary line stamped past him, showering his eyes with crimson slime, then a team of six I Dacia legionaries leapt on him at once. Pavo whipped his shield over himself, sheltering him through the first few sword blows. Sura fought to clear the waves of attackers but they were relentless and then Pavo felt his shield being torn from his grasp. He held on so he was lifted from the ground with the shield, letting go and swiping his sword round at the legs of the group who surrounded him. One fell and Pavo seized on the heartbeat of respite to scramble to his feet. His skin prickled as realisation dawned; Sura and he were in an ethereal mire of death, behind the main enemy lines. Then, loose pockets of I Dacia trailing behind turned to them. The sky filled with the roar of thunder again and five I

Dacia surrounded them, grinning with malicious glee as they hefted their swords for an easy kill.

Sura braced behind him. 'We're on our own.'

'Stop!' A gruff voice barked. Through the throng, a stocky silhouetted figure barged into the circle. Lightning tore at the heavens and lit up the man's sneering features. Festus. 'Time to open you up, Pavo!' Two of the I Dacia disarmed Sura and pinned him in the filth underfoot.

Pavo lifted his spatha, his arms numb, but his heart thumping with the rush of battle. 'I'll die in battle, gladly. But for my empire, Festus, and not at the end of your sword.'

The five surrounding them roared with laughter.

'Look around you, you bloody fool. Your relief army is crushed already, just like your precious XI Claudia. They're all dead men.' Festus snarled and then braced. 'And it's time for you to join them!' The giant legionary darted in with a flurry of sword strokes.

Pavo leapt back, parrying. Festus was eager. Too eager. He thought of Brutus' words on the training ground. Another barrage of blows came and Pavo focussed on defending, and waiting. He fired a glance to the battle; Vitus was roaring and rallying, but the numbers were telling. The precious few extra thousand Hun troops had streamed from Chersonesos and were managing to repel the Roman attempts to surround them, and were in turn surrounding the Roman lines. But Vitus was signalling – but what at? He yelped at the smash of Festus' sword flat into his wrist, and dropped his spatha.

'Don't let him break away,' Festus grinned to the five I Dacia, who spread into a circle around them. 'You're finished now,' he growled, stalking forward.

Pavo whipped his dagger from his belt. 'You always were a fool, Festus, just too stupid to realise it!'

Festus' face reddened and his eyes narrowed. The bull of a man leapt forward, his spatha tip battered Pavo's dagger from his hand. Defenceless, Pavo ducked and dodged Festus' wild hacks. The big man was tiring, but so, too, was Pavo. The next swipe of the spatha presented Festus' ribcage to Pavo as he crouched under the blow. Hammering his fist up, he winced at the crack of his fingers on Festus' mail shirt, but Festus bawled in agony and crumpled to the dirt, dropping his spatha.

Pavo dived to grasp the sword from the mud.

'You're dead...' Festus roared, but his words choked to a halt as he swivelled round to face his own spatha point, held to his throat by Pavo.

'Get him!' Festus roared to the I Dacia who surrounded them. They raced forward, swords drawn, while Festus scrambled clear. Pavo spun to face each of them in turn, but they were too fast and he was exhausted.

He roared in defiance, spinning the spatha around in a desperate hope of taking one or two of them with him as he went down. Then hot blood sprayed up and over his face. No pain, no blackness. He opened his eyes. Festus swayed, his eyes dilated in shock, mouth wide as if to shout, and a plumbata quivering in his throat. All around him, the five I Dacia crumpled, lanced by darts. Sura stood, equally bemused.

'That was some nice sword work!' A voice yelled. A broad and stocky silhouetted figure stood before them with a man on either flank.

'Spurius?' He spluttered, staggering backwards.

Spurius raced in to barge one lingering I Dacia soldier to the ground, despatching him with a clean slice below the armpit. Then he strode over to the stilled body of Festus, and grappled the plumbata shaft lodged in his gaping mouth. 'All those coins the Blues promised you...well you can take your cut in Hades...*whoreson!*' He grunted, ripping the plumbata from Festus' throat, spitting on his stunned expression. He glanced up at Pavo and Sura, both fixated on the sight of Festus' corpse. 'Get alongside me, or we're dead meat!' He roared, pointing behind them.

'Oh, bugger!' Pavo spat, as the rain thrashed across them. The Hun lines had turned, hundreds of spearmen were almost wrapped around them, and the three stood like twigs against an oncoming tidal wave. They backed onto each other as the Huns surrounded them. Their heels pushed into the dirt but with nowhere left to run. 'Last stand, lads – let's make it a good one?'

The clutch of stranded Romans roared in defiance as the circle around them raised their spears to strike, but suddenly, their twisted sneers opened up into panic. All at once, they simply turned and ran – back into the Hun ranks.

'Reinforcements!' Sura cried.

Pavo spun to the south. There, pouring into the valley in an arc toward the Hun right flank was the towering wave of fresh Gothic spearmen, closely followed Valens' contingent of candidati. The tide was turning; the Hun army was surrounded, backed in on all sides. Vitus had pulled off another masterstroke – sending a detachment around the valley side unnoticed. Giddy at the sudden liberation, he roared out at the onrushing reinforcements, ducking to grab his shield and readying himself to join the push into the Hun rear. He caught sight of the grin on Sura's face and the determined grimace on Spurius'. His heart hammered and he felt his bronze phalera judder on his chest with every beat.

'Time to finish this!' He barked.

As they poured against the Hun ranks, Pavo felt a gutsy smile creep across his face at last.

'For the empire!' He cried.

In the tumult of the raging storm, Balamber rampaged between the collapsing wings of his army, hacking at the foot soldiers who dared to flee. His cavalry remained loyal, but they were being pummelled and beaten back from both sides.

The I Dacia ranks were all but obliterated. Only a peppering of legionaries scurried around Wulfric, who roared at them, eyes bulging, smashing his sword hilt into their backs as they collapsed together. Nobody noticed the small figure of Menes as he drifted in behind Wulfric, tilted up on his toes and reached round across the Goth's neck to draw a fang-like dagger across the skin. Blood erupted like a geyser, and Wulfric's face rippled in confusion as he raised his fingers to the gaping wound. His face greying and his legs wobbling, he turned to Menes.

'My master's orders are complete,' Menes spoke gently, before closing his eyes and clasping the golden cross hanging from a chain around his neck.

The legionaries surrounding Wulfric stumbled back in horror as their leader slumped onto his knees and then toppled forward like felled timber. Their faces twisted from fear to rage; impotent to stop the crush of the allied army, they fell on Menes like a pack of dogs. In a flurry of sword blows, the little Egyptian was reduced to a butchered heap of bone and torn flesh.

Balamber hared past the scene, his mount rearing up as he spotted Wulfric's body. Fury and satisfaction curdled in his guts at the sight, and then he looked to the crimson streaked twenty who remained of the I Dacia – a sorry straggle who would only hold him back now. He turned to his nobles and bared his teeth. 'Destroy them!'

He turned away from their screams as a volley of arrows hammered into them at point blank range, and guided his mount up to the crest of a small rise. Everywhere he looked, the Roman relief force hemmed them in. He smashed his fist into his palm; the balance of numbers had been tipped with a deft outflanking manoeuvre.

Balamber beckoned the nearest noble over. 'Can we retreat to the city?'

'No, Noble Balamber,' the noble cried over the ever-closer clatter of the allied front line, tightening around them like a noose.

'What do you mean, no!' Balamber spat, grappling his noble by the throat.

'I beg your forgiveness, Noble Balamber. But it is too far for a safe retreat. And if we retreat inside the city then we would lose too many men. Our number would be too few to hold the walls. We become just like the Romans on the hilltop – trapped like rats. Forgive my speaking out of turn, but we must flee for the freedom of the plains.'

'Then so it must be.' Balamber hissed, his eyes narrowing.

The noble gulped before replying. 'But...Noble Balamber,' the Hun noble cowered and lowered his voice to a harsh rasp, 'we need to keep the Romans engaged...so the fastest of us can make it to safety.'

Balamber cast a glare across the warring Hun riders and spearmen, locked in deadly combat – and losing. They would die but he would live. Shame gripped him, but the greater good would be served if he could live to fight again, to raise another army. He swept an arm derisively across the collapsing mass of his army. 'Let them bleed, they have failed me! Gather the nobles and ready them to punch out of this noose!'

The noble gawped at his leader for a moment, and then dropped his eyes to the ground. 'Yes...Noble Balamber.'

Balamber formed up inside the triangle of his nobles, just under eighty strong. They spurred forward as one, trampling their own and building up to a charge, hurling out a war cry as they hammered into the line of Gothic spearmen. Bodies sprung upwards from the impact and the allied line buckled briefly, but just enough for the front half of the triangle to push out onto the empty valley floor. The sixty or so left behind were pulled down from their horses and they disappeared in a riot of Gothic spear shafts.

'Onward!' Balamber cried. 'Do not spare a thought for the cowards who will die behind you.' He waved his nobles on into a full gallop.

'Leave them,' Vitus called down to the group of equites as he eyed the fleeing Huns, 'let's finish this; here and now!'

The equites wheeled around and piled in with the allied army as they strangled and flattened the Hun number. A moan broke out from the Hun circle as they realised their leader had deserted them. At the clatter of thousands of Hun spears and bows dropping to the earth, Vitus closed his eyes.

'Victory is ours, sir!' One legionary called out.

'Sir,' another voice called. He opened his eyes to see the filthy figures of Pavo and Sura. 'The hill fort – it's still under attack!'

Rain hammered down. The Hun riders swarmed at the tiny bunker in the centre of the fort, throngs dismounting and pouring inside past the ram and through the gaping fissure it had rent in the rubble mound blocking the entrance. Their fervour to prise the Roman stragglers from the bunker like clams from a shell had gripped them. It had also blinded them from the fate of the main body of the Hun army.

Pavo stumbled at the head of the legion as they swept uphill and onto the plateau, his hands bloodied and numb as he scrambled over a tangle of rocks and corpses, and his bristled scalp slick with a glue of rainwater and blood. 'Come on – they're still fighting!'

'Steady lad, we're on top of them now,' Vitus yelled, grinning.

'But they're in there,' Sura cried, catching up with his friend and the tribunus. 'If the Huns are still fighting then some of the Claudia still live! The fort has been breached – they can only have moments left, we've got to hurry!'

Vitus grinned, puffed his cheeks out and whipped his sword up, wheeling round to rally the front line. 'Our brothers' lives hang in the balance - full charge!' The exhausted legionaries perked up to give a roar, rallying the ranks behind them who poured onto the plateau, and like a riptide, they crashed forward.

Pavo roared at the head of the charge. A thought flickered through his mind as the Huns to the rear turned in realization, eyes bulging in shock; he was walking in the footsteps of his father now – the military hero. Would this be the moment he joined him in the underworld? Not today, he swore, thrusting his sword forward.

# Chapter 78

The storm had died to a whimper, and the sun had prised apart the clouds, sending shafts of warmth down on the soaked plains. As the rainwater began to evaporate, the air filled with vapour and the scent of wet grass, and then the sound of thundering hooves pierced the air.

Balamber galloped all out, still enveloped by the nobles and his personal bodyguard. He kept his body low and eyes straight ahead – like a good Hun rider. They were clear of the battlefield now; this next valley lay untouched by the scarlet gore of the one they had left. He scanned the flat of the northern horizon; the plains of home called him. But deep in his heart failure taunted him, jeered him and cooked a bitter brew of self-hatred. *Tengri* the sky god would disavow him and honour would be lost, but the one voice he could hear inside was that of his father. He almost welcomed the cold fear that traced his skin as he remembered the fate of their last leader; surely his nobles would turn on him now that he had been defeated in battle. Snatching a glance to one side, he saw the noble there dutifully keeping an eye on the land up to the horizon on his side, checking for threats. His heart slowed a little at this, until he turned to his other side - catching the eyes of two nobles. Until now he had viewed them as his most loyal, or at least most awestruck and fearful, nobles. They looked away sharply, but it was too late; the seeds of doubt had entered his men's minds, and as the history of his people had proved time and time again, treachery was sure to follow along with the spilling of his own blood.

He turned to his personal bodyguard, riding by his side, and gave the faintest nod. Then he slid one hand underneath his furs, feeling for the hilt of his scimitar. He flexed his fingers around the hilt firmly and cast one final glance around to check that nobody was watching him before he made the move to slay his once-loyal servants. Then for the second time that day, a white cloaked figure caught his eye.

Bishop Evagrius was sodden with mud up to his knees, stumbling down the hillside like a drunk, scrambling on all fours to right himself. Balamber grinned as his mind feasted on the possibilities.

'There is the traitor!' He cried like a snake spitting venom. His nobles snapped to attention and they slowed to behold the sight. 'After him,' he hissed, sliding the scimitar out with an iron rasp. The nobles set off after him at a trot and rounded on him with ease, chuckling amongst themselves as they glared down on the bishop.

Balamber ambled forward, nudging his way inside the circle of his nobles. The sight of the kneeling bishop repulsed him: eyes bulging, skin as white as his robes and the mop of hair crowning his physical meekness. Evagrius' eyes darted round each of the mounted nobles, searching for even a hint of mercy and finally they rested on Balamber.

'Noble Balamber?' Evagrius asked. 'Great King of the Huns,' he added, shivering. 'Today has been a dark day for both of us. But together, we can still overrun the Roman Empire, just as we planned. Your place by my side at the throne of all Rome is there for the taking!'

Balamber ignored the bishop's words, snapping the chain and gold Chi-Rho cross he wore around his neck and weighing the trinket in his palm momentarily. Wulfric had been right; his people had been played like pawns in this plot. Dispensable grunts for a 'greater' cause. So much blood had been spilled, blood of his brothers, blood that had turned his most loyal men's thoughts towards treachery. He tossed the gold cross into the bishop's face.

'This dog is responsible for the events of the day!' Balamber glanced round to his men; their faces were etched with suspicion and their narrowed eyes fell on the bishop and then Balamber in turn, hands resting on sword hilts. *Seize the chance*, he thought, *destroy all before you*. 'He led the Roman relief force against us – flagging them forward. You all saw him wave them forward from the ridge. We have paid dearly for his gold with the blood of our kin.'

Gradually, the nobles turned to Evagrius, their faces smirking, their eyes glinting with bloodlust.

'Let us take vengeance in my honour,' Balamber continued. 'Bind him and put him on a horse.' He hesitated for a moment as he saw the bishop's jaw waver to begin protest. The silver-tongued holy man would talk himself free if given half a chance. 'But cut out his lying tongue first,' he motioned to his personal bodyguard by his side. Evagrius cried out, clawing at his face as two nobles hopped down and pinned him to the ground.

'When we return to our people, we will gather and melt the finest metals to fill his poisonous throat!' He growled. His nobles at last responded in the manner he had hoped, roaring in agreement as his personal bodyguard crouched over the screaming Evagrius with a rusted dagger clutched in his hand. The bishop's blood sprayed across the grass and his screams died to a whimper as the bodyguard held up a bloody sliver of severed tongue.

'Now we move back to the east. It may take a generation, maybe two, but we will return. And when we do, our army will be greater than ever before. One day Rome and all her lands will burn at our feet!'

*Destroy all before you.*

# Chapter 79

Pavo slumped back against a rock. It was jagged and gore-spattered, but it felt like a silk cushion as he let his leaden limbs relax. Victory could gild even the harshest of things.

The sun had prised the clouds apart like curtains, bathing the allied army and orchestrating a warm, musty breeze in a dance across the plateau. Looking down at his sword arm, he felt a numb urge to retch at the sight; a sliver of entrails had wrapped itself round his wrist, and a rough paste of bone, gristle and black-blood held it in place. His fingers trembled as he tried to move his shield arm to wipe the mess away. His head lolled back onto the rock and a sigh escaped from his lungs. All around him, the cheers of the allied army gradually hushed and were replaced by an iron rabble as they dug at the rubble-heaped entrance to the bunker. The Hun detachment had been smashed, but not before they had poured inside the bunker. What was left inside there would lift or shatter the air of victory. Suddenly, cries broke out from the bunker and rippled across the ranks. Pavo sat up with a jolt, his eyes pinging wide open.

'On your feet, Pavo!' Sura croaked, his grinning face coated in blood and the rubble-dust of the fort. 'Seems like we did it!'

'We did it?'

'We did it! Look...' Sura tailed off, pointing into the sunlight.

Pavo squinted into the brightness. A shape moved in the glare.

'Pavo?' a voice called.

Pavo's eyes flicked up to the armoured silhouette towering over him, a halo of orange light framing him. For the briefest of moments, his mind played tricks on him; the broad shoulders, the gravel voice – for a heartbeat he was transported back to the dusty tenemented street as a seven-year-old on demob day. He found strength where there was none and struggled to his feet. Then the wolf-like face of Gallus materialised as the figure stepped forward.

'Sir?'

'I didn't think that plan would come off – not for a moment – when I sent you away. The legion, or what's left of her, owes you lads her life. And the empire…if that horde had been allowed to descend on her, to cross the Danubius…' Gallus turned and craned his neck to gaze at the sky, the sunlight bathing his face. He looked gaunt, pale and utterly shattered. 'And what of Felix?' He added gently. 'Did my optio fall on the mission?'

'No chance, sir!' Felix yelled out. Twenty paces back, Felix hobbled on his crutch. 'Couldn't get my spatha dirty today but I bagged myself some of those buggers on the ballistae!' Horsa and Amalric trotted up behind the optio, saluting Gallus and throwing Pavo and Sura exhausted grins.

A warmth poured into Gallus' features, bringing a flush of colour to his pallor. Pavo's brow wrinkled at the sight of his centurion without the cool wolfen glare.

'You did it – you actually made it all the way to the emperor,' Gallus shook his head. 'Either you're good, very good, or the city lads need a good, solid kick up the arse!'

'How many left, sir?' Pavo croaked, licking his cracked and stinging lips.

Gallus' face fell back to the usual iron expression, like a dark cloud passing over the sun. 'Thirteen,' he replied.

Pavo held his gaze. Thirteen men left from the thousands who had set off just a week previously. All those faces from the training ground, all those veterans he had looked up to. All cold and still on the ground. Avitus, Zosimus and a crutch-bearing Quadratus hobbled up to join their centurion. So the few men who made up the core of the legion had survived. Those who had fought and bled to earn the title of veterans would live on. Probably why they were veterans in the first place, he mused.

'Nice work, lads,' Zosimus half chirped, half winced, grabbing at the bloody splatter on his ribs. Behind him, the handful of surviving XI Claudia legionaries trudged around the plateau, silent and thoughtful, eyeing the blue sky, some mouthing prayers.

Pavo's eyes hung on the pale, crimson-streaked legionary corpse only paces in front of him. This was the end Father had met, but today the gods had spared him. He shivered, recalling the darkening nightmare of Father calling to him from the sandstorm.

'Take heart, Pavo,' Gallus spoke, 'That you saved any of us is a miracle,' he pointed to Zosimus, who was lifting the legionary standard. The filthy and torn red bull rag flapped defiantly as it caught the wind. The allies rasped out an exhausted cheer.

'But all these men, dead,' he croaked, his eyes staying on the grey legionary corpse. The myth of the 'soldier's skin' seemed distant now.

'Loss is something a legionary must relive every day,' Gallus spoke, his eyes searching the horizon. 'Every one of those lads who fell today will haunt my dreams, Pavo. I have legions of them now, and it never gets any easier.'

Pavo looked up into his centurion's eyes. For the briefest of moments, he saw the cold pain inside the man, in behind the stony façade. 'Will their families be looked after?' Pavo remembered the day in the street, the funeral payout and the legionary with the dead eyes.

'I'll be seeing to that personally,' Gallus spoke firmly.

'The legion is bare now, how will we…'

'We'll recruit, Pavo, we always do.' Gallus fixed his eyes on him, and then something odd happened. The centurion's lips lifted at either side. 'But I know I can count on the men who survived today to see us through this,' he smiled.

Pavo felt his skin prickle with pride.

'Centurion Gallus?' A voice boomed from behind. Vitus strode over and offered his forearm. Gallus turned to clasp it as the XII Fulminata tribunus bellowed with laughter, still riding on the wave of victory. He gestured down at Pavo and over to Sura. 'I thought we would be too late – but these lads you sent back to the city were special – they must have had the emperor like putty in their hands!'

Gallus clapped one hand on Pavo's shoulder and one on Sura's shoulder. Then he spoke solemnly; 'Fine representatives for the XI Claudia, sir. This legion doesn't recognise defeat!'

# Chapter 80

Constantinople shook from the cheering. Buccinas sang out from the rooftops of the Baths of Zeuxippus and from the column-tops of the Augusteum as the triumph rolled down past the Hippodrome to the Imperial Palace. The streets swayed back and forth with a sea of citizens, striving to get the best view of the procession. The six white horses that led the gilded chariot at the head of the column wore every piece of decorative armour they could carry. In the chariot was the austere figure of Valens standing straight and tall, skin flecked with silver paint and hair combed forward pristinely. Despite neither raising a sword nor shedding a drop of his own blood, this would go down as his victory. It was he who had readied the relief army on his basis of his suspicions. And it was he who had gifted the Bosporus peninsula to Amalric as a federated kingdom – a magnanimous gesture that had thrilled the Goths and cemented the alliance with Fritigern.

Behind Valens, another, larger and unadorned chariot rolled along bearing Dux Vergilius, Tribunus Vitus, the newly promoted Tribunus Gallus and a rather bemused looking Amalric. Gallus slapped a hand on Amalric's shoulder in reassurance while he lapped up the adoration of the crowd.

Behind them, the first century of the XI Claudia marched in perfect order, a paragon of empire far removed from the reality of the battlefield; intercisa helmets sparkling, their shark-fin crests bobbing like a field of iron crop; shields repainted freshly in ruby and gold, emblazoned with the bull emblem and matching the freshly embroidered banner fluttering under the eagle standard; tunics whitened to perfection and newly dyed with the distinctive purple trim. A visit to the fort at Durostorum had seen them pick up an extra hundred and fifty fledgling soldiers to repopulate the century for the triumph. Indeed, the legion now numbered barely two standard centuries in total, but the cold hard facts could be dealt with tomorrow.

In the front rank, Pavo pulled in a lungful of dusty air – the old city smell teased the poignant memory of that day Tarquitius had bought him from the slave market. But in the six months he had been away with the legion, so much had changed for him that he felt like a giant. He had lived in the city as the senator's slave. He had left the city as a freedman, doomed to die on the end of a barbarian sword. Now, he had returned to the city as a man, a citizen and a legionary; to all intents and purposes a veteran. A grin wriggled across his face and then an itch stung just behind his eyes, *if Father could see me now.*

'When are you meeting her?' Sura bawled into his ear beside him.

'Eh?' Pavo uttered, craning his neck towards his friend. 'Oh, Felicia?' His neck burned. On the stop off at the legion fort by Durostorum he had begged for a brief leave and thundered across the plain to the town, barging through traders and sentries to get to *The Boar and the Hollybush*. Stumbling into the tavern like a drunk, he had scrabbled in his knapsack to find the Gothic necklaces he had bought with his pay, but the emptiness of the place stopped him; no laughter, no roaring. Just Felicia's father, standing with his hands on his hips behind the bar. He had mumbled an introduction while the man glared at him, searching him with his eyes. 'You're the toerag from the night of the brawl!' He had growled. Pavo stuttered an apology and then added an invitation to the triumph to him and Felicia before leaving the necklaces on the bar and scuttling back outside. Maybe he wasn't such a worldly-wise man quite yet, he thought, his cheeks glowing red now at the memory. 'She...she's probably held up – you know what the roads are like when there is a triumph on?'

'Sod it; there'll be plenty of girls happy to look after the heroes. There are hundreds of them – look!' Sura jabbed an elbow into his friend, nodding to the throngs of painted faces, all shapes and sizes, throwing kisses and winks like confetti.

Pavo afforded a half-grin as the palace gates up ahead creaked open and Valens entered. Shortly after, the emperor would address the crowd from the walls, and in the meantime, the rest of the column would merge with the crowd and the party would begin.

He sucked in another breath as the tidal wave of revellers closed in all around them – letting the fresh promise of the early summer air wash over him. A tingle rippled up his spine as the roar of the crowd grew deafening. Men slapped his back, held sacks of wine to his lips and hoisted him onto their shoulders. He caught sight of Sura being swept away likewise, eyes wide and roaring with laughter. A chuckle of disbelief tumbled from his lips too as he was passed along on top of the crowd. So this was glory, this was the moment to savour, he mused.

'Let's hear it for the Claudia!' He roared, punching the air as the men set him down and handed him the wine sack. He gazed into the azure sky as the bittersweet liquid rolled down his throat.

Felicia's stomach was in knots. She barged through the ruddy-faced and grinning throng on the streets, all vying to get into the heart of the celebrations in the Augusteum. Every character she bundled from her path embodied the emotions she wished to feel once again.

But all she could see, feel and hear was her long dead brother, *Curtius*. Her heart ached as she saw his face again, a weak, pining expression. Curtius had played the reluctant conscript and played it well. He had once told her that an imperial agent could not be conspicuously competent. However, to be found slain, throat cut from ear to ear, inside his own fort...she closed her eyes, blinking back the tears.

Wading into the centre of the Augusteum, she thought of Pavo; a sweet boy, a boy she could see herself with if life wasn't so...complicated. No, her life was all about infiltrating the XI Claudia now, all about finding those responsible for the death of Curtius. All about finding the counteragent, the hired dagger in the ranks of the XI Claudia. Despite the legion's losses, the culprit was still serving in her ranks – one of the veterans, apparently, or so her sources told her. Pavo was her new key into that dark stony bulwark back at Durostorum. She *would* obtain justice, she grimaced, justice dealt with her own hand. Blood would be let, she shuddered, and let in the gallon.

She saw Pavo at last, tipping a wine sack to his lips. Still the skinny, hawk-faced creature she remembered fondly. She wiped her eyes dry, took a deep breath and smiled. They could still have some fun before the storm...

Confetti swirled lazily amidst the warm breeze as the triumph party roared on. The streets of Constantinople continued to effervesce as the population cheered, drank and danced in waiting for Valens' speech. After that, the celebrations would continue long into the evening.

Meanwhile, Pavo remained in a lasting embrace with Felicia under a small archway in the shade. Seemingly invisible to the crowd at last, he nuzzled into her sweet scented neck and ran a hand back and forth through her tumbling amber locks.

'I thought you'd have forgotten about me?' He asked, holding her chin in his hands, gazing into her blue eyes and drinking in her beauty.

'Well, maybe I had for a while. But you're my free pass to a triumph, and I couldn't miss out, could I?' She teased. 'My father's down for the weekend trading anyway, so like a good girl I offered to come and help him…'

They fell silent for a moment again, before Felicia looked up into his eyes.

'So when you go back to Durostorum. Are you there to stay?' She asked.

Pavo felt his mind drift to the previous day in the legionary fort. The debriefing had involved talk of an emergency vexillatio from the remainder of the legion being sent north of the Danubius, where Athanaric's Gothic armies were rebelling against Fritigern and teetering on a full-scale invasion. Something was wrong up there. Badly wrong. He felt the onset of a frown, before checking it with a laugh.

'Next thing for me is to go for a drink and to properly meet your father!'

He wrapped his arms around her waist tightly, pulled her as close as he could and pressed his mouth firmly against her soft cherry lips.

'Pavo!' A gruff and familiar voice roared.

Pavo twisted round in alarm. Three faces grinned back at him; Felix, flanked by Zosimus and Sura.

'Permission to fall out granted!' Felix cackled, before they disappeared again into the midst of the revelry.

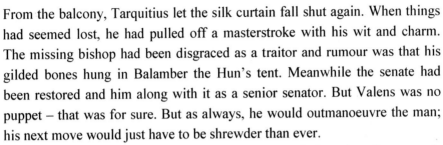

From the balcony, Tarquitius let the silk curtain fall shut again. When things had seemed lost, he had pulled off a masterstroke with his wit and charm. The missing bishop had been disgraced as a traitor and rumour was that his gilded bones hung in Balamber the Hun's tent. Meanwhile the senate had been restored and him along with it as a senior senator. But Valens was no puppet – that was for sure. But as always, he would outmanoeuvre the man; his next move would just have to be shrewder than ever.

He grinned, sipping his watered wine and inhaling the afternoon air through his nostrils. The comeback didn't end there, he gloried; young Pavo had been little use to him as a slave. But now, *now* he had a contact right in the heart of the army. And at his meeting with Athanaric the previous week, he had promised a strong network of military contacts to smooth the coming Gothic invasion.

Maybe, he mused, it would be prudent to play dice with the young man whom he had magnanimously freed from the bonds of slavery. What else did he have over the boy, he mused? Then he remembered the old crone from the slave market that day. Her words hissed in his head and he shivered. The curse had chilled his very blood. No, some things he could never tell another soul. But it was the person who had sent the crone that could be most useful. Yes, maybe it was time to play that card…to his advantage, of course.

Pavo's father might well have a part to play in this game, he grinned…

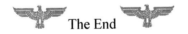 The End

*Ave,* Reader!

I hope you enjoyed this work, and I would like to thank you warmly for reading. If you would like to find out more about me and my work, please visit www.gordondoherty.co.uk. Here you can read my author bio, my blog, find links to my social networking pages (Facebook etc.), see what I'm working on next and read some free short stories I have published online!

Yours faithfully,
Gordon Doherty

CPSIA information can be obtained at www.ICGtesting.com
Printed in the USA
BVOW020931260613

324339BV00003B/510/P